ASYLUM FOR A DUCHESS

SERIES BY NELLIE H. STEELE

Cate Kensie Mysteries

Shadow Slayers Stories

Lily & Cassie by the Sea Mysteries

Pearl Party Mysteries

Middle Age is Murder Cozy Mysteries

Duchess of Blackmoore Mysteries

Maggie Edwards Adventures

Clif & Ri on the Sea Adventures

Shelving Magic

ASYLUM FOR A DUCHESS

A DUCHESS OF BLACKMOORE MYSTERY

DUCHESS OF BLACKMOORE MYSTERIES
BOOK THREE

NELLIE H. STEELE

This is a work of fiction. Names, characters, places, and incidents either are the product of the author's imagination or are used fictitiously. Any resemblance to actual persons, living or dead, events, or locales is entirely coincidental.

Copyright © 2023 by Nellie H. Steele

All rights reserved.

No part of this book may be reproduced in any form or by any electronic or mechanical means, including information storage and retrieval systems, without written permission from the author, except for the use of brief quotations in a book review.

Cover design by Stephanie A. Sovak.

❦ Created with Vellum

CHAPTER 1

A shriek pierced the fetid air of the dimly lit room. Thunder rumbled overhead, and lightning tore through the sky, flashing through the window and illuminating the space enough for me to make out exactly how dirty the tile floor was.

I wrinkled my nose as I stared at the streaks of filth across it. After another moment, I dug in the reticule that dangled from my wrist, in search of my handkerchief. I pressed it to my nose in the hopes of dampening the rancid scent. It did little good.

My mind regressed to the visits I'd made to my wayward brother-in-law when he faced murder charges and found himself in prison. Those cells had smelled better than this.

As I waited on the hard bench in the entryway, my leg bobbed up and down. I licked my lips as the tension in my body grew with every passing second.

Perhaps I had made a mistake. Yes, I was almost certain that I had, I concluded. I rose from my perch on the bench, the handkerchief still pressed to my nose, and stepped past the legs of my husband, who waited beside me.

"Lenora?" he questioned as I darted past him, heading for the large wooden doors leading to freedom.

I lowered the handkerchief from my nose to answer when another voice echoed in the large entryway. "Lenora?"

I froze, my shoulders rising to my ears, and my throat going dry. I spun around slowly to face the woman who'd called me.

Before I could address her, my husband leapt from his seat and strode forward. "It is, Your Grace," he corrected. "I am Robert Fletcher, Duke of Blackmoore. This is my wife."

"My apologies, Your Grace, I hadn't realized. Her Grace gave her name simply as Lenora."

Robert raised his eyebrows at me as I meandered forward, my legs threatening to betray me.

The woman glanced at me, her hands clasped in front of her white apron. "Your Grace, you may follow me."

Robert took a step to follow the woman as she spun and stalked across the dirty tiled floor. I held up a hand, stopping him. "Please, Robert, I prefer to go alone."

His forehead crinkled in confusion, and a momentary expression of displeasure flitted across his gray eyes.

I clutched his hand in mine and squeezed. "I apologize, dear, but it really is something I must face on my own. At least this time."

He forced a smile onto his face and offered me a nod. "Of course, dear. I shall await you here." He shuffled across the room and took a seat on the terribly uncomfortable bench with a stoic expression.

His devotion, however subtle, brought a slight curve to the corners of my lips as I reminded myself of how lucky I was to have married such an understanding man. I broadened my smile and nodded to him before I shoved the handkerchief into my reticule and clutched at the strings in a desperate attempt to steady my trembling hands.

I turned to find the nurse waiting for me on the fringes of the dark room, mainly visible because of her white apron. I strode across the space, the heels of my boots clicking along the blue tiles.

A large set of wooden doors closed off the entryway. My guide tugged a large key ring from her pocket and fiddled with it for a moment before she shoved a key into the lock and twisted it. She held the door open for me, and I preceded her into an equally dimly lit hallway.

The shrieks were louder on this side of the door, I noted. I clutched my purse strings tighter as I followed her down the long corridor. Closed doors filled the hall on either side of us.

A sharp hoot sounded from behind one as we passed. Behind another, the woman inside grasped at the bars closing off the small window, sticking her nose and lips through as she extended her tongue toward me.

I swallowed hard at the odd display and glanced at my guide, who continued along as though nothing odd had happened. She must be used to such behavior, I concluded as we paraded further along.

On my left, the sound of desperate sobbing echoed. My heart broke for the poor unidentified soul who wept behind one of those closed doors.

We reached a central chamber. A large, octagonal desk filled the center of the space. Two other women, clad similarly as my guide, bustled behind it.

We stopped, and the woman charged with leading me through the facility held her arm out to bar me from proceeding further. I shot her a questioning glance, but the reason soon became abundantly clear.

Shrieks filled the air as two burly men dressed in white wrangled a wild-eyed, wild-haired woman through the space. In a dirty nightgown, she struggled against them, her hands balled into fists and raised in the air.

"No! No!" she howled. "No! Leave me be! Leave me be!"

I swallowed hard, arching an eyebrow at her. She spotted me across the room and set her crazed gaze upon me. She reared back and lunged toward me, leaning away from her captors.

"Help me! Help me!" she shouted. "They are evil."

A man in a white coat raced toward the woman, a large needle in his hand. He jabbed her in the arm with it, depressing the plunger. With his chest heaving from the effort, he pulled back, adjusting his wire-rimmed spectacles to watch for her reaction.

"Evil! Evil! They are...e...ev...evil," she slurred out as her eyes slid closed and she slumped to a limp, lifeless state.

My eyes went wide at the scene. "Sedative," my guide said simply as they dragged the poor woman away, her bare feet skimming over the dirty floor as they carried her between them.

"This way, Your Grace," she added and led me across the large room and down another hallway.

Doors lined this corridor, too, though it seemed quieter than the first hallway we'd walked. My muscles stiffened and posture straightened as she came to a halt outside of one door. I clutched at my purse strings again, twisting them in my hands. My heart thudded against my ribs, and my throat went dry.

I shuddered, suddenly wishing for the comforting warmth of the fire in my tower room at Blackmoore Castle. I considered turning and fleeing back to the grimy entrance, where my husband awaited me. I second-guessed my decision to leave him there, cursing my desperate need to cling to my independence.

Perhaps I had made a mistake, I pondered as the woman

fiddled with her large key ring. I licked my lips, opening my mouth to give her my apologies and excuse myself, but I found myself mute, and I failed to stop her from sliding a key into the lock.

The door swung inward on creaky hinges. The woman stood aside and signaled for me to enter. I forced a fleeting smile onto my face and gave her a curt nod.

With a deep inhale, I took one step forward, my knees wobbling underneath me. I, again, considered changing my direction and fleeing, but I firmed my resolve and took another step. Odd, I considered as I forced myself into the tiny cell beyond the door, that I feared encounters with the living more than those I had with the dead.

In the twenty years I had lived, I'd always found more comfort among the dearly departed than the living. Until one month before my eighteenth birthday, when I married Robert, the Duke of Blackmoore. My life took a sharp turn from unwanted orphan to wife and eventually mother. Despite ours initially being a marriage of convenience, I found more love in my new home than I had in any of my previous residences.

Still, despite Robert's acceptance of me, I struggled to deal with most others around me, finding it easier to understand and connect with those who had already passed over from this life.

I swallowed hard and took a step over the threshold, setting one foot in the tiny room. I drew the other in, and the door closed swiftly behind me. I twisted to stare at it, my lower lip trembling and panic setting into my body.

My only escape was closed to me. I startled as the lock clanked, ensuring I could not leave. A face appeared between the bars, ghostly white against the darkness.

"The cell doors must remain locked. Call when you are ready to depart."

I tried to force words out of my parched throat, but none came. The woman spun away from the door, and the clicking of her heels diminished as she strode away from me.

I twisted to study the small cell. A cot stood against the far wall. A single flame flickered from the wooden night table next to it. Even in the dim light, I could make out stains on the sheets.

Moonlight streamed through a barred window that overlooked a small courtyard garden outside. The white light shining down on the dilapidated courtyard gave it an eerie appearance. Thorny roses climbed a broken trellis near a ramshackle bench that appeared to be in desperate need of repair.

I followed the long shadows of the bars the moon cast upon the floor to the opposite corner. A woman sat unmoving in a chair, her back to me. Her graying hair hung limply down her back, covering most of her yellowed nightgown.

I sucked in a sharp breath as I caught sight of her. With my lips pressed together to stop my jaw from trembling, I took a step toward her.

"Hello?" I called.

I received no response. The single flame of the candle flickered, coming close to extinguishing as a draft of an unknown source blew through the room. I hesitated before I took another step, my eyes fixed on the woman.

"Hello," I tried again as I inched closer.

My stomach somersaulted as I skirted the chair. The flickering candlelight cast shadows across her gaunt face. My heart seized as I caught sight of her face.

I stared at her gray, sagging skin and sunken eyes. Her slightly parted lips were cracked and pale.

A flood of memories poured through my mind, each fighting for attention. My mind repainted her features, filling in her cheeks, painting her skin with a rosy glow and darkening her hair.

I gazed into her dark eyes. Today, they stared without seeing, blank and lifeless. My mind's eye conjured a memory of a time long since passed. In it, her eyes blazed with fury, lit by candlelight then, too, as the woman straddled me, speaking a strange language.

My breathing turned ragged as I fought to control my mind. My forehead pinched as I flicked my gaze away from her gaunt form to the white orb outside. Another memory fluttered across the fringes of my mind. The sensation of thick rope being wrapped around me while I stood against an oak tree under a full moon burned through my mind.

Vision upon vision of abusive behavior bombarded me, and tears welled in my eyes. I blinked them away, struggling to regain my composure. My fingers tugged at my purse strings, snapping them in two.

I longed to return to the comfort of Blackmoore Castle, to my husband, my children, and even my wayward brother-in-law, Edwin, who had promised a surprise upon my return to the castle.

I squeezed my eyes closed, picturing their faces, the rooms of the castle, my snow-white horse, and the gardens in spring bloom. I allowed these more recent memories to soothe me as I fought to steady my breathing.

I snapped my eyes open, focusing them on the pitiful creature in front of me, frail of body and feeble of mind. She could not be held responsible.

I licked my lips and stepped closer to the woman. "Hello, Mother."

CHAPTER 2

The woman stared blankly ahead, not acknowledging me or my greeting. I studied her face in the flickering light. Perhaps her hearing had declined along with her mind.

I tried again, this time louder than before, emboldened by the lack of recognition on her part. "Hello, Mother. It is Lenora. Your daughter."

The woman continued to stare at the corner, almost appearing to look through me rather than at me. I swallowed hard as my lower lip trembled again. "I am afraid I know little about your condition, as I have not spoken with the doctors yet. However…"

My voice died off as she fidgeted in her seat. I arched an eyebrow, leaning sideways to study her eyes.

Her forehead crinkled, deep wrinkles running the length of it.

"Mother?" I questioned as my gloved fingers toyed with the frayed strings of my reticule. "Can you hear me?"

Her lower lip trembled for a moment, and tears formed in her eyes.

"Mother? It is your daughter, Lenora. Do you remember me?"

Her eyes slowly rose upward, finally focusing on my face. A tear rolled down her cheek as she stared wide-eyed at me. I straightened, unable to force a smile onto my face but doing my best to appear pleasant.

"It is Lenora," I repeated.

She stared at me without a glimmer of recognition that I could glean. Perhaps she did not recognize me, I mused. When she had seen me last, I had been a child of only five. At age twenty now, I must look quite different. And given her condition and placement in an asylum, she may not even recall having had a daughter. Particularly given the manner in which we'd been separated.

My mind regressed to that fateful moment. A moment that had embedded itself in my childhood brain, burrowing deeply inside and rooting itself into my very existence.

Mother had packed a suitcase for me early that morning, telling me we were going on a special trip for my upcoming birthday. We'd traveled to the city, our carriage wheel breaking midway through the trip.

Mother had fretted over its fixing, inconsolable and insistent that the coachman fix it posthaste and we continue along. We'd driven into Glasglow. I had marveled at the city, bouncing in my carriage seat as the buildings filled in around us.

I'd inquired about a toy store, though I did not know our first destination would be our last. I'd played in the light cast through the stained glass windows of the entryway to the convent. Mother had spoken with Mother Superior quietly as I'd waved my hands under the colored light.

The nun had whisked me away to a courtyard garden, leaving me in the care of one elderly and one young nun as she fluttered away, robes flying, to speak with my mother.

I waved to her as she gave me one final glance before disappearing with the nun, not realizing it would be the last time I would see her. She would not return to collect me that night, nor any other. My life, once settled and safe as the daughter of a doctor, spiraled into a desolate and lonely existence as an unwanted orphan.

An unwanted orphan who suffered from an odd ability. The ability to communicate with those who had passed from this life. I would be shunned for it by most, and it was the sole reason I'd been abandoned by my mother some fifteen years ago.

My mind snapped back to the present as a groan emanated from her cracked lips.

"Do you remember me, Mother?" I questioned again as she seemed to exhibit signs of cognizance.

"It is Lenora. I am grown now, and I have my own family. I–"

"You," she whispered, her lower lip trembling again.

"Yes, your daughter, Lenora," I repeated. "You may not remember me. I am quite a bit older now. I have married, and I have two children. I–"

"You," she repeated, this time the word sounding distinctly more derogatory. Her voice dripped with disdain as her features morphed into a twisted mask of hatred. The blank expression that had previously graced her ashen face and dead eyes changed in an instant. Her nose wrinkled, tugging her lips into a sneer. Her eyebrows squashed together, framing eyes filled with rage and ire.

"You," she spat out again, poking a finger in my direction.

I swallowed hard, my features penitent as they usually were when she scolded me as a child, even if I hadn't realized the reason for her anger. "I'm sorry, Mother," I said, tearing at the frayed ends of the purse strings again. "I have disturbed you, though it was not my intention. I had only hoped to visit."

She glared at me, her bony fingers clenching the chair's arms. Her long yellowed fingernails dug into the wood, marring it as she clawed the arms.

My limbs began to tremble again, and I lowered my gaze, staring down at the reticule. "I should not have come. I'm sorry."

I took a step to circle around her and call for the nurse when she lunged at me. With her yellow teeth bared, she launched from the chair, her fingers spread wide and reaching for me.

I stumbled back a step, crying out as she clamped her hands on my shoulders with a force I did not expect possible from her frail body.

"Please, Mother!" I cried.

"You little wretch," she growled at me. "You demonic little monster!"

She raised a hand and slapped me across the cheek. I let out a yelp, grabbing my smarting cheek with my gloved hand, again surprised by the strength she exhibited.

She grasped me by my shoulders again, shaking me hard. "Get away from me, devil!"

I fought back against her as she shoved me into the corner with another sharp slap across the face. Breaking free from her, I bolted across the room and banged frantically against the door, shrieking at the top of my lungs for help.

From the darkened corner, my mother emerged with the sneer still on her lips. Her hair hung limply around her ashy skin. The moonlight gave her an eerie appearance as she stalked toward me.

A nurse raced down the hall. "Hurry!" I called to her, sticking my fingers through the bars.

She skidded to a stop outside the room, desperately

searching her key ring for the correct key. I groaned as her shaking hands dropped the keys to the floor. She swiped them and began her search again.

A growl sounded behind me, and I spun to face the horrific site of my mother lunging at me with her teeth bared again. I pressed my back against the door as she plowed into me, her jaw snapping as she tried to tear my flesh from the bone with her teeth.

"Stop, Mother!" I screamed. Pressure pushed into my back, and I realized the nurse was attempting to open the door.

I fought to move forward as the woman on the opposite side of the door screamed for help. The door shoved at me, and I collided with my mother. We fell in a tangle of limbs as two bulky men swept into the room. Strong arms pulled me to my feet before rushing to hold down the shrieking banshee I had once called "Mother."

I backed up a few steps, my jaw unhinged in horror as another nurse raced into the room, jamming a needle into my mother's arm. She continued to spew foul words at me until her voice slurred and limbs went slack. She collapsed back to the floor, her eyes sliding shut.

A tear fell to my cheek and my knees wobbled as I took a step from the room. I glanced back at her slack form on the floor as I gasped for breath, fighting to contain the tears welling in my eyes.

What had I expected? I chided myself for being so foolish. The woman had left her five-year-old child at a convent after performing multiple questionable acts on her. I recalled being tied to the oak tree in our back yard under a full moon and left there until morning. She'd freed me, and when I'd collapsed, she'd left me to lay in the grass until I dragged myself inside.

And that was only one of the cruel punishments I'd

endured as a child. My lower lip trembled, and I wiped at the tear that clung to my chin.

Had I really expected her to welcome me with open arms? I should not have come. At the very least, I should have allowed Robert to accompany me inside. Perhaps then I would not have been accosted again by the woman who had born me into this world.

I stared at her as my pulse stopped pounding. She lay still and quiet on the cold floor as the nurse withdrew the needle. Guilt rushed through me. The woman was mad. She had likely been mad when I was a child, though I could not understand that at the time.

I sniffled and rolled my shoulders back as the orderlies wrested her from the floor and dragged her to her bed. Her slack bare feet skittered across the floor. They dropped her on the small cot and stepped away as the nurse flung her dangling foot onto the small bed.

I stepped to the open door and stared at the sleeping woman, my heart filling with sorrow. Sorrow for the mad woman lying in a cold cot at a rundown asylum. Sorrow for the hope I'd had when I'd arrive. Sorrow for the life that had been ripped away from me.

I crept to the bed as the nurse folded my mother's hands over her belly. With a sniffle, I reached out and grabbed one gnarled, cold hand.

"Goodbye, Mum," I whispered.

Like in a chilling tale told by candlelight, her eyes snapped open, and she shot upward. With her teeth bared, she hissed at me, her hands forming claws. She clamped onto my arm, spewing more vicious utterances.

I stumbled back, my eyes wide, and tried to tug away from her. Her bony fingers grasped my wrist with such force, I worried she'd crush it. I winced as the nurse grabbed hold of her.

My mother shook the woman off as though she were no more than a fly.

"No, Mother, please!" I cried.

"You foul child!" she shrieked, her face twisting into a ghoulish display. "You little demon! You haunt me even to my dying day!"

She reached for my neck, her icy cold, bluish fingers wrapped around it and squeezing. I felt the pressure of those thin fingers against my throat. They pushed with a force surprising to me, and I felt my windpipe closing. I gasped for breath as I choked and coughed.

I wrestled against her as the nurse screamed for help before tugging her backward. The small woman leapt onto her back, wrapping an arm around her neck and yanking her away from me.

My mother growled as outrage filled her over her failed attempt to end my life. Fueled by her fury, she found a new victim for her attack. She wrapped those crooked fingers around the nurse's arm, her long, yellowed fingernails digging into the woman's sleeve. Her mouth opened wide, and she sunk her teeth into the woman's flesh.

The nurse howled in pain as blood squirted from the wound, soaking the fabric of her dress. A spray of blood splashed onto my face and dress. My eyes shot wide, and I stood shocked for a moment as the warm, wet liquid spattered on my skin.

I raised my hand to my face and swiped at my cheek and mouth. When I pulled it away, red blood stained my gloves. I tasted the metallic tinge of blood on my tongue.

The nurse shrieked as she grasped at her bitten arm. She let go of her patient, gripping her arm as tears streamed down her face.

My mother used the momentary lapse of restraint and lunged at me. Her mouth dripped with blood as our faces came within inches of each other. She wrapped her hands around my neck again and squeezed, shaking me like a rag doll.

"Die, you little devil, die!"

I struggled to stay upright from the savage attack. The orderlies raced into the room. They grabbed hold of my mother. A nurse and doctor ran in after them. The woman attended to her fellow caregiver, while the doctor stabbed my mother's arm with another syringe.

Tears streamed down my cheeks as my mother continued to reach for me, screaming with her bloodstained lips.

I raced from the room as the nurse jabbed her with yet another needle. Her voice slurred as I stumbled around the corner. Her wild and hateful shrieks faded as my feet pounded across the filthy tile floor.

I spilled into the central area and slammed into the nurse's station, grasping the worn wood as I gasped in a breath and righted myself. I pushed myself to pivot and race down the hall through which I'd entered. Skidding around the corner, my feet scrambled to find purchase on the slick and worn tile before I found traction and burst forward.

The doors at the end of the corridor raced toward me as my fleeing footsteps echoed. I smashed into the wooden barriers. They stood firm and unyielding.

Tears streamed down my face, and panic welled inside me. I grasped the handle and twisted it, pushing and pulling on the door in the hopes of opening it.

It would not budge. I pounded against the splintered door, filled with scratches from those held inside them. "Help!" I shrieked. "Help! Robert, help me!"

CHAPTER 3

I continued to bang against the doors, shrieking at the top of my lungs as hysteria flowed through every fiber of my being. I jiggled the handle again, jimmying the door in the jamb.

Hands clamped down around my arm. For one frenzied moment, terror raced through me as I feared my mother may have escaped once again and followed me to finish the job.

I leapt backward, lashing out at the figure. As I pressed against the wall, my jaw gaping open and gasping for breath, I stared into the face of another, younger woman.

Her unkempt hair appeared as if it needed a thorough brushing. She wore a tattered pale blue dress marred with dirt on the edges.

She stared at me with dark eyes, deep set in her pale face. Her sunken cheeks and the black circles under her eyes betrayed a difficult life.

"Help me," she said.

My brow furrowed as I attempted to piece together the situation after my own calamity. My jumbled mind refused to understand the request.

"What?" I breathed.

She approached me, closing the gap between us. I pressed against the wall, trying to escape her, but she backed me into the corner.

She grasped my arm again, her grip tight. "Help me," she said with a clenched jaw.

I wrinkled my nose at the stench assaulting my nostrils. Her noxious breath, coupled with the putrid smell of unwashed linens and unclean hair, threatened to overwhelm me.

"Please," she said, barring her rotted teeth.

Her dark eyes bore into me, and I opened my mouth to inquire after her need when a shout sounded down the hall. We both snapped our eyes in the direction of the cry.

She shot one last pleading glance at me before she dropped my arm and hurried down the hall, her arms pinned to her sides and chin tucked to her chest.

I stared after her as she shuffled away. When the nurse rounded the corner, she shrank into the shadows on the opposite side of the hall, pressing her pale face into the wall to hide.

The nurse continued past her toward me, keys rattling in her hand. She closed the distance between us, studying me with wide eyes.

She stared at the blood on my dress and reddish-brown smudge on my cheek. "Your Grace, do you require medical attention?"

I shook my head at her as I caught my breath. "N-no," I stammered. "I am unharmed."

She arched an eyebrow at the stain on my clothing before she jangled the keys in her hands, searching for the appropriate one.

She shoved it in the lock, twisting it. "Your mother is resting peacefully now. She is quite unwell, Your Grace.

Please understand, anything she said cannot be held against her, as she is very unstable."

I forced a fleeting smile onto my face and nodded as she pushed the door open. I darted out of the opening without another word. The door slammed shut behind me, and the clicking of the lock echoed in the massive, dimly lit entryway.

The woman behind the desk flicked a sideways gaze at me, lowering her eyes and busying herself with her work as I collapsed back against the door, sucking in breaths.

I licked my lips as I realized how I must appear. A lock of my hair had escaped its pins and hung limply, part of it plastered itself against my skin, sticky with tears.

Blood stained my dress. My complexion, likely blotchy and red from crying, probably added to the disarray that was my appearance.

Across the space, Robert leapt from his seat, a concerned look squashing his features. I cast one look into his gray eyes, and my knees wobbled again. With a dismayed groan, I raced across the deteriorating foyer and flung my arms around his neck.

"Lenora? What is it? What's happened?"

My shoulders shook with sobs, and Robert wrapped his arms around me, holding me close. Tears streamed down my face again, this time from relief. Relief to be back in the arms of someone who accepted me despite my affliction. Relief to be away from the woman who tossed me away like a rotting piece of fruit. Relief at being alive.

I quieted my blubbering, wiping at my face as I pulled back. Robert's gray eyes stared at me, filled with concern. He wiped at a fallen tear with his thumb as I clumsily attempted to tuck the wayward string of hair into place.

I sniffled and flicked my gaze up to him, forcing a smile on my face. He returned the expression before it faded, replaced with a face pinched with concern. His eyes widened, and his jaw gaped open.

"Lenora! Is that blood?" He focused on a dark red splotch on my dress.

I lowered my eyes to it and offered a nod. I tugged open my reticule and fished out a handkerchief, pressing it to my runny nose. "Yes."

Robert's grip tightened, and he guided me to the bench, easing me onto it. "My God," he said as he continued to stare at the blood stains. "Nurse! Nurse! My wife requires medical attention!"

I shot to my feet, shaking my head, and clamped a hand onto his forearm. "No!" I called across the room to the woman behind the desk. "No, I am quite all right."

"Lenora, you are covered in blood!" Robert exclaimed, his dismay apparent.

"It is not mine, dear. I assure you, I am quite all right." I pressed the handkerchief to my nose again and sniffled.

Robert's features twisted with frustration. "What in God's name happened back there?"

I squeezed my eyes shut as images of the events flashed across my mind again. I tightened my grip on Robert's arm as my legs threatened to betray me.

His arms wrapped around me, steadying me.

"Please, dear, let us speak of it at the inn. Or in the carriage." I flicked my gaze across the room to the nurse who studied me despite her lowered chin. She quickly averted her gaze, pretending to fiddle with something.

Robert squashed his lips into a thin line and shot a glare at the woman. He agreed with a grumble, guiding me toward the large wooden doors leading to the drive.

Outside, our carriage awaited, drawn by four chestnut horses. I regretted making them wait in the cold November weather. At least, I mused as Robert steered me through the doors, no rain fell from the skies.

The cool, damp air hit my moist face as I stepped outside. On any other occasion, I would have nestled further into my fur-trimmed cape, but on this one, I relished the icy smack against my skin. It signified my freedom from the horrid asylum.

Mr. Jones, our coachman, leapt from his perch, pulling his hands from under his arms and whipping the carriage door open. Robert helped me into the space, and I collapsed in my seat, breathing a sigh of relief.

He climbed in behind me, and the door shut out the cold air. The buggy shimmied as Mr. Jones climbed to his seat and cracked the reins. The carriage lurched forward, and the *clip-clop* of the horse's shoes sounded against the cobblestone.

I let my head fall back against the carriage wall, and my eyes slid shut for a moment. My fingers curled into fists, and I swallowed hard as my nerves began to settle.

The massive asylum, set in a rambling manor home in a desolate area, faded on the horizon as we traveled away from it into the nearest town of Staghearst. The tiny hamlet offered us refuge for the night in the form of a small inn.

Robert had grumbled over the accommodations, but given our last-minute travel, other arrangements could not be made, and in the end, the stay over proved the more palatable option than the trek back to Blackmoore, high in the Scottish Highlands.

I almost sided with him as the lights on the hill grew smaller and we passed through the stone archway housing the black iron gates boasting Stagheart Asylum.

I shivered as the moonlight cast an eerie glow over them. Exhaustion coursed through me, though, and I welcomed a warm bed anywhere.

I slid my eyes open, finding Robert's gaze fixed on me.

With a lick of my lips, I leaned forward and grasped his hand. "I will explain everything. I just needed a moment."

Robert patted my hand. "We shall discuss it when you've settled at the inn. I certainly hope the blasted establishment can make a toddy."

He set his discontented gaze out the window, his chin resting in his hand.

With all the chaos I'd just experienced, chaos so reminiscent of my childhood, the statement struck me as comical. Perhaps it was the juxtaposition of the simplicity of the hot toddy as Robert's response to any misfortune with the violent attack I'd witnessed, but in any case, a giggle burst from me.

I attempted to hold it back, but it turned into a full chuckle. Robert snapped his gaze back to me, his expression incredulous.

"Oh, I am sorry, dear," I said, still laughing, "but I do love you."

His features softened as I spoke the last three words. He leaned forward, taking both of my hands in his. A slight smile crossed his face as he gazed into my eyes. "And I love you, dear, which is why I am so distressed to see you like this. And why I must insist on a toddy the moment we arrive."

I sucked in a deep breath and leaned back. "I have grown to find them comforting. And I certainly could use the comfort."

I bent forward, taking his hand again. "Though your comfort is the most important to me."

"I am willing to provide it, but if you prefer not to speak of it—"

"I only preferred to postpone the discussion until we were away from that horrid place."

He nodded as the carriage leveled out, having reached the village below the asylum. I stared up at it, high on the hill above, cast in the white glow of the moon and ringed by fog in the valley below. Another shiver ran up my spine.

"Are you cold?" Robert inquired, tugging his jacket off and settling it around my shoulders.

I nestled inside, grateful for the warmth despite my chill being caused by something other than the weather.

Our carriage slowed to a stop outside of The White Stag Inn, a quaint three-story structure on the outskirts of the town. The coachman dismounted, and we alighted from the carriage. Robert shuttled me inside and up the stairs to our room. He left me seated in an armchair by the fire, tossing on another log before he left in search of the toddy he'd promised.

I stared into the dancing flames, tugging his jacket tighter around me, appreciating the comfort it provided. I let my head rest against the armchair's wing and closed my eyes.

Robert strode into the room moments later, a drink clutched in his hand. I opened my eyes, catching sight of another soul in the room. I sat straighter for a moment until Robert stepped between us, cutting off my view.

"Can you believe brandy is the best they can do?" he scoffed as he handed me the glass.

"It will be just fine, dear," I assured him, taking a sip before settling the glass in my lap.

"The damned place cannot even manage a toddy. If we ever return to this desolate town, I shall send Henry on before us to find a suitable location to stay."

"I am uncertain there are many others."

"I will hire out an entire house if I must and bring the staff, too."

Robert's disagreeable nature stemmed from his worry. A worry I had failed to put to rest by withholding the information from him. I studied his features, wrought with concern, as the firelight lit them. His hands, pressed against the mantle with a forceful grip, also betrayed his anxiety over the events of the evening.

"Sit down, dear," I said as I rose from my seat and guided him to the armchair across from mine. I handed him what remained of my brandy. "Here. You could use this."

"Do not be ridiculous, Lenora. I am not the one covered in blood and looking as though I've lived through Hell."

I left the remaining brandy with him and eased into my chair. "I am hardly covered in blood. And it was not as bad as Hell, though I do not wish to live through it again."

He flicked his eyebrows upward as his gaze rested on the brandy glass he'd chosen to sip from after all.

"I am quite fine, Robert," I assured him, "only a little shaken from the greeting I received from my mother."

He raised his eyes to mine. "Was she able to speak with you?"

"Unfortunately, yes. She was capable of speaking."

"What does that mean?"

I sighed, casting my gaze to the flames dancing on my left. "It means she feels the same way about me now as she did when I was a child." I flicked my gaze to Robert, who studied my face. "She detests me."

Robert's face twisted into a mask of surprise. "She said that?"

"More or less. At first, I do not believe she recognized me. She seemed unresponsive when I began speaking to her, but after a few moments, realization dawned on her. She–"

My voice trailed off, and I bit my lower lip as images of the encounter flitted through my brain.

"Yes?" Robert prodded, leaning forward in his chair.

"She leapt from her chair and tried to strangle me."

"She did what?" Robert leapt from his seat, stalking around the small sitting room. "Where the devil were the nurses?"

"They came as quickly as they could and–"

"Do you mean to say they left you alone with a mad woman?" Robert snapped his gaze to me.

I shrugged my shoulders at the statement. "I suppose she hadn't been violent in the past."

My husband shook his head at the events. "If she tried to strangle you, how did you become covered in blood? Was it hers?"

"No," I admitted, clasping my hands on my lap and avoiding his gaze. "The nurse injected her with some medication that put her to sleep. I thought it would be safe to say goodbye, but she awoke and lunged for me again. When the nurse pulled her back, she–"

Robert leaned forward, his chin jutting out as he hung on my words. I flicked my gaze up to him and pressed my lips together before revealing the gory tidbit. "She bit the woman. The blood is from the nurse."

"Good God!" Robert said, flinging his arms in the air as he paced away from me.

I dropped my gaze to my lap, tears welling in my eyes. I had made a serious miscalculation when I'd decided to visit the asylum housing my mother. I'd expected to find closure, perhaps even a penitent woman. I had not expected the violent and vicious greeting I'd received.

Why I hadn't expected it, I do not know. In the nearly six years I spent with the woman, I'd known little beyond cruelty, particularly after my father departed for India.

How foolish I had been, I concluded. My features twisted as the tears threatened to spill onto my cheeks and I sank my forehead into my hand.

"I am sorry, Robert," I sobbed.

Robert appeared in front of me, rushing to my side and kneeling. He took my hands in his. "Whatever for?"

"I was a fool to pursue this. To insist upon a visit. I have upset our household for no reason."

"Do not be ridiculous, Lenora. You have upset nothing other than yourself. As usual, you expect the best from others. The turn of events must be terribly distressing to you."

I licked my lips as I nodded and sniffled. "Yes, it was. I had hoped time would have healed any wounds. However, they still seem to be gaping for her."

"My poor darling. We shall return to Blackmoore Castle straight away tomorrow. Perhaps a visit with our children will cheer you."

I squeezed his hand and offered a weak smile. "A visit with Sam and Sarah always has the power to cheer me."

He kissed my fingers and smiled up at me before he rose. "Then it is settled. We shall put the matter to rest and never speak of it or return to that foul place again."

I flicked my gaze toward the door. The space occupied when Robert had returned stood empty now. With a sigh, I realized that would likely not remain the case.

"I am not certain I will be able to hold to that."

Robert twisted to face me, his thick eyebrows furrowed over his gray eyes. "Whatever do you mean? Surely, you did not intend on visiting her again."

"My mother, no, I do not. However…"

"Yes?" Robert prompted.

"After she attacked me, I fled from the room, racing through the halls and to the main doors in a panic."

"Undoubtedly. I expect I would have behaved quite the same."

"Obviously, the doors are locked, and as I banged against them to seek escape, a woman approached and begged for my help."

"Surely, a mad woman. She probably didn't know what she was saying, Lenora. Leave it to the doctors, who are undoubtedly well-suited to handle the situation." He glanced down at the rug under his feet. "Though I suppose they left something to be desired when it came to handling your mother."

I shook my head at him. "That's just it, though. The doctors are not the best suited to handle this."

Robert raised his eyebrows, clasping his hands behind his back as he stared at me. "Surely, Lenora, you are not suggesting you are better suited to handle the ravings of a lunatic?"

"She isn't a patient there."

Robert's eyebrows smashed together. "A nurse?"

I shook my head. "No. At first, I assumed as you had. She was simply mad."

"But?"

"But then she appeared here near the doorway. And I realized I hadn't spoken with a patient while I waited to depart. I had spoken with a dead woman."

CHAPTER 4

Robert sank into his chair, his complexion turning ashy, as it often did when speaking of the dead. He swallowed hard and rubbed his chin. "Perhaps the dead woman is as mad in death as she was in life."

"Perhaps."

He raised an eyebrow at me. "Though you do not believe so."

"I do not believe she will allow me not to pursue whatever it is she needs help with, no. Otherwise, she would not have appeared here earlier."

Robert's eyes darted around the room, and he craned his neck to glance at the doorway. With a grimace, he flicked his gaze to me. "Where is she now?"

"Gone," I reported. "I believe you may have startled her when you entered."

Robert leapt from his seat, stalking around the room. "*I* startled *her*?"

"The dead do become startled by the living at times. It's likely she sought me alone and you interrupted what she expected to be a private moment."

Robert's bushy eyebrows furrowed and his face formed a frown as he stared into the flames dancing in the fireplace. "I shall never become used to this, I fear."

"You have already grown quite accustomed to it, dear," I said. "I am quite encouraged by the strides you have made."

He slid his eyes sideways to glance at me, his eyebrows lifting. "You give me too much credit."

"I disagree. I do not believe I give you enough."

Robert flopped into the armchair again, shaking his head. "You must be dismayed that I grumble each time you encounter a specter. And I should not. You cannot control it."

"I understand how disconcerting it must be, particularly when you cannot see or hear them."

He stared at me, searching my face. "I imagine it is more disconcerting for you who can!"

I wiggled my eyebrows as I settled back into the chair. "In any case, you handle the situation admirably, grumbling and all."

"You are too kind, Lenora, though you always have been."

"As are you. I regularly speak to the dead, and to date, I have been thrown from a tower, nearly murdered by Sir Richard, gotten us embroiled in a murder investigation to save Edwin, and exposed myself to being accused of a lurid affair. And on top of it all, you have not once tried to throttle me as my own mother did. Admirable, dear," I said with a coy grin.

Robert squashed his lips into a thin line and narrowed his eyes at me.

"What?" I questioned, my expression innocent.

"Not throttling you is hardly admirable, Lenora."

"I find it so."

Robert laughed in spite of himself before he settled back into the chair again, his arms crossed. "I must admit, this is not the life I expected to lead. Though I suppose you keep it quite interesting. And of course, I could not have asked for a more extraordinary wife."

"Nor I for a more exceptional husband than you."

He grinned at me as we sat by the warm fire. After a period of reflective silence on both our parts, Robert flicked his gaze back to me. "Do you expect our return to Blackmoore Castle to be delayed? Will you visit the Staghearst Sanitarium again tomorrow?"

I shivered as I considered the prospect of ever returning. "No. No, I believe I need some space from the institution. If the woman there who needs my help requires it immediately, she may seek me out here."

He bobbed his head up and down, returning his gaze to the fire. After another moment, he studied me again. "Would you mind terribly if I returned before we depart tomorrow?"

Confusion crept onto my features. "Why would you return there?"

He lifted his shoulders in a shrug. "I would like to discuss your mother's condition with the doctor, to be sure she is properly looked after. The woman clearly requires a great deal of medical care. I would like to ensure that she receives it."

My bewilderment gave way to a smile, and I blinked away the tears that formed in my eyes. "I do not object, no, though I do not require it from you either."

"I know you do not. Which is why I feel compelled to do it."

"Thank you, Robert. Despite the strife between us, I do wish her some peace in life. If that peace comes from me remaining far away from her, so be it."

"Then I shall go to the sanitarium early tomorrow morning, before we begin our return trip to Blackmoore."

I nodded at the plan. "I do look forward to returning to both the castle and the children. And oddly, Edwin."

"Oh, please," Robert said, waving his hand in the air at me to dismiss the statement, "what in heaven's name could have you looking forward to seeing my cad of a brother?"

"He hinted at having some sort of surprise. Have you any idea what it may be?"

"Surprise?" Robert questioned, his face forming the frown they often did when it came to matters involving Edwin. "I haven't a clue. And I shudder to think what it may be."

"From his ramblings about it, he seemed to think it would be well-received."

"That means nothing. Edwin's surprises are never positive."

"I beg to differ. I find Samuel quite positive."

"I find the child pleasing, too, though the sudden knowledge of his parentage left something to be desired, dear."

I chuckled at Robert's statement, recalling the realization that the child we had adopted when my friend Tilly died giving birth was, indeed, Edwin's illegitimate son. Robert had taken the knowledge in stride, though, as always, he'd grumbled about it when he'd first learned of it.

I sucked in a deep breath, unable to make any progress on the mystery tonight, and rose from my chair. "If you do not mind, I think I shall retire."

"Of course, dear," Robert said, rising from his chair as I stood. "Sleep well, Lenora. I love you."

"I love you, too," I said as I pecked his cheek and disappeared from the room.

As I slid between the sheets after changing from my soiled dress, I worked to push the memories of the encounters at Staghearst Sanitarium from my mind. Tears welled as I realized I may never achieve the closure I hoped for.

I rolled onto my side. Was it closure I sought? Or something else? Love, perhaps. Acceptance? Whatever it was, I concluded as I shifted to my other side, I would likely never find it.

My mind turned to the way I'd found my mother. An odd turn of events that had upset the careful balance of the life I'd built, despite my affliction.

I licked my lips as the memory rushed into my mind. Two months after I'd given birth to my first daughter, Sarah, Robert and I strolled through the streets of Edinburgh. I pushed the pram with my infant daughter inside as our first child, Sam, strolled next to me, clutching Robert's hand.

He chattered away to us about the summer weather and trip to the city when our conversation was interrupted.

"Lenora?" a man's voice called from behind me.

I furrowed my brow, wondering if one of the deceased had reached out from beyond the grave, though perplexed as to how they had known my name. Had it been someone known to me?

"Lenora Hastings?" the man's raspy voice said again.

I ceased my ambling, twisting to face him as I clutched tightly to the pram's handle. Robert spun, too, and I realized the man must be of the living, since Robert had heard him.

The grizzled man approached me, his jaw hanging slightly open. A thick beard covered his gaunt features. Dark circles blackened the underside of his sunken eyes. He approached in his threadbare coat, staring at me with green eyes.

Something about him seemed familiar.

As he closed the distance between us, his hand reaching for me, Robert whipped Sam into his arms and stepped between us. "What is the meaning of this?"

The man looked past Robert's shoulder, a forlorn sadness etched across his thin face. "Is it you?"

Robert's lips turned down in a frown as he continued to shield me. "You are addressing Lenora Fletcher, Duchess of

Blackmoore, and my wife, sir. Now, I ask again, what is the meaning of this?"

The man's lower lip trembled as he stared at me before flicking his gaze to Robert, whose agitation grew with each passing second.

After a moment, he cast his eyes down to the sidewalk below us. His forehead crinkled. "Fletcher?"

Robert's eyebrows shot upward at the man. "Yes, I am Robert Fletcher, Duke of Blackmoore. Now, unless you can explain yourself, I shall wish you a good day, sir."

The man sniffled, tears welling in his eyes as he flicked his gaze back to me. "Your eyes," he murmured.

I wrinkled my forehead at him, trying to place the familiarity that plagued me.

"Who is it, Papa?" Sam questioned Robert.

The word triggered my memory. My eyebrows shot up to my hairline, and my jaw flapped open. I grasped the handle of the pram tighter to steady myself as I sucked in a sharp breath. My eyes went wide. I stared at his face. Wrinkles etched it. I mentally removed them, softening his features, trimming his beard, and coloring it brown. I considered his eyes without the dark circles underneath.

My lower lip began to tremble as Robert muttered an answer to Sam. I forced my jaw closed and swallowed hard, searching for my voice.

"Father?" I questioned.

His eyes rose to mine, and a tear dropped to his cheek.

I licked my lips and clarified my statement as Robert snapped his gaze to me. "Are you John Hastings? Dr. John Hastings of Glenrock?"

"Lenora, what are you saying?" Robert whispered.

I held my hand up to him, impatiently awaiting the man's answer.

His features twisted in a mask of both anguish and joy.

More tears welled in his eyes, some falling to his cheeks, running down to moisten the thick gray scruff that grew on his face. His lower lip shook as sobs wracked his shoulders. He nodded his head. "Yes," he cried.

I stumbled backward a step, and Robert caught my arm as he held Sam, steadying me.

"Is it you, my little Lenora?"

Tears pricked my eyes, and my knees wobbled as I struggled to stand. "Yes," I gasped.

Robert studied the scene, his face a mask of concern. My father and I stared at each other, each of us speechless.

Robert cleared his throat, glancing around the area. "Perhaps we should move this conversation to a more suitable location."

I flicked my gaze at Robert, fluttering my eyelashes as I nodded. "Yes, I think that would be best."

Robert lifted his eyebrows as he stared down at the man's tattered clothing. "If you will follow me, sir, we have accommodations at the Stratford."

I spun and clutched the handle of the pram. Sarah gurgled inside, kicking her feet and glancing up at me. At two months old, her eyes remained blue, similar in color to mine.

I marveled at the events as I pushed the buggy forward with my children next to me and my father trailing behind me. Could it be true? He certainly looked like the John Hastings I remembered, though the last time I had laid eyes on him was just shy of my sixth birthday.

But he had known my name and remembered my eyes. Heat washed over me as I pondered where he had been for the years I spent in the St. Mary's Orphanage for Girls.

Questions shot through my mind faster than I could process them. We rounded the corner and approached our hotel. Robert, still holding Sam close, held the door as I pushed the pram inside and we continued to our room.

In short order, we handed the children off to Nanny West, who traveled with us, and settled in the sitting room of our suite. Robert pulled me aside before I sat, asking for a private word.

"Lenora," he said as he glanced over his shoulder through the partially open door to the sitting room, "are you certain he is your father?"

I arched an eyebrow as I stared over Robert's shoulder at the man settling into the chair near the fireplace. I weighed my words carefully as I studied him. "It has been so long. I cannot be certain, no. But he resembles him."

Robert squashed his lips into a thin line. "You understand for your protection, I must question him. To ascertain his identity, in the event it may be false."

My stomach somersaulted, but I did understand Robert's impulse to protect us from scandal. I nodded. "I understand."

Robert raised his eyebrows and flicked another gaze over his shoulder before focusing on me. "You also understand that even if his identity proves true, he may still be a charlatan."

My chin sank to my chest as I realized the truth of his words. "Yes, I do."

Robert's shoulders slumped, and he pulled me closer to him. I wrapped my arms around him as I laid my head on his chest. "Oh, dear Lenora, I only wish to protect you from harm."

I pushed back from him and forced a smile onto my face. "I realize that, Robert. And I appreciate it so. I do hope your impulse to protect me proves unnecessary, but I do understand it."

Robert offered me a tight-lipped smile and nod. "Then let us proceed. And I do hope, for your sake, he proves true."

We strode back into the sitting room. As I settled into the

seat across from him, I studied his face while Robert poured brandies for everyone.

He handed one off to my father, and when he reached for it, I noticed the barely perceptible shake of his hands. He took a long sip as Robert handed me the half-filled glass.

I nodded my thanks to him, setting the glass on the side table next to me and leaning forward to stare at my father. Robert retrieved the glass and handed it to me again. "Drink it, dear, you need it."

His voice caused my father to lift his gaze to us. He stared at me for a moment, his eyes searching my face. "I cannot believe it is you. My little child, Lenora, whom I thought lost to me forever."

"Forgive me, sir," Robert said before I could respond, "but you do not mind my asking for some explanation or verification of your tale?"

My eyes widened at his statement. He truly thought this man a charlatan.

Robert glanced down at me and placed a hand on my shoulder. "You can understand a woman in Lenora's position may be...taken advantage of."

"Lenora's position," he murmured before his gaze rested on me again. His eyebrows scrunched at me.

I forced a weak smile onto my face, though I could feel it faltering as my lips trembled. My mind raced ahead, wanting answers, but I allowed Robert to guide the situation.

"Yes, Lenora's position. A duchess. Given her background, surely you can understand how a charlatan may hope to take advantage by selling a wild tale about being a long-lost parent."

The words stung me as I realized the possibility did exist. I swallowed hard as I studied his tattered clothes and his ramshackle appearance. Had he heard of me and decided to run a con?

My heart ached for more information, but Robert had a point, and I was determined to allow him to see his inquiry through.

"A duchess. My little baby," the man said.

"Sir, I really must insist."

My father flicked his gaze back to my husband, a weak smile on his lips. He cleared his throat, sipping at the brandy again as he held the glass with both shaking hands. "Yes, of course."

Robert firmed his lower lip and nodded at the man across from me. "My name is Dr. John Hastings. I had made my home in Glenrock in eighteen forty after meeting and marrying Lenora's mother, Helen. We were blessed with a baby girl. She was born with the bluest eyes I had ever seen." He flicked his gaze to me, tears welling in his eyes.

He paused for a moment as he gathered himself before continuing his tale. "When Lenora was nearly six, I went to India on a medical expedition. I did not realize it would be the last time I ever saw my child."

The man collapsed forward and wept for a moment. I leapt from my chair and hurried to him, kneeling in front of him and taking his hands in mine.

"This is information anyone could have," Robert answered.

The man stared down at my face, then raised his eyes to Robert. "You are correct. And may I say, I admire that you go to such lengths to protect my daughter."

Robert offered him a nod as he sipped his brandy.

"When Lenora was small, she had a doll. A raggedy thing, but she clung to it no matter the circumstance. It became so worn, the color of the doll's dress, once burgundy, could barely be made out. She called the doll…"

I waited with bated breath to hear the correct name. His features pinched together as tears welled in his eyes again.

"Loulou," he finally said.

I twisted to glance at Robert and nodded. Robert lifted his eyebrows, but before either of us could speak, my father continued.

"And when Lenora was quite small, no more than three, she waded into the stream that passed near our home. The water made the rocks in the bed quite slippery, and she fell and struck her chin on one sharp stone. She required three stitches. I sewed them myself. She has a tiny scar just here."

He reached out and rubbed the underside of my chin. A smile crossed my features, and I flung my arms around his neck. "Father," I cried.

I pulled away from him and noted the tears shining in his eyes.

"I am sorry for the inquisition, Dr. Hastings, though you do understand my position."

My father nodded as he held my hands in his.

Robert asked one final question. "May I ask, sir, why have you not sought your daughter out before this chance meeting?"

My father stared at him a moment before flicking his gaze to me. "Your mother told me you were dead."

CHAPTER 5

I stared up at the ceiling of the bedroom in the Staghearst Inn with my father's words echoing through my mind. "Your mother told me you were dead," I whispered.

A chill shot up my spine as I considered the sorrow my father undoubtedly experienced when my mother uttered that false tale.

My mind returned to our conversation.

"What?" I questioned when he confessed the story to us.

"When I arrived home from India, I found Helen in the back garden. I inquired as to your whereabouts. I expected to find a thriving seven-year-old. Instead, she confessed to me you had died. From fever, she said."

My father stared at the rug under his feet, his eyebrows furrowing. "She said it as casually as she'd report a lost button. With a shrug, she moved on to tending to her flowers. I collapsed onto the ground, heartbroken. Helen continued with her business as though she hadn't just admitted our only child had died.

"When I found my voice, I inquired further. When? How

had you become sick? Had she tried to send word to me? Where were you buried?"

"And?" I asked.

My father pressed his lips together into a thin line. "I became aware through the conversation how very sick your mother was."

I rose from my place at his feet and wandered back to the chair, collapsing into it. Robert grasped my shoulder, giving it a squeeze. I reached for his hand, threading my fingers through it.

My father shifted in his seat. "Your mother told me you'd taken ill suddenly about six months after I'd departed. She had not tried to contact me, as it would have done no good. I hoped to visit your grave, but she told me she…"

My father paused, his voice cutting off as he struggled to finish the wild tale. He sucked in a deep breath and continued. "She told me she burned your body on a funeral pyre."

My face twisted into a grimace. "And you thought her mad because of it?"

"We argued. I could not understand why she had not had a Christian burial. 'She was our baby,' I said, 'she should have been laid to rest properly.'"

My father licked his lips and studied his hand for a moment. "And then she told me the vilest things. 'She was a demon,' she said. 'A filthy little monster. We are better off without her.'"

His face contorted with pain as he spoke the words. "I couldn't understand it. How could she speak of my little Lenora this way? You were nothing but a delight. I didn't know what to answer. I collapsed into the kitchen chair in shock. When I recovered a bit, I inquired about which doctor she had consulted.

"She acted as though she hadn't a clue what I spoke of. I

pressed her, and she admitted she'd not sought care. She told me we were better off without you again."

"So, all this time you thought me dead."

My father shook his head at the statement. "No. Well, at first I did, yes. For many years. I assumed Helen had killed you. On purpose or by accident, I did not know. But I assumed you to be dead by her hand."

I screwed up my face. "At first?"

"I had Helen committed to an asylum, fearing she may do harm to someone else or herself. I spent all I had seeking treatment for her at an asylum."

My eyebrow arched, understanding his unkempt appearance.

"I visited her dutifully for years, hoping for some improvement in her condition. Truthfully, I had hoped for some moment of clarity so I might learn the truth of your fate. The dubious explanations I'd received caused my mind to conjure all sorts of things."

"I struggled to sleep, my mind imagining the torture you must have lived through in your final moments. Had she drowned you? Had she burned you alive? Had she strangled you? Or stabbed you?"

My father's face fell and his forehead crinkled again as tears welled once more. "My poor little child. Killed by her own mother."

"But I was not," I answered. Robert squeezed my shoulder again and offered me an appreciative smile.

"No, I…" He paused, collecting himself, his hands digging into the plaid fabric of the armchair. "On one of my visits to the asylum, she mentioned something odd. As we strolled through the gardens, she smirked at me. 'Filthy little demon is someone else's problem now,' she said.

"I stopped her and inquired after her meaning, but she shrugged it away. I insisted, demanding to know her meaning. She confessed to me that she had dumped you somewhere. She'd inquired after you later but found you were gone. Assuming you survived whatever happened to you after she'd left you, you were still alive, but she did not know where.

"My heart soared at the prospect that my little Lenora may be alive, and I tried to seek information but found very little. The neighbors in Glenrock did not know much. Only that Helen had taken a carriage trip one day and it was the last time they'd seen you.

"Helen had claimed you were in the garden or upstairs or some other thing when they'd call, but they began to realize you were not. They saw no sign of you, and eventually Helen admitted to your death to them. They believed her. Nothing more was said."

I fidgeted with the lace trim on my dress as I considered the story. "I see."

"Oh, Lenora, I should never have left you alone with her. I did not realize it, but she must have been mad even before I went to India."

"If she was not, she turned shortly after," I answered. "While she did not murder me, she performed all sorts of odd things on me in a desperate attempt to rid me of what she perceived to be a foul proclivity."

"Let us not speak further of it. We have determined the woman to be quite mad," Robert said. "We should not dredge up whatever drove her to it."

"My father should know," I said, flicking my gaze to Robert.

"Know?" my father inquired.

I set my gaze upon him, studying his beleaguered and confused face. "I can see and communicate with the spirits of those who have passed from this life. Mother found it foul, though as a child I did not understand why. My behavior, which I believed to be normal, caused her to perform many odd and, in some cases, painful experiments to rid me of the problem. After a time, she left me at a convent. The nuns cared for me for a little over a year before they, too, seemed to rid themselves of me, taking me to St. Mary's Orphanage for Girls."

My father's eyes widened. "All this time, you have been in Glasgow right under my nose, and I could not find you."

"No," Robert interjected, "only until just shy of her eighteenth birthday. We wed one month before it, and she has been mistress of Blackmoore Castle since."

"I'm sorry, Father," I said. "I thought you dead in India. I never expected Mother to lie to you. I assumed if you returned, you would seek me."

"I did not know until seven months ago."

"Seven months?" I questioned, my muscles going stiff. "Then...is Mother..." I could not bring myself to finish my statement.

My father understood my meaning and nodded. "She is very much alive and in the Staghearst Asylum."

My mind snapped back to the present, and I rolled onto my side. Why had I decided to visit my mother? The signs had all warned me against such a fool's errand, yet I still insisted.

With a sigh, I squeezed my eyes shut as tears threatened again. Within a fortnight, I found both my parents after years of wondering about them. Neither relationship, it seemed, withstood the devastation caused by my mother's decision.

Robert had offered my father a home with us, though he had declined. Our estrangement proved too much for him, and he withdrew back to Glenrock after one night within Blackmoore Castle. Perhaps instead of our estrangement, it was my ability. I had been candid. Had I been too honest?

Robert assured me he'd come round, and that, if he didn't,

he was not worth my time. I convinced myself it mattered not. I had lived this long without my parents, going forward without them would seem normal.

Yet I could not stop myself from going to Stagheart Asylum, seeking something. I opened my eyes and bit my lip, focusing on the newest addition to my room.

Unfortunately for me, I had not found what I sought at the madhouse. But instead, something had found me.

I focused on the wisp of a woman huddled in the corner, her red-rimmed eyes staring back at me. The same woman who had begged for my help at the asylum now stood before me again.

I propped myself up on my hand and raised my eyebrows at her. "Hello."

She did not speak, merely stood staring at me from the dark corner.

I cocked my head as I studied her. She hadn't been shy at the asylum. She'd approached me, clamping onto my arm and speaking to me immediately.

"You said you needed help," I tried. "Might you explain further?"

Her pale face gleamed back, her features steady and unmoving. I cursed communication with the dead. I wondered if it would ever become easier as I shoved back the bedding and swung my legs over the side of the bed.

"Can you at least tell me your name? I haven't the slightest–"

The door to the bedroom swung open, obscuring my view of the corner. Robert strode in, stopping short and eyeing me as I sat perched on the edge of the bed.

"Lenora? Have you not yet slept?"

"I am afraid I have not," I informed him. "The events of the evening have given me little rest. Though, to be fair, it is not this evening my mind has dwelled on, but rather the odd circumstances surrounding the meeting of my father."

Robert breathed out a sigh, his flexing jaw visible from the flickering flame he held at his chest. "I wish you wouldn't continue to torture yourself with this."

I pressed my lips together in a thin line as I slid my slippers onto my feet. "I cannot help that my mind continues to ponder it. Never fear, dear, I am certain I should have a new mystery to ponder soon enough."

I stood and pulled my dressing gown around my shoulders, waving for Robert to move away from his spot.

"Mystery? Whatever do you mean?" he asked as he stepped further into the room.

I swung the door shut. My shoulders slumped, and I clicked my tongue against the roof of my mouth before I huffed.

"What are you doing, Lenora?"

"My ghostly visitor from the asylum reappeared, though this time she was mute. I hoped to speak with her, but she is gone. You must have spooked her."

"Me?" Robert said, his voice incredulous. "The idea is absolutely preposterous. That I could spook a specter. Really, Lenora, I do not understand how these things happen."

He shook his head as he slid the candle onto the bedside table. I meandered back to bed, pulling off my dressing gown and tossing it across the foot of the bed.

"I have little more knowledge than you, in all honesty, though I do know one thing. This is the third time the woman has appeared to me. And if past instances are any indication, she will not be satisfied until she receives the help she seeks."

Robert tugged off his dressing gown, tossing it near mine before sinking onto the bed's edge. "Then I suppose she should speak up and ask for it."

"Funny, dear," I said, sliding between the sheets again. "It is almost never that easy."

With a sigh, Robert leaned back against his pillow. "What do you propose?"

"I propose nothing," I answered, lying back next to him. "Though I suspect I may need to visit the asylum again."

Robert stared at the ceiling, his palms drumming against the mattress. I glanced at him, aware of the displeasure coursing through his veins over my last statement.

"I do not plan to go tomorrow. I shall give it several days after we return to Blackmoore at least before I make any decisions."

"I said nothing."

A smile crept across my lips, and I kissed his cheek. "I know you did not. But I also realize you are not pleased."

He sighed again. "I am neither pleased nor displeased. I do wish you could live somewhat of a more normal life instead of being plagued by this constantly."

I laid my head on his shoulder, and he wrapped an arm around me.

"But then I remember it is the sole reason we met and married, and for that, I cannot be more thankful." He kissed the top of my head.

I snuggled against him, a smile on my face. "I feel quite the same way, and despite being faced with my past of late and wondering what may have come if things progressed differently, I find myself quite pleased they did not."

Robert clasped his hand around mine as I laid it against his chest. "Come what may, we shall face it together."

With those words and his thumb rubbing my skin, my eyes slid shut, and my mind finally settled. I slipped off to sleep in the comfort of my husband's arms.

When I arose the next morning, I found myself alone. Robert, true to his word, had already departed for the asylum to speak with the doctors. A noble effort, I reflected as I dressed. I would not have required it of him, yet he offered it anyway.

I sat at the window, awaiting his return and wondering about our travel plans as dark clouds loomed on the horizon.

Before any deluge began, the carriage trundled down from the hill above, coming to a stop outside the inn. Robert disembarked and strode into the building.

I collected my reticule and stood awaiting him as he pushed through the door.

"Ready, dear?" he asked.

I nodded my answer. "I am quite anxious to be at home."

"Come along, we shall leave as soon as the final pieces of luggage are loaded."

He led me to the carriage, and we climbed aboard. I settled in my seat and glanced at Robert at the seat across from me.

My heart skipped a beat as I realized Robert had returned from the asylum with a new friend.

CHAPTER 6

The carriage rocked and swayed as the coachman loaded the last of the luggage and climbed to his perch. Robert settled into his seat with a huff and glanced out at the dreary day. A few drops of rain fell from the bleak sky, smacking into the street and the carriage. Drips rolled down the windows, and Robert issued a grunt.

"At least we made it inside before the rain," he said as the carriage lurched forward. He glanced at his pocket watch before clicking it closed and returning it to its fabric compartment. "We should arrive home in time to see the children before tea."

I forced my eyes to focus on him and offered a smile. I swallowed hard, considering broaching the subject of our visitor. With several hours' journey ahead of us, I found myself loath to do so. While Robert no longer detested the presence of the dead, he did not enjoy it either. I feared what informing him of his seatmate may do to him.

"Are you quite all right, Lenora?" he questioned, his eyes studying me.

I cleared my throat, broadening my smile, and flicked my

gaze back to him from our otherworldly visitor. "Yes," I said, sounding a bit too breathless.

I pushed out a chuckle and pressed my lips together, offering him a shrug. "Merely wondering what the result of your morning excursion was, though I was hesitant to broach the subject."

Robert settled back into his seat, his arm brushing the deceased woman who sat next to him. He shifted, wiggling his shoulders. I assumed a chill shot through him at the touch. Once settled, a smile crossed his face. "It went quite well. You should have no reluctance to bring up any matter to me, Lenora. We are husband and wife. You may approach me with anything."

"It is not an unwillingness to approach you, Robert, but rather my own uncertainty about the subject matter that kept me mum."

"Ah," he answered with a curt nod, "I see. Well, I shall disclose only the details you wish me to, though I believe the trip to be a success."

I smiled and nodded before flicking a gaze out the window. Rain fell more steadily, and I wished to be home. I pictured the entryway with its curving staircase inviting me up to my grand suite. I longed to climb the circular stone stairs leading to the turret rising above the sheer drop and settled into my window seat with my fur blanket tucked carefully around me and a roaring fire in the fireplace across the room.

My eyes slid closed, and I imagined Sam's tiny arms squeezing my neck and the weight of Sarah against my chest. My brow furrowed as other thoughts crept into my mind uninvited. I pressed my lips together in a thin line and snapped my eyes open, shaking my head.

I focused on Robert. "What do you mean by 'success?'"

Robert pulled his gaze from the passing scenery before

answering. "I have ensured your mother shall receive the best care for whatever life she has remaining."

I offered a tight-lipped smile and slow nod as I processed the statement. "Thank you, Robert. It is not your responsibility, though I do appreciate your efforts."

My gaze fell to the floor.

"No thanks are needed, dear. Your mother, however estranged and disturbed she may be, is still your mother. And you deserve the peace of mind to know she is receiving quality care."

The words brought tears to my eyes, and my features pinched as I fought to hold them back. Robert shifted in his seat, and his warm hand wrapped around mine. I struggled to steady my nerves as emotions coursed through me faster than I could process. Sorrow, shame, and heartbreak. Yet at the same time, my heart soared as the warmth of Robert's hand permeated my skin. He offered a gentle squeeze, unwilling to pry but wishing to offer support.

I swallowed the lump in my throat. I continued to stare at the carriage floor. "She is very sick, yes."

Robert's shoulders slumped, and he bent lower to catch my eyes. "She will be cared for properly now."

My brow furrowed, and I bit my lip before sucking in a deep breath. "Yes, thanks to you. Though her care is not the source of my consternation."

"Oh?"

"The truth is, Robert, as much as I wish to put the incident behind me, I cannot. And my mind continues to question the details of anything that may have been mentioned to you by her doctors."

"I see," Robert answered, straightening but keeping hold of my hand.

"So, I feel I must ask for all the information."

Robert knit his brows, concern settling into his gray eyes. "Are you certain? There is no need for you to know."

"As disturbing as it may be, it is more so to be kept in the dark. Please spare no details."

He flicked his eyebrows up and shot a glance at the stormy skies. "It seems your mother suffers from…" He paused, avoiding eye contact.

I raised my eyebrows as I hung on his last word, awaiting the description.

"Several afflictions," he settled on, waving a hand in the air. He finally settled his gaze upon me again. His lips parted to speak, but no words came.

After a moment, he knit his brows again and said, "Lenora…" He paused again, pulling his mouth back into a partial grimace.

I waited for several breaths as the carriage trundled along.

After a moment, he closed his gaping mouth. "I must confess, I am uncertain how to say this."

I flicked my gaze to our deceased traveling companion, then back to my husband. "Perhaps it is best, Robert, to speak plainly. I am not as delicate as you may imagine."

He squeezed his mouth shut and nodded. "One of the ailments noted by the doctor was delusions. On more than one occasion, she has spoken to…" He lifted a shoulder. "Persons who were not there."

Robert's gray eyes fell upon me as we swayed with the carriage. I pressed my lips together, clutching at the edge of the seat below me as I avoided his gaze for a moment. I flicked it back to him and nodded. "Likely, she suffers from the same affliction I do."

"Yes, I expect so. Did you know?"

I shook my head. "No. As a child, I can recall no times when my mother showed any signs of seeing the deceased.

She did not see my grandfather when he appeared shortly before she abandoned me. At least, she gave no indication of seeing him."

"Perhaps her gift is less pronounced."

"Perhaps. Or she attempted to ignore it to the best of her ability. Unfortunately, mine cannot always be ignored." I flicked my gaze to our riding companion as silence fell between us.

My gaze fell to the floor again as I contemplated telling Robert about his riding partner. Before I could bring myself to mention it, another question popped into my mind. I glanced up at him again. "You said several afflictions. Are there others?"

Robert pressed his lips together and focused on the passing scenery. "Yes, apparently there are several."

I raised my eyebrows, gripping the seat's edge tighter. "Such as?"

Robert cocked his head, a worried expression settling onto his dark features. "Perhaps it is best left with the doctors, Lenora."

"Robert, I must know."

"As always, you are correct. She is your mother. You deserve the truth."

"Not for that reason," I said, more sharply than I intended. I breathed a shaky breath as I bit back tears and swallowed the lump in my throat. "What if I suffer from the same?"

Robert's features softened, and he leaned forward to grasp my hand. I quickly flicked away a tear from my cheek. His fingers caressed my chin, gently raising it. My eyes remained downcast as I struggled to contain my fears and emotions.

"Lenora," Robert's voice cooed at me, his finger lingering on my chin.

I raised my eyes to meet his, tears threatening.

"You are not disturbed as she is."

"But I suffer from–"

"From being too kind. Not of the cruelty she exhibited. You suffer from making the best of every situation that has been thrust upon you. Not from seeking the worst in them. You, Lenora, suffer from being an exceptional person. Not of the things she suffers from."

The answer caused more tears to fall to my cheeks as I grasped his hands and squeezed.

"Oh, Lenora, she has been disturbed since your childhood. Likely even before then. The doctors say she has little chance to recover as her mind is quite gone. I am sorry to give you that news. I know you hoped for something more. For a reconciliation, perhaps. Or an understanding at least. But I am uncertain it will happen."

I licked my lips, flicking a few tears away that clung to my jawline. "I expected nothing from her. My tears are not from my mother's condition, but your acceptance of me."

Robert kissed my forehead as I composed myself before he patted the seat next to him. I slid my eyes closed for a moment as his hand passed through the woman sitting next to him.

I shook my head at his silent request.

"Do not be coy, Lenora," Robert prodded. "I would very much like to comfort you in your time of need."

"It is not reluctance based on shyness."

Robert furrowed his brow. "Then what? Surely, you can allow yourself this moment."

I opened and closed my mouth several times as I tried to find the words. My eyelashes fluttered, and I offered him a sheepish glance. "There is a spirit sitting next to you, and I should very much not like to sit in her lap."

Robert's eyes widened, and he leaned away from the woman. "What?" He stammered around, his lips bobbing up and down as he searched for words. "How long has it been there?"

I sucked in a shaky breath, my nerves settling as the conversation turned from my troubled mother to something more normal to me. "I assume since you visited the sanitarium."

"Good God," Robert exclaimed, his muscles stiff as he pressed himself against the carriage's side.

With the roles reversed, I took his hands in mine, providing comfort to him as he had to me moments ago. "She is quite quiet and not gruesome at all. Just rather…" I paused and studied her for a moment. "Disheveled."

Robert pressed his lips into a thin line and slid his eyes sideways. His face, several shades lighter than normal, pinched.

I tightened my jaw as his reaction almost elicited a chuckle from me. This time I beckoned to him, patting the seat next to me.

He dove across the carriage and settled in next to me, wrapping his arm around me and pulling me close. I wasn't certain if he intended to comfort me as he had offered moments ago or hoped to place a barrier between himself and the deceased woman, but no matter the case, I relaxed into his embrace.

After a few moments, Robert spoke again. "So, I have picked up a stray."

This time, I could not hold back the chuckle. I patted his chest and lifted my head from his shoulder. "Indeed, you have."

I glanced up at him.

An amused expression crossed his features, and he offered a half-chuckle. "And I thought you were the one who brought home the strays."

We laughed over the comment for several moments.

Robert patted my leg as our chuckling died down. I wiped at my eyes where tears had spilled over again, this time from relief and amusement rather than fear and pain.

He flicked his gaze toward the woman, an empty space for him, then focused on me. "Is she still there?"

I nodded and intertwined my fingers through his. "Yes. Still silent, staring ahead."

Robert's chest heaved, and he frowned at the empty seat across from him. "I wonder what it is she wants."

I smiled at the statement, pleased Robert's curiosity finally won out over his fear of the deceased. It marked progress on his part. "Help is all I have determined thus far."

"They all want that, Lenora. That doesn't aid us in pinpointing what she needs."

I lifted my eyebrows at him, the corners of my mouth turning upward.

Robert shot me a glance, his brow furrowing at my expression. "What?"

"Your newfound interest in the subject pleases me."

He flicked his gaze away, lifting a shoulder in response as he set his face in a frown. "I merely wish for you not to be tortured by the spirit's dubious behavior."

The smile on my lips grew, and I struggled to hold in a chuckle. He studied me again, his frown deepening before he tugged at his pocket watch and stared down at it.

"Do not laugh, Lenora. I speak the truth."

I slid my arm through the crook of his and leaned closer to him. "I think you rather enjoyed the last mystery we solved and are looking forward to another."

Robert snapped his gaze toward me, a look of surprise on his features. "I most certainly did not!" He waved a hand in the air. "Traipsing about, sticking our noses into business that was not ours. Arguing with the police. And the danger. I should not even begin to discuss the danger all our lives were placed in. My God, Lenora, Edwin nearly met his end!"

"Yes, he did, and I would have been very sorry if Edwin had been my next visiting spirit."

"As would I. You would not have had a moment's rest with him."

I chuckled and patted his arm, recognizing the truth in his statement. "Yet we came through it, saved Edwin's life in more ways than one, and identified the guilty party."

"And I would have been perfectly happy to leave the mysteries behind," Robert said with a sharp nod.

I smiled up at him before flicking my gaze to the passing scenery. We rolled along the flat road as the horses' hooves pounded the cobblestone.

"Though I do wonder about the nature of her request."

My lips turned up again as I kept my eyes trained on the buildings filling my view. Despite his cantankerous attitude, the mystery proved too enticing. He desired to solve it. Which would make my involvement easier.

I opened my mouth to answer him, twisting to face him when I froze. My jaw dropped further open, and I knit my brows.

"What is it?" Robert questioned.

I lifted my eyebrows and waved a hand at the empty seat across the carriage. "She's gone!"

"Gone where?" Robert asked, shrinking in the seat whilst his eyes darted around the carriage.

"I haven't a clue!" I exclaimed. "She is not here. She was here just moments ago."

Robert straightened his posture, lifting his chin as I informed him she was not lurking over his head or behind his back. "Perhaps it is for the best. Perhaps now you will be rid of her."

I puckered my lips into a deep frown as I stared over at

the empty seat. I doubted I would be rid of her, as Robert suggested. And even if I was, I pondered what had driven her to seek me out on three occasions. The mystery proved enticing to me, at least.

I hadn't much time to consider it further before chaos erupted. The carriage lurched sideways. A frightened squeal broke through the steady patter of rain on the roof. We spun to face the front. The horses reared, stamping their feet and attempting to break free of their harnesses.

"What the devil is happening?" Robert questioned.

The carriage shimmied as the horses refused to move, fighting against the coachman as they tried to turn around.

"Wait here," Robert instructed as he flung the door open and stepped into the rain.

"Jones! What's happening?" he shouted.

"I don't know, Your Grace. Something's spooked the horses. They–"

His words cut off as the steeds pulling the carriage whipped around in the opposite direction, tipping the carriage onto two wheels.

I struggled to cling to my seat as the conveyance threatened to tip. The door Robert had used moments ago banged closed before swinging open again. The horses bolted in the direction from which we'd just traveled.

The carriage slammed back down onto all four wheels. The force dislodged Jones from his seat. He tumbled from the perch, landing hard on the slick cobblestones.

I clutched at the seat again as the carriage bounced along, dragged by the wild horses. I stared out the back window at a stunned Jones and equally stunned Robert.

My stomach sank as I realized I was at the mercy of the four frenzied equines that pulled the carriage, and me along with it.

CHAPTER 7

Buildings passed by my window at lightning speed. Within moments, the view turned to fields as we left the town behind.

The horses blazed a path to some unknown location. I sat inside the carriage, powerless to do anything. The door continued to bang open and shut. Rain splashed inside as we flew along.

I lunged toward it as it smacked against the carriage's side and grabbed the latch. It threatened to fly open again and drag me with it, but I held firm to it and collapsed backward, managing to pull it closed and latch it.

I blew out a shaky breath as I solved one of my issues, though, unfortunately, it was the smaller of the two problems. The larger still loomed large on the fast-moving horizon.

I clung to my seat as my mind scrambled to find a solution. Short of waiting for the horses to tire and slow themselves, I could not find one.

I stared out the window, wondering if a brave rider might

come to my aid. The vast fields that stretched on either side of me dashed my hopes. Not a soul in sight. Living or dead.

The carriage rumbled along, approaching the town we'd stayed in overnight. On the hill above, shrouded in misty fog, the rambling asylum loomed.

My brow furrowed as I stared up at it, wondering if that was my final destination. The town passed by in a flash as the horses continued their race. I twisted and ducked to glance out the window toward the front.

Could I climb to the perch and grab hold of the reins to stop the horses? I shook the ridiculous idea from my head as the scenery whisked past, replaced by the question of whether I could survive a leap from the runaway conveyance.

I dismissed the idea, but it popped back into my mind as the horses turned a corner and the carriage leaned precariously to the side. The wheels lifted from the ground as the horses thundered around a bend leading away from town.

I squeezed my eyes closed, shifting my weight in a desperate attempt to stop the conveyance from tipping over.

A yelp escaped my lips as the wheels bounced back onto the rough road. We continued zooming along, the horses still galloping at full speed. The carriage tilted and I pitched forward as we began to climb the grade to the asylum.

Perhaps the slope would slow the horses enough to allow me to disembark, I pondered. As we continued to climb, I reached for the door, squeezing my eyes closed as I wrapped my hand around the handle.

I swallowed hard and snapped my eyes open, biting my lower lip hard as I swung the door open. The wind caught it, blowing it out of my hand and slamming it against the carriage's side. I shrank back, clutching at the seat again as the road whipped past me.

A sensation of vertigo passed through me at the dizzying

sight, and I squeezed my eyes shut as my stomach turned. Even if I dared make the jump, I'd likely injure myself or worse. I had not realized the narrowness of the road when we'd ascended it in the dark last night.

Beyond it, the land dropped off sharply. I pressed my lips together as the steep drop-off raced past the open door. Injury may be the least of my worries if I went through with the reckless plan to leap from the carriage, even if the horses slowed on the slope.

Though they showed no sign of yielding, continuing at a frightening pace, even up the hill. We approached the gates to the sanitarium. Perhaps this would stop them.

I steadied my breath and reached for the door as it swung closed, latching it again and waiting for the gates to stop our forward progress. I switched seats so I could stare out the front window.

Rain mixed with sweat glistened on the rumps of the running horses. I chewed my lower lip as I spotted the stone pillars rising on either side of the road. The horses showed no signs of slowing, and I worried we may plow into the gates.

I clung to the seat, readying for the impact. I blew out the breath I'd been holding as we passed between the stone columns. The gates stood open, and the horses proceeded further, unfettered by anything.

We wound around the last bit of the climb at breakneck speeds. I fretted over whether or not the carriage would topple over the steep drop-off and plunge me to my death along with our four beautiful horses, though they managed to keep to the road.

The asylum grew larger and larger in front of me until it obliterated most of my view. My forehead crinkled as I worried the horses would race past it. What lay on the other side was beyond my knowledge. Perhaps the drive ended in another sharp cliff and we'd plunge over it.

I held my breath again as we pulled next to the large structure, squeezing my eyes closed as a cry escaped my mouth.

A moment later, I pitched forward, nearly slamming into the opposite seat as the horses slid to a stop, splattering mud in a wide spray as their back feet dug into the ground. The carriage lurched, and I sat clinging to the seat.

Panic still coursed through my veins, and my heart pounded in my chest, despite the motion having subsided. The horses whinnied and nickered, bobbing their heads up and down, steam blowing from their widened nostrils.

A sob escaped me as I thanked a higher power that I arrived intact and unharmed. I flicked my gaze to the large building rising to my left.

The destination could not be an accident. The horses did not bolt, leaving both Robert and Jones behind, and drove me unbidden to the sanitarium we'd visited the previous night. The asylum where I'd encountered a soul who had begged for my help and then appeared to me on three separate occasions.

"Rather an extreme course of action," I grumbled under my breath as I reached for the door handle.

I pushed the door open and stumbled from the conveyance, my legs like jelly. I held tight to the door as my knees threatened to betray me and send me crashing into the mud below. I stared up at the dark stone walls, crawling with leafless ivy, and swallowed hard.

The cool air caressed my skin, and I gulped it in as I forced my nerves to settle. Gentle rain pattered down. After a moment, I turned my attention to our horses. I inched toward them, keeping my hand on the carriage in case my legs did not hold me.

I patted their hindquarters, circling around them. They seemed no worse for wear. I studied the mechanism connecting them to the carriage, wondering if I could disconnect it and somehow climb atop a horse to ride back toward Robert.

I dismissed the ridiculous idea immediately. My eyes rose to the coachman's perch. Perhaps I could scramble up to his seat and drive the horses back. I glanced at the large wooden doors leading to the hospital. I could go inside and seek help. In fact, perhaps this is exactly the course of action the spirit wished from me.

I glanced around in search of her. If she had been the reason the horses had bolted and driven me here, perhaps she'd make another appearance. I found no trace of her. Did she wait for me inside? I did not wish to find out.

My eyes fell back to the coachman's perch. With a nod, I firmed my lower lip and decided to try for it.

The carriage swayed as I began the climb. My shoes, slick with mud, slipped off the step, and I tumbled backward, landing in a muddy puddle. The water splashed around me, soiling my dress and hands.

I groaned as I struggled to get up, wiping at a splatter of mud that clung to my cheek. I wiped my hands on my dress and tried again. This time, I made it.

I scrambled up into the rather uncomfortable seat and sought the reins. My shoulders slumped as I spotted them in a tangle on the ground below me.

With a heavy sigh, I slid down, my feet sinking into the sopping ground. The muck sucked my feet in quickly, and I fell forward to my knees. My hands slapped against the mud to break my fall.

I shook my head as I pushed myself up and rose to stand, pulling one foot from the sludge. As I tugged the second from the thick mud, my foot lifted, though my boot did not.

I cursed the rain as I reached down and heaved my mud-stained boot free, sliding my foot into it. I stared down at my filthy clothing, lamenting what would likely be the loss of my tweed traveling suit before I bent to collect the reins.

I set them in a place accessible to the coachman's perch and climbed up. With a heavy sigh, I settled into the uncomfortable seat and reached for the reins. With my shoulders square and back straight, I snapped them as I had seen Jones do so many times before.

The horses did not respond. Undeterred, I tried again, offering a sharp "Giddy up," to them for encouragement.

One horse nickered, and another stomped at the ground, snorting at me. I narrowed my eyes at the stubborn beasts and tugged upon the reins again. *Perhaps a different approach*, I thought.

"Come on! Let's go! Move! Back down the hill. Come on, now!"

The steeds refused to budge. My shoulders slumped as I let the reins slip from my fingers.

A steadier stream of rain fell from the sky as I admitted defeat. Apparently, Jones had a special touch that I did not possess. Ironic, I could communicate with the dead but could not make horses pull a carriage.

I twisted to glance behind me. I'd need to walk the distance back to Robert. With any luck, Robert and Jones would already be closing the distance between us and my trek would be shortened.

The rain pelted me harder as I slid down from the seat, careful not to become stuck in the sludge again. I hesitated at the door of the carriage, considering ducking inside and awaiting rescue.

I rolled my eyes at myself. "Await rescue?" I questioned aloud as I shook my head at my damsel-in-distress reaction.

As a younger woman, I'd endured more than a rainy walk through the Scottish countryside.

My mind flitted to a worse experience in my youth. At the orphanage, I'd spent many nights in the cold attic with no bed or blanket, typically as punishment for my ability. On one stormy night about a year after I'd arrived, I incurred the wrath of Headmistress Williamson yet again.

The woman, who disliked me from the day I stepped foot inside the orphanage, caught me comforting the spirit of a child who'd lost her life on a similar night. Hidden in the closet of our communal room, I wrapped my arm around the poor child, no more than my own age of eight, and dried her tears.

When the Headmistress caught me, she dragged me from within the closet and gave me several swaps on the rear before she yanked me into the hall and lugged me up the narrow staircase. She flung the door open at the top and tossed me into the room.

The door slammed shut a moment later, cutting off my view of her pinched purple-red face. The click of the engaging lock echoed against the vaulted ceiling.

The storm raged louder up here. I nestled into a dark corner, shivering from the chill. Lightning lit the room from a circular window behind me. Thunder pounded against the roof, shaking the walls.

I pulled my legs up to my chest and wrapped my arms around them, letting my forehead fall to my knees.

Something smacked into the back of my head. I snapped my head up and glanced around. I expected to find the child I'd been torn away from, or perhaps another spirit, but I found myself alone.

I sank my head to my knees again. Another plunk against the back of my head. I glanced around again, still finding myself alone.

"Hello?" I called out, risking receiving another beating if the Headmistress still stood on the stairs.

No one answered. As I scanned the dark space, lit only by the lightning now and again, another plop struck me on the top of my head.

I flicked my gaze upward and studied the air above me. Another splat struck me on my forehead. I winced and wiped at my skin. My fingertips identified the source. Water.

Rain. The roof leaked, and I'd had the bad luck to sit directly underneath the leaky spot. I crawled on my hands and knees to another spot. As I'd find over the course of forty minutes, the roof leaked a fair amount in a number of places.

After sitting in a puddle, I scrambled to another spot where water dripped onto my shoulder. I moved again, and again, not finding a comfortable, dry location.

Finally, I pressed my back against the door leading downstairs. I let my head thud against the wood as I tried to get comfortable enough to fall asleep.

As my head lolled to the side and eyes slid closed, a noise startled me. I jumped, sucking in a startled breath as I glanced around. Had the child returned for comfort?

The noise sounded again. My eyebrows pinched as I attempted to identify it. Then another noise joined the patter of rain against the roof.

"Lenora," a voice hissed.

"Who's there?" I called, assuming it to be from a spirit.

"Matilda Anderson," the voice answered.

I spun, realizing it came from the opposite side of the door. "What do you want?"

"To help. Only, you're blocking the door. I cannot open it. Move away."

"What?" I questioned.

"Move back!" her small voice breathed.

I scurried backward like a crab on my hands and feet. The door creaked open, and the small form of a child my age slipped inside. Lightning tore through the sky, lighting her wide emerald eyes and flaxen hair as she stared at me.

"Have you been sent to retrieve me?"

"No," she said, hastening toward me. She unfurled a blanket and wrapped it around my shoulders before she sank down to sit next to me. "I came to help you."

She grinned at me as she tugged the blanket around her shoulders, too.

"Does the Headmistress know you're here?

She lifted her porcelain chin and shook her head, her soft curls shimmering in the fleeting light as they bounced.

"You shall be punished!" I exclaimed, wriggling from the blanket and shoving it toward her. "You must leave. And how did you open the door without permission? I heard her lock it!"

The girl waved a small object in the air. As lightning lit the room again, I squinted at it. A small hairpin stuck from between her thumb and forefinger. She gave me another toothy grin and slid it into her blonde curls.

She patted the dusty wood floor next to her. "Sit down, Lenora. You do not deserve to be alone up here."

I wrapped my arms around myself and spun away from her. "I do."

"That's ridiculous," she answered. "You're just a child, only about eight, like me. No child should be shut up in this cold attic with no blanket or bed as punishment."

"You do not understand."

"Then you must explain."

I slid my eyes sideways over my shoulder as I pouted. She patted the floor again and held the blanket out.

I pursed my lips and glanced down at my fingertips, blue from the cold. My gaze wandered back to the warm blanket the girl offered as I chewed my lower lip. After a moment, I gave in and hurried over, plopping on the floor and huddling next to her.

She wrapped the blanket and her arm around my shoulder. "You're freezing!"

"I am a bit cold. It's quite chilly up here." I shot a glance at her. "Though I am used to it. I have been locked up here a number of times."

"No one should become used to this."

Silence fell between us for a moment as I huddled deeper into the blanket.

"I do not recall seeing you in my classes," I said after a moment.

"I have only started here. My mother died several weeks ago, and the neighbor could not care for me. Too many mouths to feed, she said."

"Oh, how awful, I am sorry."

"It's quite all right, Lenora. She did not take very good care of me anyway."

My brow furrowed as I pondered the statement.

"We lived very near a pub, and she spent most of her time there. I had a brother, but he died of fever last year. Mum was too drunk to care for him."

"My goodness!" I exclaimed. "How frightful."

"There, now I've told you my story. What about yours?"

I stared into my lap, my chin nearly touching my chest. "I am a terrible person."

"That cannot be true."

"It is," I insisted. "You should not wish to be my friend if I explain it to you."

She lifted her chin and crossed her arms over her chest defiantly. "I shall prove you wrong."

"You should go, Matilda, before the Headmistress becomes cross with you."

"I will not! And call me Tilly."

"I shall not tell!"

"Oh?" Tilly asked. She tossed the blanket from her shoulders and leapt to her feet. "If you do not, I shall open the door and scream at the top of my lungs!"

"You wouldn't!" I said, my jaw unhinging at the wild statement. "You shall be punished."

"Of course I will be. And it shall be your fault!" She poked a finger at me before setting her hands on her hips. "Now, tell me your secret."

I shook my head, pressing my lips together in determination.

Tilly twisted the handle and tugged the door open. She let her jaw fall open. Her eyes slid toward me, a mischievous gleam in her eye.

I jumped up and raced toward her, covering her open mouth. "Fine!" I breathed. "Close the door and be quiet!"

She grinned at me and eased the door shut before we settled on the floor again, sharing the blanket. I traced the edge of my nightgown. "I have a terrible affliction."

"Like an illness?"

I shook my head. "No. Very much different. I should prefer an illness, I think."

Tilly wrinkled her nose and shook her head. "No, you wouldn't. Illnesses are quite terrible."

"But I am not normal, you see," I said to her, my eyes flicking up to her emerald green ones.

"You seem quite normal to me."

Tears formed as I returned my gaze to my lap. "Yet, I am not. There is no easy way to say it. I can see people who have died. They come to me for help. I feel quite sorry for them, and I try to help. I know it is horrid of me, but I did not realize it was wrong."

The tears spilled onto my cheeks, and I buried my face in

my hands. Warm fingers wrapped around my forearm and tugged it downward.

I stared at Tilly with a tear-streaked face, sniffling.

"I don't think that's wrong, Lenora. I think it's quite right." She offered a tight-lipped smile and nod.

My eyebrows squashed together as I pondered if perhaps Tilly was a member of the deceased. No, she was quite warm. Alive. Another living person who did not find me foul.

A confused but relieved smile spread on my features, and I clutched her hand. "Thank you," I whispered.

Her grin broadened, and we sat in silence for a moment.

"Now, who were you helping tonight when that old bat interrupted you?" She asked as we settled against a wall, covered in the blanket.

As I started to explain, footsteps sounded on the stairs, and a key rattled in the lock.

My eyes went wide, and I snapped my gaze to Tilly. "Hide!"

CHAPTER 8

Tilly leapt to her feet and hurried across the room as the key clanked around in the lock.

"The blanket!" I hissed.

She winced and raced back across the space, snatching the blanket I held out toward her and scurrying to a darkened corner.

I leapt to my feet as she huddled into a darkened space. My heart thudded in my chest as a crack of light appeared. The door swung further open. I swallowed hard as I spotted the figure of Headmistress Williamson limned in the light from below.

I licked my lips as she raised the candelabra she held and squinted at me.

She tossed something inside. It landed in a heap a few meters from me. "For the cold."

I grabbed the threadbare blanket from the floor. "Thank you, Headmistress."

"Don't thank me, thank Ms. Winston. Had it been up to me, I'd have left you to freeze." She yanked the door shut, and the lock engaged again. Her footsteps lumbered down the steps as I curled my fingers around the small, thin material.

"What a witch!" a small voice exclaimed behind me. "Lucky I brought a blanket larger than an infant's." Tilly reclaimed her place at my side, tossing the blanket around me.

"I could have made do with this," I said as we settled onto the floor again. "It is big enough to cover my head from the leaks."

We burst into a fit of laughter over the ridiculous offering from the headmistress. We spent almost the rest of the evening whispering, giggling, and discussing my odd ability. Tilly did not seem bothered by it. I had made my first friend on that dark, damp, chilly night.

* * *

Tears filled my eyes as I recalled meeting Tilly over a decade earlier. The rain still fell around me, matching my melancholy mood as I swallowed hard.

"Oh, Tilly," I murmured aloud as I leaned against the carriage, "why did you have to die?"

With a deep sigh, I forced myself to move forward, intending to descend the hill and make my way back toward Robert and Jones.

As I emerged from the side of the carriage, a man rounded the corner of the sanitarium. We startled one another. I nodded at him, offering a tight-lipped smile as I continued.

"Are you quite all right, madam?" he inquired, tugging the hat off his blonde hair and holding it against his drenched raincoat.

"Oh, yes, thank you," I answered. I waved back at the carriage. "The horses bolted and did not stop until they reached the summit outside the asylum. I am returning down the hill in search of my husband and coachman. The poor man was thrown from his seat when they went wild."

"Oh, how terrible," he answered. "However, you cannot walk about in this rain. You'll catch your death."

"I am certain I shall be fine. My husband is likely coming toward me and will make the trip shorter."

The man shook his head. "I cannot in good conscience allow you to wander about in the rain storm. Come inside. Perhaps we can send someone to seek your husband."

I glanced down at my soaked and soiled dress. "I'd rather not. I appear rather out of sorts."

"You shall appear more out of sorts if you continue to wander about in this weather." He held out his hand toward me. "Please. We shall ensure you receive a blanket and a hot cup of tea whilst you wait."

I glanced down the winding hill toward the village. A warm cup of tea would certainly be welcomed. And Robert would likely scold me if I did not accept and continued with my headstrong plan to wander through the village in the rain.

I pressed my lips together and flicked my gaze back to him. "All right."

He wrapped his fingers around mine and helped me over a puddle before leading me into the sanitarium. The familiar stench assaulted my nostrils the moment I stepped inside. I second-guessed my decision to stay here, wondering if the tea would even be bearable.

"Nurse Johnson," the man said to the woman behind the desk across the dirty tile floor, "Mrs., uh…I'm sorry, what did you say your name was?" He twisted to face me, his brows knit.

"Fletcher," I answered. "Lenora Fletcher." I left out my

title, certain in my current state he would not believe me anyway.

"Yes, Mrs. Fletcher has had an accident. Might you find her a blanket? She is quite soaked."

The nurse arched an eyebrow at my muddied dress.

"Nurse Johnson!" the man exclaimed as she settled her eyes on my soiled form.

"Yes, sir," she answered before flitting off into another room.

"You may bring it to the common area!" he called after her before turning back to face me. "Let's get you settled with that cup of tea."

I accepted his arm with a slight smile, and he led me toward the door leading further into the asylum. My heart sped up as we approached it, and I swallowed hard.

"It is all right, Mrs. Fletcher. You shall be safe inside. Most of our patients are quite harmless."

I forced another smile as he unlocked the door and motioned for me to enter. "Our patients? Are you a doctor here?"

"Yes," he answered, "Dr. Applebaum."

I wondered if he might be my mother's doctor. Was he the man Robert spoke with earlier?

"Perhaps you spoke with my husband earlier, then. He inquired after a patient of yours this morning."

The man led me toward the large wooden desk where nurses recorded patient information. A few of them side-eyed us as we wandered past. "Oh? I'm sorry to say I did not speak with him. I have only just arrived a week ago, so most patients are under the care of Dr. Merriweather."

I nodded at the woman as they gawked at me. "I see. Perhaps he spoke with Dr. Merriweather, then."

"Most likely, yes," he answered as we arrived in a large

room overlooking the scraggly garden. Rain pattered the floor-to-ceiling windows.

Dr. Applebaum led me to a table and tugged a chair from underneath. I eased into it, a shiver passing through me. The nurse arrived with a shabby blanket and handed it to me, her eyes searching the doctor's face for an answer.

He gave none, nodding at her and offering a thank you before he requested hot tea. When she continued to stare, he reminded her of the request again, waving a hand to signal her to retrieve the tea.

"Yes, Doctor," she said before scurrying from the well-lit space. The lighting drew even more attention to the dilapidated appearance of the room.

I swallowed hard as I tried to stop myself from staring at the grimy walls and floor, concentrating on fussing with the equally dingy fabric of the blanket. Still, I appreciated its warmth. The chilly room did little to warm me.

I tugged the blanket tighter around my shoulders, offering a slight smile at him as he sank into a chair next to me.

"Oh, I do hope they hurry with the tea. It's quite brisk in here. The fire isn't lit yet, as the patients do not use the room until the afternoon."

I stared at the cold hearth across the space and nodded at him. "Quite all right. At least I am out of the rain."

"Yes. A tiny improvement, but at least a little," he said with a chuckle that made his cheeks stick off his face like two tiny apples. He squeezed his index finger and thumb close together. "Though only just. I expect this roof to spring a leak at any moment."

We both glanced upward as though the rain would pour through instantaneously. Awkward silence broken only by the pounding of rain against the roof pervaded the air. I fidgeted in my seat as I awaited the hot tea.

Dr. Applebaum drummed his fingers on the table. "And you said your horses bolted, leaving your husband and coachman behind?"

"Yes," I answered, shifting the blanket around me. "They stopped unexpectedly, and my husband disembarked from the carriage to determine the issue. At that moment, the horses spun and charged in the opposite direction, tossing our coachman from his seat. They did not stop until they reached the sanitarium."

He adjusted his round spectacles over his rosy cheeks. "How odd. Was there anything on the road to spook them?"

I suspected there had been one former asylum patient on the road but had no confirmation of it. I pressed my lips together as I gave my head a slow shake. "No. Quite odd, I agree. And rather frightening."

"Yes, quite. I can imagine."

A shriek ripped through the air, startling me. I clutched at the blanket.

Color rose in Dr. Applebaum's plump cheeks, and he winced. "Quite normal inside the asylum, I assure you."

I smiled and nodded, lowering my gaze to my lap. The nurse bustled into the room with the tea, sliding a tray onto the table.

"Thank you, Nurse," Dr. Applebaum said as he poured a cup and slid it toward me.

"Thank you," I said just above a whisper as I poured in cream and added sugar. After a quick stir, I lifted the chipped porcelain cup to my lips and sipped it.

The doctor picked up his own tea, mustache wiggling as he slurped at the hot liquid. "Oh, quite hot!" He offered a clumsy chuckle as he wiped at his chin.

"But most appreciated," I answered, lifting the cup to him before imbibing another sip.

He smiled at me, his gaze lingering on me longer than I preferred. "You said your mother is a patient here?"

"Yes," I said, swallowing hard, uncertain I wanted to discuss the matter.

"I am sorry to hear that. I hope her prognosis is what you hope, though with Dr. Merriweather, I've no doubt she is receiving excellent care."

I smiled as I set the cup into the faded saucer. "That is all we may hope for."

"Dr. Merriweather provides some of the most advanced care in the country."

"Oh?" I questioned as my finger absentmindedly traced the rough porcelain chip on my cup.

"He performs some of the most unique care I've ever witnessed. I am so pleased to be here to learn new techniques."

I smiled at him and nodded. He fluttered his hand in the air before pressing it against his forehead and raking it through his wavy blond hair. "My apologies. I'm certain you do not wish to hear about the latest in psychiatric care."

"Actually," I answered, "I am not opposed to discussing it, though I am not certain I can hold up my end of the conversation. Though I would not mind knowing more about how patients are cared for. I visited my mother last evening, and the call seemed to disturb her greatly."

"I am sorry to hear that. Though it is not uncommon. Many disturbed patients react poorly to any changes in their environment, even from family members."

"I'm afraid we had a rather tenuous relationship at best. My presence may have disturbed her regardless of the care she received."

The man pressed his small lips into a thin line and gave me a curt nod before he sipped at his tea.

He let the cup clatter back into his saucer and glanced

around before slapping his thighs. "Well, I suppose I should determine if arrangements can be made to search out your husband. He must be worried terribly."

"I would very much appreciate it. Thank you."

He nodded at me again and rose, adjusting his glasses. "Will you be all right to sit here?"

"Yes, perfectly fine," I assured him as I adjusted the blanket around me.

He toddled across the room, checking his pocket watch as he disappeared around the corner. I reached forward, allowing the blanket to slip off my shoulders, and poured more tea into my cup.

I stirred in cream and sugar and settled back into my chair. I stared out the window at the falling rain. It dripped down the windows like tears.

The dormant plants outside the window gave the shabby garden an eerie appearance. I wondered if it looked any better in bloom.

I lifted the cup to my lips while my eyes remained trained on a battered statue of a woman holding a rose at the garden's center. As my gaze focused on her missing nose, the chip in the rim of the teacup tore into my lower lip. I gasped, my muscles tensing as I winced.

I settled the teacup into the saucer, my forehead crinkling at the sight of the drop of red blood floating in my tea.

Another droplet splatted onto my dress, mixing in with the mud already splattered there. I wiped at my lip, staining my finger with more blood.

I clicked my tongue against the roof of my mouth as I licked my lip, wincing again as my tongue stung the cut. The metallic taste of blood raced across my taste buds.

I rubbed my thumb against my blood-stained finger, spreading it all over my hand. I sighed as my lip continued to bleed and glanced around in search of something I could use to clean my bloody palm and press against my wound.

A white handkerchief waved in front of my face. I flicked my gaze to it as I grasped it, concentrating mostly on the blood smeared across my hand and my dress.

"Thank you," I murmured to the figure standing next to me. I moistened the cloth with my tongue before scrubbing my skin. Reddish-pink stains bloomed on the white fabric as I wiped away the blood.

After removing most of the sticky substance, I found a clean corner, dampened it, and rubbed at the splotch on my dress.

I licked at the still-bleeding wound again before another drop stained my clothing. "I'm afraid I've made rather a mess. The teacup is chipped and cut my lip.

"My carriage is stuck outside in the mud with my reticule inside it, so I haven't my own handkerchief."

I lightened the stain, though I was not certain it mattered much, given the mud soaking the material. Blood still filled my mouth whenever I pressed my tongue or teeth against my lip.

I pressed the handkerchief against my wound and raised my eyes to the woman standing in front of me. I expected to find the nurse who had delivered the hot tea, but I did not.

My jaw dropped open, and I leapt from my seat, stumbling back a step. The flimsy chair scraped across the floor before toppling over with a loud crash against the already cracked tiles.

I sucked in a breath as I stared into the eyes of the dead woman who had begged for my help only the night before.

CHAPTER 9

"You!" I gasped, the handkerchief still pressed against my now-swollen lip. I stared at her for another breath with my eyes wide.

She stared back, her hands clasped in front of her. The dirt smudges on her thin nightgown matched the dark circles hanging under her dark eyes. Her mahogany hair hung in tangles around her face.

I swallowed hard before I continued. "Are you the reason the horses bolted? Did you bring me here?"

Her pale mouth formed a sneer as she lowered her chin to her chest. For the first time, I noticed the clammy sweat on her pale gray skin.

I took a step toward her when she whipped her head toward the hospital. I glanced in the same direction for a moment, spotting nothing.

She returned her gaze to me for a moment, her eyes filled with fear. She clamped a cold, damp hand around mine, tugging it away from my lip.

"Help," she breathed.

"But–" I began when she faded in front of my eyes.

I pitched forward as the pressure on my arm disappeared. "No! Wait!" I called.

"Mrs. Fletcher?" Dr. Applebaum's voice echoed in the large room.

I glanced toward the entrance, finding the round man adjusting his glasses as he furrowed his brow and strode toward me.

"Are you quite all right?" he asked as he wound through the many tables set up.

I stared at the empty space that had once been filled before I cut my gaze to him. "Yes," I said with a tentative nod.

"What happened?" he inquired, hurrying toward me and peering at my lip.

I pressed my lips together, wincing as the cut stung again. "Oh, silly, really. The cup is chipped, and it cut my lip."

I waved toward the teacup on the iron lattice-work table as I pressed the handkerchief against my lip again.

"I'm afraid," I added, my voice muffled by the cloth pressed against my mouth, "I toppled the chair when I jumped."

"Oh, how awful." Dr. Applebaum side-stepped around me and reset the chair before he wrapped his arms around my shoulders and eased me into it. "Sit down."

He squatted in front of me, adjusting his wire-rimmed glasses. "Let me take a look."

I lowered the handkerchief, and he squinted at my battle wound.

"The good news is, you will live." He offered a toothy grin, a lock of his blond hair springing forward as he bobbled his head with a silly laugh. "I shall clean the wound for you."

"Really, it is not necessary. I am quite fine."

"Nonsense, nonsense," he said, waving a hand in the air. "We would not wish to return to you to your husband worse for the wear. He may wonder what sort of facility we are running." He chuckled again as he straightened.

I pressed the handkerchief against my lip again as he scurried from the room in search of the supplies he'd need to cleanse the laceration on my mouth.

As he disappeared around the corner, I let my gaze dart around the room. "Hello?"

I held my breath as I scanned the space. Thunder rumbled overhead, and the rain intensified.

"Hello?" I tried again.

No one answered or appeared. Another boom of thunder shook the large windows overlooking the garden before a streak of lightning lit the sky. A shiver shot up my spine, and I suddenly wished I had not entered the asylum.

I rose, wondering how close Robert may be. I did not have long to consider it as Dr. Applebaum flitted back into the room with a nurse in tow.

He scurried across the room, waving me into the seat. "Sit, sit. This will only take a moment."

I sank back into the chair, the handkerchief still pressed against my lip. After pulling a chair closer to me, he gently tugged my hand away.

The nurse carried a solution and pile of gauze with her, of what I did not know.

Dr. Applebaum adjusted his glasses again and stared at my mouth. Heat rushed into my cheeks as he eyed it.

"Really, I am quite fine," I said, my lower lip feeling clumsy as it swelled around the cut.

"Nonsense. I recently saw a presentation by Dr. Joseph Lister. He insists that cleaning wounds is vital to their healing and the patient's well-being. Fascinating, and the evidence he presented was quite compelling."

Dr. Applebaum grabbed a piece of the gauze and poured some of the solution on it. "I understand they may even attempt to form some sort of business over all this. I'm not certain if it will take off. I can't imagine the average person being knowledgeable about wound care in the home, but nevertheless, they disagree with me."

He pressed the moistened gauze against my lip. It stung like the dickens, and I pulled backward, wincing. "I cannot imagine it will catch on at all. The remedy is worse than the illness!"

He chuckled at my statement, thrusting his glasses higher on his nose as they slid down from his jovial laughter. "I do apologize, Mrs. Fletcher. But I assure you, it is well worth it. Just a few more moments, and it shall be finished."

My forehead pinched as he pressed the gauze to my mouth again. The burning intensified as the liquid seeped into my wound.

He pulled away, tossing the bloody gauze onto the tray the nurse held before grabbing a dry piece and tapping it against my lip. "There we are. Try not to bite down on it or lick it."

He threw the piece of now-bloodstained gauze onto the tray and dismissed the nurse. She curtsied quickly, offering a meek, "Your Grace," to me before she nodded to Dr. Applebaum.

Dr. Applebaum leaned back in his chair, his features scrunching as his arms fell to his sides. "Your Grace?"

"Yes," I answered as the nurse disappeared from the room. "I am the Duchess of Blackmoore."

He arched an eyebrow at me, his posture stiffening. Color rose into his apple-like cheeks, and his lower lip bobbed up and down under his mustache, though no sound came out.

He closed his jaw and fiddled with his glasses again. "Oh, Your Grace, forgive me, I had no idea."

I waved his concern away as I shoved the soiled handkerchief up my sleeve. "There is no need to apologize. I did not inform you."

He swallowed hard again. "The nurse seemed to know."

"I met her yesterday while visiting. My husband informed her."

He pressed his lips together and nodded, his face still a reddish-purple color.

"I assure you, Dr. Applebaum, I am a normal person just like you."

He offered a nervous chuckle. "Oh, well, yes of course. Forgive me, I...well, I...I suppose I should find a more comfortable space for you to wait for your husband."

"Were you able to send someone to fetch him?" I inquired.

"Oh, yes. We sent one of the orderlies. I hope he is able to locate him. He was instructed to offer him the horse to come at once."

"Thank you," I answered. "And I do apologize for all the trouble. If only the horses were not so stubborn, I could have turned the carriage and met him myself."

"Nonsense! You couldn't have driven the carriage in the rain! You would have been soaked."

I glanced down at my soiled dress. "I am not certain I spared myself much."

He chuckled at my humor, clutching his hands over his protruding belly. He squeezed his left hand with his right over and over.

"If you have matters to attend to, Dr. Applebaum, I am capable of waiting here alone. I do not wish to interrupt your day any further."

"Nonsense! No interruption at all. And I shouldn't like to leave you sitting alone."

I smiled politely at him and shifted in my seat. I wondered if my deceased friend would reappear. Likely not, given the doctor's presence. She seemed quite shy.

I drummed my fingers against the table as I scanned the space. "Are there many rooms like this in the sanitarium?"

He stared up at the ceiling before letting his gaze flick around the room. "Oh, none like this, but we do have several spaces for patients to recreate outside of their rooms."

"Ah," I answered, sucking in a deep breath.

"Perhaps I can show you," Dr. Applebaum said, rising from his chair and offering his arm. "Some of the rooms are quite lovely."

I considered declining but decided against it. A tour of the facility may lead me to my mysterious visitor again. And would be a better option than sitting in one place and staring at one another.

With a smile pasted on my face, I rose and slipped my hand around his elbow, dragging the blanket along with me to hide part of my soiled dress. "How long has the asylum been here?"

"Oh, several years now. It was a former country estate for the Gregorson family. However, Sir Lloyd passed on without an heir, and the house was sold."

We passed back into the hall and strolled toward the central desk. "Oh, how terrible for his wife."

"He had no wife at the time. She died in childbirth, along with the baby. Terribly sad for him. He turned into a recluse. Never remarried."

"How sad for him," I murmured as I considered how similar the circumstances were to Robert's situation. Had he followed a similar path, we never would have married, and my life would have been far emptier.

Oblivious to my ruminating, Dr. Applebaum tugged me toward another hallway and continued his explanation. "Mmm, yes. Poor man killed himself right here in this house."

My chin drew back toward my chest as I wondered if I

would run into another ghost roaming the edifice. My eyebrow arched as another notion flitted across my mind.

I snapped my gaze to him. "Did his wife die here as well?"

Dr. Applebaum pressed his lips together in an exaggerated pucker. "Hmm, no. No, I do not believe so. She died in their London home if I am not mistaken. She did not die here. It is one of the reasons Sir Lloyd shut himself away here. This house contained no memories of his wife.

"She was a French woman, you see. She did not enjoy the Scottish weather. And refused to travel to the estate."

I chewed my lower lip, immediately regretting it as my tooth hit my cut, sending a sharp pang of pain through it. Could the woman I had been seeing be Sir Lloyd's wife? Would the woman travel in death to an estate she refused to set foot in during her life?

Perhaps yes, I concluded as Dr. Applebaum pushed open a set of double doors. Perhaps the woman sought her husband who had disappeared here after her death. Did she hope to find him? To connect with him in the afterlife?

Perhaps she sought her husband in her death. Was this the help she hoped to find? If I could find the late Sir Lloyd, my task may be made simpler.

I pulled myself from my thoughts and smiled as Dr. Applebaum motioned for me to enter the room he'd just opened. I stepped inside the darkened space, lit only by the muted daylight.

A large grand piano filled a corner across the space. Rich burgundy chairs framed a large fireplace, above which hung a portrait of a dark-haired man with a shock of gray hair above each ear.

I approached it and stared up at him.

"That's Sir Lloyd," Dr. Applebaum said from behind me.

I narrowed my eyes and studied the man, wondering if his soul still roamed the property.

"This is the music room. We kept most of the furnishings intact. We sometimes have small concerts for the patients."

I glanced around the room at the luxurious seating arrangements placed expertly to allow for conversation and enjoyment of music. A harp poked from a corner near the door. Next to it, a violin stood on a stand.

"Do you bring in musicians?"

"No, Dr. Merriweather plays the violin quite well, actually. I have some skill at the piano and harp, and of course, Lady Havershire plays the piano beautifully. If she is feeling up to it, she will entertain us."

"Oh, how lovely. Is Lady Havershire married to Dr. Merriweather?"

Dr. Applebaum rocked on his feet as he chuckled. "No, no, Lady Havershire is a patient here."

My eyebrows shot up, and color rose in my cheeks. "Oh, my apologies, I did not realize–"

"Did I hear my name?" a voice answered from the doorway.

A slight woman in a dark blue dress stepped into the room. "Ah, Lady Havershire, yes. I was just telling Her Grace about your musical ability."

The woman offered a soft chuckle, casting her eyes down to the floor before snapping them demurely back to the doctor as she fluttered her eyelashes. "You flatter me, Dr. Applebaum."

"I do not," he answered, keeping his gaze focused on his toes. "You are quite gifted."

I wondered if he avoided her flirtatious gaze because of my presence or preferred not to indulge her. And was she as gifted as he said, or was it merely a form of flattery?

He finally lifted his eyes and waved an arm to the piano. "Perhaps you will entertain Her Grace and I with a song."

She tilted her head, sweeping a lock of her mahogany hair back and casting her eyes in my direction. "Her Grace?"

I tightened my grip on the blanket still wrapped around me and stepped forward. "Yes, I am the Duchess of Blackmoore."

The woman's dark eyes ran the length of me, landing on the dirty bottom of my dress. She arched an eyebrow before she let her eyes rise back to mine. "Well, Your Grace," she said with a small curtsy, "I shall play you a song."

I forced a smile onto my lips, certain she mocked me with her behavior. I wandered across the room as she seated herself on the thick, tufted burgundy cushion balanced on the delicately-curved, mahogany legs. She adjusted her dress as she raised her chin and set her fingers on the keys.

I sank onto a chair as I awaited the concert. I should soon find out if Dr. Applebaum's words were true or undue adulation.

Lady Havershire stared at a spot on the wall as she slid her shoulders down her back, straightening her posture before she leaned into the keyboard and pressed the keys.

Music floated from the piano, quite pleasant to the ear. Dr. Applebaum's praise had not been unwarranted. Lady Havershire's talent was obvious.

She finished the piece with a loud clap of one of the bass keys before spinning to face us, her face expectant. I clapped my hands as I rose to my feet. "Brava, Lady Havershire."

"Excellent as always, Lady Havershire," Dr. Applebaum added with a nod.

She rose from her seat and smoothed her dress as she eyed me curiously. "Will you be joining us at the asylum, Your Grace?"

"No," I began when Dr. Applebaum interrupted me.

"Oh, no, no. Her Grace's horses went wild and drove her

here. She is merely awaiting her husband's return to retrieve her."

She cocked her head and stared at me with a curious expression on her features, her eyes roaming up and down me again. "Oh! Interesting. Have you any musical talents, Your Grace? Perhaps we could duet."

"Unfortunately, I do not. I never had the opportunity to learn."

She pouted her thin lips. "Unfortunate, yes. Music provides such a soothing effect."

"I find reading offers the same," I replied with a smile.

She arched an eyebrow, a coy expression turning up the corners of her mouth. "Careful, Your Grace. Reading too many novels is what landed me here. Good day."

She offered me one final smirk before she spun on a heel and paraded from the room.

I stared after her, my forehead wrinkling as I considered her words.

"Good day!" Dr. Applebaum called after her.

He turned his attention to me. I hurried to close my gaping jaw and forced a smile onto my lips. "She is a lovely pianist."

"Yes, yes, she is. Music soothes many of our patients. Though, of course, some of them react poorly to it."

"How interesting," I offered. I fiddled with the blanket, attempting to push the odd information about the reason for her stay from my mind. I found myself unable to, and before I realized it, the words spilled from my mouth. "What did she mean by her comment about novels being the reason she was committed? Surely, it was a jest."

Dr. Applebaum threw his head back in laughter. "Yes, quite."

He bobbled his head around for a moment and waved a hand in the air. "Well, only slightly."

My eyebrows shot toward my hairline as I considered the ghastly idea. Committed for reading too many novels?

"Reading too many novels is a valid reason to commit women."

I collapsed into the chair behind me, my eyelashes fluttering as I pondered the ridiculousness of the idea. I flicked my gaze to him. "Why?"

"Oh, it is believed that it fills their heads with wild ideas. That women's brains are not capable of handling intense topics. Novels shouldn't do much damage, since they are frivolous. Newspapers, though, well, that's something that could prove damaging to a woman's delicate psyche."

I stared at him, uncertain of what to answer to the preposterous notion.

"Most novels are quite all right for women, though some may prove too much. Too many novels is a valid reason, though Lady Havershire's difficulties stem from, well, other issues as well." He smiled politely at me.

I remained silent, trying to imagine Robert sending me to this dank place for the sheer volume of novels I kept in my reading tower alone. I shuddered at the idea when a scream floated through the air, breaking the silence in the room.

Dr. Applebaum snapped his head in its direction. "Oh, dear, that sounds quite frightful."

Shouts rang out, followed by another shriek. Footsteps pounded down the hall. A wide-eyed nurse poked her head into the door as she skidded to a stop on the hardwood floor outside

"Doctor! Come quick! It's Mrs. Flynn."

"Oh, no, has she had another attack?"

The woman gasped for breath as she nodded. "She's bitten Miss Robbins and Nurse Walker."

"Oh, dear." Dr. Applebaum shoved his wire-rimmed glasses up on his nose and glanced at me.

"I shall be perfectly fine waiting here," I assured him before he asked.

"Thank you, Your Grace. How kind of you."

The nurse waited as Dr. Applebaum crossed the room, padding over the thick red and gold area rug before exiting into the hall.

"She bit Miss Robbins's ear, claiming that…" Her voice trailed off as they hurried down the hall to deal with the unruly patient.

I sucked in a deep breath, my mind still pondering Dr. Applebaum's claim that novel reading ruined a woman's mind. A sickening notion, though second to the perception that a woman's brain lacked the capability to handle profound subjects.

I rose and stalked toward the cold hearth, staring up at the portrait hanging above it. "Are you still here, Sir Lloyd?" I whispered.

Thunder rumbled overhead, punctuating my statement. The painting did not respond to my query. I glanced over my shoulder at the empty space.

Perhaps Sir Lloyd roamed a different part of the house, I thought as I wandered to the golden harp in the corner. My fingers reached for the taut wires stretched from top to bottom. I plucked a few, sending scattered notes in the air.

I swept my hand across several of them, creating a discordant cacophony of sound. Interesting, how harpists made it appear so easy to create beautiful music with a brush of their fingertips.

I twisted and eyed the piano. Perhaps I'd have better luck there. Lady Havershire certainly made the task look quite easy.

Perhaps I should secure musical education for the children. If my daughter Sarah's feeble mind could handle it, my brain echoed. I rolled my eyes at the statement.

Lightning tore across the sky outside, and thunder clapped. The dim light in the space darkened even more as thick, dark clouds sped past.

The rumble of thunder died out, plunging the room into silence again. My fingers touched the neck of the violin as I considered instruments best suited for my children when another sound filled the air.

Hinges creaked behind me. The hairs on the back of my neck stood up, and my flesh turned to goosebumps. The door clicked closed.

I swallowed hard, concerned about who may have entered the room. Was I trapped with a deranged patient? Perhaps Mrs. Flynn, who bit people.

I licked my lips and slid my eyes sideways as I slowly twisted to determine who had ensnared me inside the music room.

CHAPTER 10

*D*ark eyes bore into mine as the clicking of the lock echoed into the room. I arched an eyebrow at the woman, my shoulders sliding down my back as I raised my chin.

"Hello, again," I said to my ghostly visitor. "You have returned."

She lowered her chin to her chest and stared at me through her eyelashes.

"Will you speak this time? You've spoken before. You asked for help. What help do you need?"

She opened her lips to speak, sucking in a breath. I found myself leaning forward as I awaited an answer, holding my breath.

A loud banging interrupted any response I may have received. The doors behind the spirit shook. She snapped her head in their direction, her eyes growing wide.

"Your Grace?" Dr. Applebaum's voice called.

The woman backed away, a hiss escaping her mouth at his voice.

I hurried toward her as the pounding continued. "Please," I began.

The ghost whipped around to face me, a sneer on her features.

"Do not leave," I begged her. "Tell me how I may help you."

The pounding sounded again, and Dr. Applebaum called from outside. "Your Grace? Your Grace!"

"Yes, Dr. Applebaum, I am here," I called. I flicked my gaze to the door, then back to the spirit. My shoulders sank as I stared at a blank space in front of me. The woman disappeared again, likely frightened off by the banging and shouting.

With a frustrated sigh, I skirted around the furniture in the room and made my way to the paneled door. The doorknob twisted and turned, and the doors rattled in the jamb.

"Your Grace, open the doors!" Dr. Applebaum shouted.

I twisted the knobs and pulled them toward me. The doors did not budge. "The doors are locked!" I called before pressing my ear against the door to listen for his response.

"Turn the key, Your Grace," his voice answered in a slow and deliberate fashion.

I arched my eyebrow and pressed my lips together as I shook my head. The good doctor must consider me quite dim.

I stared down at the empty keyhole before setting my eyes on the wooden barrier in front of me. "There is no key, Doctor," I answered.

"No key? That cannot be! The doors are locked, and I did not lock them when I departed."

"I assure you, Doctor, there is no key."

The doors rattled as he jiggled them again. "You must have turned it earlier and locked yourself in."

"I did no such thing. The doors blew shut while I studied the harp. There is no key."

"Your Grace, listen carefully to my instructions."

I tugged one corner of my lips back into a half-grimace at both his words and tone.

"Cast your eyes down toward your feet, Your Grace. Is there a key? Perhaps it fell from the lock. Look in a wide area around the door, it may have bounced further than you may think."

I heaved a sigh as I studied the floor in front of me. "There is no key," I replied after a moment.

"Check under the closest furniture piece! It must be there!"

"I tell you, Doctor, it is not! I have made a careful search and come across no key."

"Oh, dear. Oh, dear, oh, dear," he murmured from the hall.

"Doctor!" I called.

"Yes, Your Grace? Are you quite all right? Please remain calm. We will find a way to get you out. Perhaps you should sit down lest you become faint."

I could not hold back the eye roll at these words. "I am perfectly fine, Doctor. What I wanted to ask was about the key you used earlier to open the door. Can you not use it now?"

"Oh, an excellent point. Though I did not use a key earlier. The music room remains unlocked. Lady Havershire prefers to be able to access it to soothe herself at any time."

I collapsed into a chair with a heaving sigh. "Well, I suppose we must find another way."

"No, no. You are quite right. There *is* a key somewhere. We must locate it. Please, Your Grace, sit down whilst I inquire about the key. Surely, one of the nurses or Dr. Merriweather should know of one."

Silence fell, and I assumed the doctor had left in search of a key. But a moment later, he spoke again. "Try to remain calm, Your Grace. I shall return as soon as possible."

I fluttered my eyelashes in annoyance at his insistence that my delicate sensibilities may be overtaken by something as simple as being locked in a music room. "I shall be quite fine, I assure you. I am calm."

"Very good. Deep breaths, Your Grace, deep breaths."

His footsteps departed down the hall, and I blew out a sigh, more from frustration with the doctor than my situation.

I plopped into the deep armchair and leaned back, studying the portrait over the fireplace. The woman who had just visited me flitted across my mind again. Was she his wife?

I had no better idea of who the woman was than when she had first appeared to me. "Hello? Spirit? Are you still there? Dr. Applebaum is gone. You may come out."

I waited for her to appear, but no one came. I sucked in a deep breath, allowing my head to fall back between my shoulders, my mind returning to another time I spent locked in a room by another.

The image of a young Tilly flitted back into my mind. Another spirit I could not speak to at will. She appeared to me on occasion but could not make contact with me at Blackmoore Castle.

I could not fathom why. Our bond in life should have made it easier. I even suspected after Edwin, her love and the father of her child, she may be able to appear, but alas, nothing.

My frustration over my lack of communicative abilities with those who had passed rose to a new high. I let my mind regress to a different time.

Tears filled my eyes as I recalled giggling with Tilly that first night she'd snuck into the attic with me. It would not be the last time she would sneak inside. And she would pay dearly for her trickery.

On more than one occasion, she was caught upstairs or left locked upstairs. Poor Tilly had risked so much for me. I again recalled that first rainy night on which we giggled over our future plans. The more optimistic of us, even at eight, Tilly imagined herself married well with six children and a lovely home.

"You are a dreamer," I told her.

"Do you not dream, Lenora? I should think your dreams are more vivid because of what you experience."

"I do not dream much. I do not have much cause to dream. My affliction–"

"Ability," Tilly said. "Not an affliction."

I furrowed my tiny brow and wrinkled my nose at her. "Ability? Affliction is the proper word. I have been roundly thrown from both domiciles I've inhabited due to it."

Tilly merely shrugged at the statement. "Foolish of those with whom you lived if you ask me."

I arched an eyebrow at her. "I do not believe every person I have come into contact with has been a fool."

"I do. If you are basing it at all on Headmistress Williamson, I know it. The woman is not very bright. I do not understand how she came to be headmistress."

"So is not very dimwitted," I retorted.

"She is so!" Tilly said, sticking her hands on her hips.

"She is quite talented when it comes to dealing with people."

Tilly poked a finger at me. "And *that* is why she is the headmistress, not because she is bright."

I puckered my lips as I considered her statement. "Perhaps so, but it does not explain why my mother abandoned me or the nuns. Surely, they were not all fools."

Tilly raised her chin. "Of course they were. What of your father?"

I stared at the floorboards as the rain continued to patter against the roof. "He went to India."

"And did he consider your gift an affliction?"

"I am not certain he realized the extent of it."

Tilly drew her knees to her chest as she spun to face me. "Did he leave when you were very young?"

I shook my head. "No, he left shortly before my mother took me to the convent."

"Then he knew and did not care."

My brow furrowed. Had my father known about my affliction and ignored it? Or even more puzzling to me, accepted it?

Tilly took my hand in hers and squeezed it. "He did not care, Lenora. There are people who will not. You may count me among them."

I smiled at her and squeezed her hand back. "And I am pleased to do so, however, you are in the minority."

Tilly shook her head and grinned at me. "One day you shall find others who accept you, too. You will settle into a happy home. And your husband shall adore you. And you shall have two children…no, no…three children! You shall have three children who adore you!"

A giggle escaped me at her wild dreams, and I covered my lips with my hand. "Tilly, you are quite comical."

She poked at my belly. "I am not! It is no jest. Mark my words, Lenora. You, too, shall be happy one day! And then we will visit each other. And our children will grow up together. Perhaps one of mine will marry one of yours. And we shall be proud grandparents shortly after."

My chuckling turned into a full-bellied laugh. "Oh, Tilly, stop. You are really too much."

"You'll see, Lenora. You'll see!"

* * *

My eyes clouded as tears formed in them. The reality smacked me in the face that my dear friend, Tilly, who had been so full of life and optimism, was no longer of this world. She would not raise those children. She would never see her grandchildren. I thought back to her face that night, lit only by the lightning that tore through the sky.

Her porcelain skin glowed and rosy cheeks made her green eyes sparkle as she detailed what her life would become. We continued talking for hours. Only the creaking of the door interrupted our speech.

I wiped at my nose, squeezing my eyes shut as a tear streaked down my cheek. I sank my forehead into my palm, resting my elbow on the chair's arm.

The moment seemed so real to me that I could almost hear the creaking door at this very moment.

I sniffled again, wiping at my cheeks as I tried to compose myself. Surely, once Dr. Applebaum freed me from my prison, he'd assume my outburst stemmed from the overwhelming situation on my feeble mind.

I snapped my eyes open, sucking in a deep breath. It caught in my throat, and I froze as I stared ahead.

The creaking I'd thought I'd imagined had been real. Across the room, one of the wood panels near the corner had disappeared. A gaping hole replaced it.

Inside stood the ghost I'd begged to stay only moments ago. She lowered her chin to her chest and beckoned for me to follow her.

I stared at her for a moment before she disappeared into the dark passageway.

"Wait!" I called, leaping from my seat and racing to the entrance.

The spirit flitted around a corner and disappeared from

my sight. I huffed at her, cursing the constant tendency for the dead to be difficult.

"I will not follow you!" I called into the passage. "It's dark and dim, and I do not wish to become lost!"

No one responded. I arched an eyebrow, stamping my foot on the floor. "I will not follow, I tell you! My husband will arrive at any moment, and I shall leave!"

I squinted into the hidden corridor for any sign of a response. None came. I pressed my lips together and shoved back my shoulders. I turned my back on the passage and stalked away from it.

I squeezed my eyes closed and shook my head. With a sigh, I clutched the blanket tighter around me and strode back to the passage. With a tentative lick of my lips, I slid my foot inside. My fingers glided over the wall as I took another few steps inside.

"Hello?" I called out. I marched two more steps down, squinting into the darkness. A cobweb brushed past my forehead, and I swatted it away, blowing air from my mouth as my hands waved in front of me.

"Spirit? Could you at least tell me your name, so I do not need to call you 'spirit?'" I asked, pausing before continuing forward.

A rush of air gusted past me from within the chamber, tickling my cheeks. I swallowed hard, a tremor shuddering through me. My chest heaved as my heart pounded against my ribs. My ears detected an unearthly voice on the breeze, but I could not make out any words.

"Hello? I did not hear you. Please come back," I called.

With a sigh, I continued a few more steps into the passage. I peered into the darkness looming at the end of the hidden corridor. No ghost stood at the end. She'd disappeared earlier around a corner that led to an unknown destination.

I sucked in a breath and pressed my lips together. I glanced over my shoulder at the music room behind me. *I should go back*, I thought as I returned my gaze down the passage.

The spirit had presumably caused my carriage to return here. Perhaps I should continue to follow. I took one more tentative step when another breeze wafted past me.

My stomach turned as the unearthly but undistinguishable voice floated by in the air. A chill snaked up my spine, and my eyes went wide. I gasped as I stumbled back a few steps, my lower lip quivering.

"I cannot," I called down the hidden hall before I spun and raced toward the opening.

Before I reached it, the panel snapped shut. The meager light from the music room disappeared. I slammed into the closed panel, banging my fists against it. It did not budge.

I gasped in a breath as I continued my incessant pounding, despite its futility. After a moment, I let my arms slide to my sides and leaned my forehead against the panel. My chest heaved in deep breaths as I groaned at the latest turn of events.

"Ugh," I moaned, spinning to lean against my prison door. "Spirit? Let me out!"

I received no response to my demand. My nose wrinkled as I pulled myself to stand and spun to face the panel that opened to the music room. In the darkened space, I could barely make out the features around me.

I breathed in a deep sigh and pressed my hand against the panel. There must be a trigger that opened the mechanism from this side. I would find it and free myself.

I firmed my jaw with determination and felt around blindly for the release. My fingers swept over the rough surface in search of anything that may liberate me from my surprise prison. I poked and prodded at any imperfection my fingertips stumbled across. None produced the desired effect.

I balled my hands into fists as frustration filled me. My nostrils flared as I shook my head. A simple panel would not defeat me, I vowed. I had survived far worse, including being tossed from a turret window. I would free myself.

I pressed my shoulders down my back and lifted my hand, feeling along the walls again. On a side panel, I found a lever. My fingers ran up and down the length of it before I curled them around it.

I yanked on it, trying to pull it upward. It did not budge. I pressed down, but the lever did not move. I tried wrenching it in several more directions, to no avail.

With my other hand, I pressed against the panel as I continued wrestling with the lever. Nothing worked. I chewed my lower lip as I gave up.

"Lenora," a voice whispered.

My eyes went wide, and I stared into the darkness. "Is that you, Spirit?"

No one answered me. I huffed out a sigh and flung my arms in the air. "Must you be so coy? I returned to the asylum! I wandered into the dark passage! What more do you want from me?"

"Here," a hiss called on the wind.

"I cannot follow. I can barely see my hand in front of my face. I will not be able to see."

Light bloomed inside the chamber from some unknown source around the corner.

"A lovely trick," I called, "yet I prefer you to come to me."

"Come, Lenora," the voice called again.

"Fine, fine," I acquiesced, pushing myself straighter and wandering to the light. "If only to gain my freedom."

I inched toward the lit corner and peered around it. The

light continued to elude me, slinking around another corner as I sought its source.

"This behavior is not earning you any marks in my book, you know!" I shouted as I stepped into the new corridor and continued.

The light moved ahead of me steadily, guiding me through the vast and winding corridors hidden behind the walls of the asylum.

I arrived at the top of a spiraling and crumbling staircase. The light circled around, disappearing into the darkness below.

"Where are you taking me?" I shouted down the circular stairs.

The light hovered at the bottom before disappearing. Had it moved again or simply snuffed itself out? I could not say unless I followed. And I remained uncertain I wished to follow.

"The stairs are not stable. I cannot follow–"

A force pressed against my back, and I stumbled forward, nearly pitching down the stairs head first. I dug my feet into the floor, stretching my fingers out to clutch the walls and prevent my forward motion.

"Stop!" I shouted. "Stop this at once!"

I fought against the unseen force shoving at me, but my efforts proved ineffectual. The pressure on my back overcame me, and my foot slipped, sliding onto the first crumbling stone step.

The stone's edge collapsed, disintegrating into dust. I lost my already perilous footing and slid further down. My fingers desperately gripped at the corners of the wall, trying to remain upright.

I hovered in the air, winning the battle momentarily. My heart thudded as I sucked in breaths and slid my dangling foot back up to the first stair.

I blew out a soft breath when my eyes widened. An unseen force pried at my fingers, slowly removing them one by one from their grasp on the walls.

My lower lip trembled as I lost my grip on one wall. I desperately attempted to hang on with my other hand, but it proved impossible. The weight of my body hung on my smallest finger, bending it back at an impossible angle before I felt it slip.

I pitched forward into the darkness below.

CHAPTER 11

The air rushed from my lungs as I tumbled down a few of the stone steps. My arms flailed as I sought to cling to anything to stop my fall. My hand banged off a rung on the railing, but I failed to grasp it. Pain shot through it all the way up to my shoulder.

As the stairs curved, I smashed into the wall, bouncing off and continuing my roll. The contact with the stone surrounding one side of the stairs slowed my motion and allowed me to grasp hold of the rusty iron.

I wrapped my fingers around the metal. My shoulder burned with pain as it wrenched from the weight of my body. My feet kicked until they stopped slipping, and I scrambled up a few steps to relieve the pressure.

I gasped in breaths as I assessed my injuries. Everything hurt. I winced as I contorted my body to ensure all my limbs still worked properly. After a few moments of movement, most of my pain subsided. By luck, I had only sustained minor scrapes and bruises as far as I could assess.

I breathed out a sigh, glad the simple task did not elicit

any pain as I glanced around the dark space. With a shaky hand, I smoothed a lock of hair that escaped its pins back behind my ear.

For several moments, I did not move further than that, uncertain I wanted to continue, but unsure I could go back. Would climbing the stairs result in another angry retaliation from the spirit? I did not wish to tumble down the stairs a second time.

I convinced myself to move forward, though I waited for several moments until I felt certain my legs would hold me. Bracing my hand against the wall and gripping the railing, I pulled myself up to stand, keeping a tight hold for support. My knees wobbled, and I fought to steady them, squeezing my eyes closed and biting my lower lip as I firmed my muscles.

When they no longer shook under me, I opened my eyes and, keeping careful hold of the rusty iron railing, proceeded down the spiral steps one by one.

I reached the bottom and shuffled onto the floor. Light flickered at the end of the corridor, beckoning me further.

"You could have harmed me irreparably!" I shouted as the light dimmed, moving further away from me.

I inched away from the stairs, finally letting go of the railing and stepping forward tentatively. My legs gave no protest, not even my ankles, which I feared may have become battered in my wild spill down the less-than-forgiving steps.

"This has really gone too far," I shouted as I wandered toward the light. My fingers traced the rough stone wall next to me. "First my horses, and now this. Really, this is too much! Are you attempting to harm me?"

I received no answer as I pressed closer to the light source. Flames flickered as the dank corridor spilled into a chamber. I gaped around at the cavernous space that yawned in front of me. Torches burned on the edges, and several contraptions lay scattered about on the floor.

What was this place? "Spirit?" I called, my voice echoing off the stone walls.

A sobbing resounded from an unknown location.

"Hello?" I called, still hovering at the entrance. "Are you there? Show yourself."

The sobbing subsided, and I ventured a bit further into the space, scanning the various objects strewn around the room. My brows pinched as I wondered about their use.

I crouched over a large stone box in the middle of the room. My fingers skimmed the water that filled it nearly to the top. I frowned down at it as I shook the water from my fingertips. What was the purpose of the odd device?

I stared at my reflection, rippling in the water I'd disturbed, wincing at the frightful sight. My hair stuck from my head at odd angles, and a dirty smudge graced my right cheek. I drew my chin back to my chest as I considered the notion that Lenora Fletcher did not stare back from the pond, but rather some madwoman who appeared as though she belonged in the sanitarium.

I tried to tuck my hair into some semblance before I dunked my hand into the cold water and rubbed my cheek. The dirt gave way. I swiped at my cheek with my dry hand as I returned the other into the water to cleanse it.

"Robert may leave me here, given my state," I murmured, my voice echoing again.

I wiggled my fingers in the chilly water, rubbing them with my thumb to clear them of dirt. After a few seconds, I withdrew my hand. As my fingers lifted free of the pool, a pale gray hand shot out of the water and grasped my wrist.

Bony fingers clasped around it, tugging me closer to the water. I shrieked, terrified by the sudden action, and tried to yank my arm away.

The anemic arm held firm, refusing to let go of my wrist. Was someone in the water? No one could be. I breathed a few panicked breaths before I swallowed hard and wrapped my own fingers around the wet, bony wrist.

The gray fingers unfurled from around my arm, their bluish-gray fingernails poking into the air. I tugged on the arm, attempting to pull the source from the water. I made little progress.

I wrapped my other hand around the arm closer to the elbow and slid it down into the water. My eyes grew wide as my fingers slipped past the crook of an elbow, then up a bare arm to a shoulder.

A body lay under the water. My heart sped up. Perhaps this was my ghost. Had she drowned in this pit? Is this the help she required?

"All right," I said through clenched teeth as my hand banged off a piece of metal. My brow furrowed, and I clasped my fingers around it, feeling up and down the length of the bar. "What in the world?"

I licked my lips and cast my wonderment aside as I continued to try to tug the woman upward. "I'm trying!" I called to her spirit.

At last, the arm began to move upward. I tugged at it, climbing to my feet and straining to pull.

Water splashed out, sloshing onto my dress and drenching it again. A figure rose from the water. I gasped at the sight and lost my grip on the arm before falling backward.

A skeleton rose from the water. No flesh covered the bones on the grinning skull. I covered my gaping jaw with my hands as I suppressed a shriek.

My feet kicked in front of me, seeking to drive me back from the grotesque scene. A screech filled the chamber, and I imagined it came from the skeleton that taunted me from its watery grave. I squeezed my eyes shut and clapped my hands over my ears as the sound rattled against the stone walls. The sound of blood rushing through my ears replaced any other noise as my heart worked overtime, thudding in my chest at a quick pace.

After a few moments, my labored breathing slowed, and I risked a glance at the water pit. I pulled my hands away from my ears, my brow furrowing. I cocked my head and crawled forward toward the stone bath.

No skeleton poked from it. Had the bones sunk into the water again? I reached the edge and, with a hard swallow, peered over the edge. I spotted only my reflection in the calm water. No sign of the remains existed.

They must have slipped below the water's surface. I rolled my shoulders back and thrust my hand into the chilly water again. I felt blindly around, my hands touching nothing but the cold metal I had felt moments ago. My fingertips detected no bones.

I pulled my arm from the water and shook it, squeezing the sleeve of my dress to wring as much water as possible from it. I studied my reflection in the rippling water. What had I just experienced?

I sat back on my heels, chewing my lower lip as I contemplated the odd events. Was this the doing of the spirit who sought to drive me here and keep me here? What was her aim?

A quiet sobbing diverted my attention from my ruminating. "Spirit? Is that you? What is it you are trying to show me?"

I steadied myself against the edge of the stone vat and rose to stand. My eyes scanned the chamber in search of my ghostly friend. "You must tell me what it is you seek from me."

The sobbing intensified, though I spotted no specter.

"Hello? Please appear to me! I cannot help you as it is. You must make me understand."

The weeping noises softened, almost disappearing. My shoulders slumped at the coy behavior. "Why must the dead prove so frustrating?" I lamented aloud as I pressed my palm against my forehead.

My gaze fell upon a large wooden box with a rectangular hole cut into it near the top. I furrowed my brow at it. Perhaps the box was the ghost's final resting place. I moved toward it, running my hand over the rough surface. With a lick of my lips, I eased it open, expecting to find a gruesome scene. Instead, I found a box devoid of anything outside of a spider who scurried for cover as light shined upon it.

The wailing resumed as I closed the box. I tried another plea. "I understand how overwhelming this may be for you. I can help, but you must help me to help you. Do you understand? Acknowledge if you do by communicating in some way."

The sobbing sound shifted as though the spirit moved around me. I took it as a signal and closed my eyes, trying to ascertain the direction of the noise.

It now came from my left. I snapped my eyes open and searched the area. Something flitted into the darkness across the dim chamber. I stepped toward it, squinting at the wall. I reached forward toward the stone, but my hand hit no barrier.

There was an opening in the stone wall. With a determined stride, I backtracked and approached one of the flaming torches. After a battle, I managed to wrangle one from the wall and held it overhead as I approached the darker area of the chamber.

A hole gaped in the wall, now highlighted by the flickering flames of the torch.

I stepped into the narrow passageway and inched forward. The walls closed in around me, so tight in some places that I needed to turn sideways. I squeezed through a narrow space before the passage curved in a new direction.

"Hello?" I called into the unknown looming ahead of me. Nothing answered.

My feet slipped as the floor sloped away and I began to descend further into the cavern. Water dripped somewhere ahead of me. Perhaps I would reach an egress and be able to escape from this uninviting space.

A cool breeze gusted past me. The flame of my torch fluttered, threatening to blow out before it revived. "Air," I murmured. "This must lead outside."

My heart leapt with anticipation of being free, and I pressed forward with the promise of escape at the forefront of my mind. The tight stone passage closed in around me again before spilling into another round chamber.

I waved the torch around as I scanned the new space. In the room's center, a stone well stood. It must have been the source of the water sound echoing throughout the chamber.

I approached it as I continued to search for a way out. The sobbing resumed, and I froze for a moment. "Spirit? Are you there?"

The weeping cut off suddenly. My brows knit as I pondered why the ghost acted so oddly. Was it some sort of clue?

As only the sound of the dripping water echoed off the stone walls, I continued forward toward the well. I stretched my neck to peer into the water hole. I could spot nothing from the distance at which I stood, though given my last experience with water, I remained leery of stepping too close.

With a deep inhale, I inched forward and held the torch

over the hole. I stared into the seemingly endless blackness of the well. A gurgling sound emanated from within.

I pressed my lips together as I squinted into the darkness, searching for any features. A long rope disappeared from my sight several meters down. The bucket must still be at the bottom of the well. I set the torch in a holder on the stone wall and returned to the well.

The rope wound around the spindle stretched above the hole as I rotated the wheel. I cranked and cranked the handle until wet rope began to appear, wrapping around the dry cord.

After another moment, the bucket handle appeared, followed by the rim. Water filled it to the brim. I turned the handle a few more revolutions and reached for the bucket swinging over the well.

My fingers reached the edge, but the bucket slipped away as it wobbled on the rope. With a determined flex of my jaw, I stretched my arm further as the wooden water holder twirled back toward me. My fingertips caught the rim this time, and I let go of the crank and dragged the bucket toward me.

I balanced it on the stone and peered inside. Something glittered at the bottom of the bucket. I squinted my eyes at the object, clouded by the murky, rippling water.

"Is this what you wished me to find, spirit?" I questioned aloud, my voice echoing off the chamber's walls.

I received no answer. The sediment settled over the object, obscuring it from my view. I would need to bolster my nerves and reach into the dirty water.

A shiver snaked up my spine, as the last time I reached into the water while on this odd journey through the cavern, I'd had a less-than-desirable experience.

I slid my eyes closed and shook my head as I firmed my

resolve. I popped my eyes open and plunged my arm into the icy water before I could change my mind.

My fingers searched blindly, slipping across the slimy bottom of the bucket. My nose wrinkled at the mucousy muck. After a few seconds of searching, something struck my hand, floating through the water.

I fluttered my fingers toward it, seeking the object that had struck me. My open palm banged into it again, and I closed my hand into a fist, yanking it from the water.

I grinned at my closed hands, my smile fading quickly as I noticed the brownish-green sludge clinging to them.

My nose wrinkled at the sight, and I rubbed my fingers across my dress to wipe away the muck. With the amount of dirt already sullying the garment, I didn't see what a little more would harm.

After cleaning my hand to the best of my ability, I raised my still-closed fist to examine what I'd caught in my fishing expedition. My fingers uncurled, revealing a small gold key.

I squinted down at it, studying its tiny yet ornate details. Questions filled my mind. How had this key fallen into the well? To whom did it belong? And was it what the spirit hoped me to find?

"Is this what you wanted?" I called out aloud as I held out my palm. "I have found the key! Are you pleased?"

I waited for a response but received none. How typical, I mused, puckering my lips at the situation. The dead never seem impressed, even when you cleverly work out their request.

"Perhaps you can tell me the significance of this?"

A gurgling noise emanated from the well again as I finished my question. My eyebrows shot up as I considered it progress toward receiving an answer.

I took a step toward the well and continued asking my questions. "Was it your key? What does it open?"

Another burbling bubbled up from the well, almost sounding like a chortle. "Hello?"

I leaned over the well, peering into the blackness in search of the source. Another bubbling noise that turned into a gushing sound met my ears. The blackness seemed to race toward me. It morphed into a horrid face with red eyes and sharp fangs.

CHAPTER 12

My eyes widened as the horrid face shot out of the well, flying toward me with its mouth hanging open.

"LENORA!" a wicked voice rumbled as the disembodied head barreled toward me. The sound raked my ears, stinging them.

I trembled all over as a sense of evil surrounded me. It squashed my senses and soul.

I stumbled backward as the head rose from the well. I lost my footing and fell onto my back. The air rushed from my lungs, and my limbs flailed. The key flew from my hand, skittering across the dirt into an unknown corner.

The blackness rose past the edge of the well, dispersing into a massive cloud of bats. I pushed up to an elbow as they fluttered around. They shrieked, the frightening noise only dampened by the frantic flapping of their wings. I stared in terror at the bat colony as it dispersed.

After a few moments, only a few stragglers flitted around the chamber before ducking out through an exit I could not discern from my position. I lay on the ground for several more gasping breaths as I allowed my senses to return to normal.

When my heart no longer pounded, I pushed up from my elbows to my palms, then climbed to my feet. I dusted off my dress. Why I did not know. Given its current shape, dust was the least of the problems.

I eyed the well suspiciously. What had I encountered moments before the bats burst from inside? I shivered as the terrible sense of evil burned through my mind. Had I imagined it?

I wrapped my arms around my midriff and chewed my sore lower lip as I pondered if I had given in to foolish notions after my terrible morning.

I glanced in the direction the bats had flown moments ago. Perhaps an egress existed. I no longer heard their screeches echoing off the cavern walls. *Had they escaped? Could I?*

With a determined stride, I retrieved the torch from the wall holder. I took one step toward where the bats had flown before I retraced my step. I waved the torch around nearer to the ground until I spotted the glinting of a golden object.

I snatched the key from the tan dirt and shoved it into my pocket before spinning on a heel and traversing the length of the cavern to the opposite side.

I waved the torch around in search of an exit, hoping it was large enough for me to fit but worried I would find a tiny bat-sized crack.

After a moment of searching, I located a narrow passage. I squeezed into it. Stone rubbed against my shoulders, and I twisted sideways, inching through with the torch held in front of me.

A stone jutted out toward me, and I contorted my body to weave around it. After the tight spot, the passage widened, allowing me to walk normally. I breathed a sigh of relief as I continued forward.

My heart leapt for joy as a slight breeze tickled my cheeks. *Could the end be in sight?* I quickened my pace, hurrying forward in search of an exit.

The slope of the passage curved up. My breathing increased as I worked to climb the steep grade.

Finally, light not from my torch spilled into the stone hall. The corners of my mouth turned upward, and I dropped the torch and raced toward the bright daylight. Moments later, I burst forth from the cave.

Gray clouds floated overhead, still blocking out the sun but not producing any rain. I would not have cared if the precipitation poured down upon me. *I was free!*

I sucked in a breath as I pressed my hands against my head and raised my gaze to the sky, smiling at it. I spent a moment basking in my freedom before my mind pushed me to take action.

I glanced at my surroundings, trying to determine my location. Above me, the sanitarium loomed high. I wrinkled my nose at the building, though it provided the best place for me to seek shelter and await Robert's arrival.

This time, though, I thought as I climbed the hill toward the sprawling structure, I would not enter any secret passages. I would wait in the entryway for Robert. I did not even wish to view or relax in the parlor, the billiards room, or any other recreation area.

I pressed my hands against my thighs as I struggled up the steep grade, scrambling onto the drive with some effort. I gasped in breaths before I pressed on, shuffling up toward the front door. My feet kicked the gravel, creating an awkward trail behind me.

My carriage and horses still stood outside, obediently awaiting orders from someone other than me. My hand caressed the carriage as I took a moment to steady my breath. A fleeting thought raced across my mind, and I wondered if I may climb aboard and drive away on the carriage, having no desire to re-enter the building.

I concluded it to be a terrible idea, and with a sigh, I slogged to the front door and pushed inside.

The woman behind the large wooden desk's eyes widened, and she leapt from her seat. "Your Grace!"

"Hello. I became lost and–"

"I shall take you to Dr. Applebaum. Follow me!"

"No, I would prefer–"

The girl flitted away from me faster than I could decline, her shaky hands retrieving her keys and unlocking the door. My shoulders slumped, and I shambled behind her. I passed through the door back into the asylum with my palm pressed against my forehead.

Hair hung in stringy pieces around my face. Dirt and grime covered my dress, and likely my face, too. My lip, which I had forgotten about during my daunting experience, remained swollen and I imagined now sported a bruise. I must look a fright. The poor woman probably sought the doctor for fear I had sustained some injury.

She raced around the corner, and I quickened my pace to keep up with her. We wound through the halls until we reached the dreaded music room. She waved a hand to the inside and nodded to me, an expectant expression plastered on her features.

As I approached the now-open door, a familiar voice floated from within.

"… mean to tell me my wife became locked in this room and then disappeared? Tell me, Doctor, how she managed to disappear from a locked room?"

Dr. Applebaum's tentative voice responded, "Please, Your

Grace, she was here when I went to search for the key. We spoke. I told her to remain calm and I would find a key—"

"And when you returned, she was gone? Do you keep such poor track of your patients? Do they, too, elude you, even when locked away?"

An unfamiliar voice filled the air. "Of course not, Your Grace. I cannot imagine what may—"

The unknown voice cut off as I appeared in the doorway. I scanned the room, finding Robert pacing the floor near the piano. His jaw dropped as our eyes met, and he hurried toward me.

I raced to him, flinging my arms around him. Tears filled my eyes, and I squeezed them shut as I pressed my cheek against Robert's shoulder.

"Lenora," he whispered, wrapping his arms around me and squeezing me tight. One hand pressed against the back of my head as he held me close.

After a moment, he pulled back, his hands cupping my face. "Are you all right, dear?"

I nodded, my lips twisting into a smile for a split second. "I am all right. Shaken, though unharmed."

I reached for his hand, wrapping my fingers around it as he rubbed my cheek. He studied my face, likely dirty, his eyes landing on my bruised lip before rising to my eyes.

"I am quite fine, I assure you."

Dr. Applebaum approached, along with the other man who had been speaking when I arrived. Dr. Applebaum shoved his glasses up on his nose and studied me. "Your Grace, what happened?"

Robert huffed at him. "Really, Doctor, can you not see my wife has suffered a trauma? And yet your curiosity cannot wait even a moment?"

Dr. Applebaum's face reddened as his lower lip trembled

under his blond mustache. "No, of course not, Your Grace, merely–"

"It is quite fine, dear," I assured Robert. "I am certain Dr. Applebaum only means to determine how I disappeared to prevent harm from coming to anyone in the future."

"Quite right," Dr. Applebaum said with an appreciative half-smile at me. "And I do wish to ensure your own safety. I cannot imagine what may have happened, but I would very much like to ensure no harm came to you in this fiasco."

Robert guided me to a chair and eased me into it. "Sit down first, dear. And might we have a toddy brought to settle her nerves? Or a brandy at the very least."

"I shall see to it right away, Your Grace," the nurse, who still hovered outside the room, said with a curtsy. She darted away in search of the nerve-settling beverage.

"Thank you," Robert called after her, running his hands through his unruly dark hair. He heaved a discontented sigh and set his gaze upon me. "Are you sure you are all right? My goodness, Lenora, it looks as though you've been beaten and strung up!"

"I am certain, dear," I said, grasping his hand and squeezing. "Much of my state came from my feeble attempts to wrangle the carriage back down the hill after the horses bolted."

Robert shook his head at the statement. "I am very sorry, dear. Had I known they would have done that, I would not have alighted from the carriage."

"You could not have known," I assured him, "and Dr. Applebaum took very good care of me. He offered me a blanket–" I leaned around Robert to eye the fair doctor. "I'm sorry to say I lost it, though. And some tea. A chip in the teacup cut my lip."

Dr. Applebaum waved a hand in the air as the other

stroked his mustache. "The lost blanket is of no consequence. Your safety is all that matters."

"And thank God she is safe," Robert spat at them, "or I would have this institution shut down!"

The other man stroked his chin, shooting his gaze at Robert. "Really, Your Grace, there is no need for that." He waved a hand in my direction. "She is quite safe, as you can see."

Robert's eyebrows shot up, his features twisting into an incredulous expression. I squeezed his hand, hoping to prevent an outburst.

Dr. Applebaum chimed into the conversation, interrupting an argument between them. "Forgive me, Your Grace, but how is it that you disappeared from this room?"

I pointed in the direction of the panel that had moved. "A panel popped open leading to a passage. I followed it in the hopes of freeing myself. Thankfully, it led outside."

"A panel?" the other man inquired.

"Yes," I said with a nod. "A panel opened, and I followed it, hoping it would lead me to freedom."

Dr. Applebaum wandered to the wall and stared at it, tugging at his mustache. "This one?" he asked, running a hand along the wall.

"No, the one next to it." I pointed to the next panel over.

He furrowed his brow and stepped toward it, running his hand over it. "How did you trigger it?"

The nurse flitted into the room with a steaming toddy on a tray. I accepted the proffered drink with a smile and sipped at it before answering.

"I did not. It popped open," I claimed. I recalled Dr. Applebaum's earlier statements about the feminine mind's lack of ability. If he believed me stupid, I should play the part when needed.

"Hmm."

"Most interesting," the other man said. "We shall look into it, and until further notice, no patient should be in the room alone." He clasped his hands behind his back. "I am quite sorry, Your Grace, that you experienced this, however, at least we can prevent it from happening to one of the poor souls in our care in the future. Now–"

Robert interrupted his speech, flailing his arms in the air. "Quite frankly, Doctors, I am still in utter shock that this happened at all. What kind of institution is this where a woman awaiting the arrival of her husband is injured by a teacup, locked in a room, and then forced to wander through Heaven knows what to find her way back?"

"Just a moment, now, Your Grace," the other doctor, whom I assumed to be Dr. Merriweather, countered.

I rose to stand, interrupting his speech. "Really, Robert, there is no harm done. We should be on our way. I would very much like to return home and see the children." I glanced down at my clothing. "And change."

Robert stared at me for a moment before he nodded. "Quite right. Into your bedclothes and straight to bed after this." He shot a pointed glance at Dr. Merriweather. "And I shall be summoning our doctor to examine you."

"Oh, please do write to let us know of Her Grace's condition," Dr. Applebaum said as he adjusted his glasses, oblivious to the threat Robert intended.

"I most certainly will," Robert snapped, offering an unimpressed frown at the man as he tugged the toddy from my hands and set it on the nearby table. "Come, dear. We shall return home at once."

Goodbyes were called after us as Robert guided me from the room and through the halls to the main doors. The nurse at her station leapt from her seat as Robert flung the doors open and waved me out.

I stepped into the light rain, finding Jones huddled near

the door and the carriage turned around and waiting to depart. "Your Grace, thank the good Lord," he said as he rushed ahead of me to open the carriage and unfurl the stairs.

"Her Grace assures me she is all right," Robert said before climbing in and settling into the seat next to me. "Straight home, please. And this time, try to keep hold of the horses."

"Of course, Your Grace," Jones said with a nod before securing the door and climbing to his perch.

"Do not be so hard on him, Robert. It is not his fault," I said as the carriage lurched forward.

"Do not be hard on him? Lenora! Because of his ineptitude, this carriage drove away with you inside it! You could have been harmed or worse."

"I do not believe his ineptitude caused it."

Robert raised his eyebrows at me as he tugged a blanket from the opposite seat and placed it around me.

"Moments before the horses bolted, our quiet traveling companion disappeared, remember?"

Robert's eyebrows rose even further to his hairline. "Are you saying…"

I nodded. "She frightened the horses and sent them racing right back to the sanitarium."

Robert's lips formed a frown, and he fidgeted in his seat. "I am quite worried now. Perhaps she will never allow us to return home."

"I certainly hope she does. And I am optimistic she will. I may have found what she hoped for me to find. At least for the time being. I've no doubt I shall need to return to Staghearst."

"What did you find? Lenora, what happened when you disappeared? I had the distinct sense you were holding back in your story at the asylum."

I nodded again, grabbing Robert's hand and squeezing it.

"Yes, I was. I could not recount the entire tale without the doctors admitting me for treatment."

"Over my dead body!" Robert roared. "In fact, I am beginning to wonder if we should consider moving your mother from the place. It is clear they are incapable of running a hospital. Good heavens, imagine if one of the patients slipped away as you did."

My eyes stared at the floor, focusing on nothing. I bit my lower lip, wincing as I hit the cut again. "Though I wonder if that is not exactly what happened."

"Whatever do you mean?"

"I wonder if a patient stumbled upon the secret passage and died in the caves connected to them."

CHAPTER 13

Robert stared at me with his jaw hanging open for a moment. "Good Lord! Whatever happened to you in these caves that you believe a woman may have died there?"

"The experience was not pleasant," I answered with a shake of my head.

"How did you find your way in there to start with?"

"Dr. Applebaum suggested a tour of the facility. I took him up on it, since I preferred not to sit staring at him in the garden room and because my visitor had dropped by and I hoped to find some information on her. He took me to the music room.

"One of the other patients appeared and played a tune on the piano." I flicked my gaze to him. "Did you know you can commit a woman for reading too many novels?"

Robert's eyebrows squashed together and he shook his head as the carriage hit a bump and bobbled us. "What does reading novels have to do with anything?"

"Apparently, it fills our feeble minds with nonsense."

"Feeble minds? You have one of the sharpest wits of anyone I have ever met in either sex."

A grin formed on my face, and I patted his hand. "Thank you, dear."

"The idea is preposterous. And should anyone suggest you or my little daughter, Sarah, be too feeble-minded to read, I shall throttle them."

"I very much appreciate that, Robert."

He smiled and nodded at me before he waved a hand in the air. "Please, continue."

"Right. Where was I? Oh, a nurse fetched Dr. Applebaum about another patient. He left me in the music room, and my new friend appeared again. She locked me inside. When Dr. Applebaum returned, he could not open the doors, as no key existed on either side. Whilst he sought a key, the panel opened.

"My friend beckoned to me. I told her I would not follow, though I did. After I entered the passage, it closed, and I could not free myself. I could only continue forward. I reached a curved staircase and refused to go any further."

Robert raised an eyebrow, likely wondering what made me proceed further. I did not wish to share the reason with him, certain he would object to any future involvement with this investigation. As though I could control it.

"When I reached the bottom—"

"Just a moment," Robert interrupted, holding up a hand. "When you reached the bottom? I thought you said you refused to descend the stairs?"

"At first I did."

"What changed?"

I pressed my lips together and flicked my gaze out the window before answering.

"Lenora?" Robert prompted when I failed to answer.

"I—well—that is to say, I did not have much choice."

Robert narrowed his eyes at me. "What does that mean?"

"I...the ghost forced me down the stairs."

"Forced you?" His eyes grew wide as realization dawned on him. "Do you mean to say this spirit threw you down the stairs?"

I chewed the inside of my lower lip. "'Threw' is such a strong word."

"Damn it, Lenora," Robert said, slapping his hands against his thighs. "You could have been killed!"

"I would have preferred not to roll down the stairs either. My own obstinance is to blame, I suppose. I had grown quite tired of these games already. Apparently, the ghost has not."

Robert heaved a sigh and shook his head. "I suppose you have little control over it."

"Correct."

"All right. What happened next?"

I described the odd water chamber and skeleton that rose from within. Then I imparted the information about the chamber with the well.

"In the well, I found a key." I retrieved it from my pocket and showed it to him.

Robert picked it up from my palm and studied it. "What could it be for?"

"I am not certain. I am not even certain of the woman's name to try to track any information. She is quite elusive." I fixed my gaze on the passing countryside as our carriage continued to rumble along.

"Perhaps that is for the best. She nearly killed you!"

I flicked my gaze back to Robert. "I am wondering if she was not the one who almost injured me."

"Who, then?"

I stared into space as I considered the question. "I am not certain, though something quite odd happened to me whilst in the well room."

"Odd? I should say so, Lenora!"

"Odder than normal," I said with a slight smile. "After I found the key, a noise came from within the well. I wondered if perhaps the woman had drowned. I glanced inside, and I saw…"

My voice trailed off as I tried to come up with words for what I'd experienced.

Robert's chin slid forward, and he raised his eyebrows. "Yes?"

"I am not certain. It appeared to be a face. An evil, horrid face. It flew up at me, growling my name. I fell backward. Bats shot out of the well moments later and disappeared from the chamber. It is how I found my way out. I followed their escape path, finding my own."

"And you believe this…evil voice and face were at fault?"

"I conjectured it, yes. I am not certain, though."

"I do not like this, Lenora."

I patted his hand again before slipping my arm through the crook of his. "I know, dear. You never do. Though I often have no choice in the matter."

He wrapped his arm around me and pulled me close, kissing the top of my head. "Yes, I realize that. Though I do not like when these…people involve you in their tragedies. I wish for you a moment's peace."

"They wish for peace, too. That is why they seek me."

"You are kinder than I," Robert said, stroking my hair with his hand.

I stifled a yawn, exhausted after my bizarre experience under the sanitarium. "I am not."

I let my eyes slide closed as I laid my head on Robert's shoulder and drifted off to sleep, lulled by the rhythmic motion of the carriage.

* * *

Random images flitted past me, causing me to tremble all over. A skeleton rising from water, the evil face with red eyes, a dark cavern I'd never seen before. Water dripped somewhere, and a dreadful cold permeated me. Fog formed in front of my lips as I blew out a breath, spinning in a circle to study my surroundings.

I did not recognize them.

"Hello?" I called, my voice echoing off the cold stone surrounding me.

I took a few tentative steps forward as I searched for a clue to my location. "Hello!"

Only my own echo answered me again. The screeching sound of bats filled the air, and I ducked as a group of them fluttered past overhead.

I followed their flight, hoping to find an escape. I shivered as it turned colder. My feet slipped as I descended further into the cave.

"Hello?" I called out again. My fingers began to throb from the cold, and I shook them before shoving them under my arms.

"Lenora!" a voice called out to me.

I whipped my head in its direction, searching for the source. "Who is it?"

I squinted into the distance, trying to discern anything in the icy cold chamber. Had my ghost returned? Where had she taken me? And what did she want?

"Lenora," the voice said again in a whisper that floated on the cold breeze.

"I am here. Where are you?"

"Trapped. Help me, Lenora."

I froze, trying to stop my body from shivering as I furrowed my brow and listened hard again. "Who is it?"

"Help me, Lenora."

My eyes widened, and I raced toward the voice. "Tilly?" I

called, my voice breathless. "Tilly! What is it? What's wrong? Where are you trapped?"

I stopped running and glanced behind me over my shoulder, then returned my gaze forward. I hadn't moved. Despite all my running, I stood in the same spot. Nothing had changed.

What was this place?

"Help me, Lenora," Tilly said again.

"Tilly, where are you? I'm trapped, too. I keep trying to find you, but I'm stuck. I cannot move forward or back."

"We are trapped. You must help us."

I shivered again, my teeth chattering. "I'm trying, Tilly, but I cannot find you. And I cannot find a way out."

"Help us," she repeated on an endless loop.

"Tilly! Yes, I will try but–"

The walls began to crumble around me. A large rock crashed to the floor, breaking to pieces. A stalagmite toppled over, chunks of icy rock skittering across the brown dirt below my feet.

The ground shook, and a giant fissure formed. I inched back several steps away from it. A red river glowed from inside, rushing toward one of the stone walls and disappearing below it.

"Tilly!" I screamed, searching the air for her or a way out.

"Help us," she continued.

The ground beneath me tilted, and I lost my footing, sliding toward the red water. I dug my feet in, desperately trying to stop my progression toward it. I lost the battle, picking up speed as I careened down toward it.

My mouth opened, and a loud scream emerged as I faced certain doom.

* * *

I jolted awake as the carriage jostled me around.

Robert shifted in the seat next to me. "Nearly there, dear."

I glanced out of the window, realizing the carriage climbed a steep grade. The turrets and towers of Blackmoore Castle rose high above us with their banners waving proudly. Dark clouds gathered over top, as always. Thunder rumbled overhead, but no rain fell from the gray skies.

"We may beat the rain," Robert said.

"I'm not certain it matters much in my case," I said, flicking my gaze to him.

He chuckled at the statement and pulled me closer to him. "Soon, you shall be settled in your bed with a hot toddy and a bed warmer at your feet."

"That sounds marvelous," I said as I settled in next to him and stared up at the imposing silhouette of my home. "I will be so happy to be home."

Robert rubbed my arm. As we approached nearer to the castle, the disturbing dream I'd just experienced flitted across my mind. Why had I dreamt of Tilly, and why in such dire circumstances?

In truth, I'd had little luck reaching her whilst at Blackmoore. I assumed Edwin's presence may open the channel, but sadly, I'd had no contact with her even after he'd taken up residence in the castle.

With my pregnancy and Sarah's birth, I hadn't the opportunity to visit her at her gravesite.

"Have you any plans to visit Glasgow soon?" I inquired.

"Glasgow?" Robert inquired, fidgeting next to me.

I picked my head up off his shoulder and glanced up at him with a nod. "Yes. I haven't spoken with Tilly in quite some time, and I would very much like to see her. Perhaps introduce her to Sarah."

"We shall make arrangements, though perhaps it can wait until spring?"

I licked my lips and offered a nod, hoping it could. The message in my dream sounded urgent. Though perhaps my mind had merely knit together some of my more frightening experiences into a nonsensical nightmare.

"We may go earlier if the opportunity presents itself," Robert said, sensing my consternation.

"There is no need to go out of your way, dear. But just now I had a strange dream about her and find myself unsettled by it. I shall give it a few days and see if it passes. If not, perhaps we may go earlier."

"Of course. After everything you've been through, perhaps it is just the duress."

"Yes, I'm certain my feeble mind cannot process it," I said, my lips curling into a coy grin as I flicked my gaze up to him.

He pulled one side of his mouth back in a half-smile at the statement. "Remind me to throttle that doctor if we return to that horrid place."

"Honestly, I am hoping we do not, though given the lengths this specter has gone to, I cannot imagine we will not."

Robert's smile faded, replaced with a wrinkled forehead and puckered lips. "And there is the matter of your mother as well. Perhaps we shall have her moved."

My shoulders heaved as I sighed and stared out the window at the castle again. "I shall leave the decision to your good judgment."

"I am sorry the meeting did not go as well as you hoped, Lenora. I realize you may not wish to discuss the matter, but perhaps take a few days away from it before you consider what may be best."

I snapped my gaze to him and offered a weak smile and slight nod. "I shall."

I squeezed his hand as the carriage rumbled to a stop outside the door. The staff, led by Buchanan, awaited our return. Jones leapt from his perch and flung open the door. Robert stepped out after the stairs were rolled out and reached back to collect me.

I disembarked from the conveyance as thunder rumbled overhead. Buchanan's eyes bulged as he studied my rumpled and soiled clothing.

"Quickly, Buchanan," Robert said as he wrapped his arm around me and guided me to the door, "have Sinclair prepare a toddy and bring it to Her Grace at once. She has had a terrible experience and must go to bed immediately."

"How terrible! Of course, Your Grace," Buchanan said with a nod, shooing the servants back to their posts as he dashed off to find my ladies' maid.

"Really, Robert," I said as we stepped into the expansive foyer, "it is not as much of an emergency as you make it sound."

"It bloody well is. You've been traumatized. You must rest. Really, I should call the doctor, however, I will wait and only call if you take a turn."

I held back rolling my eyes at Robert's apprehensive nature as I tugged off my gloves. Nanny West awaited us with Sarah in her arms. I did not spot Samuel, though.

Robert strode toward her and scooped our daughter from the woman, giving her a kiss on the forehead. She gurgled as she studied him.

"My word, Your Grace!" Nanny West said as I smiled over Robert's shoulder at my baby. "What happened?"

"An accident with the carriage. Nothing to fuss over. I am quite fine. Where is Sam?"

Nanny West threw her shoulders back and shimmied. "With his Uncle Edwin. Getting into trouble, no doubt."

"That would be Edwin, yes," Robert concurred as tiny footsteps echoed from the back hall.

Little feet slapped against the stone, and Sam raced across

the foyer, his arms thrown in the air. "Mummy!" he called as he careened toward me and threw his arms around my soiled skirt.

I swept him into my arms and showered him with kisses. "Hello, my little darling. Have you missed me very much?"

"Yes, Mummy," he said, clapping his chubby hands together. "Did you miss me?"

I grinned at him and kissed his cheek. "I did, yes. I wished to see you every moment I was away. And what have you done whilst Papa and I were gone? Nanny says you got into trouble with Uncle Edwin."

"Of course we did," a new voice said from across the space.

I flicked my gaze toward it, finding Edwin grinning at us as he strode over.

"Really, Edwin," Robert said, "you mustn't ruin the child."

"Hardly ruining a child to let a boy play in the mud."

"The little master came back covered from head to toe," Nanny West said. She lifted an eyebrow and stared down at my dress. "Much like you, Your Grace."

Edwin's eyes traveled up and down my form, and his mouth pulled into a wider grin. "My goodness, Lenora, it appears you, too, have been playing in the mud."

"There was a mishap with the carriage," Robert explained.

Edwin cocked a hip and shoved a hand into his vest pocket. "Oh, dear. And did you make poor Lenora fix it?"

"Certainly not!" Robert snapped, pressing his lips into a thin line and shaking his head. "Never mind."

"Relax, brother, only a joke."

"Yes, yes. Everything is a joke to you, Edwin," Robert said, handing Sarah back to Nanny West.

"'Tis time for the children's naps," Nanny West said, glancing at the child in my arms.

"Of course," I said, giving Sam one last kiss. "Sleep well, my darling."

Nanny jostled Sarah into one arm and reached down for Sam's hands as I set him on the floor. "Come along, Sam."

He waved his little hand at us as Nanny pulled him along.

"All right, Lenora, up to bed," Robert chided after they disappeared into the back hallway.

"Sent to your room after playing in the mud?" Edwin chimed in.

"Lenora has had a most awful experience courtesy of a delinquent spirit. Really, Edwin, try to grow up and not make light of everything."

"I find making light of things a most enjoyable way to deal with life. Particularly now that I am dry."

Robert's features turned stony, and a grumble escaped him.

Edwin grinned and hinged at the hip, meeting Robert's gaze. "Smile, brother. Do not be so dour." He righted himself and turned his attention to me. "And what was this awful experience?"

"The damned ghost sent the carriage racing away with only Lenora in it. It drove her to the asylum and then shoved her down a flight of stairs and nearly killed her in some underground cave."

Edwin's eyes widened, and he stared at me. "Is this true?"

"Somewhat," I explained. "Robert has embellished a few details."

The arrival of Sinclair interrupted any further conversation. She bustled into the room, skidding to a stop near me and grasping my hands. "Oh, Your Grace! Buchanan tells me you've had a terrible accident!"

"It wasn't very terrible, Sinclair. I'm afraid His Grace and Buchanan are making it more than it–"

"We certainly are not," Robert interrupted. "Her Grace

has had quite a terrible experience. As you can see, she has sustained quite a bit of...damage. You should assist her in changing into her dressing gown and ensure she remains abed for the rest of the day."

I swiveled my head to stare at my husband, fluttering my eyelashes at him. At least he did not find my mind feeble, though apparently he considered my physical constitution to be as fragile as Dr. Applebaum considered women's minds.

I returned my attention to Sinclair and squeezed her hands. "I am really quite fine, though I would like to change from these soiled clothes."

"And then you shall climb into your bed and remain there. You have been through an ordeal. Soaked through and muddy. You risk pneumonia! I will not have it, Lenora. Sinclair, ensure your mistress is well looked after, please."

Sinclair bobbed her head up and down, and I resigned myself to being fussed over for the remainder of the day. I would not prevent her from completing the job with which she'd been tasked by my doting husband.

"Oh, but..." Edwin began, his nose wrinkling at the conversation.

Robert twisted to stare at him, a wide-eyed expression on his face. "Have you something to say, Edwin?"

Edwin lifted a shoulder and held up a hand. "It's only that I had planned to take Lenora to see her surprise. And we are already behind schedule due to your late arrival."

Robert's jaw unhinged at the statement. I winced as I prepared for the oncoming lecture.

"Well, I am so very sorry Lenora's near-death experience has spoiled your plans."

"Near-death? Oh, Your Grace!" Sinclair exclaimed.

"Really, that is quite an exaggeration," I said with a shake of my head.

Edwin widened his stance and flung his hand in the air

again. "It hasn't spoiled my plan, though confining her to her bed will wreak havoc upon them."

I did not believe Robert's eyes could get wider, yet they did. "Do you find this humorous?"

"Not at all," Edwin answered. "Perhaps after she has changed we could depart..."

"Certainly not!" Robert exclaimed, pounding his fist against the entryway table. "Have you gone mad?"

"No! But I have gone through much planning for this, and I do not wish it ruined. Lenora has saved my life on numerous occasions, and I hope this provides some small thanks."

"Small thanks would be allowing the poor woman to recuperate after her trying experience! Edwin, this is too much. I demand you stop being so selfish! Though this poor behavior is not a surprise. You have always thought only of yourself. You-"

"Really, Robert, it is nothing to argue over," I interjected.

"I disagree! Edwin's behavior is self-centered, as always."

"Oh, here we go," Edwin murmured, throwing his hands in the air and stalking a few steps away with a pout.

"Yes, here we go. Again, brother. Because, again, you behave poorly. Really, I assumed your son may cure you of some of this childishness, but alas-"

"That is quite enough," I said. "The bickering between the two of you must cease. Robert, you are understandably distressed at the morning's events. You are taking it out on Edwin."

Edwin spun to face his brother, a triumphant expression on his boyishly handsome features. Robert's lips puckered as he stared down at his feet, displeased with my statement.

"And Edwin, I know not why you are insistent on trying Robert's patience, however, you must stop. It is clear he is distressed, and you continue to badger at him."

Robert lifted his chin and narrowed his eyes at his brother. Edwin's shoulders slumped, and he shot me a pleading glance. He did not do well with rejection.

"Now," I continued, "I shall change my clothes, and we shall continue with your plans."

Robert opened his mouth to object, but I continued. "And then I shall spend the remainder of my day abed with a toddy."

With the plans set, despite a minor protestation from Robert, I proceeded to change with Sinclair's assistance. The task proved lengthier than anticipated, given my sullied condition from head to toe.

I appeared in the entryway in a fresh dress with my hair whipped into shape by some miracle only Sinclair could perform. Edwin leaned against the door jamb leading to the sitting room. He straightened as I strode down the stairs and hurried across the room to retrieve my cape.

With a giddy grin, he slipped it around my shoulders and motioned for me to precede him through the front door.

We climbed into the awaiting carriage. I shuddered as I settled into the seat.

A fresh set of horses pulled the conveyance, and I hoped they would not become spooked as the others had this morning.

Edwin sat across from me, one eyebrow arched high and a coy expression playing on his lips.

"Are you planning to grin at me for the entire ride?" I questioned.

A chuckle escaped him before he puckered his mouth and wiggled his eyebrows at me. A smile played on my mouth, and I struggled to maintain my composure with his giddy behavior.

The small town of Blackmoore closed in around us as the

carriage slowed to a stop. The door popped open, and Edwin climbed out, waving his hand inside to collect me.

I stepped from the carriage and stared up at the empty shop. The bluish paint peeled in a few places, but overall, the shop appeared well-kept. I wondered why Edwin had driven me to an empty storefront.

He pushed open the door, its hinges protesting and motioned for me to enter. I stepped inside and scanned the space.

"Edwin, why on Earth have you brought me here?"

His features pulled back in a devilish grin, and he arched his eyebrow again. "Because this, Lenora, is the site of our new detective agency."

CHAPTER 14

I snapped my head toward him, my lips falling open and brow furrowing at the statement. "What?" was all I could manage to choke out.

He spun to face me fully and clasped his hands in front of me, the grin still playing on his features. "Our new detective agency."

He formed the words slowly, enunciating each one before he puckered his mouth in a grin, and arched his eyebrows at me.

"Are you mad?"

His coy expression deflated into the now-familiar pout he displayed when someone did not react the way he'd hoped. "No."

I glanced at the shop space again before returning my gaze to him. "Detective agency? What are we detecting?" I ran my hand over the bulky desk nearest me. "Dust?"

A chuckle burst from him, and he doubled over for a moment before he said through his laughter, "No. Police work of sorts. Though done by the common person. It's all the rage in the States, I'm told. A fellow Scot by the name of Pinkerton is doing quite a business apparently."

I furrowed my brow at him, and he paced around the creaky floor, continuing his explanation. "He supposedly foiled a plot to assassinate their president. Lincoln or whatever his name is. Gangly fellow, most unpopular with the southern states. Wouldn't be surprised if someone doesn't try to off him again."

"Edwin," I said with a huff, "will you keep to the topic at hand? What in the world are you suggesting we do in this shop?"

He stopped his pacing and faced me, swinging his hands behind his back. "Solve mysteries."

"What?" I questioned again, my brow furrowing.

He waved a hand in the air. "Murders, disappearances, missing children. That sort of thing. You know, mysteries. Things the police cannot or will not solve."

I still failed to grasp the concept of which he spoke. My words came slowly as I tried to piece together the notion. "You propose to solve mysteries with Robert. He will detest the idea."

"No, no, no, no, no," he said, his hands wiping the air as though to clear it. "Certainly not!"

I lifted my eyebrows and nodded. "Thank heavens. Robert would undoubtedly decline. He hates mysteries."

Edwin lowered his chin and stalked closer to me. "But you do not."

He passed behind me, and I twisted to face him, confusion apparent on my features. "What are you getting at?"

"I already said it. This is *our* detective agency. Not mine and Robert's. Yours and mine, Lenora."

My eyes went wide, and my jaw gaped open. I spun to face him fully, my chin sliding forward. "I no longer need to ask. I now am convinced you have gone mad."

Edwin's shoulders slumped, and he shook his head. "Surely, you jest. Lenora, you have solved two murders! You are excellent at working out things. And with your special abilities, we will have an advantage no one else has."

My jaw still hung agape as I processed the statements. One word rattled through my mind: insanity. Perhaps Edwin should join my mother in the asylum. He clearly had descended into madness.

I raised my eyes to meet his. He stared at me expectantly, a grin playing once again on his lips.

"You're mad," I spat out.

His smile faded into a pout. He crossed his arms over his chest and stamped a foot on the ground. "Really, Lenora, I expect you to be thrilled."

"Thrilled? Edwin! Do you realize what you suggest? A detective agency? With me? Robert will forbid it. He will never agree."

Edwin bit his thumbnail, narrowing his eyes at me. "And you will allow him to stop you?"

"Do you really believe a woman is an appropriate business partner, or are you merely hoping to raise Robert's ire?"

Edwin waved a finger in the air. "Ah, well, here is the interesting bit. This Pinkerton fellow often employs women. Why, you may ask, my dear sister-in-law? The answer is that they make excellent spies. Unsuspected in most instances. Able to remain undetected in their pursuits. And with your unique advantage, it is an even stronger case to be made.

"So, in short, yes. I propose you and I form the Fletcher Detective Agency right here in this space." He waved a hand around at the nearly empty office before he raised a finger in the air. "Before you dismiss it, consider the possibilities."

He wandered toward me. "We shall be able to help others. Your unique skill will be used for the greater good. And you shall be challenged with puzzles galore! Forget your dusty novels. You shall live the mystery."

"I quite like my dusty novels, as you put it," I murmured.

He circled behind me and wrapped his fingers around my arms, ignoring my statement. He guided me around one of the two large desks in the room.

With his foot, he kicked the chair out from under it and eased me into it. "You shall sit here."

He hurried across the room and plopped into the chair behind the other desk opposite mine. "And I shall sit here."

He kicked his feet up on the desk and laced his fingers together, using them to cradle his head. "Picture it, Lenora. A dreich day. Thunder rumbles overhead. Through the raindrops, a woman rushes down the street. She pushes inside and throws back the hood of her cape. 'Help me!' she cries, wringing her hands. 'You must help me!'"

I rolled my eyes and stood from my seat. "Really, Edwin. Is this only about playing the hero to a damsel in distress?"

"Of course not," he said, rising across from me. "We shall take cases from men, too. Whatever cases we choose."

"You have it all figured, do you?" I asked as I ran a finger across the desk and studied the gray dust now crusted on my finger.

"I do. So," he said, shoving his hands into his pockets, "what say you? Are you game?"

I rubbed my thumb against my finger to flick the dust away before I snapped my gaze to him. "Have you said anything about this to Robert?"

Edwin's shoulders slumped forward, and he rolled his eyes. "Robert, Robert, Robert. Really, Lenora, I thought you forward-thinking enough to make up your own mind about the offer."

I pressed my lips together and bounced on my toes as I

stared out the window at the townsfolk bustling up and down the street.

Edwin hurried toward me, sidling up to me and wrapping his arm around my shoulders. He waved a hand in the air. "Picture it, Lenora. A family member murdered. The poor bloke comes to us. We solve the crime. The family is forever grateful. Think of the number of people you can help."

I sucked in a breath and flicked my gaze sideways at him. "I am not opposed to this idea. Though I cannot imagine Robert will agree."

Edwin raised his chin and arched an eyebrow. "Leave Robert to me."

A sharp laugh escaped me. "That will only end in disaster."

I slumped back into the chair behind me and stared at the dusty desk. I puckered my lips as I imagined solving mysteries. I'd solved several, as Edwin already noted. Had I enjoyed it?

I hadn't much choice, I reflected. I'd become accustomed to helping the dead, and the enigmas I'd tracked answers to had been interesting. In fact, even when forbidden to continue, I had plowed ahead.

Again, I hadn't much choice. The dead did not play by my rules, and certainly not Robert's. And I found myself in the depths of another conundrum I presumed I would not escape from easily.

I raised my eyes to Edwin's. "We may already have our first case."

A grin spread across his face, and he slapped his hands together. "We shall be the best detectives in all of Scotland. With my people skills and your...specialty, no one shall do better than us."

I raised a hand in the air and shushed him. "Before you

become too ecstatic, we must discuss this with Robert. My duty remains first to being mistress of Blackmoore Castle."

The smile faltered on Edwin's features, but I pressed on before he could whine.

"When Robert offered marriage to me, he substantially changed my life for the better on many levels. I am appreciative of that and do not wish to upset the balance. On top of that, I love him. And for that reason alone, I do not wish to disappoint him."

"We shall speak to him together tomorrow. We will bring him by. Once he sees the place, he will be sure to agree."

I arched an eyebrow at Edwin's confidence. Sure to agree was a long stretch from what I believed Robert would be when confronted with the madness of his wife, the Duchess of Blackmoore, working as a detective.

Unfortunately for Robert, the idea appealed to me a little too greatly, and much to his inevitable chagrin, I was as eager as Edwin suggested to solve mysteries.

Edwin plopped into the chair behind the desk opposite me and grinned. "Now, did you say we already had a case, partner?"

"Partner? Equal?" I inquired, leaning my forearms against the desk after blowing the dust from it.

"Equal. Now, the case."

I narrowed my eyes at him. "And I can make decisions on my own. Without running them past you?"

"Decide away, dear Lenora," Edwin said, kicking his feet on the desk and leaning back in his chair.

"And you'll listen to me?"

"Don't I always?"

I opened my mouth to respond when Edwin flopped his feet down on the unswept hardwood, slapping a hand against the desk. "Don't answer that."

I let my chin rest against my knuckles and eyed him. I'd

not seen him this excited about a prospect in the time I'd known him. Perhaps the project would provide him with the ability to straighten his life.

"The genesis of the curious case stems from my visit to the Staghearst Asylum."

Edwin's gaze cut to me, and he rolled a hand in the air. "Go on."

"While there, a spirit made contact with me and begged for my help."

"What did she wish you to help her with?"

I lifted my shoulders and sighed. "I know not. Spirits are not terribly direct."

"Like Gerard. He could not tell you what he wanted when you sought him to clear my name."

I nodded and let my hands fall into my lap. "Correct."

"So this spirit…male or female?"

"Female."

"Right, female. This female spirit begged for your help. And gave no indication of what she wished you to do?"

"No, though she was quite persistent. She appeared in our room at the inn. And she was, in my best estimation, the cause of the mishap with the carriage."

Edwin's features crinkled, and he narrowed his eyes at me. "What did happen with that? And why were you covered in mud?"

"The horses stopped suddenly and refused to go any further. Robert disembarked to assess the problem. When he did so, the horses turned and raced off. Jones fell from his perch, leaving me alone in the carriage as it raced away."

"How did you stop it?"

"I did not. The horses raced me straight back to the asylum. I attempted to drive the carriage back to Robert myself, though it proved more difficult than I anticipated. I fell into the mud. Twice."

Edwin's eyebrows lifted toward his hairline, and his lips puckered as he worked to hold in a chuckle.

"A doctor at the asylum took me inside to escape the rain. While there, I had several more experiences with my ghostly friend."

"And did she punch you?"

I opened my mouth to continue my story before my brow furrowed. and I clamped it shut. "What?"

"Your lip. It's swollen and bruised."

"Oh, that," I said, rubbing the purple skin and wincing. "I'm afraid that is courtesy of a chipped teacup, nothing supernatural."

"Hmm, the other explanation would be far more compelling in a retelling."

I snapped my gaze to him. "I shall stick to the truth in my stories, thank you."

He rolled his hand in the air. "All right, go on with your truthful accounting. Did anything else interesting happen?"

"Quite. Whilst there, I managed to become trapped in a secret passage. A force, perhaps not the original ghost who sought my help, drew me further into an underground cave. There, I experienced several strange..." My voice trailed off as I suppressed a shiver, recalling the evil presence I felt near the well. "And disturbing events, the culmination of which turned out to be the finding of a key."

I opened my reticule and pulled it from within, holding it up between my thumb and forefinger.

Edwin rose from his chair and approached, snatching the golden key from my hand. "What is it for?"

"I know not. After I found the key, I managed to escape the underground chamber. By the time I wound my way back to the asylum, Robert had arrived."

Edwin switched his gaze from the key to me. "And was undoubtedly castigating the staff over your disappearance."

I lowered my chin to indicate the correctness of his statement.

"And did you see your ghostly friend again?"

"I did not. We managed to make it home after the incident. I am afraid I have little more information that I started with about the woman's identity, nor what this little key may uncover." I stared at the object clutched in Edwin's hands for a moment before I glanced up at him. "Perhaps it can be the Fletcher Agency's first case."

Edwin's brow furrowed at my statement. "Whatever will we investigate?"

"What happened to this woman to warrant her request for my help."

"And who will pay us?"

I stared at him for a moment with a blank expression. "Did you not wish to help others?"

"For money. That's the key thing, Lenora. The money bit."

"Really, Edwin," I said as I rose from my chair and paced around the desk. "Consider it practice."

"Practice for what?" Robert's voice asked from the doorway.

He swung the door shut, closing out the cool air that gusted inside, sending a few dry leaves swirling into the space.

"Robert!" Edwin exclaimed, leaping to his feet. "What are you doing here?"

"Collecting my wife."

"I had planned to return her when we had finished," Edwin objected, his fingers closing around the key into a fist.

Robert took a few more steps inside, his eyes scanning the dimly lit interior. His features pinched, and he shot a glance at me. "What has this to do with your surprise for Lenora?"

"Oh, ah…" Edwin stammered. He shot me a worried

glance and swallowed hard before returning his attention to his brother.

Robert raised his eyebrows, awaiting a response. "Well?" he finally prodded, tapping his cane against the dusty hardwood below his feet.

A nervous chuckle escaped Edwin. He fiddled with the key, turning it over and over in his hands.

"Oh, for heaven's sake, Edwin, you may as well tell him."

"Tell me what?" Robert inquired.

Edwin licked his lips and lowered his gaze to the floor.

"For God's sake, Edwin, say something," Robert demanded with another pound of his cane.

"I...we...that is to say..."

Annoyance showed plainly on Robert's face as he let his gaze flit around the room again. "Will someone please explain to me why on Earth my brother brought my wife to an empty shop as a surprise?"

"Edwin has had a unique idea," I answered.

"Edwin seems full of...unique ideas," Robert retorted. "What's the scheme this time, brother?"

"There is no scheme!" Edwin shouted, heat entering his voice as it usually did when he spoke with his brother.

"Oh? I shudder to think why it is you've dragged Lenora here. What is it you want from her?"

Edwin's face reddened as the vague accusation hung between them.

"Actually," I interjected, "I found the idea to be promising."

Robert pressed his lips together in a thin line. "I reserve the right to decide for myself once I've heard it. If ever."

"I was unprepared to discuss it with you."

I cringed as Robert's eyebrows shot toward his hairline again, an incredulous expression on his features. "Yet you were prepared to discuss it with Lenora. And, using her earlier distress to your advantage, wear her down to your side."

Edwin shook his head. "That's not true."

I stepped between the feuding brothers. "This can all be solved quite simply by explaining the situation. Edwin proposes opening a detective agency."

"A what?" Robert inquired.

"A detective agency. To investigate things and solve mysteries."

Robert's forehead crinkled, and his lips turned down at the corners. After a moment, they reversed direction, and his belly began to shake. Seconds later, a chuckle escaped him, turning into a full-bellied laugh soon after.

Edwin's mouth formed his familiar disappointed pout. "Why are you laughing?"

"Sorry, brother. The notion of you solving crimes is amusing."

Edwin's face set into a stony expression. "It's not that amusing. We solved Gerard's murder."

Robert choked out a few more chuckles, along with a few words. "Lenora solved Gerard's murder, lucky for you."

"I helped," Edwin whined.

"Very little. The bulk of the work fell to Lenora. You couldn't solve a mystery without her."

"Well…" Edwin said, waving a palm in the air and lifting a shoulder.

"Well, what?" Robert questioned. "You plan to hire Lenora as a detective." Another laugh bubbled up. "That's almost as amusing as you solving mysteries, Edwin."

My chest rose high as I sucked in a breath and prepared for the onslaught as I confirmed Robert's worst fear. "Actually, that is exactly what he proposed, Robert."

Robert's expression turned serious in an instant. He

slammed the cane's tip down on the ground again. "Surely, you jest!"

Edwin lifted his chin. "I do not. Lenora would make an excellent partner, and she has already agreed to the venture."

Robert's jaw dropped open, and he shifted his gaze from his brother to me. I gave a slight nod to confirm Edwin's statement.

"You're mad. Both of you. Mad." Robert paced across the room as the news sank into his mind. "I will not allow it. I simply will not allow it!"

CHAPTER 15

"Pure madness. Simply preposterous!" Robert continued his parading around the room, his cane tapping angrily onto the hardwood with each step.

Edwin waved a hand in front of him, his mouth opening to begin an explanation. I placed a hand on his forearm and hushed him. In his current state, it would only serve to antagonize Robert.

Robert spun on his heel and crossed the room in the opposite direction, shooting a glaring glance at Edwin. "She is the Duchess of Blackmoore! And you propose she trot around the countryside solving mysteries? You have finally lost your mind. Have you been drinking again?"

Edwin's posture stiffened at the accusation, and he opened his mouth again. I waved a hand at him and shook my head, pressing a finger to my lips.

Robert turned and ambled back in the direction he'd started his frantic wandering. "Really, Edwin, this is too much. Simply too much." He ceased his toddling and twisted to face me. "And you find this acceptable?"

I lifted my shoulders and offered a half-smile. "It seems to me that I must participate, whether I choose to or not. At least in this version, I have Edwin's assistance."

Robert pressed his mouth together in a thin line and pounded the cane against the floor as he stared ahead at nothing. After a moment, his lips twitched, and he thudded the walking stick against the floor again. "I suppose you've already made the arrangements to secure the space?"

I gave Edwin a slight nod, and he responded. "Yes, I have. I...may have told MacArther you approved already."

Robert's nose wrinkled, indicating his displeasure, though it also indicated his outburst neared an end. "Of course you have. Well, to go back on it now would put me in a bad spot, wouldn't it?"

He spun and studied the space again. "And I suppose the space should be put to good use while it is under our name."

"Yes, it would look rather bad if we left it to languish," Edwin agreed, shoving his hand into his vest pocket.

Robert frowned, still intent on showing his disapproval, though far closer to acceptance than when the idea was first mentioned. He sauntered over to the desk across the room and banged on its side with his cane. "I suppose this will be my desk?"

"Ah," Edwin said, darting across the room and patting the dusty desk with his palm, "no, this is my desk." He offered Robert a lopsided, nervous grin.

Robert arched an eyebrow and puckered his lips. He spun and eyed the desk opposite Edwin's. He meandered across the room and rapped against the heavy wood of the second furniture piece. "This one, then."

Edwin winced and scurried across the room, wrapping his hands around my arms. "No, that one is Lenora's."

Robert twisted to face us, his features a mask of confusion. "Lenora's? Whatever does she–" He stopped his comments and pressed his lips together. "And where, then, shall I sit?"

Edwin's mouth moved, but no words emerged from them.

Robert's chin dipped forward as he awaited an answer. "Surely, I am invited to take part in this wild adventure."

"Of course," Edwin finally managed. His mouth pulled back in a desperate wince as he searched around the room. His eyes fell upon a ramshackle table against the back wall. Next to it, a rickety chair stood.

Edwin lunged toward it and patted it, a smile creeping over his face. "Here you are."

Robert's thick eyebrow arched high, and he wandered to the desk, staring down at it with a grimace. "This?"

"Indeed," Edwin said, lifting his chin.

"This isn't a desk. It is a table."

"Well," Edwin said, shimmying the chair closer to Robert. "As the face of this outfit, you wouldn't spend much time here. Plus, you have a large desk at the castle. So, you would not need one here."

"Lenora has a desk at the castle, yet she has a desk here."

"But she…look, Robert, your work is the most integral part, but it cannot be done at a desk, so—"

Robert held up a hand, bobbing his head up and down as he glanced away from his brother. "All right, Edwin. Please stop attempting to flatter me into agreement."

He twisted and eyed me. "Are you satisfied with the arrangement?"

My features curved up in a smile, and I nodded.

"Then, I suppose I shall be, too. Well, it appears we own a detective agency." Robert tapped the cane on the floor again and lowered himself into the chair. A crack resounded in the room, and the chair shattered to pieces. Robert landed on the floor, his arms and legs flailing.

My jaw dropped, and I hurried to his side. "Robert! Are you quite all right?"

Robert glanced up at me and heaved a sigh before glancing behind him. "Yes, yes, I am. I suppose a new chair may be the first order of business."

A chuckle escaped me as Edwin pulled him to his feet. "We shall buy you a new chair, dear."

"Yes, though it must be the second order of business," Edwin said, raising a finger in the air. He held up the key. "Lenora has already found our first."

Robert's eyebrow arched again. "You intended to pursue the odd matter from the asylum as a case?"

I nodded at him and snatched the key from Edwin's hand, returning it to my reticule. "Yes, I have tasked Edwin with tracking information that may assist us in identifying the woman. Perhaps if we know who she was, we may be able to understand why she seeks help."

"Yes, about that," Edwin said, rubbing his chin, "how do you propose I do that?"

Robert huffed and glanced at his brother. "For God's sake, Edwin, you have opened a detective agency. Detect!"

"Yes, but detect where?"

I stalked to my desk and plopped into the chair as I considered the vague duty I'd tasked Edwin with. "Perhaps check the papers for a woman who passed at the asylum."

"I'm quite certain several have," Edwin answered. "How will we know?"

I flicked my gaze to him and shrugged. "I am not certain, but we must begin somewhere."

"Have you any idea of her name? When she died? How?"

I shook my head. "Nothing on any of those."

Edwin crossed his arms over his chest and puckered his lips. "Perhaps you should return to the asylum and inquire after more information with your ghost friend. Then I can–"

"No," Robert said, striking the cane against the floorboards. "If you wish to be a detective, then you must learn to chase leads. Lenora has done enough of the work already. It is your turn."

"I am only pointing out that I may not find much. Who would report the death of a woman in an asylum? Do you believe the local paper has any interest?"

Robert shot him a glance, lifting his shoulders. "I suppose you'll find out."

Edwin let his head loll to the side at the statement as Robert turned his attention to me. "Well, dear, it appears your work day has come to an end. Come, let us return to the castle."

He approached me and offered his arm. I accepted, rising and stalking to the doorway.

"Goodbye, Edwin, and good luck," Robert called over his shoulder as he tugged the door open.

"I will require traveling expenses!" Edwin called as we stepped onto the sidewalk.

Robert waved a hand in the air, giving silent approval as we approached the second carriage awaiting us on the street.

We climbed inside, my stomach somersaulting again as I wondered if we'd make it home without the horses being spooked by a specter.

Robert threw himself into the seat across from me with a heavy sigh, and the carriage lurched forward, heading toward the castle.

He studied me for a moment before he spoke. "What are your true thoughts about Edwin's scheme?"

"I gave them already. I do not find it so much a scheme as perhaps an excellent use of his time."

"Really?"

"It provides him with a focus. He did rather enjoy the solving of Gerard's murder."

"That is because he was accused of it. It was to his advantage to solve it."

I eyed my husband as the carriage rocked back and forth, climbing the steep hill. "I disagree."

"How?" Robert questioned, his expression incredulous. "He'd have spent his life in prison or worse had you not solved it."

"He seemed rather interested in chasing leads."

"That seems to have waned," Robert grumbled, turning his gaze to the passing scenery.

"He needs a bit of encouragement, and he shall be fine."

Robert's eyes slid sideways to stare at me. "I fear the Fletcher Detective Agency will be shuttered in one month if it lasts that long."

"I disagree," I said, lifting my shoulder and cocking my head. "Edwin may have finally found something in which he will excel."

"We shall see."

I settled back into my seat and glanced up at the banners snapping in the wind that always whipped at the top of the hill.

"For your sake, I hope you are correct," Robert added. "I would like to be finished with this asylum business. I do not care for it after the last episode there."

"I'm afraid I have rather the same feelings." My eyebrows pinched, and I bit my thumbnail. "Though I must attempt to separate the ghost from whatever evil presence I detected in the cave."

"Have you ever experienced anything like it before?"

I pressed my lips together into a thin line as we rumbled along and reached into the depths of my memory. The crease between my eyebrows deepened as something flitted across my mind. "I'm not certain."

"I cannot imagine you would have forgotten something so startling."

My gaze fell to my lap. "I cannot either, though…"

Robert leaned forward, catching my eye.

"Though there is something that plagues me. Something that feels…familiar about that voice."

"Familiar? Do you recognize it? Is it someone you have known?"

"No, not that I can place." I placed a palm against my forehead and sighed. "I am not certain."

Robert reached out and grabbed my other hand, squeezing it. "You are tired from our trip. Undoubtedly, the visit with your mother coupled with the…unexpected return trip has left you drained."

I forced a weak smile onto my face and nodded. "Yes, quite right. I shall enjoy the toddy you insist I drink today."

Robert tapped the cane against the floor of the carriage. "You should not have gallivanted around with Edwin. I knew it! Blasted Edwin and his schemes."

"Do not blame Edwin. I was party to the trip, too. I insisted we continue on with his plan."

"You are too kind, Lenora," Robert said as the carriage ground to a halt in front of the castle's entryway.

I offered a genuine smile this time before we climbed to the gravel drive and pushed into the entryway for the second time today. This time, no one greeted us. I stared up the curving staircase.

"Straight to bed, dear," Robert said as Buchanan hurried into the room to relieve us of our cloaks.

"I'd like to check on the children–"

"I shall have Nanny bring them 'round before their meal."

"I could–"

"Lenora," Robert said, his eyebrow arched high, "you must rest. I shall call the doctor if you do not."

I pursed my lips and let my shoulders slump. "Fine, dear. I shall go straight to my room and rest."

He smiled at me and nodded. "Buchanan, have Sinclair attend to Her Grace immediately."

Buchanan nodded as he tossed my cloak over his arm. "She awaits you in your suite, Your Grace."

I nodded at him and smiled before I climbed the stairs. My mind tumbled through thoughts. An uneasy feeling grew inside me. Something felt off. I could not place what it was, however, I could not shake the feeling.

I wound through the halls as my mind wound from topic to topic, beginning with my ghost and ending with Tilly.

I stepped into the hallway containing my bedroom suite, and a shiver passed through me. I ceased my steps and stared down the hall.

"Hello?" I called into the empty hall.

I glanced over my shoulder. My skin puckered into gooseflesh, and I swallowed hard. My heart thudded against my ribs, and my knees wobbled.

"Hello? Spirit?" I called.

No one answered me. A coldness passed over me, and I wrapped my arms around myself, rubbing at them. My breath fogged the air in front of me.

"Tilly?" I questioned.

"Help us, Lenora," her voice called.

CHAPTER 16

I sucked in a sharp breath, my eyes going wide. "Tilly?" I shouted as I hurried forward in search of her.

The door to my room burst open. I expected to find my friend there. Instead, Sinclair stepped into my path. I ground to a halt with my brow furrowed.

"Your Grace?" she asked. "Are you all right? Did you call out a moment ago?"

I glanced behind me again, confusion pinching my features. "Yes, I did. I thought I heard something."

I spun back to face her, realizing the coldness I had experienced moments ago had passed.

"Was it a ghost, Your Grace?"

"I–I am not certain. I thought so, but it was a most unusual encounter."

Sinclair's eyebrows shot up as she stared down at her clasped hands.

"More unusual than normal," I added.

A smile tugged at one corner of her lips. "I do not understand how you so easily take these experiences in stride, Your Grace."

"You would if you had lived your entire life like this."

She snaked an arm around my waist and drew me into the suite. "Come along, Your Grace. I have orders to see that you are put straight to bed after changing."

"Yes, I know," I said to her as she began to unfasten my dress. "Robert even came to collect me from Edwin's clutches."

"And what did Mr. Fletcher wish to offer as your surprise, may I ask?"

"I fear telling you may shock you more than my confession about speaking with the dead," I said with a chuckle.

The unfastening of my dress slowed. I imagined Sinclair's eyebrows pinched tightly and her lips puckering as she considered my statement.

"Perhaps it is none of my business, Your Grace," she stated after a moment. The unfastening of my dress resumed.

I smiled as I stepped out of the garment and spun to face her. "My intrepid brother-in-law has proposed the formation of a detective agency."

"Detective agency?" Sinclair asked, slowing in her work of folding my dress.

"A firm that investigates mysteries," I said with an arch of my eyebrow.

"Mysteries?" she questioned, readying my nightgown.

"Crimes and the like," I said with a nod.

She slipped the garment over my head and tugged it down. "Forgive me, Your Grace, but why is this surprise of any concern to you?"

"He proposes we work together. As partners."

"Partners? A lady detective?"

I nodded as she tugged my dressing gown around me.

"And are you interested in the idea?"

I crossed the room and sank onto the stool in front of my vanity. Sinclair stowed my dress in the wardrobe and followed me, pulling my hair from its upswept style.

"I am quite keen on it," I answered, eyeing her in the mirror.

Her eyebrows shot up again, and the corners of her lips turned down. "It sounds like an interesting prospect."

"I found it so. And I have already given Edwin our first case. The woman who begged for my help at the asylum." My brow furrowed as I cast my eyes down to the wooden vanity on which I drummed my fingers. "I wonder what we shall find."

"Well, I daresay between you and Mr. Fletcher you shall solve it. I have never known you to be stumped for long."

I smiled at her through the mirror as she finished the braiding of my hair. With it fastened at the bottom, she met my gaze.

"Now, to bed with you."

"Might you do me a favor?" I asked as I climbed between the sheets, slipping my feet down into the warmth created by the bed warmer Sinclair had placed at the bottom.

"Certainly, Your Grace," she answered as she fluffed my pillows.

"Will you have Nanny bring the children 'round now?"

"I will try, Your Grace. Though you know Nanny. I am certain she will fuss if their naps are cut short."

"Yes, I realize that. Robert promised to have them brought by before their dinner, but I feel the urgent need to see them. Please tell her I am insistent."

Sinclair tucked the covers around me and nodded. "I shall see to it, Your Grace."

"Thank you." I settled back into the pillows as she scurried from the room.

My fingers drummed against the covers as I awaited

seeing my children. The uneasy feeling settled over me, and the space between my shoulders began to ache. I fidgeted in the bed, wiggling against the pillows to relieve the dull pain.

My head began to throb at the temples. I let my head sink back into the pillows behind me and closed my eyes.

"Help us, Lenora," Tilly's voice echoed in my mind.

I snapped my eyes open and searched the room. "Tilly?"

I threw back the covers and leapt from the bed, shoving my feet into my slippers. I padded across the room, checking every corner. "Tilly?"

A knock sounded at my door, and it burst open before I could call out. Robert stepped inside, freezing for a moment as he spotted me standing in my sitting room.

"Robert!"

"Lenora." He eyed me for a moment. "I am glad I came."

"Oh? Has something happened?"

"Yes, something has."

I pressed a hand against my stomach, feeling it turn over. "What is it? Is it the children?"

"No," Robert said, wrapping his arm around my shoulders and guiding me back to my bedroom. "It is you. You are meant to be in bed, not wandering about your suite. I shall have to have a word with Sinclair about ensuring your rest."

"It is not her fault. She is fetching the children and likely the toddy you insisted upon."

"Which is why I came. Someone must monitor you before you race about the castle."

I huffed at him as I climbed into my bed again and tugged the sheets over me. "I am hardly racing about the castle, Robert. I thought I heard Tilly and rose to investigate it."

Robert's muscles stiffened, as they often did when I mentioned the presence of a spirit, and his gaze darted around the room. "And did you find her?"

I heaved a sigh, letting my eyes lower to the blanket on my lap. "No. Unfortunately not."

I shook my head as Robert's tension eased and he dragged a chair close to my bedside. I wrung my hands as he settled into the chair. "I cannot help but be worried for her."

"Tilly?"

I nodded and glanced at him. "Yes. Why can she not visit me here?"

"Perhaps because she had never traveled here in her life."

My forehead scrunched as I considered it. Had I ever experienced a visit from a ghost who had not visited the castle? "You may be correct. I believe the only spirits I have encountered at Blackmoore are Annie and that dreadful man who killed her."

"You saw Sir Richard's ghost?"

I pressed my lips together and nodded, unwilling to speak his name or acknowledge him.

"When?" Robert asked, straightening in his chair, his fingers clutching the arms until they turned white.

"Just after his death. He stood on the ridge. He appeared confused. I screamed at him to go away. He disappeared, and I have not seen him since. I assume he crossed over. Though I had more important matters to attend to at the moment, so I cannot say." I reached for his hand and squeezed it, tears filling my eyes as I recalled his limp, almost lifeless form bleeding through his shirt following their duel.

"That infernal man. Even in death, he caused trouble."

"I think he was astounded to be dead. Though I felt no pity for him."

Robert's hand curled into a fist and pounded the chair. "Nor should you have!"

"Back to the matter at hand, perhaps Tilly cannot visit because she has not been here."

"Quite right. I am certain it is nothing to trouble yourself over."

I puckered my lips as my fingers traced the edge of my blanket. "Yet she appeared in Edwin's jail cell. I am quite certain Tilly had never visited that place before."

Sinclair's arrival with my toddy interrupted our conversation. "Here you are, Your Grace. And I have informed Nanny West to bring the children 'round as soon as possible."

"Thank you, Sinclair," I answered as I wrapped my fingers around the warm mug and took a sip. I would not admit as much to Robert, but I had grown fond of the beverage.

"Would you like me to stay?" she inquired, flicking her gaze from me to Robert.

"I shall stay with Her Grace until dinner. Perhaps you could take a tray here and keep her company."

"That is not necessary," I insisted.

Robert raised his eyebrows and drew back his chin. "I beg to differ. I found you wandering the room when I arrived."

"Oh, Your Grace!" Sinclair exclaimed. "You must rest."

"I promise to remain abed," I told them both after another sip of my toddy. "I do not need anyone to monitor me."

"I shall request a tray and keep you company, Your Grace. Perhaps we can discuss your latest mystery and find a path forward."

I smiled at her and nodded as Robert's gaze cut to her. "I had not realized you'd be colluding over this meal. Perhaps I should not have asked Sinclair to stay."

Sinclair's eyes widened as she wrung her hands in front of her. I waved her away. "His Grace does not mean that. I shall see you later. We shall enjoy our meal together. And our colluding."

Robert shook his head at me as Sinclair curtsied and scurried from the room, slipping out the door and closing it behind her.

"Really, Robert. You'll frighten the poor woman away from her duties here."

"Oh, I will not," Robert said with a wave of his hand. "Sinclair is quite devoted to you."

"And to my mysteries," I said with a half-smile and wink.

"And now you have Edwin devoted to your mysteries. Lenora, are you certain you believe this a wise idea?"

"I was quite intrigued with it. Apparently, this Pinkerton fellow he has based his business off of hires women frequently."

Robert wrinkled his nose at the prospect. "Woman working. What a ghastly idea."

I held the warm mug closer to my chest with one hand as I let the other fall to the bedding on my lap. "I hope you do not believe that. I will be working. I do not wish you to find me ghastly."

Robert reached for my hand and stroked it. "Never, dear. I suppose I shall come 'round to it. I am, after all, a modern man."

The arrival of the children with Nanny West ended our conversation about my new profession. I slid what remained of my toddy onto the nightstand as Sam raced ahead of Nanny as she waddled in with Sarah. His little feet pounded against the floor, and a grin spread across his face. He slammed into the bed and tried to climb up.

I tugged him upward, despite Robert's groaning over my overexertions. "Sam, you should not tax your mother so," he scolded the child.

I waved Nanny West over and held my arms out for Sarah. She flicked her gaze to Sam, who nestled against me, his little arms clutching at my midriff.

"I am capable of handling both," I assured her.

She straightened and pursed her lips as she laid the baby in my arms. Sarah cooed and I rubbed her cheek with my finger as I stared down into her eyes, already turning gray like Robert's.

I settled Sarah in the crook of one arm and reached around Sam with the other, pulling him closer to me. "Have you had a very nice day, dear?"

He nodded, another giddy grin on his features.

"Answer, Sam. Do not simply nod and grin."

"Yes, Mummy," Sam said in his tiny voice.

I kissed his unruly hair, which had begun to darken and appear closer to his father's. "What did you do? Did you play with your trains?"

"Yes."

"And your rocking horse?"

"Ride!" he shouted, waving his arms in the air.

Even Robert grinned at this statement. He leaned forward and studied our little son's face. "Yes, ride, son. Very good. Soon you shall ride a real horse."

"Not too soon," I cautioned.

"Ride! Ride!" Sam said, clapping his hands and staring at Robert.

Robert smiled and nodded at him. "Perhaps I shall take you for a ride tomorrow. Would you like that? We shall ride together, and you shall see if you like the horse."

Sam giggled and clapped his hands again. "Horsie!"

"Yes, Papa will take you on a big horse," Robert promised with a broad grin.

I cocked my head and shook it at my overzealous husband.

Nanny held out her hand toward the boy. "Come along, Sam, it is time for your dinner."

"Will you bring them by before their bedtime?" I asked her as I passed Sarah back into her arms.

"Of course, Your Grace. Though if you are tired, I can kiss them goodnight for you."

"No, no. I would prefer to see them, though I will not be leaving my bed to make the trip."

Nanny West nodded at me, hiding her true thoughts behind an awkward smile as she led Sam from the room for his meal.

I sighed as the door closed behind them. "Nanny will be whispering about me again."

Robert crossed his arms and slouched in his chair with a frown. "Nanny should say nothing."

"Yet she likely will. I hover too much. Sarah's birth only intensified my interest in the children. I long to see how they will play together when she is old enough. I spend a great deal of time in the nursery. Did you know Sam spent an entire morning showing Sarah all the toys you bought him when he was born, and all those you bought her when she was born?"

"Really? Did he show her the rocking horse?"

I pressed my lips together into a thin line and shook my head at him. "Really, Robert. And while we are on the subject, is it wise to take him riding tomorrow?"

Robert's gaze shifted to nowhere, a confused expression twisting his features. "Why ever not?"

"He is only three!"

"Exactly my point," Robert exclaimed, tossing a hand in the air. "He is already three!"

"He is just a baby."

"He is a young man. My father put me on a horse at this age, and I turned out perfectly fine. And to be an excellent rider."

I heaved a sigh. "Do be careful with him, Robert. I worry so."

"You spoil him. If you had your way, he would be wrapped in padding and kept quiet all day."

"I am not quite that protective," I objected, raising my

chin. "And yes, I spoil him. I am his mother. It is my right.

"The child must be challenged and kept in line if he is to grow into a fine man."

"I leave challenging him to you as his father, dear. And I trust you implicitly to raise him into a fine, forward-thinking man such as yourself."

"Flattery will get you nowhere, Lenora."

I grinned at him, fluttering my eyelashes. "I beg to differ. You seem to quite enjoy it."

"We shall see how far it gets you when this mystery detective adventure goes awry. I am still worried about this venture. Edwin will merely use your talents to do his work."

"Edwin will learn to be useful in his own way. He was not useless whilst investigating Gerard Boyle's murder."

"He had his own interests in mind then. And he was."

My shoulders slumped, and I reached for my now-lukewarm toddy and took another sip.

"Well, he was," Robert insisted. "Nearly got himself killed and had to be rescued."

"By me, I may add. Perhaps I shall be the lead detective in the Fletcher Agency." I offered a coy grin at my husband.

Robert offered me an unimpressed stare. "The situation is worsening by the moment."

"I am certain you shall rally, dear, and accept it in stride as you always do."

Robert opened his mouth to reply when Sinclair pushed into the room with a tray of food. A maid followed behind her, carrying a larger tray. She flitted to the bed and set it down before she curtsied and scurried from the room.

"Well, I shall leave you to your dinner, dear," Robert said as he rose.

Sinclair replaced him in the armchair as I waved her into the vacated seat.

"Thank you, Robert," I said as he kissed my cheek. "Enjoy

your meal with Edwin. Perhaps you will have an illuminating conversation with him about the new venture."

"I have no doubt it will be interesting," Robert murmured as he stepped away. "Ensure she rests."

"Of course, Your Grace," Sinclair answered. The door swung shut, and Sinclair pushed her spoon around in the broth in her bowl. "Now, tell me all about your adventure earlier."

I detailed the rather outrageous tale to her.

"And you have not seen this spirit since you've returned?" Sinclair inquired.

"No, I have not," I admitted.

"Perhaps she has given up."

I glanced up from my nearly empty tray and tugged back one corner of my mouth.

"One may always hope for such things, Your Grace."

The other corner twisted upward in a half-smile. "I must admit, given the nefarious spirit I sensed underground near the well, I find myself hoping for the same. Though I do not hold much confidence in that theory."

"What will you do next?"

"Wait, I suppose," I said as I drummed my fingers on the bedding. "Frustrating, though typical. Perhaps Edwin will find something."

"If you should need anything, just say the word. I shall help in any way I can."

I reached for her hand and squeezed it with a smile. "Thank you, Sinclair. I can always count on you."

She nodded and stared at me for a moment, her lips quivering as though she wished to speak.

"Is there something else, Sinclair?"

"It is not my place to ask, but with all the commotion, you did not mention how the visit with your mother went."

I lowered my gaze and swallowed hard. "Oh, yes. Not well, I'm afraid."

"There is no need to discuss it, Your Grace."

I lifted my eyes and offered her a tight-lipped smile, reaching for her hand. "Quite all right, Sinclair. Though I am afraid for Mother, nothing has changed."

"Do you mean she still believes you to be a small child?"

"No, no. Though it may be better if she had. What I meant was, she has the same feelings toward me now as she did when I was only a child. She attacked me and called me horrid names."

My eyes fell to my blankets again.

"Oh, Your Grace, what a terrible shame she remains as disturbed as she was."

Exhaustion overcame me as I stared at the light blue coverlet over my legs. Tears formed in my eyes and my face pinched as I fought to hold them inside.

"Now, now, Your Grace," Sinclair said, shifting from the chair to perch on the edge of my bed. She wrapped her arms around my shoulders.

The action, despite its design to comfort me, only served to force the tears from my eyes. They spilled onto my cheeks, and my shoulders shook.

"There, there," Sinclair said with a pat on my arm. "Let it all out, Your Grace."

I wiped at my cheeks, embarrassed by my outburst. "Oh, how foolish of me."

"Not at all," Sinclair said with another pat on my shoulder. "How distressing it must have been to see your mother so ill."

I tightened my jaw and clutched at the blanket on my lap. "Ill. Yes. Perhaps I am distressed over her illness."

"Well, of course you are, Your Grace. It must have been terribly upsetting to witness."

I sniffled and rubbed the back of my hand against my jawline, where tears still dripped. "Perhaps…perhaps she is not as ill as we imagine."

"Whatever do you mean?"

"What if…what if she is correct about me? Perhaps I am an abomination."

Sinclair's muscles stiffened, and she pulled away from me, glancing down with an incredulous expression. "You shouldn't talk like that."

"But…"

"Nonsense. Suppose Sarah can also see spirits. Would you cast her out as a demon child?"

"Certainly not!" I cried.

Sinclair arched an eyebrow and lifted a shoulder. "Then you cannot consider yourself as such."

I blew out a long breath and stared ahead at the fire crackling in my fireplace. "You are correct, as always, Sinclair." I wiped the final tears that had fallen from my cheeks and sniffled again. "My mind remains shaken from the visit with my mother. And the other encounters."

"Certainly, Your Grace. Which is why His Grace insisted you rest."

"Yes," I said, slouching down in my bed. A yawn stretched my jaw wide, and my eyes grew heavy. "I suppose my husband was right again."

Sinclair smiled at me, sinking back into the armchair and patting my hand. "Sleep, Your Grace. I shall wait with you."

A weak smile flitted across my features as my eyes slid closed and I drifted off to sleep.

I awakened shortly after when the door popped open and my son raced into the room, shouting for me. Sinclair smiled down at him and lifted him onto the bed as I pushed myself up straighter.

"Hello, darling. All finished with dinner?"

"Yes, Mummy," he said as Nanny West approached with Sarah on her hip.

"And are you all ready for bed?"

Sam shook his head. "No. Nanny reads a story."

"Perhaps tomorrow night, Mummy can read you and Sarah a story."

The smile faded from Sam's face, and he shook his head. I sobered and took his hands in mine. "Why not, Sam?"

"Not with Sarah."

"Oh? She is quite young, but I am certain she enjoys the stories, too."

Sam pulled his hands from mine and covered his face. I tugged them away, squeezing them and searching his tiny face. "What is it, darling?"

"No, not with Sarah." He shook his little head back and forth, a frown on his face.

My brow furrowed, and I drew back my chin. "Why not?"

Sam glanced over his shoulder at Sarah, who waved at us and clapped. "Bad man follows Sarah."

My jaw dropped, and I stared up at Nanny West.

She glanced behind her, a stunned expression on her normally firm features. "Your Grace, I haven't the slightest clue what the little master is speaking about."

I turned my attention back to my son. "Sam, is the bad man here now?"

Sam shot a glance over his shoulder and spun back to face me, covering his face with his hands again and nodding.

I stared at my daughter as Nanny West tried to explain the situation away. "Oh, a fantastical tale, surely, Your Grace. I am certain I have been reading them too many frightening stories. I shall pick a lighter one tonight."

My eyebrow arched as her words began to fade into the background. A shadowy black image formed behind her. The dark fog curled into a figure. Features formed on its face.

They twisted into an evil smirk under a pointed nose and glowing red eyes.

"I will have your daughter, Lenora. She will be mine."

I screamed and reached for Sarah. "Nanny, quickly, give Sarah to me!"

"What? Your Grace, are you quite all right?"

My lower lip quivered as she hesitated to pass the child for just one moment too long. The chimerical creature opened its mouth into an impossibly wide hole and dove toward my daughter, consuming her in darkness.

CHAPTER 17

I screamed as I witnessed the evil entity devour my baby daughter. I attempted to stumble out of bed and save her but found myself unable to move. Sam sobbed next to me, still hiding his face.

"Sarah!" I shouted as I tried to move my leaden legs.

When the blackness finished with her, it shot toward me. The last thing I saw in front of me were two red eyes before everything went dark.

* * *

I gasped in a breath as my eyes shot open and I flew upward to sit.

"Your Grace!" Sinclair exclaimed as she startled from her dozing in the nearby armchair.

I pressed a hand against my chest as my gaze darted around my surroundings. My bedroom. Safe. The words flitted through my mind before another appeared. Sarah.

"Sarah," I gasped.

"Sarah?" Sinclair questioned, confusion still apparent on her face.

"Is Sarah well?" A groan escaped my lips, and I flung the covers off me and swung my legs over the side of the bed.

"I'm certain she is quite fine, Your Grace," Sinclair answered, rising from her chair and attempting to keep me in bed. "I shall call for Nanny West if you'd like."

"I shall go myself," I said, tugging my robe toward me.

"Now, Your Grace, His Grace will be cross with me if I allow you to roam about the castle. Please, let me fetch Nanny and the children. I promise I will return straightaway with them."

My jumbled brain began to settle as my heart slowed to a normal rate. "Yes," I said with a nod. "Yes, he will be most upset."

I settled back and let the robe slip from my fingers.

Sinclair patted my legs, encouraging me to return to bed. Despite the worry etched into my heart, I abided her, swinging my legs onto the mattress and allowing her to tug the covers over me again.

"Now, you wait here, and I shall fetch Nanny right away."

I grabbed her hand and squeezed. "Please return as quickly as possible with news of both children. And have Nanny bring both children to me at once."

"Yes, of course. I shall, though I am certain there is no need to worry." She offered a reassuring smile and patted my hand before hurrying from the room.

I closed my eyes and squeezed my lips together as silence fell. Why had I sent her? I could have rung for another servant to fetch Nanny. I regretted the decision to stay alone after that dream.

After the fear-inducing experience in the cavern, I worried it may be a warning. I snapped my eyes open and flicked my gaze to the ceiling as details of my dream flitted through my mind. I drummed my fingers against the bed covers and huffed.

Why had I sent Sinclair? I should have gone myself. I should go now. With a nod at my own thoughts, I threw back the covers again and swung my legs over the bed, sliding my feet into my slippers. I drew my robe around my shoulders and rose.

As I tied it around me, the door burst open. Robert appeared in the room, his jaw falling open as he spotted me. "Lenora! What are you doing out of bed?"

I glanced down at my robe's tie as I fastened it. "I must find Sam and Sarah."

Robert held up his hands as he approached me. "Sinclair is handling it. I came across her as she dashed through the castle. She told me you awakened and were quite upset. I came to check on you. Damned good thing I did, as I've found you wandering about again."

"Oh, Robert, really," I complained as I tried to step around him. "I am not ill, nor injured. I am perfectly capable of traversing the castle."

Robert raised a finger in the air. "Yet you shall not." He offered me a coy glance as he placed his hands on my shoulders and guided me back to bed.

I shook my head and refused to sit. "No. I must find the children."

"What has you so disturbed? I have never seen you this beside yourself. Not even when a man with a knife in his chest appeared to you."

I heaved a sigh and sank onto the mattress despite my protestations. "I had a nightmare about Sarah. An evil force consumed her. I...given the encounter I had earlier, I wish to ensure her safety."

Robert's features pinched with concern. "Oh, dear, how terrible for you." He sank onto the bed's edge next to me and slid his arm around me. "Though I am certain she is quite well."

"I would like to see for myself."

"Of course you would, dear. Sinclair will arrange it."

I pressed my lips together, reaching over to clutch Robert's hand. "Aren't you going to tell me I'm being foolish? That it was only a dream?"

Robert avoided my gaze for a moment before he flicked his eyebrows up and his eyes met mine. "I...that is...well, while I am certain Sarah will be found well, I have learned your dreams are rarely foolish."

My heart skipped a beat, and I swallowed hard. If Robert did not find my concern an overreaction, I worried even more. A groan escaped me, and I stared into the distance as I counted the passing seconds.

Robert squeezed my shoulder and pulled me closer to him. "Please do not worry. While I do not discount your dreams, I also am not certain they are to be taken literally."

"Then how shall I take them?" I cried. I squeezed my eyes closed and sank my forehead into my palm. "My apologies, I did not mean to shout."

"There is no apology needed, dear. You had several dreams about Mr. Boyle, did you not?"

"Yes."

"And while they all pointed toward something, none of them came to exact fruition."

I licked my lips and sucked in a deep breath. "While I do not expect Nanny to report a black smoke has consumed Sarah, I...what could it mean?"

"Whatever it means, we shall find out together."

I offered a weak smile to my husband, glad for his

support as the door opened again. Sinclair hurried into the room. "Both children are quite fine. Nanny is dressing Sarah for bed and will bring both the moment she finishes."

I breathed a long sigh of relief, and Robert rubbed my back. "There, dear, you see? Quite fine."

A fleeting smile crossed my face, and I nodded.

"Now," Robert continued as he rose to stand, "back to bed."

I obliged him, still wishing to hold both children in my arms but willing to wait, given the all-clear from Sinclair. As she fussed over pulling the bedcovers higher on my lap, I snapped my gaze at her.

"Did you see the children yourself?"

"Yes," Sinclair said with a nod. "Both were perfectly well, happily fed and ready for a story."

I nodded, crossing my arms and drumming my fingers against my dressing gown.

"They will be here any moment, Lenora. Try to relax."

"I would very much like to ensure their safety myself. I could have gone, you know."

"While I have no doubt you could have made it through the arduous task of roaming the castle, I prefer you did not. You have been through quite a day. There is no need to worry yourself sick over something new."

"It is not something new, it is—"

The door burst open, interrupting my words. Sam tugged his hand from Nanny's and raced across the room. I smiled at my little boy as Robert scooped him up and kissed his forehead.

Sam clapped his hands together and grinned at Robert. Nanny carried Sarah over to me. I held out my arms in a silent request for the child.

"Both are perfectly fine, Your Grace." She shot an irritated glance at Sinclair. "Miss Sinclair seemed to think something was amiss."

"Sinclair acted on my direction," I said as I pulled Sarah close to me and kissed her forehead. "I had quite a disturbing nightmare and wished to see both children right away."

"Of course," Nanny answered, clasping her hands in front of her and wiggling her shoulders, a clear sign of her agitation.

"Would you give us a moment alone?" I requested, earning an arched eyebrow from Nanny.

Her shoulders slid down her back, and she lifted her chin. "Of course." She spun on her heel, eyeing Sinclair for a moment. When my ladies' maid did not move, she stormed from the room.

I pulled my lips back in a wince. "I am afraid I have upset her again."

"Too bad for her," Robert said, collapsing onto the bed with Sam.

"She will recover, Your Grace," Sinclair added.

"And how was your supper, son?" Robert asked Sam.

"Mmmm," Sam murmured, rubbing his swollen belly.

"I am certain Cook will be quite pleased with those thoughts," Robert said with a grin.

I held out a hand and waved Sam toward me. "Come sit by me, darling."

Robert plopped him on the bed, and he scrambled up into the crook of my arm. I kissed the top of his head. "Are you quite tired?"

"Not very," he said as he stifled a yawn.

I held back a chuckle, giving him a knowing smile. "Are you quite certain? You look very tired."

He thrashed his little head back and forth to deny the accusation.

"Would you like to sit with me for a while?"

This question earned an exaggerated nod.

"Really, Lenora, you must rest," Robert chided.

I waved the comment away as I kissed Sam's head again. "Sam," I said as he nestled against me, "may I ask you a question?"

He craned his neck to stare up at me, his gray eyes focused on my face, and nodded.

"Do you promise to be honest? Even if you are afraid it may hurt me?"

Another nod. I reached up and swiped a lock of his unruly hair from his forehead. "Have you ever spotted a man near Sarah? A man you did not know? He may be frightening in his appearance."

Sam's little features pinched in thought, and he placed a finger on his lips. After a moment, he shook his head back and forth. "No. Only Papa and Uncle Edwin. Sometimes Nanan."

I nodded my head, recognizing the name he used for Mr. Buchanan.

"Buchanan," Robert corrected him.

I pressed on with another question. "And are you afraid to be near Sarah?"

He shook his head again, this time without hesitation. "No, Mummy. I love Sarah."

This brought a broad smile to my face.

Robert patted him on the leg. "That's very good, Sam. And what must we always do with Sarah?"

"Protect her," his little voice answered.

Sinclair smiled down as his response, as did I. I stroked his dark, curly hair, watching it spring back in place as the locks escaped my fingers.

"Very, very good. You are her big brother. You must always protect her, no matter what. Let no harm come to your sister."

Sam nodded as his head fell against my chest. He yawned again as I rubbed his little back.

"Perhaps we should call for Nanny. The little fellow is quite tired," Robert said, wiggling Sam's foot.

Sam wrapped his arms around me.

"Nonsense," I said, squeezing my son closer to me, "they are perfectly fine here."

"Lenora," Robert chided, "they should fall asleep in their own beds."

"There is nothing wrong with them falling asleep in their mother's arms," I argued.

"I never fell asleep in my mother's bed," Robert retorted. "I went to sleep in my own bed in the nursery until I went to boarding school."

I offered Robert an unimpressed glance before I returned my attention to Sarah, adjusting her to lay against my chest before I wrapped my arm around my son again. "I am not the sort of mother your mother was."

"Yet I think you'll agree she produced a rather wonderful son." Robert offered me a cheeky grin.

"*Almost* perfect," I joked. Sam rubbed his eyes before he traced a thread on my dressing gown.

"This will spoil him, you know."

"And I have told you that is my job as his mother. I leave his rearing into manhood entirely to you, dear."

Sam's eyes grew heavy, and his finger ceased moving. He snuggled against me as Sarah cooed contentedly.

"Sarah cries at night," he said, sleep creeping into his voice.

"What?" I questioned, the bliss on my face moments ago fading.

"Sarah cries," he answered.

"All babies do that, darling," I said, patting his back. "I'm certain Nanny settles her right away."

"She stops crying when the crib doesn't shake anymore."

This statement sent chills up my spine. "What?"

"Sam," Robert said, rubbing his leg, "are you saying Nanny shakes her crib?"

Sam shook his head as he snuggled tighter to me. "No one is there."

CHAPTER 18

I snapped my gaze to Robert, my jaw agape. "What do you mean no one is there?"

"The crib shakes, and Sarah cries. But no one is there, Mummy," Sam answered, his eyes sliding closed and thumb sliding into his mouth.

My eyes widened at the statement, and I glanced at Robert again.

"Sam," Robert called to him.

I shook my head, lowering my voice. "He is asleep."

"Then we shall wake him," Robert said, reaching to shake the poor child.

"No!" I scolded him. "The poor child is exhausted. Let him sleep."

"Lenora," Robert exclaimed in a hushed tone, "he has just made a very, very odd statement. And I, for one, would like to question him about it."

"We shall question him about it when he is awake. Though I can discern his meaning. Someone or...some*thing* visits Sarah in the wee hours. Just as my dream hinted."

Robert crossed his arms over his chest with a deep sigh

and scowl. "I would say this is preposterous, but given the circumstances we have lived through since I married you, I am afraid it is not."

"I'm sorry," I sighed.

Robert snapped his gaze to me. "Do not apologize. It is not your doing."

My stomach continued to somersault as my dream paraded through my mind again and Sam's words rattled along with it. "I fear Sarah may be doomed to suffer from the same affliction I do."

Robert stared down at the child asleep on my chest.

"At least she has a mother who can guide her through her life," Sinclair whispered. "Oh, forgive me, Your Grace, but I had to speak up."

I flicked my gaze to her. "Has there been any talk amongst the servants of odd happenings in the nursery?"

She shook her head and pursed her lips. "No. Nothing that has reached my ears. Perhaps we should ask Nanny."

I nodded as I continued to rub Sam's back. "Yes, I believe we should."

"I shall fetch her, Your Grace."

Sinclair bustled from the room, returning in a moment with Nanny in tow.

"Oh, dear," Nanny lamented as she neared the bed. "If I may request the services of Miss Sinclair to assist me in returning the children to the nursery–"

"Just a moment, Nanny," Robert said, rising from the bed, "there is something we must discuss."

"Of course, Your Grace," Nanny said. I pitied her at that moment as a concerned expression flitted across her features.

I stepped into the conversation before Robert came across too harshly. "Sam made an odd comment, and we wished to discuss it with you."

Nanny fidgeted, wiggling her arms around as she nodded. "Oh?"

"He mentioned Sarah crying at night because her crib shook."

Nanny's eyebrows shot up toward her already graying hairline. "Well, all children fuss a bit at night. I assure you I tend to her right away and see that she is fed, changed, or comforted back into her peaceful slumber."

"Of course," I said, "please do not misunderstand. I have every confidence that you attend to her needs in a more than timely manner."

Her forehead pinched as I spoke.

"What concerned us was the shaking crib. Have you noticed it?"

The corners of Nanny's mouth turned down, and she studied the floor for a moment before she answered. "No, I cannot say that I have. But now that you have made me aware, I shall be certain to watch for it."

I smiled and nodded at her. "Thank you, Nanny. If you should see it occur, please inform me at once."

"Certainly, Your Grace." She paused for a breath before she reached toward me. "I shall take the children to bed straightaway, with Miss Sinclair's assistance."

"Oh," I stammered, my voice faltering, "perhaps they could sleep here for the night. They are so content."

For a moment, I wondered if Nanny might fall over dead. She froze, her face reddening, and her eyes wide with shock.

"You must rest, Lenora," Robert chided. "And you cannot do so with the children sprawled across your bed."

My features pinched, and my lip bobbed up and down before I choked out one word. "But–"

"But nothing, dear. You have been through quite an experience, and I insist that you rest."

"Do not fear, Your Grace," Nanny said as Robert

motioned for her to take the children, "I shall keep a watchful eye on the crib tonight."

My shoulders slumped as she hauled Sam away from me and Sinclair scooped Sarah into her arms. "Thank you, Nanny," I murmured.

With a smile and nod, she bustled from the room, and Sinclair followed close behind her.

I slouched further down against my pillows with a sigh.

"She will be perfectly fine, Lenora."

I snapped my gaze to Robert, my lips pressed into a thin line. "We do not know that. What is shaking her crib?"

"Perhaps your crib was shaken when you were a babe, too. We do not know this."

I cast my eyes down, staring at my bed covers. "It disturbs me. Particularly after the dream I had. What if something is after her?"

"Then we shall protect her."

"Who shall protect her? Nanny?"

Robert arched an eyebrow at me. "Of course not."

"Yet you sent her away with only Nanny to look after her. Robert, we must keep a closer eye on her, given my recent encounter." I cast my eyes downward again, suppressing a shiver. "It still makes me shudder to recall it."

Robert perched on the edge of the bed and reached for me, wrapping me in his arms. "I shall sleep in the nursery tonight."

I squeezed him before pulling away. "No, dear, if anyone should sleep in the nursery, it is I. I can determine if something otherworldly rocks her crib."

"I will not have it, Lenora."

I held up a hand before he could continue his lecture. "Only for one night. I shall move her crib here tomorrow until the matter is sorted."

"I still object. You have been through an ordeal."

"I shall never sleep. I am consumed with worry."

"Then I shall summon the doctor. Or have Sinclair prepare a sleeping draught."

I squeezed my eyes closed and shook my head. "Robert, please. If something lies in wait for our baby daughter, I prefer to know it and take steps to fight it."

Robert's chest deflated as he considered it. "Then I shall have the nursery moved here tonight so you may rest properly."

"Nanny will not be pleased. She has likely just settled the children." I pressed my fingers against my forehead as frustration set in. "Leave it for tonight. I do not wish their rest to be disturbed."

Robert arched an eyebrow.

I waved a hand at him. "I shall check on them throughout the night. We shall discuss moving them based on what I find."

He opened his mouth to object, but I stopped him. "Robert, I insist. I shall rest in my own bed, and the children shall rest in theirs. But I will monitor them."

Robert considered it for a moment before responding, his forehead pinching. "It seems a reasonable compromise, I suppose."

"I do hope to find them sleeping soundly in their beds each time."

He squeezed my hand and kissed my cheek. "If you do not mind, I shall stay with you so we both may check on them."

I offered him a knowing glance. "And so you may check on me?"

"Is it so terrible that I wish you to rest?"

I settled back into my pillows with a smile. "Not very, no."

Robert grinned at me before he rose, kissed my forehead, and departed from the room to ready himself for bed.

We spent the next two nights monitoring the children

closely. On no occasion did we find any disturbances of any kind. No shaking cribs, or otherworldly visitors. Not even a fussy Sarah crying out in the night.

I received no additional visits from my disturbed ghost. The tension I'd felt when we'd arrived home began to ease. I stared down at my infant daughter as I pushed her in her pram on an unseasonably warm day. Sam paraded down the path next to me, babbling about the dormant garden's flora.

He went silent for a moment before he jabbed a chubby finger in the air. He hopped in the air and clapped his hands together.

"Ahoy there!" Edwin called from above.

"Uncle!" Sam shouted, clapping his hands again.

"Oh, no," Nanny breathed from behind us. "Not again."

Edwin grinned at us, waving a paper in the air. "Lenora! Come quickly."

"Go ahead, Your Grace," Nanny said, grabbing hold of Sam's hand and the pram. "I can take the children in."

"Oh, but–"

"It seems quite urgent," Nanny said, nodding her head to Edwin, who motioned for me to join him at the castle atop the hill.

"So it does," I murmured as I eyed the paper clutched in his hand. My mind darted from possibility to possibility as I climbed the steep hill toward him.

He met me at the top, the grin still broad on his boyishly handsome face.

"Good afternoon, Edwin."

"Good afternoon, dear sister-in-law. And how are you on this lovely autumn day?"

I eyed the paper, now stuck under his arm. "That depends."

"On?"

"Your urgent summons," I said, nodding my head toward the paper.

He arched an eyebrow at me, an amused expression playing across his features. "Shall we go inside to discuss it?"

I pried my eyes from the paper and glanced up at him. "Certainly."

We strolled into the castle and settled in the sitting room. Edwin paraded around the room rather than taking a chair.

I drummed my fingers on the arm. What had Edwin so flustered? Had he run into more legal trouble? No, the grin on his features did not fit.

He came to a stop in front of my chair and flung his arms out, his teeth gleaming as he smiled. "Congratulate me."

My brow furrowed, and I studied his features. "Might you give me a clue as to what I am congratulating you for?"

"I have found her."

"Who?" I asked, fidgeting in my seat. Had Edwin met a woman he intended to marry?

"Your spirit! From the asylum. I have found her! Well, I am almost certain."

I sat straighter, my jaw hanging open before my lips tugged up into a partial smile. "Really?"

"Well, don't look so shocked. Robert told me to detect, and I have. I searched and searched and managed to come across several deaths, obviously, but one which I believe may be your girl." He offered me a coy grin.

"I am not shocked, though I would like to hear what you have found."

Edwin plopped into the chair across from me and unfurled the papers he held. Handwritten notes filled several blank sheets and were crammed into the margins of newspaper articles.

He shuffled through a few before he waved a sheet in the

air. "Here. First, I listed all the deaths in recent years, of which there were many."

I nodded as he spun the sheet to face me. Several names filled it.

"I ruled out the men," he said, pointing out one of the struck-through names. "And then I ruled out those who may not fit. You described her as a younger woman. Older than you, but not elderly."

"Correct," I said with another nod.

Edwin raised a finger in the air and produced another paper. "That narrowed it down considerably to only three women, as most of these ladies died in their older age."

"First, Lady Trembly. She died at the asylum only a few months after being admitted." Edwin flashed the newspaper article to me. "Newsworthy due to her position. As the wife of the influential Lord Trembly, her death had reporters flocking for the gory details."

"Which were?"

"Lord Trembly committed her after she tried to set her children on fire and nearly burned down the family home. She threw herself from a second-story window while at the asylum."

"Oh, how tragic."

"Well, of course, rumors persisted that she was murdered," Edwin said, offering me a knowing glance.

"And was anything found to suggest that?"

"No. In fact, any inquiries resulted in the same story. Left unattended, Lady Trembly found her way to an upstairs hallway, opened a window, and threw herself to the ground below. Could she be our man, as it were?"

Edwin raised his eyebrows and held his breath for a moment before he shook his head. "No. Here's why. This woman is not at all what you described. Though younger, she did not have dark eyes, nor traces of a difficult life. In fact, she was described as having sparkling emerald eyes, a trait that drew Lord Trembly to pursue her, and a youthful appearance even after her madness."

"I see. So, you have ruled out Lady Trembly. Though I maintain she may be seeking help if, in fact, she was murdered."

"But the description—"

I held up a hand, stopping him. "May not be accurate. The dead do not often appear as they did whilst alive."

"Oh?" Edwin inquired. "What do you mean? Their eyes change color?"

"No," I said, my brow pinching as I sought to describe it. "For example, Mr. Boyle appeared at first with the knife in his chest. Then with a blood splotch, and later normal."

Edwin rubbed a finger against his chin while he processed the information and I continued with more. "Annie appeared disturbed. Dark, tangled hair. Dark eyes that turned red at times. Gray skin."

Edwin frowned. "Oh, how gruesome."

"Yes, and from her looks when she last appeared to me, her first manifestation was quite different. So, it could be that Lady Trembly is appearing to me but is unrecognizable."

"I see," Edwin answered, chewing his lower lip. "Well, we shan't rule her out entirely, then, though I still believe I have correctly identified the woman."

"All right, proceed," I said, waving my hands in front of me.

Edwin's features turned from disappointed to animated, and he shuffled through his stack of papers. "The second possibility is Ruth Abernathy." He scanned the paper before he spoke again. "Died at the age of thirty-four. Blonde hair, blue eyes, though, as you mentioned, this may not matter."

I nodded again, and he held up a finger. "However, the

reason I believe her *not* to be the woman we seek is because of her condition."

"Her condition?"

"Yes. She was simple. I doubt she would be able to communicate with you at all. Her mentality was that of a child's, and she was nearly mute. Also, the circumstances of her death were quite mundane. She died of pneumonia."

I narrowed my eyes as I parsed through the information. "I see. Yes, that does seem a safe bet, given her condition."

"Do spirits recover from mental conditions in their death?"

"I do not know. I have never encountered a spirit who has had a mental condition to my knowledge. So, I cannot say. What is the nature of the third tale that has you convinced you have correctly identified the ghost?"

Edwin licked his lips and grinned for the umpteenth time. He wiggled his eyebrows and shuffled to the final paper. "Mary McGinty."

He paused for a moment, staring at me. My eyes slid from side to side. "Am I supposed to recognize the name?"

He drew up his chest. "Perhaps."

"I am afraid I do not."

"Mary McGinty was admitted to the asylum following a very public trial in eighteen sixty-two."

"Trial for?"

Edwin's mouth curled into a mischievous smile, and he said, "Murder."

"Mary McGinty was a murderess?"

"Not just a murderess. A mass murderess. She killed multiple people." Edwin appeared almost giddy over the salacious tale.

"Was there some sort of accident in which they perished?"

"Oh, no. Mary McGinty lured them into her home, incapacitated them, and then hacked them to death."

My eyes widened as my stomach rolled.

Edwin nodded with another knowing glance. "Grim, I realize, but a perfect candidate for the asylum."

"Whatever makes you believe she is the woman seeking my help?"

"Well, first of all, Mary McGinty maintained her innocence all through the trial, despite mounting evidence. Her attorneys argued she was incompetent to stand trial. The judge agreed and sentenced her to life at Stagheart Asylum."

"Where she died."

Edwin nodded. "Under mysterious circumstances."

I arched an eyebrow. "The plot thickens. How did she die?"

"Some people claim she was murdered."

CHAPTER 19

"Murdered?" I questioned, my mind reeling.

"Exactly," Edwin said, jabbing a finger toward me. "The murderess was murdered."

"How?"

"Well, that is where the story turns murky. You see, a nurse claims another patient murdered her, but the asylum maintains that she committed suicide."

"Suicide? Another?"

"Mmm," Edwin said, settling back in his chair, "not exactly the best news, given Lady Trembly's demise. Rather another mar on their record, however, preferable to murder."

I turned pensive as I considered the information.

"Well?" Edwin prompted after a moment.

"It appears congratulations *are* in order. This is excellent work, Edwin. And I believe you may be correct. It makes sense that Mary McGinty would contact me. Particularly if the circumstances surrounding her death were questionable. Perhaps there is more to the story than meets the eye."

"Indeed. And it also explains why you may sense a malevolent spirit. It could be one and the same as your ghost. A mass murderer would carry some evilness, no?"

I chewed my lower lip, uncertain I agreed with his assessment. I did not sense the malevolence around Mary herself, but rather elsewhere when she seemed to have disappeared. Or was driven away.

Was the malevolent spirit what drove her or someone else to commit suicide?

"Lenora?" Edwin questioned.

I tore myself away from my thoughts and flicked my gaze to him. "Yes?"

He narrowed his eyes at me. "What are our next steps?"

I sucked in a deep breath as I considered it. My nose wrinkled as one thought settled in my mind. "I believe we will need to return to the asylum."

"What?" Robert's voice joined the conversation.

I snapped my gaze at him, standing in the doorway. He spun to whip the doors shut and stormed across the room. "Absolutely not!"

"Hello, Robert," Edwin said from Robert's armchair.

Robert frowned down at him, wandering to the mantle and leaning against it. "I suppose this is your doing."

"If you are referring to the fact that I did exactly what you told me to do, then yes, I suppose it is."

"Oh? And what is that?" Robert questioned, whipping around to face him. "Convince Lenora to return to the asylum to seek more information for your ridiculous agency?"

Edwin's features pinched into a mask of upset and ire. He leapt from the chair. "Now, see here!"

I rose and placed myself between them. "Stop, both of you. Edwin has done his job and found three potential suspects for our ghost. We now need more information. Information we can only find at the asylum."

"Really? I would like to see this supposed work."

Edwin snatched the papers from the table and shoved them at Robert. Robert lifted his eyebrows as he accepted the proffered papers. He shuffled through them before handing them back. "Nonsense. I can't make heads or tails of it."

Edwin squashed his lips together as he wrested the papers from Robert's grip.

"Edwin's explanation aided quite a bit in deciphering his notes," I said. "We must return to the asylum. Perhaps on our way to or from Glasgow."

"Glasgow?" Robert questioned.

"I wished to see Tilly."

"Oh, yes," Robert said with a nod as he returned his attention to the glowing fire.

"If you have too much business, I shall escort Lenora," Edwin said.

"Certainly not! Heaven knows what would happen."

Edwin crinkled his brow. "Whatever do you mean? I am capable of accompanying Lenora to the asylum to follow up on *my* leads. And if she plans to visit Tilly, I wish to be there."

I offered a soft smile at Edwin. "I am certain Tilly would like to see you, too."

"She has made no contact with you here? Even since I have been here?"

I shook my head, still confounded by that fact as well.

"Oh, for God's sake, Edwin, only you can expect a woman to follow you about even in death."

"That is not what I meant," Edwin said.

"He makes a decent point, Robert," I said. "I, too, had expected Tilly to appear here when Edwin took up residence."

"I thought we discussed the idea that Tilly could not appear in Blackmoore because she had never been here."

"That does not make sense. She appeared in the jail cell, and to my knowledge, she had never been there."

Robert arched an eyebrow at me, his lip bobbing up and down before he firmed his jaw.

"What?" I questioned.

"Nothing." He returned his gaze to the fire.

"You had a thought. Say it."

He flicked his gaze sideways. "Only that...well, perhaps she had been there. Given her profession..." His voice trailed off as he waved a hand in the air so we may infer the rest.

"Unbelievable!" Edwin shouted.

"Oh, really, Edwin. You know what she was. She was a...well, a..."

"*She* was the mother of my child. And had never spent a night in a jail cell."

"Really, Edwin, how would you know? You did not even know she was pregnant."

Edwin's face reddened, and he balled his hands into fists.

"That is quite enough from the both of you," I said, stepping between them again. "Despite Tilly's...profession, neither of us has any reason to believe she had been in that particular jail cell. And besides, there are other instances of spirits appearing in places they may not have been. Take Esme at Cameron's estate. Or our new ghost at the inn."

"Perhaps they had—"

"Yes, yes," I said, waving a hand in the air, "perhaps Esme had traveled to Melrose, and perhaps Mary McGinty stayed at the inn. But I would doubt either of those occurred. Making it likely they managed to appear in a place they'd never been. I would very much like to speak to Tilly about that."

Robert's eyes went wide, and he spun to stare at me. "Mary McGinty?"

"Yes, one of the women Edwin identified as a potential match for our ghost."

"As in the murderess, Mary McGinty?"

I nodded, surprised Robert knew of the tale.

"Then I know I shall be escorting you on this trip. Lenora, if the ghost of that crazed madwoman has made contact with you, I will not leave you to go unattended–"

"I would be with her," Edwin interjected.

"As I said," Robert answered, glaring at his brother, "I will not leave her to go unattended. The woman was a terror in real life. I will take no chances, especially given your last experience with her."

"And just what is that supposed to mean?" Edwin asked, heat entering his voice, and his hands rising to his hips.

"Exactly what it sounds like. The last time you and Lenora investigated something together, you took her to a brothel."

"For the umpteenth time, we did *not* go inside."

"I do not care if you only came within two yards of it. I–"

"Enough!" I shouted.

Both of them snapped their gazes at me. Edwin winced, and Robert's shoulders slid down his back.

"We shall all go. And we shall take the children."

Robert's forehead crinkled. "The children? Perhaps given what you plan to investigate, they should stay here."

I pressed a hand against my forehead. "I cannot shake the dream I experienced, Robert. And I do not wish to leave them here."

Edwin cocked his head, stepping closer to me. "Is Sam all right?"

"Yes, he is fine," I answered. "It's Sarah."

"Oh?"

"Lenora had a terrible dream, and then Sam told her

someone pesters Sarah at night, shaking at her crib and causing her to cry."

Edwin's gaze flicked from Robert to me. "Have you witnessed anything that confirms this?"

"No. We have watched the crib for several nights and noticed nothing out of the ordinary." I slumped into the armchair behind me, my hand pressed against my forehead.

"Perhaps we should not make the trip," Robert said. "This is obviously wearing on you."

"But we must continue the investigation!" Edwin exclaimed.

Robert pressed his lips together, shooting a glaring glance over his shoulder at Edwin. He turned back to me, taking my hand in his. "Lenora, if this is too much, we shall wait until you are comfortable to travel."

I squeezed his hand and waved the other in the air. "No, Edwin is correct."

Edwin replaced the momentary expression of surprise with a brash one, raising his chin as Robert shot him another glare.

"We cannot ignore what happened at the asylum. It is only a matter of time before it rears its ugly head again. Likely at the worst possible moment."

Robert heaved a sigh as he considered his argument.

"And I would like to visit Tilly. I am terribly worried about her."

Edwin's features pinched as I mentioned her name.

"And the children traveling with us will be welcome. I would very much like for Tilly to see her son and meet our daughter."

"Then we shall make the arrangements to travel at once," Robert said with a reassuring smile and pat on my hand.

"Thank you, dear," I answered.

"When?" Edwin questioned.

The pleasant expression on Robert's features soured at the sound of his brother's voice. He slid a fiery gaze sideways.

"Well, I must know so I may prepare."

"Really, Edwin? Prepare? What do you need to prepare? You are quite used to slogging through slums at the drop of a hat, so you shouldn't need much."

Edwin narrowed his eyes at Robert. I shook my head at him, silently hoping he allowed the comment to pass.

"Might we travel tomorrow?" I asked.

"Of course, dear. I shall make the arrangements at once. Where do you propose we travel first? Glasgow or Staghearst?"

"Glasgow. I shall speak with Tilly before pursuing the matter at Staghearst. It may take longer than we hope to solve that issue."

Robert bobbed his head in agreement before he spoke. "We shall leave tomorrow morning for Glasgow. If you will excuse me, I shall make the arrangements."

I pushed myself up from the chair. "Of course, dear. I must attend to several things as well, particularly speaking to Nanny."

Robert winced as he stepped away. "I do not envy you that. Good luck."

"Is Nanny really that bad?" Edwin inquired.

I offered him a shrug as I shuffled to the door. "Nanny has a very particular way of doing things. She does not appreciate my hovering."

"Oh. I find it quite endearing. Mother did not spend a great deal of time with us growing up. I'd like to imagine Tilly would have..." His voice trailed off, and he licked his lips, letting his gaze fall to the floor. "Never mind."

I returned to him and squeezed his arm. "She would have.

And I do hope you will accompany me to visit Tilly. She enjoys seeing you."

He did not raise his eyes to mine, instead concentrating on kicking a tassel on the area rug as he gave a curt nod.

"She will be so very proud to know about your detective agency."

A slight smile flickered across his face, and he finally let his eyes meet mine. "I do wish to make her proud."

The glistening in his eyes betrayed the depths of the emotions he still experienced over her death. He quickly wiped at his cheeks and sniffled before sucking in a deep breath. "Well, I have many things to attend to before we depart."

"Of course," I said.

He strode to the door. "I likely will not attend dinner. Too many things."

"Edwin," I called after him, stopping him in his tracks, though he did not turn to face me, "please reconsider. I would like to discuss the case further."

He hesitated for a moment before he twisted his head slightly, eyeing me sideways. "Yes, of course. For you, Lenora."

He disappeared from the room without another word. I shook my head as I headed for the nursery first, hoping the Fletcher Agency held the power to turn Edwin's life around. The tragedy he'd suffered with Tilly's loss still had the capacity to destroy him.

The long list of tasks required of me prior to our travel pulled my mind away from Edwin's troubles. After our evening meal, in which Edwin and Robert conversed about the case without nearly coming to blows, I settled in my bed for an early evening.

I flicked open my well-worn copy of Frankenstein for

what I hoped to be a relaxing re-read of my cherished novel, but I found it unable to hold my interest.

As I stared down at the page, my mind concentrated on anything but the words that appeared. After another moment, I tossed the book aside with a heavy sigh.

I wrung my hands as I stared at the blue blanket on my lap, chewing my lower lip.

"Tilly?" I called. I waited for a response of any kind whether it be a sound, smell, or even a wisp of wayward air.

As I held my breath, my eyes scanned the room, spotting nothing out of the ordinary. "Tilly?" I tried again.

My heart sank as I received no response. What stopped her from appearing to me here? Perhaps I would find out tomorrow.

I drummed my fingers against my forearm as the clock chimed midnight. "Useless," I mumbled to myself and threw back the covers.

I slid into my slippers and pulled my dressing gown over me. I paced the floor of my bedroom for ten minutes before I expanded my roaming to my sitting room.

After another few moments, I collapsed onto my chaise, letting my chin fall into my palm. I shook my head and rose, ambling to the door, this time with a clear destination in mind.

As I wound through the halls, memories from my nightmare returned to me. Robert's analysis likely proved correct. My dreams typically had some meaning. But what, I asked myself as I pushed through the door into the night nursery.

I stared down at the sleeping form of Sam, a smile forming on my face. With his dark curls stuck to his slightly sweaty forehead and tiny lips parted slightly, he breathed heavily in the throes of deep sleep.

I stroked a few locks of hair away and kissed his forehead. He fidgeted, then settled back into his peaceful sleep.

I tore my eyes from my son, flicking them across the room to my daughter's crib. Drenched in the moonlight that shone in through the nearby window, it cast long shadows across the floor.

I took a step toward it but froze immediately, my muscles stiffening. I stared ahead, my eyes wide. My heart thudded in my chest and blood rushed into my ears as my daughter's crib began to shake from some unseen force.

CHAPTER 20

"Sarah?" I croaked as the crib's shaking turned more violent.

A cry escaped from inside as I searched the area for the cause. I could spot nothing. *Why could I not see anything?*

Fear gripped me at my core, and my chest tightened. My lower lip trembled as I raced forward. Inside, my daughter fussed and cried as the crib continued to convulse. I scooped her into my arms, backing away from the shuddering cradle as I pressed her close to me.

"Shh," I murmured as I rocked her.

The commotion woke poor Sam. "Mummy!" he shouted, tears forming in his eyes as he sat up in his bed.

"I am here, darling," I said, rushing to his side and reaching for him with one hand as I cradled Sarah with the other.

Sam climbed to his feet, tears streaming down his cheeks, and clung to me. I squeezed him close to me, lifting him up onto my hip. "Close your eyes, darling, don't look."

I waddled from the room with both children as the crib began to pound against the floor.

"Mummy, what is that?" Sam asked through tears.

I kissed his head as he squeezed his arms around my neck. "It's all right, dear. Just keep your eyes closed, and Mummy will make it all go away."

Sarah settled as I hurried down the hall, though I could feel Sam's little heart pounding in his chest. "It's all right, darling. Mummy will never let anything happen to you."

"I'm scared, Mummy."

"I know you are, my love. But there is nothing to be frightened of."

I hurried through the door of my suite and crossed to the bed, collapsing onto it. "All right, dear. Can you sit back in Mummy's bed for a moment?"

"No, Mummy," he said, tightening his grip around my neck, his legs squeezing my torso.

"Sam, you are safe now. Just sit back in the bed, and I shall be back in just a moment."

"No!" Sam whined.

"All right," I answered. I slid my hand under his bottom and scooped him up as I struggled to stand.

I tottered over to the pull cord on the wall. As I struggled to grab it with my wiggling fingers, Robert strode inside. He stopped short, his face transforming into a mask of confusion.

His lower lip bobbed up and down before he hurried toward me.

"Take Sam," I said, shifting the hip my son clung to toward him. "He's terribly frightened."

"Lenora, what happened?"

Robert wrapped his hands around Sam, trying to tug him away from me. The poor child clung to me, squeezing his legs tighter around my torso and snuggling his arms around my neck.

"We shall discuss it after we've settled the children. Sam, it is all right. Go with your father."

"No, Mummy," he cried.

I wrapped my arm around him and twisted the opposite way. "Take Sarah."

Robert frowned but relieved me of the smaller of our two children, balancing her high in his arms as he continued to study me.

Sinclair raced into the room moments later. "Your Grace! What's happened?"

"Something alarming. I intend to keep the children here with me for the rest of the night. Would you please inform Nanny of their whereabouts?"

"Of course. Should I return here after to help you tend to them?"

"No, I shall stay," Robert answered.

"Thank you, Sinclair. You may go back to bed after speaking with Nanny."

"If you're sure, Your Grace."

I offered her a nod and reassuring smile before following her to the door and closing it behind her. I spun to lean against it, my free hand stroking my son's dark curls.

His little heart beat against my chest at normal speed, and he loosened his grip slightly. "It's all right now, darling. Everything is all right."

He snuggled tighter against me, one hand falling from my neck as he stuck his thumb in his mouth. "You're very tired, aren't you?"

He nodded, his head sliding up and down against me as I crossed the room to my bed.

"Let's get you settled in bed to sleep."

"No, Mummy!" he shouted again, pulling away to stare at me, his gray eyes wide with fear.

"It's all right, darling. Mummy will be right next to you. And I will let nothing harm you."

I tugged back the covers and eased onto the edge of the bed, trying to pull Sam's arms from around my neck. With surprising strength, he refused to leave me.

"Sam, let go of your mother and get into bed as you were told."

"No," he cried.

"Samuel William Fletcher, stop this nonsense at once and listen to your mother!" Robert barked at him.

I shook my head, giving Robert a disapproving look. "Darling," I said, keeping my voice steady and calm, "you must let me get into bed."

He let his arms go slack and scrambled off my lap and into the bed, tugging the covers over him to hide. I stood and removed my dressing gown and slippers before sliding between the sheets and pressing closer to him.

He slid the covers down to his nose and stared up at me.

I swiped a curl off his forehead and smiled down at him. "There we are. All safe and cozy. Lay your head back on the pillow and close your eyes."

He reached out, grabbing my hand before he squeezed his eyes closed. I motioned for Robert to place Sarah next to him.

"Whatever is going on, Lenora?" Robert whispered as he climbed into the bed next to Sarah.

I pressed a finger to my lips as I waited for Sam to fall asleep. Within minutes, safely snug in bed with his parents, he drifted off, his chest rising and falling in a rhythmic pattern.

I lowered my voice as I scooped Sarah into my arms and situated her between Sam and me. "I had a terrible feeling and went to check on the children. After I had checked on

Sam, I took a step toward Sarah's crib when it began to violently shake."

Robert's eyes went wide, and he stared down at our infant daughter. "Good heavens! Is she all right?"

"Yes. She cried, but I removed her as quickly as I could, and Sam, too. Unfortunately, he witnessed something of the frightening scene. And sensed my anxiety, which upset him further."

Robert stared down at our sleeping son. "Poor child."

"With any luck, he will have forgotten it by morning, but I did not feel comfortable leaving them in the nursery."

"Of course not." Robert reached across the children to take my hand in his. "Lenora, I think we should postpone the trip."

"Certainly not," I breathed.

"Lenora," Robert began again, heaving a sigh.

"Robert, no! I would prefer to take the children out of this house, given the recent developments. And I remain troubled over Tilly. I would very urgently like to see her."

"Then we shall go straight there and return."

I shook my head, squeezing his hand as I spoke. "No. Outside of the investigation with the former asylum patient, I..." My voice trailed off, and I sucked in a deep breath, shaking my head. "I would like to speak with my mother again."

"Speak with your mother? I must draw the line there. She attacked you last time. I will not have it."

"You may go with me if you would prefer it, however, I must seek information about what may be happening with the children. She is the best source of information."

"She is insane. She cannot provide any information."

"Is she? Or does she only believe she is insane?"

"What does that even mean?" Robert whispered to me as the candle he'd brought into the room flickered behind him.

"She likely suffers from the same thing I suffer from. If I told the doctors in the sanitarium I spoke with the dead, that I had encountered a former patient of theirs roaming the halls, they would lock me up right next to her."

"Are you saying you believe they are treating her for your own condition?"

My shoulders slumped, and I pressed my lips together in frustration. "No. I don't know. I believe she may have gone insane after what she did to me, yes. But I also believe she may see the dead and assume she is insane because of it. And that may have also driven her mad."

"You are making little sense, dear. I fear this terrible business with your mother may have disturbed you more than you are willing to admit. And I do not wish it to trouble you further."

"Avoiding the issue will not make it go away, Robert."

"I did not suggest avoiding it. Merely put it off until you feel ready to deal with it."

I sucked in a deep breath, ruminating on his suggestion before I shook my head. "No. I have never put things off in the past. I will not begin doing so now."

"You were never given much choice in the matter, I suppose. And now you have a choice. There is no need to visit the asylum or your mother."

I shook my head again, studying the blanket covering my children. "It will not help me to do so. I will not become less disturbed or troubled. I will only become more so."

I flicked my gaze to my husband. "Besides, we must solve the first case the Fletcher agency has taken on."

Robert guffawed, fidgeting in the bed as he crossed his arms and a frown settled on his face.

I snickered, my features curling into an amused grin.

"You are not going to find working with Edwin amusing in a month's time. Mark my words, Lenora. Mark them. You will be the one sitting in this bed with a frown on your beautiful face."

"If his work on the case is any indication, he may have found his calling in life."

"At his age, he should have found it ten times over," Robert grumbled.

I giggled again, pushing a lock of his curly hair behind his ear. "Stop being so disagreeable because we are speaking of your brother."

"I would very much prefer not to speak of my brother at any given moment, but particularly in the middle of the night, when we should be sleeping peacefully."

I glanced down at the children nestled between us. "They both appear to be sleeping. Shall we try to join them?"

"Yes, please," Robert said. "I would rather be asleep than discussing Edwin's virtues, however few they may be."

I leaned closer to him, brushing his lips with mine before I slid further down under the covers, relaxing back into the pillows and nestling closer to my children. As I closed my eyes, I prayed I would not suffer any additional nightmares.

* * *

My eyes fluttered open early the next morning. I stretched and glanced at the two sleeping babies next to me before they fell upon my already-awake husband.

"Good morning, dear," he whispered.

"Good morning. Have you slept at all?"

"Yes. I awoke earlier and did not wish to disturb the three angels I shared my bed with."

I smiled at him, lowered my chin, and glanced up at him through my eyelashes. "You are becoming as big a flirt as–"

"Do not say it and ruin my morning," Robert said with a groan.

Any further discussion was quashed by a knock at the door and the subsequent entrances of both Sinclair and Nanny, who was beside herself as she hurried toward the bed.

"Oh, Your Grace! You should have awoken me at once," she fretted, wringing her hands before pressing one against her forehead.

"It's perfectly fine," I answered as Sam stretched and yawned. Sarah, who had fluttered her eyelids open at the knock, waved her hands around and cooed at Robert.

"Hand the child to me," she instructed. "You have been inconvenienced long enough." She shot a glance at Robert. "I am sorry, Your Grace."

"As Her Grace already stated, it is wholly acceptable, given the circumstances."

"Which were? Forgive me, but Miss Sinclair did not provide a clear explanation."

"Ah," I began as Robert glanced at me with a questioning stare, "Sam had a nightmare and was inconsolable."

Nanny shook her head, reaching for Sarah again. "You did not need to do all this work, Your Grace. I could have soothed him. Please, in the future, do not tax yourself."

"It is not taxing, Nanny. We rather enjoyed having the children."

Nanny arched an eyebrow as I handed Sarah over to her. Sinclair held my dressing gown out for me to don as I climbed from the bed. Sam crawled over and reached for me.

"Come along, Sam," Nanny said, reaching for him. "Mummy and Papa must prepare to travel. And we must get your breakfast."

"No!" he cried as he reached for me again.

"Now, Sam…" Nanny began as Sinclair finished with my tie.

I scooped my son into my arms and kissed his head as

Nanny tried to suppress a huff but failed. "It's all right, darling."

"I'm scared, Mummy."

"I know you were very frightened," I said as I carried him to my chaise and sank onto it. He hugged me tightly, refusing to let go.

"But it's all over now. Mummy and Papa made certain you were safe. Remember you slept in Mummy's bed last night?"

I felt his head bob up and down. I rubbed his back and continued to soothe him. "And now all the bad things have gone away. But now I need you to be a very brave boy and go with Nanny to eat your breakfast."

"No."

Robert crossed to us, tying his dressing gown around him. "Sam, you must listen to your mother."

"Yes," Nanny interjected, "come along. Nothing will happen to you under Nanny West's watchful eye."

His response was to squeeze me tighter, nestling as close to me as he could.

"Sam," I said, keeping my voice calm and measured as I spoke, "you know we are taking a trip today, don't you?"

His head rubbed up and down against my neck.

"And you wouldn't want to stay at home, would you?"

"No!" he shouted, leaning away from me and staring at my face.

I smiled at him, kissing the tip of his nose. "Then you must eat your breakfast with Nanny. Otherwise, you would not be able to go."

"But Mummy–"

"No 'but Mummies,' dear. You must have your breakfast. And if you go right now and be a good boy for Nanny, you may ride in the carriage with Mummy, Papa, and Uncle Edwin."

"Do you promise?"

I nodded, and he clapped his little hands together. "I sit with Uncle Edwin!"

"Yes, I am certain he will enjoy that. Now, go along with Nanny, and I shall see you soon."

I placed him on the floor, and he tottered over to Nanny's outstretched hand, waving at Robert as he passed.

"Come along, little master. We must get you fed and washed."

"I don't want to wash," I heard him tell Nanny as she led him down the hall.

Robert glanced through the open door as their chattering voices faded away. "Thank goodness Nanny has a firm hand, or else he may run rampant in that nursery."

"I am certain she is quite disturbed that the children will ride with us. But I hoped to go straight to the graveyard when we arrive."

"Certainly, dear. I shall leave you to ready for the journey." Robert leaned over and kissed my cheek before he departed.

Sinclair, already readying my traveling attire, dropped the dress on the bed and followed him, closing the door behind him.

"Poor children," she said as she crossed the room toward me.

I plopped onto the stool at my vanity table and shot her a glance through the mirror. "With any luck, the change of scenery will make Sam forget all about the frightening experience."

"It sounds like it still troubles him greatly."

"Yes, though children are more resilient than we think. What troubles me more is the source of the disturbance and how to prevent it in the future."

"And you saw nothing?"

"No," I said with a shake of my head as she brushed my hair. "Why?"

"Perhaps spirits roam that even you cannot see."

"Undoubtedly," I answered, "certainly spirits can remain hidden. In fact, Annie caused quite a disturbance when I first came and remained unseen during it. However, if they are causing a disturbance, they typically want something. What is it that this spirit wants?"

Sinclair continued to fashion my hair into its usual style as I rambled on about the disturbance. "More importantly, why go to Sarah? That's really the frightening thing."

"I hope you shall find out soon, Your Grace. For both your and Sarah's sake."

I smiled at her through the mirror as she put the final touches on my hair. We continued with my morning routine before I joined Robert for an abbreviated breakfast and we collected the children and climbed into the carriage.

Edwin awaited us inside.

"No breakfast?" Robert questioned as the carriage lurched forward and we left the castle behind.

"No," he answered. "I felt it would not agree with me."

Robert narrowed his eyes at his brother, and I wondered if he thought he may have spent an evening drinking, however, I detected no evidence of that. I assumed Edwin's avoidance of his morning meal stemmed more from the prospect of being in Tilly's presence than anything else.

I patted Robert's knee as Sam climbed from my lap, reaching for Edwin. "Uncle Edwin."

Edwin smiled at the boy and lifted him onto his knee. "Hello, fellow! Did you sleep well?"

Sam shook his head and frowned as I settled Sarah on my lap and drew a blanket over us.

"Were you too excited for the trip?"

"No, I was scared."

"Scared? Of traveling?"

Sam shook his head again. "Sam had a terrible nightmare," I explained to Edwin, "in which he saw someone shake Sarah's crib. But we have already explained that it was not real." I offered him a knowing glance I hoped would translate properly.

Edwin narrowed his eyes at me and offered the slightest of nods. "Well, it seems Mummy and Papa have the matter well in hand. I'd bet that dream will trouble you no further."

I glanced out the window as Edwin's words rang in my ears, praying they were true.

After several hours, the buildings of Glasgow surrounded our buggy. The carriage behind us, bringing Robert's valet, Sinclair, and Nanny veered off behind us, heading for the hotel as we continued on to the St. Agnes Cemetery.

Edwin fidgeted in his seat as we approached, awakening a sleeping Sam. The child glanced around with a sour expression until he became cognizant of his surroundings. He rubbed his eyes and glanced out the window, clapping his hands.

"Almost there, darling," I said with a smile.

After a few more moments, the carriage slowed to a stop. Gravestones littered the space before us. I scanned them as I climbed down from the carriage with Sarah in my arms. Robert reached into the conveyance, pulling Sam into his arms.

Edwin emerged last, a disconcerted expression on his boyishly handsome features. I stared up at him for a moment, understanding how my friend could have fallen in love with him. I glanced at my husband, holding Tilly and Edwin's child in his arms, a child he had accepted into his home as our own, and smiled. Boyishly handsome or not, I had the good fortune to fall in love with the better brother.

"Ready, dear?" Robert prompted.

I nodded at him, feeling my stomach roll as we strolled through the chilly November air toward Tilly's final resting place. I prayed I would find my friend there waiting to speak with me. Though I worried I would find something much, much worse.

CHAPTER 21

I shivered as the icy wind whipped past me again. The bare branches shuddered overhead, and the few remaining leaves scurried away, as though searching for a warmer hiding place. The sun began to disappear past the horizon, and with it, a coldness filled the air. I wondered if it signified something more than just the setting of the sun.

Tears filled my eyes as I wrapped my arms around my midriff.

"Perhaps we can try tomorrow, Lenora," Edwin said, sliding an arm around my shoulder.

Robert had long since taken the children back into the shelter of the carriage to wait for me. My features pinched, and I glanced down at the gravestone in front of me. "Where is she?"

"Perhaps she had something to do," Edwin said.

I glanced at him sharply, and he offered me a tentative, lopsided grin.

"That was a terrible attempt at humor," I said, though a chuckle escaped me.

We waited over an hour. I had called to Tilly many times,

but she did not appear. She had not reached out in any way. My concern for her grew. Given the odd dreams I'd had, the latest development only added to my worry.

"Just a moment longer," I requested.

"Lenora," Edwin said, squeezing my shoulder, "she is not here."

I licked my lips, holding back the tears that threatened to spill onto my cheeks.

"I wish she had been, too, but night is nearly upon us. It is growing cold. You'll catch your death out here, and Robert will blame me."

"Robert will not blame you," I said with another laugh as I flicked away a tear that escaped.

"He will, too, and you know it."

"Always concerned for yourself," I teased.

He lifted his chin, offering a slight smile. "Always. You know me. Edwin, Edwin, Edwin."

My eyebrows pinched, and I reached for his hand and squeezed it. "All right. For your sake, I shall give up on my quest for tonight."

"We shall try tomorrow before we depart for the asylum."

I nodded at him as I slipped my hand into the crook of his arm, and he led me back to the waiting carriage.

We climbed inside, and I quickly pulled the blanket over my legs before rubbing my arms to rid them of the chill.

Sam climbed onto Edwin's lap after he'd settled in, and I reached to take Sarah from Robert's arms.

"Well, it's about bloody time," Robert said. "I thought you planned to stay the night."

"About bloody time," Sam repeated with a clap of his hands.

My jaw dropped open before I clamped it shut and shook my head at my son.

"Now look what you've done, Robert," Edwin said with a cheeky grin. "You have the poor child swearing."

Robert huffed, crossing his arms over his chest and deepening the frown on his face. "Hardly swearing."

He glanced at me, and I attempted to hold back a chuckle. "I assume you did not make any contact?"

The smile playing on my lips faded, and I shook my head. "No, unfortunately not."

My brow furrowed as I turned pensive. "Where could she be?"

"We shall try again tomorrow, before leaving for Staghearst."

"Edwin suggested the same. He also suggested we leave for the night. I preferred to wait a bit longer."

Robert glanced at his brother, who bounced Sam on his knee, raising his eyebrows. "Perhaps opening the Fletcher Agency has had a positive effect on you, brother. It seems you have begun to use your brain."

Edwin offered Robert an amused grin. "I could be insulted, though I believe I will take that as a compliment."

The corner of Robert's mouth tugged up into a half-smile. I flicked my gaze between the brothers, finally not snapping at each other and bonding over something as simple as stopping me from spending too much time in the cold.

We arrived at the hotel and shuttled the children inside to a fretful Nanny West. "Well past their bedtimes," she murmured as she took Sarah from my arms.

"They had plenty of naps in the carriage," Robert assured her.

"You must learn to be more accommodating, Nanny," Edwin said with a wink. "Children's schedules needn't be so rigid."

Nanny arched an eyebrow at him, his boyish grin and charm having little effect on her. "Children are best kept to a tight schedule. I am certain Her Grace agrees, otherwise she would not have engaged my services."

"Thank you, Nanny. I do appreciate your attention to detail," I said before she tugged a sleepy Sam behind her to ready them for bed.

After she departed, I said my goodnights to both men, excusing myself for an early evening.

Despite my weariness, though, I found myself pacing the floor of the bedroom in my dressing gown and staring up at the moonlit sky. How many times I had dreamt of or recalled fond memories of Tilly in this room I reflected as my forehead leaned against the frosty windowpane.

It was in this very room I had made the realization that my precious Sam, Tilly's first and only child, was fathered by Edwin. I had recalled memories of Tilly at the orphanage.

As I stared out the window, another flitted across my mind. During my second year at the establishment, a teacher tasked us with writing an essay about the challenges we faced in life.

I very foolishly wrote about my ability, thinking the teacher would gain a better understanding of me from the information I provided. It did not have the intended effect.

Instead, the young woman, a Miss Weatherby, passed the paper on to Headmistress Williamson. The Headmistress visited the class with my paper in her hand.

"I cannot control my odd affliction," she read from the paper, "and I did not wish for it. But I hope to help those souls who seek me out if I can."

She pulled her reading glasses from her face, letting them dangle from a chain around her neck. "Girls," she said in her shrill voice, "let Miss Hastings's essay be a reminder of the dangers of lying."

The woman sneered at me as she held my paper up with one hand, using the other to tear it in two. She turned it and tore it again, repeating the action over and over until it had been torn into tiny pieces. She scattered them on the floor, narrowing her eyes at me.

"Miss Hastings, clean up this mess at once." She glanced at Miss Weatherby and nodded before she strode from the room.

I scurried from my seat and began to pick up the scraps of paper while the other girls giggled. Miss Weatherby stared down her hooked nose at me before she turned her attention to the class. "Miss Hastings will receive a zero on her assignment for lying and will write one hundred times *I will not lie* as a substitute assignment for which she will receive no credit. The importance of honesty is vital, girls, along with the art of being discreet. Particularly if you are to be engaged in a prestigious household."

I bit back tears, realizing honesty was only prized if it fit their mold. Cool air brushed my skin as one of the girls approached Miss Weatherby's marred oak desk at the front of the room. I glanced up finding Tilly's flaxen curls bouncing as she grabbed for the stack of papers on the desk's corner.

"Miss Anderson, what do you think you're doing? You were not told you could leave your seat."

"Are these the other assignments from the rest of the class?"

"Yes," Miss Weatherby said with a curt nod, her ringlets bouncing.

Tilly stared down at them for a moment before she turned them on their side and tore them in two.

"Miss Anderson!" Miss Weatherby shouted.

Tilly tore at them again and again, shredding them into pieces.

"Stop this at once!" Miss Weatherby cried. She raced to Tilly and waved her hand in the air. Tilly raced away, still tearing them to bits before she flung them into the center of the room. They rained down from the sky, showering the girls and desks in the room.

"Now they are all destroyed and we shall all take zeros!" Tilly grinned from ear to ear, clapping her hands together.

Miss Weatherby's jaw dropped open, and she marched toward my friend. With a reddened face, she slapped her across the cheek. The amused expression on Tilly's face faded, replaced by an angry one. She glared up at the teacher, her hands curling into fists. "It is you who should learn the importance of honesty, Miss Weatherby. And of fairness before no one respects you."

Miss Weatherby's lips turned into a sneer before she stormed from the room, calling for Headmistress Williamson in a shrieking tone that curdled my blood.

The headmistress hurried back into the room and stared at the scene. "Miss Anderson took it upon herself to ruin all of the assignments. She tore them to shreds, then lectured me on honesty."

Headmistress Williamson narrowed her eyes at Tilly, who raised her chin and her eyebrows, daring the woman to confront her. Instead, she flicked her gaze away, finding me still crouched on the floor, holding a stack of bits of paper.

She marched to the front of the room and tugged me to stand by my hair. "This is your doing."

"It is not!" Tilly shouted at her. She raced around the desks and pressed herself between me and the headmistress. "I did it."

"Because your friend was punished. This is Lenora's fault. She is the source of the trouble."

"You are the source of the trouble, you bitter old woman. You cannot stand that Lenora is special!"

"Tilly!" I warned in a hushed tone.

"Do not dare to speak, girl!" Headmistress Williamson

said, cracking me across the cheek hard enough to send me sprawling across the floor.

As I recovered, my eyes went wide at what I spotted. Tilly cocked a fist and punched the headmistress in the gut. She let out a gasping breath, doubling over before she slapped Tilly, too. She hauled both of us up by our hair and dragged us from the room. "You both shall be punished severely for this."

"Lenora does not deserve it! She did the assignment, and she did as you asked after you ruined hers!"

"You will both be punished. Lenora for her disgusting practices communing with the dead, and you for your poor judgment, behavior, and flippant mouth."

"She has already been punished," Tilly shrieked as the headmistress dragged us into her office.

"Not enough," the woman growled. She strode to her desk and tugged open a drawer, pulling a large switch from within. She wiggled her finger at me. "Put your hands on the desk."

Tears brimmed in my eyes as I gripped the edge and felt the first lash across my back. I received four more flogs before she instructed me to step back. I straightened, my back still smarting from the flaying, and clasped my hands in front of me, backing away from the desk with my head bowed.

"You miserable old bird!" Tilly shouted at her, kicking her in the shin. She grabbed the whip from the woman's hands and flailed it wildly toward her. It cracked her on the shoulder, then thrashed her across the cheek. The last smack injured her, drawing a thin line of blood.

Headmistress Williamson's features pinched as she raised a shaky hand to her cheek, flinching as her fingertips touched the gash. She pulled her hand away, her eyes wide as she spotted the red smear.

Tilly stood unyielding in front of her, fire still raging in her eyes.

"You little brat," she spat at her as she reached for her. Tilly raced away, scrambling around the desk in an attempt to avoid the headmistress's wrath.

They darted around for a few moments before Miss Weatherby pushed into the room at the worst moment for Tilly. Tilly ran straight into her, and Miss Weatherby grabbed hold of her.

"She attacked me, the little devil," Headmistress Williamson growled. She jabbed a finger in my direction. "It is *her* doing. She is a bad influence on the girls here."

"No, it isn't! It had nothing to do with Lenora!" Tilly shouted, fighting against Miss Weatherby as she wrapped her arms around her shoulders and held her back.

With a hateful expression, Headmistress Williamson stripped the whip from Tilly's small hands and strode toward me. She gave one final ire-filled glance at Tilly before she cracked me across the face with it. It split my lip open, the wound continuing to tear my skin up to my cheek. I cried out as the taste of blood filled my mouth.

"And now," she said, striding back to Tilly, "you will be punished for your impudence. Turn her around, Miss Weatherby, and hold her still."

Miss Weatherby stood with her jaw agape, still staring at me before she glanced at the Headmistress.

"Turn her around," the woman screeched.

Miss Weatherby, her lower lip trembling, stared at the headmistress.

"Miss Weatherby! Do as you are told before I must flog you for insolence."

Miss Weatherby swallowed hard, her gaze shooting sideways to me again before she slowly spun Tilly around. Both of them jumped with her lash, and a tear slid down Miss

Weatherby's cheek. She quickly flicked it away and firmed her jaw.

Tilly wept openly as Miss Weatherby let go of her shoulders. She slid to the floor in a heap.

"Get up," Headmistress Williamson barked at her. "You will both sleep in the attic tonight."

My heart broke for Tilly at those words. I was used to spending nights in the attic. Sometimes Tilly even joined me to pass the time, but to be forced to sleep on the cold, hard attic floor after reaching over a dozen lashes to her back would prove difficult. Even a forgiving mattress would have made for an uncomfortable night.

Headmistress Williamson herded us upstairs and into the attic, locking the door behind us as darkness fell over the orphanage. Tilly still sobbed, curled in a tight ball on the floor. I pulled her head into my lap and stroked her flaxen hair.

"I'm sorry," she whispered.

"Whatever for?" I questioned.

"My poor behavior made things worse for you," she said, sniffling and trembling.

"There, there, it is nothing to cry over."

"Nothing to cry over? You would have merely taken a zero on your assignment, but now you have been whipped and put to bed in the attic without supper."

"A blessing," I answered.

"Blessing?" Tilly choked.

"We can spend the evening giggling together," I said with a grin as she flicked her gaze up to me.

My lighthearted take on things only served to make matters worse. Tilly burst into tears, sobbing into my skirt. My brow furrowed as I failed to understand her reaction. It marked one of the first times I could recall dealings with the living being more challenging than those with the dead.

As I tried to parse through it, Tilly wiped at her cheeks and rolled to glance up at me. "Only someone as special as you could find a blessing in a punishment."

I smiled down at her, peeling a lock of hair plastered to her cheek by her tears. "Every moment I spend with you, dear friend, is a blessing, no matter what the circumstances."

She sat up and flung her arms around my neck. I wrapped my arms around her, careful to avoid the wounds on her back, and we sat for a few moments, comforted by each other's presence.

* * *

I bit my lower lip as I stared out the window at the moon, recalling the memory as my eyes welled with tears. It was another instance of a moment that bonded Tilly and me for life. And beyond. Which made it odd as to why I could not contact her now.

I stalked across the room, recalling walking out of the attic the next morning hand in hand. When we went to class the next day, we found Miss Weatherby gone. The whispers of the other girls informed us she had packed and departed in the middle of the night after a raucous row with Headmistress Williamson.

I wrapped my arms around me recalling Tilly's slight smile as she confided to me that this meant we had won.

A faint smile crossed my own face now before it faded, replaced by concern. I wrapped my arms around myself. Worry consumed me, welling in my heart and filling it with sorrow. "Where are you, Tilly?"

CHAPTER 22

I breathed a shaky breath as I stared at the stormy skies the next morning. Angry thunder rumbled overhead, and lightning tore through the sky.

"Perhaps we should go straight on to the asylum," Robert suggested, rousing me from my musings.

I lifted my forehead from the windowpane and glanced at him, a pinched expression on my face.

He licked his lips and nodded, understanding my answer even without me speaking. "Nanny wondered if she should take the children to the castle straightaway."

I bit my lower lip, understanding her urge to keep the children out of the dreary, damp weather, though I still hoped to introduce my daughter to Tilly.

Perhaps it was selfish, but I wanted the children with me.

Before I could answer, Robert strode to me, tipping up my chin. "I shall tell her no."

I heaved a sigh and offered him a weak smile. "I am sorry."

"There is no need to apologize. May I ask if it is the

reunion with Tilly that has the tears welling in your eyes, or if it is the return to the asylum?"

"Tilly," I admitted. "I am worried."

Robert ran his hands up and down my arms. "You did say you tried to contact her before and could not find her."

I nodded, grabbing one of his hands and squeezing it. "Yes. During the murder investigation, I attempted to contact her several times and could not find her. I assumed her to be spending her time with Edwin. Though this time–"

"May be no different," he interrupted.

I sucked in a deep breath. "You are likely correct. My agitation over the asylum visit is likely seeping into my emotions about Tilly."

"We do not need to visit the asylum. Edwin can give up on his first case. It will not be the first time he's abandoned an unfinished project."

"I refuse to give up, and not just for Edwin's sake."

"So, it is somewhat for Edwin?"

I flicked my gaze up at him and gave a coy smile and slight shake of my head. "If I do not follow through, it is likely this spirit will rear her head at the worst possible moment. *That* is why I will not alter our plans."

"Then alter them we shall not!" Robert exclaimed, poking a finger in the air.

I smiled at him before I stole a kiss. A knock at the door interrupted any further close moments between us.

"Yes?" Robert called.

Edwin burst through the door. "Good morning. Are we ready?"

Robert's posture stiffened, his annoyance growing with the appearance of his brother. "In a hurry?"

"Is there some reason we should not set off? We *are* still planning on visiting Tilly's grave, are we not?"

"Yes," I answered. "And taking the children. We shall part ways there and continue on to the asylum."

"Shall we discuss a plan for seeking out information there on the trip?"

"Lenora plans to visit with her mother first. Depending on how that plays out, we shall make a decision about pursuing other information after."

Edwin's eyebrows raised toward his hairline. "Oh? I thought the first visit with your mother did not go well?"

"It's not really your concern, is it, Edwin?" Robert barked at him.

Edwin rolled his eyes behind his brother's back as Robert squeezed my hands. "I shall go speak with Nanny."

"Thank you, dear," I said, adding a kiss to his cheek before he departed.

Edwin glanced over his shoulder as Robert slipped from the room. "Care to tell me what prompted the visit with your mother?"

"The incident with Sarah. Like it or not, she has the most information about my childhood and whether or not this may have happened to me."

"Is she cognizant enough to impart anything worthwhile?"

"It is sometimes amazing to me how much you and Robert really are alike."

Edwin guffawed, shooting me an incredulous glance. "Please, Lenora. With talk like this, I will wonder if you belong in the institution."

I returned the cheeky grin he gave me and shook my head. "Robert said the same. Though it is my conjecture that my mother suffers from the same affliction I do. And this is partially why she is in the asylum."

Edwin offered his arm and led me toward the door. "Interesting. Do you believe it to be a family condition?"

"I do not know," I answered with a shrug. "Though I will feel quite awful if Sarah suffers from it."

"You should not. Sarah will not lead the life you led. She already knows acceptance from a family."

I glanced up at Edwin, offering him a genuine smile. His insight often surprised me.

Robert met us at the door to our suite, Sam in his arms. He clapped as he saw us, waving with a toothy grin.

"Hello, love," I said as he leaned for me to take him. I set him on my hip and showered him with kisses.

"Mummy, are we going to the dead again?"

My eyebrows knit as I stared at him. "What?"

"Do you mean the cemetery?" Robert questioned.

Sam raised his chubby palms in the air.

Edwin poked a finger at Sam's chest, tickling him. "Are you meaning where we visited last night?"

Sam nodded. "The dead."

Robert tugged our son from my arms, informing him about the correct name for our first stop as we made our way to the carriage.

We climbed aboard as the rain continued to pound against the roof, drowning out any attempt at conversation. I wrung my hands as the carriage trundled along through the streets on the way to St. Agnes Cemetery.

Despite Robert's reassurances, worry continued to consume me. I had never gone this long without contact from her. And when she had been unreachable before, she had been with Edwin. But now even Edwin's presence could not conjure a visit from her.

I sucked in a breath as we passed through the gates to the graveyard. Robert reached over and patted my knee, offering his silent support. I offered him a fleeting smile, returning my eyes to the passing headstones.

The carriage wound toward Tilly's final resting place

before coming to a stop. I climbed from the carriage with Robert's help, my eyes flitting to Tilly's marker. I hoped to find her already standing there waiting for me, but I did not spot her. My heart sank.

"Perhaps we should leave the children in the carriage until she has appeared," Robert suggested as he held an umbrella over my head.

I nodded in agreement, taking the umbrella from him as Edwin alighted. He popped open his umbrella as his eyes went to the same spot as mine. He shot a glance at me, and I shook my head.

"Perhaps if we are closer," he said, offering his arm.

I nodded and accepted his arm as we picked our way among the other markers to Tilly's. When we arrived, there remained no sign of her.

"Tilly?" I called.

Thunder rumbled overhead, and the rain seemed to intensify the moment I spoke her name. I shivered against the icy rain, and Edwin slipped his arm around me. "Anything?"

"Nothing," I said, my voice breaking. I firmed my jaw, holding back the emotions that threatened to bubble over.

"Tilly! Please come to visit us. I have brought Sam. And Edwin."

"Please, darling," Edwin called. "If you are there, show yourself to Lenora. She worries terribly over you."

He glanced at me. I chewed my lower lip for a moment as I scanned the area before flicking my gaze to him and shaking my head.

"I really thought that would do it," he said with a sigh.

The statement brought a cursory smile to my face at his ego, though it did not prove enough to relieve me of the worry that grew in the pit of my stomach.

"Tilly!"

I received no response.

"Perhaps we should go," Edwin said.

"No," I cried, my lower lip quivering and fog puffed from my mouth.

"Lenora, it is pouring rain and terribly cold. Please, let us go. I realize how frustrating this is for you, but falling ill from exposure will not help."

My breath came in ragged gasps as I fought back all the emotions that brewed within me. "Please give me a few moments alone."

"Lenora, I–"

"Please, Edwin," I said, more harshly than I had intended.

He sucked in a breath, blowing out a deep sigh as he fidgeted from foot to foot before he nodded. "All right. Only a moment, though. Please do not leave me alone for longer with Robert, lest one of us become the next spirit you see."

I shot him a narrow-eyed glance at the droll statement, and he tugged one corner of his mouth up into a cheeky smirk.

Edwin squeezed my shoulder before he strode back to the carriage, lowered his umbrella, and tugged open the door.

A snippet of Robert's voice floated from the carriage as the door opened and closed. "...the devil is..."

Edwin may prove correct about leaving him alone with Robert, I mused as I wrapped one arm around myself, shivering. Water dripped from my umbrella in small puddles around me.

"Tilly?" I called again, my voice breaking as a sob threatened. "Where are you?"

I waited a moment before I continued my plea. "I am alone. If you prefer not to speak in front of Edwin, you may appear now. It is only I. I sent him back to the carriage."

Only the patter of rain on my umbrella filled my ears.

"Please hurry. Robert may murder Edwin at any moment."

No one answered me. I stood alone in the graveyard, a unique concept for me. I flicked away a tear that escaped to my cheek. "I will return as soon as I can, Tilly. I hope you are safe, friend."

I stared down at her gravestone, marking the years of her short life as sadness and worry overcame me.

I swallowed the lump in my throat and pushed myself to return to the carriage. Robert spilled from within, taking my umbrella and urging me into the conveyance. I pulled Sarah from Edwin's arms and kissed her forehead as I settled into my seat, desperately trying to contain my emotions.

"Nothing?" Robert inquired as he climbed inside.

I shook my head, pressing my cheek against my baby's forehead as I clutched her close.

Robert slid a hand onto my back, giving it a slight rub. "I am sorry, dear."

My features pinched as the simple gesture threatened to bring me to tears again. I twisted to face away from him, staring at Tilly's wet gravestone.

A glint of light flickered in front of the stone, blotting it from my view for a moment.

"Tilly!" I exclaimed, my eyes going wide.

My heart thudded against my ribs as my pulse quickened. I passed Sarah to Robert, stumbling past him and flinging the carriage door open. I plowed into the rain without an umbrella or hood, racing around the carriage to the grave.

"Tilly! I am here!"

Icy rain smacked my head and face, feeling like pins pricking my skin. "Tilly!" I called out again, spinning in search of her.

"Lenora!" Edwin called from behind me.

I spun to face him. Water dripped from his chin. My eyes narrowed as rain clung to my eyelashes. "She was here!"

He raced to me, searching around me. "Where? Is she here now?"

"No," I moaned.

He pressed his lips together and stared down at me. "Perhaps you only assumed you saw her."

"She was here. I saw the pink dress I'd seen her in so many times. Pink fabric. It was her, Edwin. She is trying to reach me."

I pressed a wet hand against my forehead. "Why can she not?"

Edwin squinted into the rain, his shoulders rising to his ears as the rain drenched us both.

"Let me fetch an umbrella at least."

I nodded at him. "I shall wait here."

Edwin trotted back to the carriage, tugging the door open to retrieve an umbrella.

Though I could hear his raised voice, the rain drowned out most of Robert's rantings. Edwin held his hands out, speaking slowly to his brother.

I realized how frustrated Robert would be with my decision to race into the rain and then stubbornly stay there. Though I could not abandon my friend if she had tried to reach out.

My heart began to return to normal speed as Edwin pulled back from the carriage, opening an umbrella over him and palming another. He skirted the wheel, heading toward me.

I sucked in a deep breath, spinning to face Tilly's gravestone.

"Oh, Tilly," I moaned as my fingers reached for the rough stone, "where are you?"

My fingertips scraped against the rough stone and a jolt

shook my body. My muscles stiffened and trembled. My neck swung backward, forcing my eyes to stare up into the rainy sky.

"Lenora!" Edwin shouted.

His pounding feet marked the last sound I heard before the world went black around me.

CHAPTER 23

Water dripped somewhere in the distance. An icy coldness whisked past me as my eyelids fluttered open.

I stiffened as my eyes adjusted to the blackness. "Hello?"

My voice echoed off unseen walls.

I pushed myself up to sit. The ground below me sent a shiver through me with its coldness. The scent of mossy dirt floated to my nostrils.

"Hello?"

"Lenora?" a voice answered me.

My eyes grew wide, and my heart skipped a beat. I sat straighter, peering into the darkness. "Tilly?"

"Lenora!" she answered with a note of relief in her voice.

"Tilly, where are you? I cannot see you."

"I am here, Lenora."

Fingers wrapped around my hand before interlacing and squeezing me. A figure moved in front of me, though I still struggled to see in the almost-black space.

"Tilly, is that really you?"

"Yes. I have waited for you to come."

"Oh, my dear friend, where have you been?"

The outline of her face formed in front of me, and I tugged my hand from hers, reaching for her face.

"I am stuck."

"Stuck?"

"I cannot reach Blackmoore as much as I try. Something blocks me."

"But I have come to your grave. I brought Sam, Edwin, and my daughter, Sarah. But I could not find you."

Tilly sucked in a shaky breath. I felt a tear wet my fingers as it rolled down her cheeks.

"Tilly, what is it?"

"I–I–" she stammered. Her face fell away from my hand. I reached for her, my hand falling onto her shoulder. It shook with sobs.

"What is it? What is wrong? Please tell me so I may help."

"I desperately tried to come to Blackmoore. I saw the castle." She grasped my hand and squeezed, sniffling. "Oh, Lenora, it is beautiful. I am so thankful my son will grow up in such luxury."

"Tilly," I said, trying to refocus her onto the question at hand, "what happened when you attempted to visit Blackmoore."

Her hand trembled, and she pulled away from me. A tremor shook my body, too. I assumed it to be from the cold that permeated the air.

"Please tell me," I insisted.

"As I approached the castle–"

"Lenora!" a muddled voice called overhead.

"Tilly, please!" I shouted at her. "Tell me."

I shook all over again before I began to slide backward. I reached for Tilly, my fingertips grazing the fabric of her dress, which I desperately tried to cling to.

"No!" I screamed as the fabric slipped from my grasp.

ASYLUM FOR A DUCHESS

I barreled backward through the blackness screeching for my friend. My fingernails dug into the dirt below me, becoming sore as the dirt became embedded in them.

"Lenora!" the voice shouted again. Another loud screaming filled my ears. I became weightless for a moment before I felt myself moving. I tried to force my eyes open but found myself unable. Murmurs filled the air around me, though they were unintelligible at first.

Something creaked, and my body settled onto a hard surface.

"Lenora!" Robert's voice said, patting my cheeks.

I tried to answer but found myself unable. *What was wrong with me?*

"Lenora, please wake up," Edwin's voice croaked.

Warm hands wrapped around mine. The back of my hand was pressed against warm flesh.

"For God's sake, Edwin, pull yourself together. Do something useful. Fetch a doctor!"

My hand fell through the air until it struck something. I fought to open my eyes again or to speak.

"Wait," Robert said, "she is coming to. Lenora, can you hear us? It is Robert. Please come back to us."

My eyes fluttered open. Two blurry faces hovered over me. I blinked several times, finding Robert and Edwin's concerned faces staring at me as I half-sat, half-lay in the carriage.

"Lenora, thank heavens," Robert said, breathing a sigh of relief.

"Robert," I murmured, squeezing my eyes closed again as I crinkled my brow. A dull ache still thudded at my temples.

"Are you still ill? Edwin, do something useful and fetch a doctor."

The carriage shook as Edwin shuffled around to alight and race away for a medicine man.

I popped my eyes open. The dim beams of light coming from the still-gray sky stung them. "No."

"Lenora?" Robert asked, holding my hand.

"Help me to sit," I requested.

"Are you certain?"

I nodded and squeezed his hand. "Yes, I am. Please help me up."

Robert tugged me upward, and I shimmied back on the seat, leaning into it and letting my head rest against the side wall. Edwin leaned in from the outside, drizzle still pattering on his back. His wet hair still dripped onto his face.

My clothes remained soaked, as did my hair. I shivered from the cold as it struck me. Robert wrapped the blanket around my shoulders and pulled me closer to him, settling onto the seat next to me.

Edwin climbed inside, pulling the door closed and shutting out the cold, damp air. "What happened?"

"For God's sake, Edwin, give her a moment before you pry, will you?"

I snuggled deeper into the blanket and inched closer to Robert. "It is all right. I am fine. I merely have a lingering headache."

"We should go straight home," Robert said. "I shall inform Jones at once."

"No," I argued as a knock came at the window.

Robert popped the door open, and Sinclair popped in her head. "My apologies, Your Grace. Nanny West wishes to inform you the children are still quite fussy after Her Grace's episode."

I leaned forward, my heart skipping a beat. "Bring them at once."

"Lenora!" Robert scolded. "Now is not the time to be tending to the children. Leave it in Nanny's very capable hands. Sinclair, I am certain Nanny is able to manage them for the time being. Her Grace has been through quite an ordeal."

"Have the children brought at once. They are likely worried after witnessing my episode."

"Leave them in the other carriage."

Sinclair's eyes darted back and forth between the two of us as she wrung her hands. Her lower lip bobbed up and down while she attempted to formulate a response.

"Robert," I pleaded, "they are frightened. I am certain a few moments will be all it takes to settle them. I should not wish them to be unnerved for the duration of the return trip to Blackmoore."

"You may comfort them when you are settled in your bed with a toddy in your hands."

"We are not returning to Blackmoore. We have business to attend to at the sanitarium."

"You cannot be serious," Robert said with a guffaw. "First, you raced into the rain, and then you fainted dead away. You are soaking wet and very likely ill. The doctor should attend to you at once."

"I am not ill. While I do not fully understand what happened when my fingertips touched the gravestone, I am certain it has little to do with a normal illness."

Robert's jaw flexed, and he breathed out an angry sigh.

"Please, Robert. Poor Sinclair will be the one who falls ill if we do not allow her to return to the carriage."

Sinclair waved a hand at me, a reassuring smile on her face. "Quite all right, Your Grace. I am made from sturdy stock."

"Bring the children," Robert grumbled with a wave.

Sinclair nodded, slamming the door shut and hurrying to the carriage behind us. It shimmied back and forth before she wrapped Sarah in her arms. Nanny climbed down with

Sam, and they both hurried toward us with the children in tow.

The door popped open, and Sarah's wailing cry floated inside. Sam scurried into the carriage and scrambled onto my lap, throwing his arms around me.

"Mummy," he said, his little forehead pinching together.

"I am quite all right, darling," I said to him, kissing his head before I reached for Sarah. "Pass her to me."

"Lenora," Robert began when I waved away his scolding.

Edwin grabbed the child and held her out to me. I lifted her from him and settled her on my lap. She continued to cry in a mewling whimper, though she no longer screamed as she had before.

"Give your mother some room, Sam," Robert said, trying to tug him onto his lap.

Sam clung to me, fussing.

"Leave him," I said, wrapping my arm around him and patting his back. "It is all right, my loves. I am fine."

"Mummy, you died," Sam said.

"No, darling, I did not. I merely fainted."

He leaned back and stared into my face.

"I fell asleep suddenly," I explained. "But now I am awake and perfectly fine, as you can see."

He placed his chubby hands on my cheeks and stared into my eyes.

I grabbed his hand and kissed it, offering him a smile. "See?"

He settled back into my arms, laying his head against my shoulder. I took the opportunity to situate Sarah, kissing the top of her head as she finally settled.

Nanny fidgeted outside of the carriage. I realized she likely hoped to be on her way to Blackmoore by now, so as to minimize further disruption to the children's schedule.

"And now, dear, you are going to return home with Nanny and Sinclair."

"No!" Sam shouted.

"Sam, screaming no at your mother is most unacceptable," Robert scolded him.

"Your father is correct."

His little face pinched. "But I do not wish to go."

"Yes, I know. But we do not always get our way. And I am counting on you to be brave and take care of your sister."

"But Mummy–"

"No, Sam," I said with a shake of my head, "you must go home."

Sam's lower lip trembled as tears welled in his eyes.

"Sam," Edwin said, tapping his shoulder.

Sam twisted to face him, and Edwin grinned at him. "I have a secret to tell you."

"Secret?" Sam asked.

"Yes," Edwin said, "come closer."

Sam put his arms out to Edwin, and Edwin tugged him onto his lap. He whispered something into his ear, and Sam's forehead wrinkled.

Edwin rubbed his little back and whispered something further. Sam twisted to face him, a confused expression on his features. Edwin nodded at him.

Sam bobbed his head up and down before he climbed down from Edwin's lap. He flung his arms around my knees and said, "I love you, Mummy." He stepped to Robert, passing along a similar message as he grabbed his legs.

"Ready for Nanny?" Robert asked.

Sam nodded, wiping his nose and sniffling. Robert opened the door, and Nanny scooped him into her arms. I passed a now-settled Sarah to Sinclair after giving her a kiss and burrowed down into my blanket again.

"Lenora, I really believe we should discuss this before

charging off to the asylum," Robert said the moment the door shut.

"We are not charging anywhere," I argued. "By the time we arrive, I shall be dry and fully recovered."

"You should be sitting in bed, sipping a toddy, not racing about the countryside, trying to solve four mysteries."

"Three," I corrected, counting them on my fingers. "Sarah, Tilly, the phantom patient. We cannot gain further information on two of those without going to the asylum."

"She is correct," Edwin said.

"Pipe down, Edwin! No one asked you," Robert barked.

"Sitting her in bed with a drink will not resolve anything. And likely will only add more stress to Lenora as she continues to be plagued by these troubles."

Robert narrowed his eyes at his brother. "I asked you to refrain from comment. Are you incapable?"

"Robert, please. The point I am making is summed up well by Edwin."

Robert's eyes slid closed in annoyance. I grabbed his hand and squeezed it. "I understand you only wish to take the best care of me that you can. But I cannot put off seeking information. I will rest, I promise. You may take care of me to your heart's content after we've done our work."

"And I will," Robert said gruffly, shifting in his seat.

The corner of Edwin's lips tugged up as we won the battle.

Robert waved his hand at Edwin. "Tell them we proceed as planned."

Edwin knocked on the window behind him, waving Jones on. The carriage lurched forward, and we trundled along toward Staghearst.

I snuggled closer to Robert, and he pulled me tighter to him, rubbing my arm. "Are you warm enough?"

"Yes," I said, my voice muffled by the blanket as I burrowed deeper.

"What happened, Lenora?" Edwin asked as we passed under the gates and onto the street.

Robert shot him the evil eye. I slid my hand from under the blanket and squeezed Robert's arm. He wrapped his hand around mine and patted it. "Whenever you are ready, dear, you may tell us."

"There is not very much to tell, the end result is that I am more worried about Tilly than when we came to Glasgow."

"How does a case of the vapors lead to more worry?" Robert inquired, his brow furrowing.

"That is just it, Robert," I said. "It was not a case of the vapors. I did not faint."

"You most certainly did so," he argued. "You went limp in front of my very eyes. The children were frightened beyond belief, as was I. Even Edwin was shocked."

"I do have feelings, you know," Edwin said with a roll of his eyes.

"You slumped to the ground. I flew from the carriage as quickly as possible. Thank heavens Nanny had the presence of mind to meet me and take charge of the children. You were limp in my arms as I carried you back to the carriage. Lenora, I worried you had–" His voice cut off as he firmed his lower lip, suppressing the emotion threatening to bubble over.

My shoulders slumped, and I squeezed his hand before sliding my arm through his. "I am perfectly fine, Robert. Though I realize it must have been terribly frightening for everyone."

"Indeed," Robert answered with a curt nod as we continued to rumble along through a small town.

"What happened that led you to become more worried about Tilly?" Edwin questioned.

"When I touched her gravestone, something happened to me."

"You fainted," Edwin said.

"No, as I said, I did not. I..." My forehead crinkled as I sought the words to describe my experience. "I was called somewhere. My consciousness went to another place."

"What?" Robert asked, a guffaw in his voice.

"I am not certain I can explain it in any better words than that. I went to another place. A dark, cold, damp place. Tilly called to me. I was finally able to speak to her."

Edwin leaned forward, his eyes widening. "What did she say?"

"She said she had tried to come to Blackmoore." I sucked in a breath as the conversation flowed back through my mind. I gasped. "She said she had seen the castle. But something prevented her from entering. She started to tell me when I revived."

"And not a moment too soon. We were both beyond worry."

"My apologies for worrying you, though I wish you'd waited just a moment longer before shaking me back into this world."

"Lenora," Robert said, an unimpressed expression settling onto his features.

I held up a hand, stopping him from lecturing me. "Only a joke, dear."

"Next time, we shall hold off shaking you until you have gathered all the information," Edwin said with a grin, causing Robert to guffaw again.

"I shall need to work out a way to give a signal to you from beyond."

"You cannot be serious," Robert said with a snort.

I tried to hold back a chuckle, but it bubbled forth from

me. I giggled as Edwin also laughed. "Of course not, dear," I promised.

Silence fell between us as I patted poor Robert's arm again. He settled closer to me with a sigh, resuming his rubbing of my arm. My brows knit as I turned pensive again. My mind whirled as we continued our journey north, and I began to worry I would never see my friend again.

What had Tilly been trying to tell me? And what prevented her from reaching Blackmoore Castle?

CHAPTER 24

I awoke with a start, surrounded by blackness again. I strained my ears, listening for sounds of water dripping. Had I wandered back into my unconscious state?

"Tilly?" I shouted, flailing my arms.

Something grabbed me, restraining me. I fought to shake it off.

"Lenora," a familiar voice called to me.

It took my tired mind a moment to adjust and realize it was not Tilly, but Robert calling to me.

I sucked in a breath as I allowed my eyes to take in the scene surrounding me. The carriage rumbled underneath me as the small village of Staghearst passed by my window. I swallowed hard and flicked my gaze to my husband. "My apologies. I must have dozed off."

"Yes, you did. I had hoped you would get some rest, but you were moaning terribly."

I pushed myself straighter, fidgeting as I realized my dress remained damp. The cold fabric pressed against my clammy skin. "I must have been dreaming. I do not recall."

"With the manner in which you attacked Robert, it must have been quite disturbing."

My jaw unhinged, and I glanced at my husband. "Oh, dear, I am terribly sorry."

"I survived it," Robert said. "Lucky I have been through pub brawls in the past, so I was prepared." He cracked a coy smile at me.

"You were quite good in a fight if I recall, brother," Edwin responded.

"You were quite good at starting them, I was better at finishing them," Robert answered.

"I am pleased to know I could not harm either of you with my antics."

"I do wish you had gotten more rest."

"I got enough," I assured him as I flicked my gaze out the window. Dark clouds gathered on the horizon, shrouding the asylum in darkness.

Thunder rumbled overhead. I wondered why it always seemed to be storming near this place. We passed through the gates and continued up the hill to the sprawling institution. I licked my lips as I stepped from the carriage and stared up at the stone facade.

Robert ushered me inside and out of the damp weather, announcing us to the woman who sat behind the desk at the front.

"She is with another visitor, Your Grace," the nurse reported. "Might you wait?"

"Of course," Robert said with a nod, stalking back to the hard bench Edwin and I had perched on.

With a sigh, he squeezed in next to me. "Your mother has a visitor at the moment."

I nodded, no words coming from my lips as I struggled not to fidget. "Perhaps," I began when the door across the room opened.

I shot from my seat as the man stepped into the lobby area. "Father!"

He stopped short, his eyes wide as he stared at me. "Lenora? What are you doing here?"

My lip bobbed up and down as I attempted to explain, shooting a glance at the nurse who eyed the exchange discreetly. "Perhaps we could step inside the garden room to speak?"

"Yes, that would be most appreciated," Robert said to the nurse. "Could you let us in?"

She nodded and disappeared, reappearing at the door my father had just stepped through and ushering us into the back. She led us to the garden room where my ghostly visitor had appeared to me on my last visit, and my father and I settled at a table as Robert wandered the room.

"I had hoped to speak with Mother," I said when we were left alone.

"With your mother?" my father inquired. "She is quite ill."

"Yes, I know," I said, my shoulders slumping. "And the sight of me disturbs her greatly." I shot my gaze to my father, my posture straightening. "I wonder if, perhaps, you could help."

"Help? With what, Lenora?"

"Do you know if Mother suffers from the peculiarity I do?"

"You mean," he said, lowering his voice and leaning closer, "speaking to the dead?"

"Yes," I answered, "did Mother? Is it the source of her madness?"

My father stared down at the dirty tile floor, murmuring for a moment before he shook his head. "No, not to my knowledge."

I heaved a sigh, shooting a glance at Robert as Edwin stalked into the room.

He whispered something to Robert who nodded before he approached our table. "I am sorry, I do not believe we are acquainted. Edwin Fletcher. Lenora's brother-in-law." He thrust out his hand.

My father slowly shook it. "Dr. John Hastings."

"Yes, you stayed with us for a night in Blackmoore, though we never had the pleasure."

My father looked at him curiously for a moment, then flicked his gaze to me. My new life continued to overwhelm him. Edwin shot me a glance, wiggling his eyebrows at me and signaling something that I did not understand.

I turned my attention back to my father. I hoped to make more progress with him, though the introduction of Edwin into the situation agitated him. "Father," I tried, "were there ever any incidents with me as a baby?"

"Incidents?" My father searched the air. "You were quite a pleasant baby. Often able to soothe yourself. Your mother rarely needed to tend to you. You had a fever when you were about six months old, but nothing else of note."

"Nothing...out of the ordinary?"

He stared at me curiously. "What do you mean?"

"Were there ever any unexplained incidents regarding me as a child? My crib shaking with no explanation, for example."

My father pulled his grizzled chin back to his chest before shaking his head, his brow furrowing. "No."

I breathed a slight sigh, frustration filling me as I nodded. "Thank you."

He glanced at me, then at Robert. "Your mother is most unwell, Lenora. Perhaps you should rethink visiting her."

"Thank you, Father. I appreciate your concern."

"She is quite ill, Lenora," he said, his forehead crinkling as he reached forward, grasping my hands.

"I know," I said. "I have visited her. She was most

disturbed to see me. I had hoped time would have healed her, but it had not."

He shook his head, tears welling in his eyes again. "If only I had not gone to India."

I offered him a fleeting smile, squeezing his hands. "We cannot change the past, Father. If it is any consolation, your departure has led me to the happiest moments of my life with Robert and my children."

"Treasure them, Lenora. They are gone too quickly," he said, sobs filling his voice as he attempted to hold them back.

"Dr. Hastings, may I walk you out?" Edwin inquired, clapping a hand on the man's shoulder before he went to pieces.

"Yes, yes," my father said, wiping at his nose as he rose. "Yes, I must be going." He turned to face me, offering a nod as his lips bobbed up and down before he decided to remain silent. He spun to face Edwin and nodded at him.

Edwin led the way from the room, chattering away to my father about something or another.

"I am so very sorry, Lenora," Robert said as I remained seated, lost in thought for a moment.

I lifted my eyes to his and offered a fleeting smile. "I am not certain Father has recovered from the ordeal. He suffers as Mother does, only in a different way."

Robert arched an eyebrow. "I do wish his suffering upset you less. It is you who has endured the worst of it."

I rose to stand, grabbing his hands in mine. "I do not agree."

"You give me far too much credit, Lenora. The life you endured at such a tender age would have ruined so many. Yet you remained a kind, loving, exceptional woman."

"What my life has become more than makes up for that."

"I am pleased to have offered you something in that way."

"You offer me more than just something."

He smiled at me, nodding before he changed the subject. "Are you certain you still wish to visit your mother?"

I heaved a sigh and pressed a hand to my forehead. "No. Though I do wish to learn if she knows anything." I flicked my gaze to him. "I hate to ask this, but–"

"You wish me to speak with her alone."

I winced and nodded, gnawing at my still-sore lip again.

Robert's eyebrows shot up. "I must admit, I prefer this. Even with me at your side, I do not wish for you to visit with your mother."

"I do not wish it on you either," I admitted.

"For Sarah, I would do anything, dear. Wait here, I shall return as soon as I have finished."

I nodded and squeezed his hand again before settling into my seat as Robert strode toward the door. I blew out a sigh of relief as he departed, though guilt coursed through me almost the moment he disappeared from my sight.

I drummed my fingers against the table, staring out at the gloomy day. Perhaps the weather remained gloomy here, no matter the day. In any circumstance, the gloominess matched my mood.

Melancholy settled in my chest, despite my best efforts to stop it. I pictured the faces of my husband and children. I had everything I wanted in life. Why did seeing my parents upset me so?

I supposed a part of me clung to the hope of achieving acceptance from them. I had not thought much of it before, having no contact with them. Now that I did, I desperately sought it. Why, I did not know. I chided myself for it.

The clicking of a man's shoes on the tiled floor interrupted my thoughts. I flicked my gaze to the door, expecting Robert. Instead, his younger brother strode in. His features transformed into a coy mask as he eyed me. "Oh, good, you understood my signal."

"Signal?" I inquired as he strode toward me.

"Yes, signal. I signaled to you that I would get rid of Dr. Hastings whilst you directed Robert's attention elsewhere so we could investigate."

My brow furrowed, and I shook my head at him. "I have little to no idea what you are speaking of."

"Lenora," he said with a chuckle, "obviously, you did take my meaning."

I rose from my seat, confusion still crinkling my features. "Are you referring to that odd thing you did with your hand?"

He nodded, his eyebrows wiggling at me. He repeated the gesture, swiping his finger across his throat.

"I had no idea what you meant."

"Yet you managed to get rid of Robert."

"Robert kindly offered to speak with my mother for me. I found myself suddenly reluctant."

"So you did not understand my secret signal?"

I shook my head.

Edwin pressed his lips together, a dejected expression on his features. "We shall need to work on that. It is important that we be adept at communicating silently." He sucked in a breath, but before I could answer, he continued. "No matter. We should abscond as quickly as possible before anyone returns."

He grabbed my arm and tugged me toward the door.

"Abscond?" I inquired as I shuffled along.

"Yes, discreetly slip away. Really, Lenora, as a bibliophile, I fully expected you to understand the term."

I yanked my arm from his grip and rolled my eyes at him. "I understand the term quite well. What I do not understand is where we are absconding to?"

He wrapped his fingers around my arm and pulled me

through the door. "To the doctor's office. All the records are kept there."

"Edwin!" I said, wriggling under his grasp. "How do you propose we enter the office?"

"Oh, I have that handled," he answered as we rounded the corner.

After a quick glance up and down another hall, we hurried across, rounded another corner, and approached a set of double doors. A nurse milled around outside them. She caught sight of us, the expression on her facing changing to an easily recognizable one.

I held back, rolling my eyes as she fluttered her eyelashes at Edwin. "You must be joking," I hissed.

"I use what is readily at my disposal," he murmured. "Do not ruin it." A grin spread across his face as we approached the girl. "Hello, again, Agnes. I am sorry to have made you wait."

"It is no trouble, Mr. Fletcher–"

"Oh, please, Edwin," he said, leaning closer to her with a broad grin.

Her shoulders raised to her ears as she giggled, casting her eyes downward, her face flushing. "Edwin," she whispered with a giggle.

"We're all friends here," he said with a wink.

I narrowed my eyes at the exchange, wondering how many women fell for this nonsense. I silently asked how Tilly could have as the nurse fiddled in her pocket before extracting a set of keys.

Her hands shook for a moment, and she swallowed hard. "I could get in so much trouble–"

"Oh, no, no," Edwin said. "We will only be a moment. We will not even leave the tiniest of traces. No one will know, Agnes, I promise. I would never risk endangering your position."

She flicked her gaze up at him.

"I am a professional," he said.

She nodded, biting her lower lip, her cheeks flushing to an even deeper red as she fiddled with the keys, shoving one into the lock and thrusting open the door.

Edwin offered her a smarmy smile, staring into her eyes for a moment longer than appropriate. "Thank you," he whispered with another wink.

I bit back bile, eyeing the nurse fluttering her eyelashes as Edwin guided me into the room, pressing his finger to his lips.

"Shh, it's our secret," he breathed as he slid the door closed behind him.

He spun to face me, and I raised my eyebrows at him. "Really, Edwin?"

"What?" he questioned.

"That was a shameful display."

"We must each use our talents to further the business. You can charm the dead, and I can enchant women. We must each play our part."

I shook my head at him as I glanced over my shoulder at the large wooden desk cluttered with papers.

"Come on, we haven't much time." He hurried to the wooden cabinets along the wall flanking the door and tugged open a drawer.

"What is it we are searching for?" I inquired as I perused the papers on the desk.

"Information on Mary McGinty."

I freed a paper covered in odd illustrations from the jumble and studied it. Edwin slammed the drawer shut and yanked open another, pawing through the contents. He cursed under his breath as I stared at crudely done drawings.

Edwin moved to another cabinet, raking through the

folders before he snatched one, grinning at me. "I've found it!"

I hurried over, the paper still clutched in my hand, and peered over his shoulder as he flipped open the patient chart.

The notes began in a steady hand, discussing the patient's intake. Mary McGinty had been determined criminally insane, though she maintained her innocence, even in her early interviews.

After three months at the asylum, Dr. Merriweather made the determination she had repressed the memories of the killings. He noted perhaps she behaved as another person during them and hence had no memory of them whatsoever.

"What is this bit here?" Edwin inquired.

I read over the information. "Hypnosis," I murmured. I read the fantastic accounting of how the doctor had sought information about Mary's early life through a technique employed by a French doctor.

"I waved the pendant in front of her over and over until I lulled her into a state similar to sleeping, though she could speak and respond to commands," Edwin read.

"How fantastic," I breathed.

Edwin's eyebrows shot up as he turned the page and read the next part of the entry. "Oh, my, even more fantastic is the tale she told while under this...whatever it's called."

"Hypnosis," I repeated.

"Right," he said, pointing a finger at me before he drew my attention to the salacious tidbit. As a young woman, Mary McGinty had endured abuse from her father, of several natures.

"How awful," I murmured. "It is no wonder she snapped."

"She killed only men," Edwin informed me. "This would explain why."

"Hmm," I murmured, pressing a finger to my lips, "however did she overpower them?"

"Poison? Sleeping draught? She incapacitated them in some way."

I flicked my pensive gaze to Edwin. "What way? Did the reports say?"

Edwin shook his head. "No, though they all had some trauma to their skulls."

"Did she hit them over the head?" I pondered aloud.

"Perhaps."

"We shall need to investigate that further. For now, we should read on." I wiggled a finger at the notes.

"Quite right," Edwin said, shuffling the papers. The notes continued discussing Mary's treatment. In more recent months, the handwriting became sloppier, and the treatments more experimental. Eventually, most details ceased beyond simple notes, such as "treatment given, no progress."

Edwin turned to the last page and snapped his gaze at me. The final chilling words merely read: PATIENT DIED.

"That's rather odd, wouldn't you say?"

"You would think more attention to the cause would have been given or noted."

"Patient died? What if a formal inquisition was made? This is all they have?" Edwin snapped the folder closed with a huff before stuffing it back into the drawer. He stalked away, rubbing his chin with his finger.

He spun to face me, his lips parting to speak when another noise intruded. "Yes, of course, Dr. Merriweather! I shall bring tea right away!" a woman's voice yelled down the hall.

"Thank you, Agnes," a man's voice answered from the other side of the door as a key sounded in the lock.

Edwin's eyes grew wide, and he shot me a glance. I swallowed hard, my stomach turning over as I realized we were trapped and about to be caught.

CHAPTER 25

"Hide!" Edwin hissed.

"Where?" I whispered, throwing up my hands.

"Under the desk!"

I shook my head. "Are you mad? We will never fit under there."

"Well, we must go *somewhere*."

My gaze darted around the room, gauging potential hiding spots. We would be spotted in any location easily. No nooks existed where we could tuck away unseen whilst the doctor worked in his office.

Across the room, a wall of medical volumes filled the shelves. Next to it was a large window with thick draperies. "Quickly, behind the drapes!"

I waved a finger toward them as I darted across the room. Edwin followed as I tucked myself behind the thick, velvety material.

"I will not fit!" Edwin hissed as the lock released.

"Doctor!" the woman's voice called again as the door knob turned.

"Yes?" the man's voice answered.

"Go to the other!" I said, waving a finger toward the adjacent window.

Edwin clicked his tongue at me as he slipped along the wall toward the other window. His shoulder smacked into the sconce, knocking it askew. A clicking noise echoed in the room. I snapped my gaze in its direction as Edwin desperately attempted to fix the wayward candelabra.

"Damn it," he cursed as I stepped from behind my curtain.

A smile crossed my lips, and I hurried to the bookshelves. I wrapped my fingers around the edge of one and tugged, widening the gap between it and the neighboring bookcase. "Edwin, help!"

Edwin snapped his gaze to me, his eyes going wide before he scurried toward me and yanked at the heavy wooden bookcase. Together, we managed to widen the gap enough to slip inside. Edwin grabbed the leather pull on the opposite side, easing it closed just as the door swung open.

"Whew," he hissed as darkness surrounded us. "That was close. Thank goodness I saved us, eh?"

"You must be joking," I said as my eyes adjusted to the dim light streaming from the slim opening between the bookcases.

Edwin grinned at me, wiggling his eyebrows.

"You stumbled upon that completely by accident."

"Most women express their gratitude over things like this."

"I am not most women. You should know that already, business partner."

Voices floated through the bookcase. It seemed Dr. Merriweather's tea had arrived. He thanked the nurse, and the door thudded shut moments later.

Edwin sighed as violin music began to play. "Who is playing that?"

"Dr. Merriweather is adept at it, from what I understand."

"Oh, perfect," he moaned, "we are stuck in here whilst he performs, drinks his tea, and does bloody-who-knows-what-else."

I leaned back against the wall behind me.

After a few moments, Edwin slumped back next to me. "Did Robert really not woo you?"

"What?" I questioned.

"You seemed quite taken aback by my flirting with the nurse. Did Robert really not behave in such a way to win you over?"

"Robert and I married within three days of meeting."

"Oh, right. He did rather do things in an interesting way, didn't he? I suppose the congratulations go to him. He demanded marriage from the moment you met yet ended up with a devoted wife. He is the luckier brother."

"Hardly demanded," I answered. "Offered is more like it."

"Offered? Really?"

I nodded. "He made it quite clear I could refuse."

Edwin arched an eyebrow. "Yet you did not. What drew you to agree?"

"He seemed honest. And truly needed the help. And of course, the life he offered would match no other offer I could hope to receive."

"Ah, so the money did it." He snickered as he offered me an amused grin.

I shook my head but found myself chuckling alongside him. "Yes, the money did it."

A moment passed, and the violin stopped for a moment before starting again. Edwin crossed his arms and shuffled around. "Though you now love him."

"Yes."

His forehead crinkled. "Why?"

"What do you mean?"

"He has not wooed you in any way."

"You mistake flirting for wooing. Robert provides me with more acceptance than any other living person outside of Tilly."

Edwin pouted, casting his gaze to the floor. "I am hurt."

"Why?"

"I provide you with acceptance."

"You do, yes. And I am very grateful for that. Though you did not care for me much at first."

"The mistakes of a drunken dolt."

"Drunken dolt?" I said with a giggle.

"Had I not been such an ass, perhaps…"

I squeezed his arm as his voice trailed off, turning wistful. "There is no sense in lamenting the past. We must continue to strive toward a better future."

He twisted his arm, sliding his hand up to squeeze mine. "I have made a mess of things."

"We all make messes of things. It is how we move forward that counts."

"Robert is a lucky man."

"We are both lucky."

"As am I to have you both. Though do not tell Robert. He'd be quite unimpressed to hear me blather on about family and such."

"Robert cares more for family than you give him credit for. But I shall keep your fondness for him to myself."

The violin finally went quiet. Edwin shot up and approached the panel, pressing his ear against it.

"Nurse! Nurse!" a voice shouted.

The door opened, and the nurse's voice answered.

"Let's go over the patient's charts if you do not mind."

Edwin's shoulders slumped as he sighed and dragged himself back to the wall, slouching against it again. "Unbelievable."

I shifted around again. "It is not the way I hoped to spend the afternoon either. Perhaps the visit with my mother would have been preferable."

"Robert is likely finished by now."

"And searching for us."

"He will be cross with me for–"

A loud bang sounded from the room beyond, catching our attention. "What is the meaning of this?" Dr. Merriweather's voice demanded.

"I'd like to know the same, Doctor!" Robert's voice answered.

Edwin's face morphed into a mask of surprise. "Robert," he whispered.

"You burst into my office. I demand to know why."

"Where is my wife?"

"How would I know?"

"This is the second time she has been left alone in your institution and gone missing. What type of establishment is this? I demand you search the premises for her at once."

"I cannot be responsible for your wife's wanderings."

"Uh oh," I murmured to Edwin.

"My wife's...how dare you, sir? In the last instance, your assistant physician took her on a tour, left her in a room that she became locked in, and she disappeared. Not wandered away."

"Perhaps she went back to that room."

"And perhaps one of the deranged patients harmed her or dragged her away. I demand this looked into at once." The pounding of Robert's cane punctuated the words.

"He is furious."

"As he was in the last instance." I narrowed my eyes as I considered it. "The last instance..."

"What of it?"

"I found my way out eventually by wandering through

the passage the spirit opened for me." I twisted and glanced into the darkness past Edwin. "I wonder if this hidden passage leads to an exit."

Edwin glanced into the black hole beyond us. "How do you propose we navigate it? It is dark!"

"Are you frightened?" I inquired.

"Certainly not," he said, straightening. "But we may stumble."

"We shall be careful. Come along." I pressed my fingertips against the wall and inched my way further down the path.

"Lenora," Edwin hissed from behind me, "wait. Do not leave me behind."

I reached backward, jabbing him in the stomach with a hand before his hand found mine. I squeezed it and tugged him forward. My feet searched the ground in front of me as I took each step.

"We must be careful not to tumble down any stairs we may come across."

"Tumble down stairs?" Edwin questioned, his hand clutching at mine. "I did not realize this would be so dangerous."

"You really are frightened, aren't you?"

"I am not. But I do not wish to fall down any stairs. I just recovered from a life-threatening stab wound. I have no desire to be laid up in bed again."

I felt my way forward, my fingertips curling around a corner. "There is another hallway to the right." I side-stepped my way to my left, bumping into the wall and issuing a sharp sigh. "And one to the left."

"Which way?"

I mentally calculated where we may be within the sprawling institution. "If we go to the right, we would be going further away from the center of the institution."

"And left would lead us closer. We should go left."

"All right. We shall go left."

"Wait!" Edwin shouted behind me.

"What is it?" I questioned.

"Is there a way forward? Perhaps we should not veer off."

I stuck my arm out in front of me and staggered through the dark until I smacked into the wall. I slid my hand along it until I reached a corner and waved my hand into the opening. "There is a straight passage. We shall go straight."

"No wait, that may be worse."

"So, left," I resolved.

"But what if—"

"For heaven's sake, Edwin, pick a direction."

"Give me a moment!" he hissed at me. "I must think. Right, left, or straight."

The sound of his shuffling shoes filled the silence between us as he stalked around in the dark. After a moment, a *thud* sounded. "Oof, damn it."

Air rushed past me as Edwin's shoes tapped off the floor rhythmically. *Was he hopping?* Seconds later, he bumped into me, trampling on my foot.

"Ouch!" I cried. "Edwin! Whatever are you doing?"

"I kicked the corner and stubbed my toe. And now I've bumped into you whilst hopping about to relieve the pain."

"Stop hopping," I said, laying a hand on his shoulder.

He ceased his crazy movement, shaking his leg.

"If you would only pick a direction, we could move on."

"I told you, I'm thinking. I must vet through the options."

"How much vetting can it require?" I inquired. "Perhaps we should—"

My words cut off as light bloomed in the distance. I stared into it, wondering if someone stumbled into the tunnels in search of us.

"We should what?" Edwin asked.

I took a step toward it, surprised Edwin had not reacted.

"Lenora, where are you going? What should we do?"

"Hello?" I called, shielding my eyes as I took another step.

"Yes, I am right here," Edwin answered. His hand bumped my arm before sliding down it and grasping my hand.

"Who is there?"

"I am. Edwin. Have you lost your senses?"

I clicked my tongue at him and waved at the light. "No, of course not. Someone is there!"

"Where?" he asked, his gaze shooting forward as he squinted.

"There! Holding the light."

"Light?" he questioned. "There is no light. It is pitch black in here."

I flicked my gaze back to the bright beam shining down the hall. "No light?" I murmured.

"Of course not. Wait, are you seeing light?"

"Yes, a bright beam. We should follow it." I started toward the light.

"Just a moment," Edwin said, tugging me back. "Didn't you fall down the stairs the last time you followed the light?"

"I also found my way out. Come along."

Edwin hung back as I wandered a few more steps forward. "Lenora," he hissed behind me. "Wait!"

He hurried toward me, grasping my hand and squeezing it. "I will not allow you to go alone."

The light disappeared around a corner. I quickened my pace, hurrying to the hall's end and peering around the bend.

"Is the light still there?" Edwin asked.

"Yes. It disappeared around a corner and now shines in the distance."

He nodded, staring ahead blankly. I squeezed his hand, realizing it must be difficult to wander through the darkness.

"This way," I said, pulling his arm to the left. He followed beside me, wrapping his arm around mine.

I groaned as we approached the end of the hall.

"What is it? Is it a ghost?"

"No, it's stairs. I propose we traverse down them before I am thrown down them again."

"All right," Edwin said with a hard swallow.

"I shall guide you. Hold tight to me."

A slight tremor shook my arm as Edwin struggled to move forward, feeling for the stairs with his foot.

"Almost there," I said, wrapping my arm around his waist and holding tight to him. "First step is just in front of you. Step down."

He wobbled forward, his foot hitting the step hard. He pulled himself back abruptly to avoid pitching down the stairs.

I tightened my grip on him, grasping at the rail with my other hand. "Slowly. One step at a time."

The light still glowed at the bottom of the stairs, lighting Edwin's features. He arched an eyebrow as I pressed closer to him and encouraged him one step lower. "Hmm, are you quite certain you are in love with my brother?"

"Quite certain, yes," I breathed out as I tugged him forward again.

"Mmm, the way you are clinging to me suggests otherwise." He offered an amused grin in my direction, though his gaze suggested the light still hid from him.

"Even in the darkest of places, your humor shines through, Edwin."

"Is it any wonder my charm causes so many women to fall in love with me?"

"No wonder at all," I said with a chuckle as we reached a platform and circled around before beginning our descent of the remaining stairs.

"Do not worry, dear sister-in-law, I shall not breathe a word of this to Robert."

My chuckling continued as we stepped down from the last step. "Done," I reported, releasing my grip on Edwin and smoothing my dress.

"Where is the light? Still there?"

"Just ahead. There appears to be a doorway."

He reached out for me, and I slid my arm through the crook of his, leading him forward. I passed through the opening and ground to a halt, my breath catching in my throat.

"What is it? Has the light gone out?"

"No," I said in a whisper. "It is Mary McGinty."

CHAPTER 26

"The murderess?" Edwin shouted, his eyes going wide.

"I believe so," I answered, narrowing my eyes at the specter glowing across the room. "Of course, I cannot be sure. She has yet to give her name or speak."

Edwin winced, clutching tight to my hand.

I cocked my head and stared at the woman in her dirty blue dress. "Hello. Are you Mary McGinty?"

The specter lowered her chin, staring at me through her eyelashes. Her gaunt grey face with the dark circles under her eyes created a macabre appearance. She flicked her gaze to Edwin, who still stood staring blankly ahead. He likely only saw darkness, whereas I could see the light shining behind the ghostly woman.

I patted his shoulder. "This is Edwin. He is helping me help you."

"Do not tell her my name," Edwin hissed.

"Why not?" I questioned, flicking my gaze to him.

"Now, she will know me. And haunt me."

I held back from rolling my eyes at the statement and

looked at the spirit. "Do not haunt Edwin. He will do you no good anyway. Can you tell me your name? Are you Mary McGinty?"

The spirit made no move to approach us or speak.

"Perhaps we were incorrect on the identity," I whispered to Edwin, my eyes never straying from the ghost. "She is not acknowledging anything."

"Perhaps she is mute."

"She spoke on our first meeting. She asked for help. What were the other possible names?"

Edwin flicked his blind gaze upward as he tried to recall the others we'd ruled out. "Lady Someone-or-another. Teacup. Treeweather. What was it?"

"She is not reacting to any of those names. Unsurprising, I suppose, as they are ridiculous."

"They are not," Edwin contended, his forehead pinching as he considered the name.

I sighed, flicking a quick glance at him. "Lady Teacup? Really, Edwin?"

"Trembly!" Edwin exclaimed, snapping his fingers. "Lady Trembly! ARE YOU LADY TREMBLY?"

I placed a hand on his arm. "You need not shout."

"Perhaps I do. Perhaps she is hard of hearing, and that is why she does not answer."

"Try the other name," I murmured.

"I will as soon as I recall it. Just a moment." He drummed his fingers against his forehead. "This may be her. She was simple, remember?"

"Rita. No. Ruth. Ruth Abernathy." He grinned into the darkness in front of him, and I realized as he stood unable to see me, but smiling just the same at his feat, why Tilly had fallen in love with him.

My poor, beautiful friend danced across my mind, and I felt a deep sense of melancholy as I realized how much she, I, and Edwin had lost. But now was not the moment for wistfulness. The ghost stood in front of me, and I had the chance to elicit information.

I flicked my gaze at the woman. "Are you Ruth?"

Her unmoving eyes continued to bore into me. In an instant, she was on top of me. I stumbled back a step.

"What is it?" Edwin whispered.

"Ruth?" I questioned.

"Innocent," she hissed. "Help me."

My brow creased, and I stared at her for an instant. "Innocent?" I repeated.

"What is happening, Lenora?" Edwin questioned, gripping my arm.

"The ghost has moved to stand directly in front of me. She said 'innocent' and reiterated her request for help."

"Innocent?"

"Yes, which makes me believe she is Mary." I kept my eyes trained on the ghost as I said it. "Are you Mary? Please tell me if you can. I must know, so I may help you."

"Innocent. Murdered. So many murdered," she said.

I stared into her dark eyes. They did little to betray the evil that supposedly lived inside her. Did she not realize her crimes, as the doctor suggested?

"Is there someone else there? Someone...not Mary?"

Edwin licked his lips, cocking his head as he awaited any information. How terribly frustrating for him, standing in the dark, unable to see or hear the spirit with us. Though my end wasn't faring much better.

"Help me," the ghost repeated.

"Please tell me your name. Nod if you are Mary. Do something so that I might know your identity."

"Anne," she said before she snapped her gaze over her shoulder. She shot a glance back at me, her eyes filled with fear.

"Help me," she moaned once more before she vanished.

"No, wait!" I shouted, stumbling a step forward as I groped the air. I issued a groan as my hand fell to my side.

"What is it? Is she behaving terribly? Will she haunt me?"

"No, Edwin, she will not," I said with a sigh. "She has fled. Again. With little to no explanation of who she is."

"Did she say the name? Or give any indication."

"She said, 'Anne.' Who is Anne?" I questioned.

Edwin puckered his lips in thought. "I cannot recall Lady Trembly's first name, though I do not believe it to be Anne."

I scrunched my features as I attempted to recall the name scrawled on Edwin's notes. "No, it is not Anne. Lydia."

Edwin snapped his fingers. "Yes, that's it. Good memory, Lenora. Well, I suppose we should continue on now that the ghost has left. Did she happen to leave the light on for you?"

I chuckled at Edwin's question and opened my mouth to answer when a breeze fluttered the fabric of my dress. I twisted to stare in that direction.

"Lenora? Say something. I am becoming incredibly uncomfortable standing in the darkness with no answer from you directly following a visit from a ghost."

"The light remains, but now I feel a breeze. Perhaps it will lead to a way out."

"I felt nothing," Edwin said, thrusting his hand out in front of him. "Let's find out if we might escape, shall we?"

I grasped his hand and pulled him forward. "Yes, before Robert commits a crime in the name of finding us."

"Well, you. Robert would gladly leave me to wander these secret passages until I rotted away."

"He would not," I contended as we approached the doorway across the room where the ghost had once stood.

I ducked through it into another chamber. Lit torches filled it, along with an odd metal contraption that stood across the space.

I glanced at Edwin, wondering if he could spot the light. "Can you see now?"

"Of course not," Edwin answered. "It is pitch black."

I furrowed my brow as I stared at the flaming torch next to me. I stretched my arm out toward it, snapping it back as the flames licked my fingers. "Ouch!"

"What happened? Is it the ghost? Has she harmed you?"

"No. There are torches lit around the room. And I–"

Edwin snorted a laugh, interrupting me.

"What?" I questioned.

"Lenora, this room is pitch black, just as all the others." He rolled his eyes.

"I saw that."

"Saw what? The ghost?" he questioned, his grip tightening on my arm.

"No. The roll of your eyes. I can see it because there are lit torches in this room. I burned my fingers reaching for one to ascertain if it was real or not."

He squinted, staring ahead at nothing as his eyebrows pinched together. "If this room is truly lit up, tell me, then, what face am I making right now?" He stuck his tongue out and crossed his eyes.

"You are sticking your tongue out and crossing your eyes."

His features snapped back to normal, his eyes widening with surprise. "How is it that you can see the torches and I cannot?"

"I do not know, though I assure you the room is lit in a warm glow, though it feels anything but warm. In fact, I'm finding it quite disturbing."

"Because of the ghost?"

My shoulders slumped. "No, of course not. The ghost is long gone, Edwin."

Edwin reached his hand out in front of him. "Where are these torches? Put my hand near one."

"You may become burned," I cautioned.

"I shall take the chance to test a theory. Put my hand nearer the flame." He wiggled his fingers in front of me. I grabbed them and tugged him a step to the side, inching them ever closer to the blaze.

"Can you feel warmth?"

"No, nothing."

I crinkled my brow, wondering why I could but he couldn't.

"I am quite close. My fingers feel the heat."

"Odd," he said as he pulled his hand away. "I feel nothing."

"I suppose we should continue on and determine if this may lead to an exit."

"Quite right. I would very much like the light to apply to both of us again. It is rather unfair that only you can see."

"Another tragedy in your life," I said with a giggle as I looped my arm through his and led him forward.

"Quite right. It is a wonder how I continue to survive when I am constantly–"

His words cut off, and I stumbled forward a step as the pressure of his arm pulling back against me ceased.

"Constantly what?" I asked, my eyes glued to the odd metal contraption in front of me.

I received no answer from my partner. I reached out to touch the large metal box, my eyebrows furrowing before I twisted to glance at Edwin.

"Constantly wh–" I began when my heart dropped. I stood alone in the chamber.

"Edwin?" I called, my voice echoing off the stone surrounding me. "Edwin!"

I stormed back toward the entrance, wrangling a torch

from the wall and retreating into the previous chamber. "Edwin?"

I received no answer and found no one. *Where had Edwin gone?*

My brow pinched as I returned to the chamber containing the metal container. I still stood alone, though now a breeze tousled the flames. I crossed to the opposite side of the chamber, ignoring the metal box and entering a long corridor. The flames bounced off the tight walls as I pressed forward.

The narrow hall opened into a wider chamber. I recognized it as the stairway I had fallen down on my last visit. "Edwin!" I called again, hoping by some odd circumstance I may stumble upon him.

I did not have any such luck. I glanced behind me as I hovered in the doorway to the chamber with the pool of water. I could navigate out easily now. However, I did not wish to leave Edwin behind. Though I knew not where he'd went.

I took a step toward the water chamber. I could escape from the odd chambers under the asylum, report Edwin's disappearance to Robert, then return to search for him.

I bit my lower lip, hesitating in the doorway. I should not leave Edwin behind. I had the good fortune to be able to see. He was left in the dark. I would return to find him.

I swung around and retraced my steps. Perhaps he had become caught in the odd metal contraption. Or perhaps he had stumbled into another chamber or passage I had not spotted.

"Edwin!" I called again as I traversed down the narrow hallway. "Edwin, where are you?"

A faint voice reached my ears. "...ora..."

"Edwin?" I called, quickening my pace.

"Le...a."

"Edwin! Edwin!" I called, entering the chamber with the metal container. "Where are you?"

I spun in circles, searching for him. My eyes settled on the metal contraption. I wandered closer to it. The flames reflected off the shiny metal, dancing inside it.

"Edwin?" I questioned, squinting at the two holes just above my eye level. "Edwin, are you in there?"

My fingers clasped around the large handle poking from the container. I tugged it open slowly. The door creaked on unseen hinges. The screeching noise assaulted my ears and echoed off the walls.

I shifted the torch to light the interior of the odd standing casket. My blood ran cold as the light revealed what it held. I stumbled back a step, dropping my torch, a scream sticking in my throat as my stomach turned.

CHAPTER 27

I trembled all over as I stared at the interior of the metal case. Spikes stuck from the door, dripping with blood. I covered my mouth as I gasped. Had Edwin somehow wandered into this contraption and become impaled?

Tears welled in my eyes as I wondered if the weak cry I'd heard had been his final words.

"Edwin," I choked out as a lump caught in my throat.

I sniffled and wiped at my eyes, raising them slowly and forcing myself to stare at the body. My brow furrowed as I caught sight of gray fabric. Edwin had worn a suit much darker. I realized the fabric formed a skirt, not trousers.

Edwin was not in the deadly coffin. But who was? I lifted my eyes to the face. A woman, marred by a spike sticking through her cheek and another poking one of her eyes out of its socket. The other stared back, unseeing.

I covered my mouth and spun away. I did not recognize her at first glance, though I did not wish to study her further. I had seen the dead in all manner of states, but this was one of the more gruesome.

I sucked in a shaky breath and composed myself, reaching down to collect the still-burning torch. I would report her body after I returned to the asylum and saw a search party dispatched for Edwin.

I glanced over my shoulder one last time at the horrifying scene before I forced myself away from it. I could do nothing to help the woman, living or dead. Her soul did not reach out to me. I made a slow search of the rest of the space, finding nowhere Edwin could have slipped away.

I continued through the narrow passage, searching every inch of it. I found no hiding spots. With a deep sigh, I hastened past the fated stairs I'd rolled down and into the water chamber. The pool sat in the middle, and I swallowed hard as I recalled the odd incident the last time I'd been here.

I wondered if many lost souls roamed here. It would explain the unusual events I'd experienced. I considered giving the watery pit a wide berth, however, I worried Edwin may have fallen into it. It did not appear deep, but perhaps he hit his head and drowned.

With my jaw clenched, I approached the pool and peered in, catching sight of my own reflection in the still water.

The murky tank did not reveal any further details. "Oh, Edwin," I murmured as I lowered to my knees. "Why did you wander off?"

I reached toward the water, wrinkling my nose as my fingers dipped into the cold liquid. My fingers hit something metal, and I yanked my hand back. I blew out a long breath. Not Edwin, at least, I told myself as I forced my hand back into the water to the elbow.

There seemed to be some sort of cage submerged. My brow furrowed as my fingertips explored it. I had little idea what it could be, though it did not appear Edwin had fallen inside.

My mind turned to the well in the next chamber. Had he

fallen into the well? I pulled my arm out and shook the water from it, squeezing my drenched sleeve.

As I climbed to my feet and stepped toward the next chamber, a breeze floated past me. It carried on it a whisper.

"Murder," a voice said.

I stopped, spinning in search of the voice's source. "Hello?" I called.

No one answered me or appeared. My eyes fell to the pool again. An unsettled feeling lodged in the pit of my stomach. I tore my eyes away from it and pressed on to the next chamber.

"Edwin?" I called out as I entered the cavern with the well.

A quick scan showed no one inside. With a sigh, I trudged forward toward the opposite wall in search of the exit. I passed the well, eyeing it suspiciously.

I paused just before I passed it and slid my eyes sideways. What if Edwin had fallen inside? He could be hurt. Or worse. No, I thought with a shake of my head.

"If he had died, his ghost would be pestering me," I murmured as I stalked toward the well reluctantly. "Edwin?"

I inched closer to the stone and stretched my neck to peer into it. I could not spot anything from my angle. I would have to get closer and lean further over.

After the last experience, I loathed getting any nearer, but for Edwin's sake, I forced myself.

I licked my lips and held my breath as I stepped toward the well's opening and peered over the edge. Only the blackness looked back at me.

"Edwin?" I called out in a voice meeker than usual. I swallowed hard and cleared my throat. "Edwin!" I shouted in a steadier voice.

No answer. I held the flame over the opening, shifting it around for a better view. I saw no bottom. I considered tossing the torch down. What if Edwin lay at the bottom, I wondered? I could not tell without light, but throwing the torch down may harm him.

As I waffled back and forth on my decision, a rattling noise floated from within the well. My heart stopped. I clutched the edge of the stone, searching the bottom with wide eyes.

"Edwin? Edwin? Have you fallen?"

The chittering sound turned into a groan. My heart skipped a beat, and I held the torch further within the stone circle. "Edwin! If you are there, I am going for help!"

I still could see nothing at the bottom of the well. I shook my head, my features pinching as I searched for any sign of my wayward companion. My mind raced with worry as I considered methods to extract the poor man from the well.

Before I could back away to seek help, another groan sounded. This one seemed closer. I leaned over again. My jaw dropped open as a hand rose from the blackness.

"Edwin!" My mind whirled. Had he somehow climbed out? Before I could consider it further, the hand reached for me, grabbing hold of my wrist and tugging.

"Edwin! Stop! You'll drag me in. I cannot balance your weight."

The arm tugged against me. I tried to pull away as my feet began to slip.

"Edwin, no!" I cried as my feet lifted from the dirt below. I wobbled on the edge of the stone before I began to pitch forward. The force pulling on me continued to drag me further into the dark well.

I opened my mouth in a wide scream as I plunged forward and the growl that had emanated from the depths of the hole surrounded me as it sounded again.

My stomach flipped as I fell further and further, wondering when I would hit the bottom and how hurt I would become. Would I become a spirit and roam the earth as the ones I encountered?

The blackness continued to rush toward me until I began to feel woozy. I fought to keep my eyes open as I fell, but they slid closed, and my senses dulled.

Finally, my body shook, pulling me back to reality. I must have finally smacked into the bottom. Everything seemed hazy. Had I fallen into water? Was I floating?

My body shook all over as my senses began to return more fully. A sniffle sounded, and my body rose in the air before being cradled. "Lenora, please wake up."

Edwin! I tried to speak to him, but my lips would not move, and my eyes would not open. My leaden arm refused to reach for him. I swallowed hard and forced my eyelids open. Darkness filled the room. I could not see my own hand in front of my face.

Memories rushed back to me. We had been roaming in the underground chambers under the asylum. I had obtained a torch, however, only I could see the light.

"Edwin?" I murmured.

His muscles stiffened, and he gasped in a breath. "Lenora!"

I struggled to push up to sit, smacking him in the head with my forehead. "Ouch, oh, I am sorry," I said as I pressed my palm against my head where it smarted.

"Quite all right. I am more glad to have you back and do not plan on complaining about the bump."

"Edwin, not complaining? Whatever is the world coming to?" I teased. "How long have I been unresponsive?"

"Several moments. You fainted suddenly. I caught you and tried to revive you, but with no light, I could not assess the situation very well. Though several times you moaned or moved, which I am glad for, since I knew you remained alive."

"I did not faint."

"You did," Edwin began.

"No," I interrupted. "I disappeared again. Well, I thought you had disappeared. You stopped speaking suddenly, and then you were not there. I searched for you and could not find you, though I found several other gruesome things."

"Gruesome things?" Edwin questioned.

"Yes. A woman who had been impaled inside a metal contraption. And a cage in a pool of water. Someone whispered murder. Then I went to the chamber with the well. I worried you had fallen in, and I searched for you after hearing your voice. Something pulled me into the pit, then I awoke here."

"Goodness. I am quite glad I do not suffer from what you do, Lenora," Edwin said.

"I grow weary of it myself," I said as I rose to my feet and dusted my dress off, despite not being able to see the dirt. "The good news is, I know how we can escape from this place."

"You do?" Edwin asked, the direction of his voice indicating he remained on the ground.

"Yes. Assuming my unexplained roaming whilst unconscious is an accurate representation of these chambers, all we must do is find the exit in this room near the metal container, pass through the narrow hall, and then go through the chambers I navigated through on my first underground visit."

"Oh, how exceptionally simple," Edwin said with a groan. A scuffle sounded, which I interrupted to mean Edwin had climbed to his feet. A hand reached out, bumping into my shoulder before it traveled down to my elbow and fingers closed around it.

I reached for him with my other hand and grabbed his arm, leading him forward. I stretched my other arm in front of me as I inched along in search of the opening in the blackness.

"This was much easier when I had a torch."

"Indubitably. I am just pleased to hear your voice again and have a way out."

"Please keep talking to me," I said as my fingers bumped into cold metal. I shivered as I recalled the gruesome scene I'd seen in the alternate version of this room. I slid to the left a few steps and continued forward.

"It is a tight fit," I said as my fingers slid forward, no longer deterred by the stone walls.

"Wonderful," Edwin groaned as we slipped inside.

The sides scraped my shoulders, and I twisted sideways to continue my journey. Edwin huffed behind me. "Tight fit is not the word."

"Almost through," I said. Within moments, the walls receded, and we spilled into a slightly lit chamber.

I made out the dark form of the stairs to my right and used it to navigate to the opening in the wall across from it.

"We must be careful. This chamber contains a pool of water, and I do not wish to end up in it," I said as I hugged closer to the walls and crept around the room.

"And the next room has a well?"

"Yes," I said as I continued across the room by feeling my way along the wall. A gust of wind blew through the chamber, and I froze.

Edwin bumped into me. "Lenora! You must say something if you plan to stop."

"Shh," I hushed him. "I heard something."

"Really? A gh–"

"Do not ask if it is the ghost," I interrupted with a shake of my head, even though he could not see me. I pressed my lips together and narrowed my eyes as I strained to hear.

"Murder," a voice repeated.

My heart skipped a beat. The same thing had occurred in my unconscious foray through these chambers just before I had been dragged into the well.

"Lenora," Edwin hissed, fidgeting around next to me. "What's happening?"

I swallowed hard, listening for more from the phantom voice, though the breeze died down and I heard nothing further. "Nothing. I heard a voice, but it is gone now."

"What did it say?" Edwin inquired.

"Never mind. Let us focus on finding a way out."

Edwin tugged back against me. "Lenora! What did the ghost say?"

"Murder," I answered with a sigh.

"Murder? Was it Mary McGinty? Perhaps she is confessing to her crimes. Maybe she feels guilt and cannot rest until she unburdens her soul."

My fingers wrapped around the wall's edge, and I reached further into the opening, pulling us forward into the next chamber. "Why would she say 'murder' rather than something else that indicates her guilt?"

"Such as?"

I shrugged as I continued to feel my way along the wall. This way would take longer but keep us away from the dreaded well. "Such as guilt, perhaps," I answered.

"Oh, right. Good point."

We continued along in silence for a moment until Edwin spoke again. "Why murder? What is she driving at?"

I stopped dead, and Edwin ran into the back of me.

"Why did you stop? Do you hear her again?"

"No, but your question is excellent."

"Of course it is," he answered.

I imagined him grinning, pleased with himself. "Stop grinning at yourself and listen."

"Do you have a torch again?"

"No, I know you too well. Now, why murder? What is she driving at?"

"I have no idea, which is why I asked it."

"What if she isn't confessing to the murders she committed, but rather–"

"Saying someone else murdered them!" Edwin finished.

I shook my head, even though he could not see me, pressing my lips together. "No. What if she is not discussing the crimes she was accused of at all, but rather suggesting that she herself was murdered?"

"The murderess murdered. It was a possibility, though quickly dismissed by the asylum."

"Well, of course it was," I answered, continuing forward, "the asylum would not wish to admit one patient murdered another."

"But what if they did? What if that is the help she is asking for? She would like her death avenged."

"Odd," I answered, "she would like her death avenged after killing so many."

"She considered herself innocent."

"True," I said, coming to a stop again.

"Did you hear her again?"

"No," I said, my brow furrowing. "We have come 'round to the doorway we came through without stumbling upon the exit."

"Perhaps you missed it."

"I kept my fingers pressed against the stone the entire time. So much so that they are raw at this point. There was no opening."

"What are you saying?" Edwin asked after a momentary pause.

"I am saying..." My voice trailed off as I swallowed hard, then licked my lips, my brows pinching together. "I am saying we are stuck."

CHAPTER 28

"Stuck?" Edwin shouted, his panicked voice echoing off the stone walls. "No! No, no, no. We cannot be stuck."

I grabbed his hand and dragged him behind me as I returned the way I came, desperately searching for the opening again.

"Anything?" he questioned as I slowed to a stop.

"No," I said with a sigh, "nothing."

"Keep looking. I do not plan on dying in the prime of my life stuck under a batty house."

I rubbed my forehead as I thought through the situation. "Mary?" I called out.

"Again?" Edwin inquired, lowering his voice to a whisper.

"Perhaps she is blocking the exit until we have done whatever she wishes," I breathed. I raised my voice and called out again. "Mary? Are you there? What did you mean when you said murder?"

A breeze rustled my hair, and I spun toward it, my arms reaching out. Either the breeze was created by Mary or blew in from the outside. Either way, I intended on following up on it. I reached in front of me. Cold flesh touched mine. Fingers wrapped around my hand. "Help me. Home," a voice whispered in my ear.

"Mary!" I said, my eyes going wide. "Please tell me more."

"The hook," she whispered, the sound of her voice tickling my ear. The pressure against my fingers released, and I stumbled forward a step.

"Mary! Mary? No, please, wait. Tell me more."

I waited a moment, hoping to hear something more or feel the rustling breeze, but only silence and stillness met me.

"Lenora," Edwin hissed from behind me. "What's happening?"

I groaned and spun back toward him. "She is gone. And we are still trapped."

"What did she say? Did she say anything more about the murder?"

"She requested help again, then mentioned home."

"Home? Her home? Who's home?"

"I do not know," I admitted, scratching my head. "I am not certain. Home. Why? First, murder, then help, then home."

Edwin's fingers snapped together. "I've got it. We must go to her home."

"If we ever find our way out of here."

"Too bad she did not tell you how to escape from this place. Did she say anything else?"

"The hook," she said.

"What does that mean?"

I sighed, my shoulders slumping. "I have little idea."

"Perhaps she wants you to go to her home and find the hook she used to murder her victims."

"How would that help her?"

"I don't know, I'm merely trying to offer suggestions."

I pressed my lips together as I continued to consider the encounter.

Edwin sighed, reaching for my hand and squeezing it. "I suppose it does not matter, since we are stuck."

I began to nod when my head stopped moving and eyes shifted, despite still seeing nothing. "Wait. Perhaps we can escape. We got into these chambers through a secret passage. In fact, I accessed them twice through such a mechanism. Perhaps we can reopen them from this side and escape!"

"But if we burst through the panel into the doctor's office, we will be caught. Though I suppose I would prefer that to dying in this dank place."

"But *not* if we burst through the panel into the music room."

"Lenora!" he exclaimed, grabbing my hand and squeezing. "You are a genius."

"Of course I am. Which is why you insisted I become your partner in this venture." I tugged him along as I searched for the exit back into the water chamber. After a moment, my fingers slipped around the corner, and we spilled into the other room. I crossed it as quickly as possible, still clinging to the walls so I would not fall into the water pit.

We emerged near the dimly lit steps. I grabbed hold of the railing and pulled myself up, hoping I was not thrown down them moments later by my spirit friend. Edwin clamored up behind me. We used the small amount of light to find the passage I'd traversed on my last visit.

I hurried to the end and pounded against the door. "This leads to the music room. But on my last visit, I could not determine how to open it."

"Stand aside," Edwin said in a firm tone.

I ducked away, allowing him full access to the door. A thud sounded, followed by a curse. Another thud echoed in the narrow passage. "I can do nothing."

"What did you try?"

"I hit the panel, then I kicked it."

"There must be a trigger somewhere."

"But you did not find it last time," Edwin contested.

"Though I did not spend much time trying since the spirit called to me. We should search for some sort of release mechanism."

I stepped forward next to Edwin, sliding my hand up and down the panel in search of some sort of lever or button that may unlock the panel. We found nothing. I slumped against the wall next to me with a sigh.

Edwin collapsed into the wall across from me with a huff. "Ouch, damn it."

"What is it?"

Edwin straightened, spinning to glance behind him. "Something is poking in my back."

"The hook," I said.

"Yes, a hook or something similar. Poked right between my shoulder blades, and–"

"Shh," I said with a wave of my hand as I pushed around him and felt the wall for the object. I touched the lever I'd found on my last trip and slid my hands above it, striking metal. I wrapped my fingers around the hook-like object, pulling down on it. Nothing happened. I wrinkled my nose and fiddled with it again, trying to push or pull it in any direction. It finally slid to the side, and a clicking noise sounded.

The panel at my side popped open, a sliver of light from the room beyond shining into the dark space.

"You did it!" Edwin exclaimed. He tugged at the panel, pulling it open further. "After you, my ingenious partner."

I nodded at him with a smile as I traipsed into the empty music room. The doors across the room closed off the space to the hall. Voices shouted outside. Apparently, a search had been undertaken to find us.

I could imagine Robert, his arms crossed tightly over his

broad chest and foot tapping against the floor, standing in the central room as nurses flitted about the sanitarium in a frantic search.

"Come on," I said as Edwin closed the passage. "We had better seek Robert before the entire place is turned upside down on our behalf."

I hurried toward the doors and spun the knobs, to no avail. The lock prevented us from escaping. "Of course."

"Stand aside, this time I can do something."

I backed away from the doors, expecting Edwin to exert some force against them to break them open. Instead, he pounded his closed fists against them, shouting at the top of his lungs. "Help! We are trapped! Someone help us!"

"Really, Edwin," I said as a commotion sounded on the opposite side of the door, "I could have done that."

"Though I am quite a bit louder," he said with a grin as the sound of a key turning in a lock reached us.

The door popped open, and a wide-eyed nurse stared at us. "I have found them!" she shouted down the hall.

Dr. Applebaum appeared in the doorway, adjusting his spectacles. "Oh, my. Are you quite all right, Your Grace?"

"Yes, I am quite, thank you. We merely became stuck again. There is no need for–"

Robert burst through the door, pushing between the nurse and Dr. Applebaum. "My God, Lenora, are you quite all right? I have been worried to no end!" He rushed to my side and pulled me into his arms.

"As I just told Dr. Applebaum, I am quite all right. No harm done."

"And I, too, am fine," Edwin chimed in, "in case anyone wondered."

"And what would be wrong with you?" Robert snapped.

Edwin frowned at him as a new man entered the room. Dr. Merriweather glanced at me and Edwin, then at Dr.

Applebaum. "Well, I see we have found everyone safe and sound, as I suspected. There is no cause for worry."

"Of course there was cause for worry. My wife—"

"Really, Robert," I said with a shake of my head, "it is quite all right. I was with Edwin the entire time. We merely became stuck. There is nothing to cause trouble over."

"Leave this to me, Lenora," Robert said.

"Really, Robert, there is no cause for this. We were quite safe, I assure you," Edwin said. "I took excellent care of Lenora."

Robert glanced at Edwin, an irked expression on his dark features. I placed a hand on his arm and squeezed. He glanced over his shoulder at me, flicking his gaze back to Edwin for a moment, then to the two doctors in the room.

After clearing his throat, he said, "I suppose I overreacted. Thank you for your attention in helping me find my brother and wife. We will take our leave now."

"Of course, Your Grace," Dr. Merriweather said.

He opened his mouth to continue when Dr. Applebaum interrupted. "Oh, just a moment, we should ensure Her Grace has not been harmed in any way."

"Harmed?" I questioned, my eyebrows pinching together. "I am perfectly fine."

"I would prefer that we take no chances," Dr. Applebaum insisted, flicking his gaze to Robert. "Surely, Your Grace, you feel your wife should be examined by a professional before she leaves the premises?"

Robert's brow furrowed, and he glanced at me. "Really, dear, I am quite fine. If I experience any issues, we may follow up with Dr. MacAndrews."

"Oh, but—" Dr. Applebaum protested.

"All right," Robert agreed with a wave of his hand. "Quickly. I would very much prefer to have Her Grace settled in the carriage and on her way home."

"Of course," the doctor answered, adjusting his wire-rimmed glasses as he approached me with a pleasant smile.

I held back, rolling my eyes and sighing, plopping into a chair, as directed by the doctor. He gently lifted my chin and gazed into my eyes. "Have you any dizziness?"

"No, none," I answered.

He felt for my pulse, his brow pinching as it thumped against his fingers. "Weakness in your limbs?"

"No."

"Do you feel clear-headed, or is your mind in a fog?"

"Clear-headed."

"Are you certain? Perhaps you feel turned around after your escapade?"

"I do not. As Edwin has made clear, he took excellent care of me whilst we were stuck."

The man puckered his lips, glancing at Edwin, who nodded. "How did you manage to become stuck?"

"Well..." Edwin stammered, "we...the door closed and..."

"But we checked this room," the doctor interrupted.

Edwin's jaw dropped, but no sound came out.

"There is a passage. I told you about it before. It opened, and as we found ourselves trapped, we traversed it in the hopes of freeing ourselves."

"There is no such passage," Dr. Merriweather cut in.

"There is. Edwin can attest to it."

Edwin nodded in agreement, motioning toward the wall. "Yes, just here."

"Interesting," Dr. Applebaum said, adjusting his glasses again. "You both experienced this...passage."

I pushed against the arms and rose to stand. "Yes, we did. And we are quite fine, despite a bit of roaming through dark halls. Though I find myself weary and would prefer to return home. Robert?" I flicked my gaze to my husband in a silent appeal for him to end this charade of an examination.

"Of course, dear," Robert said. "Doctors, if you will excuse us, I must insist we depart at once."

"Yes, of course, Your Grace," Dr. Merriweather answered. "And please, if you should have any further questions regarding Mrs. Hastings's care, do write."

"I shall do just that," Robert promised, taking hold of my arm and leading me from the room. Edwin trailed behind us as we traversed the halls, arriving at the locked door leading to the entrance. Robert huffed as we waited for a nurse to scurry down with a set of keys and allow us to exit.

"I certainly hope you got what you came for," Robert groused as we stepped into the chilly air.

We climbed into the carriage and waited for Edwin, who spoke briefly to Jones before clambering up and plopping into the seat across from us.

"Jones knows the way home," Robert said. "No need to tell him."

"Ah, but we are not going home, are we, Lenora?" Edwin asked, a twinkle in his eye.

Robert snapped his gaze to me, his eyes wide. "What is he saying?"

"We stumbled upon several pieces of information whilst at the asylum," I said as the carriage trundled down the hill.

"And disappeared again," Robert said, crossing his arms over his chest.

"Apparently causing the good doctor to be in quite a frenzy."

"Not really. I was rather shocked, actually, at how little Dr. Merriweather did about your disappearance. He seemed rather blasé about the entire matter. Most off-putting. What happened, by the way?"

"Edwin managed to charm his way into Dr. Merriweather's office, where we reviewed the files of Mary McGinty.

However, Dr. Merriweather's unexpected return forced us to think quickly on our feet."

Robert raised his eyebrows, flicking his gaze between me and Edwin. "And?"

"Edwin stumbled upon a hidden passage. We secreted ourselves inside to await his departure. However..."

"Yes?"

"You burst into his office and spoiled the entire plan," Edwin said. "It was then that Lenora suggested we search for a way out from within the secret passage, so we did."

"Yes," I added. "We stumbled upon several underground chambers."

Edwin leaned forward, a smirk on his handsome features. "And then something odd happened."

"*Then* something odd happened?" Robert questioned. "This is the moment where you believe the tale turns odd?"

"Really, Robert, where is your sense of adventure?" Edwin asked, slumping back into his seat.

"Climbing the moors on horseback is my sense of adventure, brother, not slinking through underground passages."

Edwin rolled his eyes. "I assure you this was far more interesting than taking in the Highlands on horseback. Lenora had another episode. Thank goodness that doctor was more interested in gazing into her beautiful eyes than doctoring, or he may have noticed she fainted again."

Robert's jaw dropped open, and he shot me a glance.

"I did not faint," I said with a firm shake of my head. "What I am experiencing is not fainting, but a loss of consciousness as I wander about in some other place. In this case, it helped us navigate back to the music room at least. Though before that, I witnessed several gruesome displays in those chambers."

"How did you see them? Was it not dark?" Robert

snapped his gaze to Edwin. "And what did you mean about him staring into Lenora's eyes?"

Edwin lifted his eyebrows, leaning forward again. "Lenora had a torch, though I could not see it." He paused for a moment before continuing. "And I meant exactly what I said. Really, Robert, are you blind?"

"What are you saying?"

Edwin rolled his eyes, offering his brother a bemused look. "Robert, the man is quite taken with her. That is obvious. He used his doctor bit to be close to her."

Robert's jaw unhinged again.

"Really, brother, you cannot be this dim. She is a beautiful woman."

"Yes, of course she is. She is also a married one!"

"Love knows no boundaries, brother," Edwin said with a cheeky grin.

"Stop this talk at once! This is my wife. The man has no business loving her."

Edwin shrugged, wobbling about as the carriage hit a rough spot in the road. "I only mean to make you aware. The doctor has less of Lenora's well-being on his mind and more of his own."

"Thank you, Edwin, we shall be aware of it in the future," I answered, "but for now, we must concentrate on the information we learned at the asylum."

"Which is? And how did you carry a torch Edwin could not see?"

"I do not know, though I imagine it had to do with my spirit friend. I saw Mary McGinty. Well, who I assume to be Mary McGinty. And light bloomed. I found it to come from torches, though Edwin could not see or feel any heat from them. Then suddenly Edwin was gone, and I roamed the chambers on my own. I found a maimed body inside a curious metal contraption, a metal cage inside a water pit, and then was dragged into a well."

"Dragged into a well?" Robert spat.

"Not literally, though it felt vividly real. I awoke in Edwin's arms. And together, we tried again to escape. However, I found the previous route I'd used blocked. It was then that I encountered the ghost again. She said, 'Help me. Home.' Then whispered, 'The hook.'"

"Hook?"

"Yes, we managed to escape from the passages and into the music room using a hook that triggered the panel."

"And," Edwin added, "we assume the ghost is requesting that we visit her home. Why we do not know, however, we should follow up on this lead."

Robert narrowed his eyes at his brother, and I could see his indignation over the matter building as he realized Edwin had given Jones the order to travel to Stirling.

Before he could remark, I patted his knee. "What of your inquiry, dear?"

"What?" he questioned, his features pinching.

"Your inquiry with my mother. Did anything fruitful come of it?"

"Oh, no, nothing," he said, flinging a hand in the air to dismiss it.

"Really? Nothing? Did she refuse to speak to you?" I questioned.

Robert's lips formed a frown, an expression I recognized when he wished not to lie but preferred not to tell the truth.

"Oh, no. Did she attack you?"

"No, no," Robert assured me. "Nothing quite so dramatic. In fact, she seemed almost lucid, though I am quite convinced she was not."

"Oh? And why not?"

"Because of what she said. Utter nonsense. The babbling of a mad woman."

"What did she say?" Edwin inquired as the carriage rocked back and forth.

"Nothing important. Now, back to the matter at hand. Are we, in fact, on our way to Stirling?"

"I suspect we are," I answered, "though I would very much like to know what my mother babbled. It could contain a clue about what is happening with Sarah."

Robert pressed his lips together, refusing to make eye contact. "I should very much prefer not to repeat it."

Edwin's eyebrows raised, and an amused grin crossed his lips. "Oh? Was it salacious? Oh, please do repeat it, brother."

"You are incorrigible," Robert groused.

"Please, Robert," I asked, "I would very much like to know what she said, lucid or not."

Robert's eyes slid sideways to me for a moment, before he returned them to stare straight ahead. "She said…" He huffed and shook his head. "She said as an infant, you had been visited by a demon."

CHAPTER 29

"What?" I gasped.

"A demon?" Edwin repeated. "As in the bad sort with horns poking from their heads and long, pointy tails?"

Robert cocked his head in frustration. "No, Edwin, I took her to mean the good sort of demon, who rides unicorns and spreads cheer."

"I only asked a question. You needn't be so quarrelsome."

"Next time, ask better questions instead of infantile things."

"It is not infantile. Was she being serious or simply babbling on?"

"I fear her words to be true," I breathed, swallowing hard as I nearly choked on the words.

"Lenora, you mustn't take what she says seriously. She is mad."

"You said she seemed lucid."

"That is not what I meant," Robert retorted.

"Oh? Then what did you mean when you say my lucid mother admitted a demon visited me as a wee babe?"

"I meant..." Robert huffed, pressing his lips together as he shook his head. "I meant she did not babble or ramble. She spoke clearly and coherently. That is not to say the words she spoke were not tainted by the madness from which she suffers."

I sucked in a breath as I considered it. "No, I believe she was quite lucid."

"How can you, Lenora?" Robert questioned.

"Yes," Edwin chimed in, "you cannot remember such an incident."

"I do not remember it, no. But I feel...there is something familiar about these strange goings-on with Sarah. I wonder if she, too, is visited by a nefarious spirit."

"To what end?" Robert inquired.

"I do not know. Perhaps they are drawn to her because she can see them."

"Why could you not?"

I chewed my lower lip as I considered my husband's question. "I do not know. Though I would not discount my mother's words so easily. This incident alone may have caused her madness. Though I am quite certain she suffers from the same thing I do and that is the culprit. It certainly explains why she did what she did after my father departed for India."

"She mistreated you because she claims a demon visited you as a child?" Edwin questioned.

"Yes. She likely assumed the demon entered my body and that is why I saw the dead. She performed all manner of experiments in an attempt to expel the demon from my body."

"Oh," Robert said, rubbing his chin, "you may be correct. I do remember you telling me about them. The white bread and the odd ceremonies."

"Yes," I agreed with a nod, "I believe she considered it

some sort of cure. When it did not work, she made me someone else's problem."

Robert laid a hand on my knee and patted it. I smiled down at the gesture and patted his hand. With a sigh, I flicked my gaze out the window. "The information does little to find a solution for Sarah. I am only more troubled by the odd events. Did she say anything else?"

"Not really," Robert answered.

I prodded for more with a raise of my eyebrows.

"Her comments descended into madness after." Robert flung his hand into the air. "She claimed you to be possessed now and so on."

"Which we all know to be false," Edwin said with a definitive nod.

"Quite right," Robert agreed. "First intelligent thing you've said on this trip."

"Hardly the first, but certainly the best," Edwin countered.

"Certainly the first, and definitely the best. Remember, you are the one who has us on a wild chase to Stirling. Tell me, Edwin, what do you propose we do when we arrive in the city? Wander about in search of a dead woman?"

"I propose we go to her home."

"Ah, of course," Robert said with a curt nod, "and I am certain there will be some sort of sign announcing the home of the mass murderess, so we shall have no problems finding it."

"I know exactly where it is," Edwin said.

"You do?" I asked.

"Of course," he said. "They referenced it in her file."

"I see," I said as understanding dawned on me.

"Always know where a lady lives, so you may seek her when she is needed," Edwin responded with a cheeky grin.

Robert guffawed at the questionable saying, and I stifled a

chuckle. "Then I suppose we have a destination in mind. Though how do you propose we access the property?"

"Knowing Edwin, he will expect us to knock at the door and ask to be let in."

"Her sister lives there. We shall inquire after Mary. Surely, this will gain us admittance."

"How do you know her sister lives there?" Robert inquired.

"The file," I filled in. "Only Edwin would memorize a woman's address."

"And if needed, I shall use my charms on her."

"Heaven help us," Robert said, slouching a bit in the seat and crossing his arms as he flicked his gaze outside.

I did the same, staring at the scenery as it rolled past my window. "I am not certain what Mary meant when she said home, but I suppose this is a good start. I only hope to find out more once we arrive."

"Robert, the coach can drop us at Mary's address, and then perhaps you should go and find us lodging. I doubt we should push the horses to return us to Blackmoore tonight," Edwin said.

"Absolutely not. I shall not drop my wife on a street corner and race off to find a hotel."

"She will not be alone. I shall be with her."

"No difference to being alone. No, I shall stay with her for the duration to ensure her safety. We shall seek accommodations after. I have visited Stirling on two previous occasions, and I am certain the hotel I frequent shall have a space."

"Perhaps you should–"

"No," Robert said, his hand slicing through the air, "say nothing further on the subject, Edwin, I will not hear it."

Edwin pursed his lips and shot me an irritated glance. "Well, I suppose we all shall visit Mary's former home, then."

We rode along the remainder of the trip in relative

silence. After a long while, the countryside gave way to buildings, and we entered the city's limits. The carriage wound around to a rather derelict area of town.

Children, their faces smudged with dirt and clothes threadbare, played in the street. Rough men wandered home, their collars pulled high around the necks to keep out the cold.

Robert wrinkled his nose at the setting. "Perhaps we should return in the morning."

"No," Edwin said. "There is no harm in visiting her home now. If we cannot gain admittance, then we shall return in the morning."

Robert huffed, crossing his arms over his chest and flicking his gaze out the window as the shabby buildings passed. The carriage rolled to a stop outside a pub.

The crease between Robert's brows deepened, and his forehead crinkled. "Did this woman live in a pub?"

"Close," Edwin said. "Above it."

An angry sigh emerged from Robert as our door popped open. Edwin slipped past us onto the sidewalk and stared up at the building. "Anyone fancy a pint before we seek Mary?"

"Have you gone mad?" Robert asked as he helped me exit the carriage.

Edwin screwed up his face as he glanced at us. "I thought you may be thirsty. It's been a long journey."

"I will not drag Lenora into a rowdy pub. I cannot even fathom the atmosphere in such a place."

Edwin glanced through the window into the filled bar. "It hardly seems rowdy, but fine. Shall we?"

We passed through a small opening and climbed the stairs leading to the rooms above the tavern. A narrow, dimly lit hall stretched at the top. I swallowed hard as I stared down it, imagining my ghost wandering through it during her life.

I blew out a long breath, glancing at Edwin. "Which was hers?"

"You cannot tell?" he inquired.

"She is not clairvoyant!" Robert yelled.

"Well, I thought perhaps Mary was standing at her doorway, waving. How can I know?" Edwin asked as he led us down the hall. He glanced behind him, waving a finger in the air before he settled on a door. "This one."

He looked at me as though seeking confirmation.

I lifted my shoulders and shook my head. "Nothing. She is not here."

"She tells you to come to her home and then does not even show up to meet you? Seems rather rude," Edwin said as he banged against the door.

"I am not certain I can stand this partnership," Robert mumbled under his breath.

"He is still learning, dear. Try to be understanding."

Edwin stared at the door for a moment before he glanced up and down the hall.

"No one is here," Robert groused, "we shall return tomorrow morning."

"Just a moment," Edwin said, waving a finger in the air. He stalked away a few steps, peering into the darkness. "Hello?"

I squinted down the dark hall, barely making out the form of a woman huddled in the shadows.

As Edwin continued down toward her, she spun and hurried toward the stairs.

"Wait just a moment!" Edwin called. He broke into a half-run, chasing after her and sprinting past her to block the stairway. "Do you live here?"

The woman kept her eyes trained on the floor as she shook her head.

"Do you know someone who does?"

"No, sir," she answered.

"Do you often roam about in buildings you do not live in or know anyone in?"

The woman's features pinched, and she shook her head again. "Please, sir, I don't want any trouble."

"For God's sake, Edwin, let the poor woman go," Robert snapped at him.

I glanced from my husband back to the scene at the end of the hall. My eyes went wide. Standing next to the woman Edwin spoke with was the ghost of Mary McGinty.

We must have identified her correctly. Did she know this woman?

I approached them, my eyes flicking back and forth between the ghost and woman. "Wait," I called, "please do not leave."

I studied the sunken face of the alleged murderess, as well as the face of the timid woman trapped by Edwin. Similar faces. Similar eyes. Similar lips. Similar signs of difficulty.

My forehead wrinkled, and I stared at the living woman. "Are you Mary's sister?"

She snapped her gaze at me and shook her head. "No."

Edwin's face showed his surprise, his eyes wide and jaw dropping open. "Sister? Are you Mary McGinty's sister?"

"I am not. I have no idea what you're saying. I do not know that woman. Please, I must go."

She tried to shove past Edwin, but he blocked the way. "Just a moment."

"Help her," Mary whispered.

"Please," I said, grabbing hold of her arm. "We are here to help. Your sister sent us."

"I do not know of her. You have me confused."

I flicked a glance to Mary. "I do not believe so."

Her features pinched again, and her eyes welled with tears. "Please. If you are family members of one of the victims, I have nothing to say. Or if you wish to report on her in the papers, I will not speak to you."

"We are neither, but we do need to speak with you urgently," I said. "I promise we are not here for any other reason than to offer help."

"What sort of help?" she asked.

I bit my lower lip, wondering how to break this to her before I decided to postpone the news, hoping I would receive more information from Mary as the situation progressed. I glanced at the accused murderess before I swallowed hard and said, "Perhaps we could speak in private."

The woman's eyes flicked from me to Edwin, then to Robert.

"Please, we do not mean you any harm. I promise."

She nodded before leading us to the door Edwin had knocked on earlier and pushed inside. We followed her, entering the small one-room living space. My eyes scanned the space, finding Mary standing in a corner as her sister lit a lantern and set it on the kitchen table.

"Might I offer you something? Tea or the like?"

I shook my head and waved a hand in the air. "No, please, we are not here to impose."

"Why are you here? What did you mean when you said my sister sent you?"

I pressed my lips together as Robert placed a hand on my shoulder and squeezed.

"She sees dead people," Edwin spouted before I could say anything.

I shot him an incredulous glance, my jaw falling open. "Edwin!"

"What?" He sidestepped toward me and lowered his voice. "Oh, my apologies, should I not have said? I thought you usually were honest."

"You nitwit," Robert grumbled at him. "Please, sit down, dear lady. My wife will explain."

Mary's sister, face as white as a sheet, sank onto the rickety chair. It creaked as she shimmied around on it, her forehead wrinkling. She now eyed us with more fear than when we confronted her in the hall.

I approached the table as Robert pulled the other chair out for me. The woman sucked in a breath, leaning away from me, as I eased onto the seat.

I held out a hand in front of me, hoping to steady her nerves, though it only proved to make matters worse.

She leapt in her seat, twisting away from me. "Please, what do you want from me?"

"I am sorry for my brother-in-law's...less-than-eloquent explanation of the situation. Though he spoke the truth."

Her eyebrows lifted, and she stared at me for a moment. "You...speak to the dead?"

I nodded, pressing my lips together tightly.

She sucked in a deep breath, her gaze flicking to Robert, then Edwin, then back to me. "I...I am sorry. I have no money. If you hope to be paid a fee, I have nothing to give."

I shook my head. "No, I do not wish for a fee. I am not here to–"

"She is no charlatan," Robert said, crossing his arms over his chest. "She is not here to trick you out of your money. We have no need of it."

I shivered as the cold in the apartment sank into my bones.

"Are you cold, dear?" Robert questioned, rubbing my arms. "Might we build a fire? Edwin, perhaps you can–"

"No," the woman interrupted, bouncing from her seat.

"Dear lady, it is quite cold in here. Surely, you plan to build a fire for your evening."

She pressed her lips together as she sank into her seat again. "I haven't the money to purchase coal."

Robert's chin pulled back to his chest. "How do you plan to cook your evening meal?"

She motioned toward a basket on the table. "I will eat bread."

I glanced at the meager meal, noting the green edges of the days' old loaf. Perhaps this is how Mary hoped us to help. The poor woman had nothing to eat and no coal for heat.

"Edwin," Robert said, handing him a note, "buy coal and food."

Edwin slid his eyes sideways at his brother before his brow furrowed, and he shook his head.

Robert's eyes widened, and he waved the bill at his brother.

"You go," Edwin hissed. "I'm on a case."

"You are unbelievable. Fine, I will do what needs to be done. Do not leave this apartment until I return, and for God's sake, make sure Lenora is safe."

"There is no need for this," the woman began when I hushed her.

"There is every need. Please, whilst my husband retrieves the items, we may continue our conversation."

Robert disappeared through the door in search of heat and food, and I took a deep breath before continuing with my explanation.

"I suffer from a peculiar oddity that allows me to see and, at times, communicate with those who have passed on. I recently encountered the spirit of your sister, Mary. She *is* your sister, isn't she?"

The woman bobbed her head up and down, swallowing hard.

"She begged me for help. And after some prodding, she told me to go to her home. And when we encountered you, she appeared and asked us to help you. I can only assume she meant with your situation."

The woman's lower lip trembled as she dropped her gaze to her lap. "I...Mary..." She blew out a shaky breath and wiped a tear from her cheek.

"When Mary was accused, I was only fourteen. Our parents passed away when I was ten. She took care of me. And then she..."

"It must have been a great shock to you to find out what she did," Edwin said.

"She didn't do it," the woman shouted back, her eyes brimming with tears.

I reached for her, wrapping my fingers around her cold, trembling hand.

A sob escaped her. "Since she has been accused and... convicted, I have not been able to find much work. No one wants a murderess's sister around."

"How do you live? Eat?" Edwin inquired.

Her round green eyes glanced up at my brother-in-law, and a large tear rolled down her cheek. "I do odd jobs here and there when I can. Cleaning and the like. I'm a good girl. I don't do no prostituting." She lowered her head. "And sometimes I nip a bit." She snapped her head back up, a stubborn expression on her dirty features. "But only when I can't take the hunger no more."

My heart broke for the poor woman. Not much younger than me, her life had played out so differently from mine. I had been rescued from my terrible situation, while she had been plunged further into it. And through no fault of her own.

I glanced around the small room in search of Mary. Robert would purchase her a bit of food and some coal for the evening, but that would hardly fix the issue. What did

Mary expect of me? She had not entered the space, though. No sign of my spirit.

I met Edwin's gaze as I searched for her, and he raised his eyebrows at me. I let go of the woman's hand and stood, pulling him away a few steps. "I do not see Mary. But I cannot help but feel that one night's food is not what she hoped of us."

"What else can we do?" Edwin whispered.

I pressed my lips together as my brow knit tightly and I glanced over my shoulder. Her thin wrist flicked as she wiped away her tears and sniffled, using her sleeve to wipe at her nose.

"Do you imagine Robert would take her on in the maid's role Mrs. Thomson is seeking?"

"You plan to offer her a job?"

I shot him a pleading glance. "What else can we do? We cannot leave her here to die of starvation."

"She won't. She nips a bit if she needs it."

I shook my head at him before I started back toward the table. Edwin grabbed my arm and tugged me back. "Wait. What about the case? Is this the only reason Mary sent you? To make her sister a maid?"

"I doubt it. Though there is not much else I can do here tonight. Mary is not here. But perhaps we shall learn something from her sister."

"I shall speak with Robert about the position and signal you when we re-enter."

"I am sorry to thrust this upon you, but please make certain he agrees."

I took another step toward the table when Edwin grasped my arm again. "Wait! I cannot assure his agreement."

"You must." I nodded at him and stepped away, taking my seat across from the woman as Edwin scoffed at my request before he stalked to the door. With a last glance at me and pleading look, he stepped out into the hall to await Robert.

I opened my mouth to speak, realizing I did not know the girl's name. "I am very sorry, I do not know your name."

She sniffled and glanced up at me. "I thought Mary would have…"

"She did not. Often the dead are not as communicative as we wish. I would have preferred she tell me more, though she only drove me to find you."

The woman licked her lips and nodded. "Anne."

"Anne," I said with a nod. "Yes, Mary did mention that name. I did not realize she referred to you. Your sister implored me to help you. I suppose she knows the trouble you are in."

"It was not her fault. She was wrongly accused. I know she could not have done the things they said. Mary was the sweetest person."

"Why do the police believe she committed all those crimes? Have you any idea?"

The girl shook her head. "I do not know, though I do not believe she could have done it. She worked hard to give us both a decent life and keep food on our table. She could not have killed them."

My mind pondered if Mary could have killed them for money.

"I know what you're thinking," Anne said, "but she wouldn't do that to steal from them."

I nodded and reached for her hand. "Anne, I am hoping we can help you."

"You already have," she answered. Her eyes flitted around the room. "Bless you, Mary, for sending them! I shall have a full belly and a warm night."

"Unfortunately, Mary only appeared in the hall, though I shall pass the message along at the first opportunity."

The woman nodded as she sniffled again. "Please tell her I love her. And…miss her." Her voice broke at the last words.

I forced a smile onto my face and squeezed her hand. "Anne, I would like to make sure you have a warm bed and a full belly for more than just tonight."

"Oh, Madam," Anne said, her eyes wide, "I could not take more from you. Already I have taken enough charity from you. And if possible," she said, rising from her chair and wandering to a small desk. She fished inside the drawer for a scrap of paper, inkwell, and quill, "please leave your information, so I may repay you when I have the ability."

I shoved the paper away with a shake of my head, certain the frozen ink wouldn't allow me to leave any information behind anyway. "Anne, you said you did some cleaning to earn money?"

"Yes," she said with a nod, "though the work is difficult to find, as many people accuse me of…"

"There is no need to go further, I understand. Though I would like to put your cleaning skills to good use."

She tilted her head as confusion distorted her features. The door burst open, and Robert entered, his hands empty. Edwin followed behind him, puffing with exertion. He offered me a nod.

I glanced at Robert. "Lenora, may I have a word?"

I rose from the chair and stepped into the hall with him.

"Have you made the offer?" he inquired as he pulled the door closed.

"Not as yet. I was about to when you entered. Should I not?"

"I do not object. Edwin told me in no uncertain terms I was not permitted to object."

I grabbed his hands and squeezed. "She needs help, Robert. We cannot leave her to starve."

"I realize that. Though she is not the only person in this city in this position."

"But she is the only person in this city whose deceased sister has asked us to help. She suffers even after losing her sister."

Robert nodded, his lips forming a slight smile as his thumb caressed my cheek. "Your kindness is unparalleled. Well, let us finish this business so we may leave this freezing place."

I glanced down the hall, finding it deserted before I leaned in for a kiss. "Thank you, dear."

We re-entered the cold room. Edwin drummed his fingers against the table as Anne swept the floor with a shabby broom. I opened my mouth to address the woman when my eyes snapped to the corner. Lit by the dim lantern, I spotted another spirit.

CHAPTER 30

I sucked in a sharp breath as I stared into the eyes of a burly man sitting at the table in the seat Anne had previously occupied. My gaze lingered on him for a moment. Anne set her tattered broom against the wall, eyeing me sideways.

She likely wondered what had happened to the offer previously extended for the coal and food. I licked my lips and gave a final glance at the pale man sitting across from Edwin before I tore my gaze from him and stared into Anne's green eyes.

"Anne," I began before pausing.

She waved a hand in front of her. "You do not need to make an excuse. Times are difficult. I do not expect anything."

"It's not that," I said. "Though you are likely wondering why my husband did not return with anything promised. But there is a reason."

Anne clasped her hands in front of her, focusing on me. I flicked my gaze to the man still sitting in the kitchen chair. He stared straight ahead, unresponsive.

With a deep breath, I returned my stare to Anne. "Providing you with coal and one night's meal does not help you, really, does it?"

Anne's forehead pinched as she considered a response. "I am most appreciative—"

I held up a hand and shook my head. "I understand you would be appreciative of even one meal, though I do not believe this is the help your sister hoped for. After we leave, you will be stuck in the same predicament."

"I do not see what else is to be done, Madam," she said with a shrug.

I glanced at Robert, who offered a nod before I continued. "We currently require another maid in our household. We would like to offer you the position."

Anne's eyebrows shot toward her light hair. "Oh, that is very generous, madam, though I…I am not certain how I would travel to your home for work. Do you live within the city?"

I shook my head. "No, you do not understand. The position would require you to relocate. And includes a room and meals, in addition to pay."

Anne's lips parted as she stared at me. Her lower lip bobbled up and down for a moment as her eyes studied the floor. She creased her forehead and flicked her gaze back to me. "I…I do not know what to say."

Edwin leapt from his seat. "Say yes. It is an excellent position."

She shook her head, dropping her chin to her chest. "I cannot. I would bring scandal to your home."

"We live quite far. In the Highlands. Not many will know you there. Your reputation need not follow," I said.

Her brow furrowed, and she snapped her gaze to me.

"I realize it is quite far and a change from what you are accustomed to, but—"

"I will take the position," she blurted.

A smile spread across my face, and I nodded.

"Excellent decision," Edwin said. "Now, please, may we go to the hotel?"

"A wise idea. We shall catch our deaths in this cold."

Anne straightened her shoulders and peered between me and Robert. "Where shall I report, and at what time?"

I glanced at Robert, who stepped forward. "No, no, you shall accompany us tonight to the hotel. You may assist Her Grace for the evening, as she does not have her ladies' maid with her. Tomorrow, we make the trip to Blackmoore Castle. You shall begin work in two days' time. I hope that gives you sufficient time to settle into your new home."

Anne found herself speechless again, her eyes going wide. "C-castle?"

"Yes," I said, "Blackmoore Castle is our home. And now yours."

"But for tonight, we shall stay at a hotel, where we shall have warm beds and warm food," Edwin added, rubbing his hands together.

"Please gather your things. You shall travel with us now," Robert said.

The girl nodded, grabbing her lantern and hurrying across the room. She gathered a single garment from a ramshackle rectangular box and spun to face us. "Ready."

"There is nothing else?" Robert inquired. "We shall not return."

"No, nothing else."

I nodded before I shot a glance at Robert. "Might you settle Miss McGinty in the carriage and give Edwin and me a moment?"

"Of course, dear," Robert answered. He motioned for Anne to precede him into the hall. I offered him another nod as he swung the door shut.

Edwin's shoulders slumped as the door slammed. "What is it now? Why can we not go to the hotel and eat?"

"Really? What happened to your intrepid detectiving?"

"Detectiving? I do not believe that is a word. And to answer your question, my focus died when my stomach began to rumble and my fingers began to freeze." He wiggled his fingers at me before shoving them under his arms again.

"Good to know our business only goes by the whims of your stomach. We have important matters to attend to."

"Such as? Perhaps you can inform me." His eyebrows shot up, and his jaw dropped open. "Oh, is the ghost here?"

"A ghost is here. Not Mary's ghost."

Edwin drew his shoulders up toward his ears, his eyes scanning the space. "Where? Who?"

"I do not know, but he is just there." I pointed to the kitchen table.

Edwin stared in the direction I pointed, his features pinching. "There? Right near where I sat?"

I nodded.

"Was he there when I..." He inched closer to me and lowered his voice. "Was he there when I sat there?"

I nodded again. "Yes. He appeared when I re-entered with Robert. I do not know who he is or why he is here. He has made no attempt to speak."

"Do you think..." Edwin's voice trailed off as he stared blankly ahead at the chair.

"What?" I asked.

"Do you think...he was murdered here?"

"Yes, I would say he is a victim."

"Perhaps we should depart," Edwin answered.

"Edwin, we are here to solve a mystery. Do you not wish to solve it? It is the Fletcher Agency's first case."

"Perhaps we should start slowly and not solve it. Then we

shall have only success to look forward to and no reputation to uphold."

I pressed my lips together, shaking my head at my brother-in-law. "Really, Edwin. Don't be such a defeatist."

"I am not defeatist, but standing in a murderess's home with one of the victims lurking about makes me uncomfortable."

"You had better become accustomed to it, dear brother-in-law. Around me, there is normally at least one ghost lurking about, and they have often met a less-than-peaceful end."

Edwin frowned, swallowing hard as I stepped toward the man.

"Sir?" I questioned in a gentle voice so as not to frighten him.

He stared ahead at the wall, as though unable to hear me.

"Sir?" I tried again, this time catching his attention. "Hello."

"Mary?" he questioned, his gaze roaming around the room.

"No, Mary is not here. Can you tell me about her? Can you tell me about what happened to you?"

"Happened?" he asked.

My shoulders slumped a bit as I realized he did not know what had happened. At least not at the moment.

"What's he saying?" Edwin hissed behind me.

"He is confused."

Edwin huffed out a sigh. "Always. Why are they always confused?"

"He likely met with a very terrible end and has not processed it yet. But he seeks Mary." My eyes narrowed as I stared at him. Did he seek her because she was his killer, or did he seek her because she had provided him comfort before his murder?

"Perhaps you should remind him that he is dead and ask who did it."

"Hush, Edwin, I shall handle it the best way I can." I sank into the chair across from the man and offered him a consoling smile. "Sir, can you tell me your name?"

"Name? I'm Bill. Who are you? And where is Mary?"

I sucked in a breath, pleased to have received more than a one-word answer. Perhaps we would receive some of the information we sought. I recognized the name "Bill" as one of the victims.

"I have some rather terrible news for you, Bill. Mary is not here. And neither are you. Not really. You may not recall this, but you are dead."

His brow furrowed and he scrunched his nose as he stared down at the table. "Dead?" He snapped his gaze to me. "Had a bit of a nip at the old pub downstairs, did ya, dear?"

"No, I am not drunk," I responded as Edwin snickered behind me. I shot him an annoyed glance before I continued, "I...have the ability to see those who have passed. I am very sorry to say you are one of them. Murdered, unfortunately. Likely right in this very room."

"Are you pulling a prank?" Bill inquired. "Now, look, I like a good gag as much as the next bloke, but right now I'm hungry. And I'd like my meal. Now, where is Mary? I paid her good money to have a piping hot meal at the end of my day."

"I see. So, Mary cooked for you, did she?"

"Aye, that's right. Mary cooked for a good many of us what works in the area."

I nodded at the tale, consistent with what I'd read, and with the idea that Mary had easy access to poison her victims.

"Now, where is Mary with my meal?" he said, poking a finger at the table.

"As I explained, Mary will not be bringing you a meal—"

"Right, because I'm dead. And as I explained, I'm not in the mood for jokes."

"Please, Mr. Mitchell—"

"Wait a tick," he said, interrupting me as he threw his arm out to slice the air, "how do you know my last name? I didn't tell you that."

"No, you did not. Though I have explained why I would know it. You, Bill Mitchell, were murdered. You may not recall the events, as they were likely traumatic. But—"

I stopped as his eyes went wide and he scanned the room. He shook his head. "No. No, I—"

I offered him a sympathetic glance as the realization of his condition washed over him.

He locked eyes with me, his jaw falling open as he began to tremble all over. "Mr. Mitchell, *Bill*," I began, sliding a hand toward him when he disappeared from my sight.

My shoulders slumped and I breathed out a long sigh as I stood.

"Well? What happened? Did he tell you Mary killed him?"

"No," I answered, "he disappeared when he realized he was dead. Come along, we should not keep Robert waiting."

Edwin offered his arm. "Indeed, he is likely growing grouchier by the minute and shall take it out on me."

"You two are more alike than you realize," I said as I slipped my hand into the crook of his arm.

"Please, Lenora. You are becoming insulting."

I offered him a coy smile and head shake as we strode down the hall. "We should return tomorrow morning. Perhaps my second spirit will reappear to me in a better state and I can gather some information."

"You suggest it to Robert. He shall flog me if I even mention it."

"No, he will not," I said with a chuckle as we emerged onto the sidewalk and approached the carriage.

Robert popped out and ushered me inside where Anne sat, her dress clutched in her hands. Edwin collapsed into the seat next to her, and we set off for the hotel.

After a light supper, Anne helped ready me for bed. As I tugged on my dressing gown, Anne hovered in front of me. "That is all, thank you, Anne," I said.

She offered me a fleeting smile, clasping her hands in front of her. "Oh, Your Grace, I wanted to utter my thanks to you again. I…" Her words trailed off as she glanced around the room. "I have never seen such things as this. And have not had a meal or warm bed in quite some time. I cannot express my gratitude enough to you."

I smiled at her and grabbed her hands. "There is no need to express your gratitude any further. I am pleased you accepted the position and hope you love Blackmoore Castle as much as I do."

She offered a broad smile and nodded before she said a final goodnight. As she pulled the door closed, another individual revealed herself in the flickering candlelight.

CHAPTER 31

"Are you pleased?" I asked the ghost of Mary McGinty. "Your sister will be well-cared for now."

"Innocent."

"Yes," I said with a nod as I plopped onto the bed, "your sister is an innocent victim in all of this. But there is no more need to worry. She will not go hungry another night."

"Home," Mary said.

I offered her another nod and slid my feet under the sheets. "Yes, she will have a new home."

"Home," Mary repeated.

I smiled at her before blowing out the candles and settling back into the pillows. My eyes closed, and my last waking image was of Mary McGinty, standing at the foot of my bed.

I awoke later with a start. Mary no longer stood at the foot of my bed. Instead, she now hovered over me, her hands grasping my shoulders and shaking me.

"Home," she growled at me.

"What?" I squeaked out, though apparently not loud enough to awaken Robert, who slept soundly next to me.

"Home," she repeated before she flung back the sheets.

"No," I groused at her, tugging them back around me. "It is the middle of the night. I will not traipse about Stirling now. We plan to return tomorrow morning."

I yawned and rolled onto my side, settling into the pillows again. My eyes slid shut, and I began to drift off to sleep when the covers were wrenched from my grasp again.

"Stop that," I scolded. I lamented why the dead always seemed to need something in the middle of the night. "I already told you, we plan to visit your home tomorrow morning. And I shall—"

Mary interrupted my words by placing an icy hand over my mouth. "Now."

She released her frigid grip on me and pointed toward the door. My shoulders slumped. I recalled the last time I'd been whisked through the streets of Glasgow by Edwin's deceased friend in an effort to save his brother.

Perhaps a similar situation existed. Was someone dying? "Fine," I said with a sigh, reaching for Robert.

Before I could jostle him, Mary dragged me from the bed. I tumbled onto the floor with a thud. Not even this commotion awoke my sleeping husband, and before I could right myself, I found myself being dragged toward the door. I grabbed my slippers as my bottom slid across the floor in only my nightgown, then I desperately reached for my robe and snagged the corner with my fingers as I passed by it.

"Stop this," I said as we reached the door, which flung open on its own. I skidded over the threshold before the door slammed behind us.

In front of me stood a baffled-looking Edwin. "Lenora? What are you doing crawling about on the floor?"

"I am not crawling about," I began as I tugged the robe around my shoulders and shoved my arms through. Before I could explain further, I continued my sliding across the room.

"Help!" I cried, flailing my arms and twisting to glance behind me as Edwin followed my fugue with his eyes.

"Whatever is going on?" Edwin inquired as he rushed after me. The doors to the hotel suite blew open in front of us, and I barreled toward them. Edwin hurried after me, making it through just before they snapped shut.

"It is Mary," I said as I came to a stop on the thick runner in the hall. Edwin tugged me to my feet, and I finished securing my robe around me. "She is insisting we go to her home now."

"Mary McGinty shoved you across the floor?" Edwin questioned.

I shoved my slippers onto my feet. "Yes, after she dragged me from my bed. Robert is still asleep. I am fortunate you were not. You can accompany us."

"We should wake him–" Edwin began as I stumbled backward a few steps.

"There is no time. She is literally dragging me with her. Please, Edwin, hurry!"

Edwin glanced back at the now-closed door to our suite before racing after me. Within short order, we emerged on the streets of Stirling and continued to plod along to the rougher area of town, where Mary had resided.

"This is insanity," Edwin groused, his hands shoved firmly under his arms as we wandered through the chilly weather.

"Unfortunately, it is beyond my control," I said, my arm stretched in front of me as Mary dragged me along behind her. "At least I am not alone this time."

"This time?" Edwin questioned.

"Yes, remember during the investigation into Mr. Boyle's death, Gerard dragged me from my bed in the middle of the night and rushed me through the streets of Glasgow to his brother's home."

"At least it was in a better part of town," Edwin said, side-eying an alley where a suspicious-looking fellow loomed in the shadows.

"Indeed. I am most pleased about your presence. I am certain Robert will be, also, when he inevitably finds out about this."

"This is most inconvenient," Edwin said, his voice raised. "If possible, Mary, a more decent hour for shenanigans would be appreciated."

"My sentiments exactly," I agreed as we reached Mary's building. "Thank goodness. At least we can escape the chill."

"It is just as chilly in there," Edwin said as we stormed up the stairs.

"But there is no wind," I said with a shudder.

"You must be frozen," Edwin responded with a shake of his head. He tugged his overcoat off and put it around my shoulders as Mary flung the door open to her former home.

I thanked him as I snugged it around me before I ducked into the one-room domicile. Darkness filled the room, with only dim light filtering in from the window. I squinted into it before a lantern flared to life.

Mary held it up higher, her face illuminated by the flickering flames. It appeared diabolical from the shadows cast across it, but it was not this that made me gasp. It was the eight other figures in the room.

"What is it? Is Mary re-enacting a murder?"

I shook my head, my face searching the others in the room. I recognized one of them as Bill Mitchell, the man with whom I'd spoken earlier.

"Did she confess?"

My shoulders slid down my back as my brain pieced together the situation.

"Lenora," Edwin grumbled next to me, his hands shoved under his arms and shoulders slumped forward as he attempted to stay warm, "what the devil is going on? Why were we made to leave our lovely, warm hotel and dragged to this frigid room?"

"I am not certain yet, though I have my suspicions."

"Which are?"

"Mary is not the only spirit in this room," I answered. "It appears she has gathered all eight of the victims."

"What?" Edwin gasped. He inched closer to me, his eyes wide as they searched the room. "Do they seem angry?"

"No," I said with a shake of my head, my eyes never leaving Mary's. "But I still do not understand. Mary, why have you brought us here?"

"Innocent," Mary answered.

"What did she say?" Edwin hissed.

"She said 'innocent.'"

"Her or them?" Edwin questioned, his finger pointing randomly around the room.

I cocked my head as I stared at her rather sinister-looking features and narrowed my eyes. "I believe she means her."

"So, she has brought the victims to you to defend her?"

"I think so. This seems to be some sort of witness statement."

"Have the others said anything?"

"Not yet," I said with a shake of my head before I directed my comments to Mary. "Mary, are these men here to speak on your behalf? You have maintained your innocence in the crimes. Have you brought me to them to prove it?"

Her chin lowered and raised a few times.

"Yes," I said to Edwin, grasping his arm, "she means to prove her innocence!"

"That's all well and good, but it does little for her now. She is dead and gone. And I doubt you will be able to admit any of this into evidence, so her name will not be officially cleared," Edwin answered.

"No, but…" My voice trailed off as my eyebrows pinched. "The murderer is still at large. And could still be murdering others!"

"Good God, Lenora, you are correct! Though…why has there been no mention of more murders?"

"Perhaps the murderer switched his or her tactic. Or moved on," I mused.

I studied the men in the room. Perhaps they could easily clear this up. "I shall ask the victims. Perhaps they can identify the killer."

"Ask, but be quick about it."

I nodded and opened my mouth to inquire when I snapped my gaze to Edwin. "Why?"

"What?"

"Why must I be quick?"

"It is freezing here. Could she not have convened this group of victims within the confines of our warm hotel?"

I stared at him for a moment, fluttering my eyelids before I returned my gaze to the other spirits. "Might one of you be able to explain what happened to you?"

"What did they say?" Edwin asked.

"Nothing yet. No one beyond Mary has spoken."

As if on cue, Mary spoke again. "Murdered."

"Yes, I realize they were murdered. And not by you. But by whom? That is the question. We must know so that we may stop the real murderer from striking again."

"He gave me food. Then I fell asleep, but I was awake," one of the men said. His eyes stared straight ahead, as though unseeing. "And then he…"

"Yes?" I questioned. "Go on."

The man's pale lip trembled before he buried his face in his hands.

"What is it? What have they said?" Edwin whispered.

"One man explained that the murderer, a man by his claim, offered him food. He says he fell asleep but remained awake. He found himself unable to continue with his tale. It must distress him greatly."

"Asleep but awake? How is that possible?"

"I do not know, but perhaps it is a clue. File it away in your mind, so we may follow up on it tomorrow."

"Right," Edwin said with a mock salute. "Got it."

I raised my voice to the others in the room. "Can anyone else tell me more about this person? A man, I have gathered, and very much not Mary."

"Not Mary," another man said. He glanced over at her. "Poor Mary. She did nothing but help us. Cooking us good, solid meals after a long day of work."

"Then how did this man come to serve them?" I questioned. I glanced around at them before my gaze settled on Mary.

Her chin fell to her chest, and she did not make eye contact with me.

"Mary? How did the man come to serve them?"

"I dinnae know," she said as a tear slipped down her cheek.

"You did not know what?" I questioned.

Silence fell amongst our group. Edwin nudged me with his arm, his eyebrows wiggling. I shook my head, trying to indicate that I would inform him later. I did not wish to lose my chance to identify the murderer if possible.

"She dinnae know what he was doing. And once she did, it were too late for most of us," Bill answered.

"Threatened her sister, he did," another man said.

"Who? Who was this man?"

Mary sobbed for a few moments before she lifted her

beleaguered face. "Paid." The simple statement made her burst into tears again.

"'Twas not your fault, Mary," Bill said.

"That miserable sod took advantage of all of us," another man added, tugging at the beard on his chin. "He put something in the food Mary cooked. I could not stand. But I could see things, hear things. I could hear it when he broke my legs. And I could feel it when he busted my hands. And he did worse until I finally succumbed."

My stomach turned at the violence these men had endured at the end of their lives. I grasped onto Edwin as my knees wobbled.

"What is it?" he asked, wrapping his arm around me to steady me.

Bile crept up my throat as the sickening images of their deaths flitted through my mind. They had lived through horrors before their untimely ends. They had experienced awful things. But they had also seen the murderer. Could he be identified? I had to find out.

I swallowed hard and firmed my trembling lower lip. "Who did this? Can you name him?"

I waited with bated breath for one of the spirits to speak. After a moment, one of the men stepped from the shadows. "He called himself 'The Butcher.'"

CHAPTER 32

"'The Butcher?'" I repeated, my eyebrows pinching.

"The butcher did it? Is that our man?" Edwin asked, his fingers tightening around my arm.

"No," I said with a shake of my head. "He calls himself 'The Butcher.' One of the victims said those exact words."

"What is his real name?"

"I am not certain they know."

"How could they not know?" Edwin said with a huff. "Did they not meet the man?"

"I am not certain he introduced himself before murdering them, Edwin."

"How bloody inconvenient. Well, find out if they can tell us anything else."

I shot him an irritated glance, my lips pressing together as I shook my head.

"Is there anything else you can tell us about this man? Anything about how to locate him?"

I glanced around the room, noticing only five of the eight men remained. Another disappeared after my request. "No!" I cried. "Please do not leave. I need more information."

"Leave? Damn it!" Edwin shouted. "Do not let them go!"

"I have little control over it! And now another has left." I pressed a hand to my forehead. "Please, is there nothing else you can tell me? How can we find this man?"

"Horrible man. Did horrible things," another man said before blinking from existence.

"No," I lamented as one of the remaining three disappeared.

Two men remained along with Mary. I pressed my lips together, my hands curling into fists as I fought for more information. "Did this Butcher have another name, or can you give me any way to find him?"

Mary glanced up as one of the men wrapped his arm around her. Her glassy eyes stared at me as her features contorted. She spoke one word before they all disappeared. "Asylum."

"Ah!" I exclaimed as they all disappeared, the lantern going along with them and plunging the room into dim moonlight.

"What is it?" the room's only remaining occupant questioned.

"They're gone."

"All of them?"

"Yes," I said with a nod. "All of them."

"Did you learn the identity of the killer?" Edwin inquired, his voice strained.

"No," I lamented. "They did not give a name. I am not certain they knew it. I asked for a way to find him, and Mary said only the word 'asylum.'" I stalked away from Edwin, shaking my head and sinking into the kitchen chair.

"Asylum?" Edwin questioned.

"That is what she said in answer to my question about his identity." I let my elbow rest on the table and sank my forehead against it.

"What does it mean?"

"I don't know," I said with a sigh, the cold finally penetrating me, despite Edwin's jacket draped over my shoulders. My weariness grew, and I pushed myself to stand before I risked growing too comfortable in the cold seat. "We should go."

"Quite right. We'll catch our death in here." Edwin froze, pulling his lips back into a wince. "Sorry. Terrible choice of words, given the location."

"Quite," I said as I shivered, both from the cold and events that took place in this room. "Their deaths were...horrible."

My forehead crinkled as I stepped into the hall. The words of the victims rattled around in my brain. I had experienced much tragedy in my interactions with the deceased, however, this was likely one of the most tragic tales I had encountered.

My stomach turned again as the horrific details of their experiences paraded through my mind. How awful their final moments had been, likely realizing they would not escape and probably praying they would take their final breaths sooner rather than later.

"Those poor men," I murmured as we stepped into the street to begin our journey home.

"Yes. Murder is a horrible end, though I suppose at least it was quick."

I stopped walking, and Edwin continued for several steps before he twisted to face me. "What is it? Is something wrong? Oh, no, you haven't turned an ankle, have you? I fear I cannot carry you all the way to the hotel. I lack the stamina Robert has for such things."

"My ankle is quite fine," I said as I choked on a sob.

Edwin reached out, taking my arms in his hands. "Lenora, what is it?"

"Those men," I said, wiping at my cheek, "their death was

not quick. Not at all. They suffered. Horribly." My jaw trembled, and my teeth chattered, both from cold and from upset. "He drugged them in some manner, causing them to lose the ability to escape but remain awake. Then he…did horrible things to them. Inflicted dreadful wounds."

Edwin's posture stiffened as realization dawned on him. "I understand. And I am sorry you had to learn of such things." He pulled me closer to him, wrapping his arms around me as I choked out another sob.

I appreciated his warmth and sympathy. I pulled back, wiping at the tears that had stained my cheeks. "My apologies for going to pieces."

"Do not apologize. Remember, I am an expert at comforting women." He offered me a cheeky grin, his teeth gleaming in the moonlight.

I laughed in spite of myself. His terrible joke struck me at that moment, providing me some much-needed levity.

He squeezed my arms and offered me a tight-lipped but genuine smile. "I realize the tales they told you may have been disturbing, but the best thing we can do for them now is solve this case and bring the killer to justice."

I stared up at him, his face lit with the dim moonlight. In moments such as this, I could easily see why Tilly had fallen in love with Edwin. "Sometimes, Edwin, you are quite wise."

"Only sometimes?"

"Yes, only sometimes," I said with a chuckle, slipping my arm into the crook of his. "Do you want your jacket back? You must be quite cold."

"No. I am very cold, actually. But I would never allow you to catch a chill."

"Quite the gentleman."

"In truth," he said as we turned a corner and the wind smacked us in the face, "I fear the wrath of Robert if I return in full dress and you only in your dressing gown."

I gave him a light smack on the chest as I shook my head. Light began to streak the sky as the hotel came into view ahead of us.

"It is true. I may soon become one of the spirits that haunts you."

"Really, Edwin, you exaggerate."

"I do not!" he said as we traversed the halls, warming finally washing over us after being out of the wind.

We both chuckled as he unlocked the door to our suite and pushed it open, motioning for me to enter.

Robert stood inside near the fire, a brandy in his hand despite the early hour. He spun to face us, his jaw flexing. "Where the devil have you two been?"

"Pub," Edwin said. "A few early morning rounds to settle our nerves."

Robert's jaw dropped open, and his eyes widened. He snapped his gaze to me, his voice gruff. "Tell me he is joking."

"He is, dear," I assured him as I relinquished Edwin's jacket and warmed myself by the roaring fire.

"What a terrible jest. Not funny, Edwin. Not humorous in the slightest. I awoke and found my bed empty—"

"Tragic, though hardly surprising," Edwin answered, donning his jacket and spreading his hands in front of the fire.

Robert's posture stiffened, and his cheeks turned red.

I placed a hand on his shoulder. "Robert, we have had quite an unexpected turn of events, thanks to our latest troubled spirit."

"Oh?" he asked, tearing his eyes away from Edwin and glancing down at me.

"Mary tossed me from our bed in the middle of the night. By sheer luck, Edwin remained awake."

"Unsurprising," Robert grumbled.

"Rather a stroke of luck, if you ask me. I saw Lenora

being shoved across the floor and raced after her so she would not be alone."

Robert puckered his lips, studying the brandy in his glass. "I suppose I should be thankful for that."

"Indeed. And given our destination, you should be most pleased. That spirit dragged us back to that frigid little room we visited earlier to collect Anne."

"You went back to the McGinty home? In the middle of the night?"

"We had little choice!" Edwin groused. "I would have preferred her to convene the victims here in the safety and warmth of our hotel room, but apparently the woman had something much more dramatic in mind."

"Convene the victims?" Robert asked, his eyes wide. "Lenora, might you explain what the devil he is babbling about?"

"Please sit, dear," I said as I sank into a chair.

Robert perched on the edge of the armchair nearest mine, leaning toward me.

"Mary took us to her home, where all eight victims had gathered. She insisted on her innocence, and the victims corroborated her claim. Apparently, a man killed them. He used some sort of drug and…"

My voice trailed off as I cast my glance to the floor, wringing my hands. Edwin stepped toward me, placing a hand on my shoulder. "There is no need to go into it. Suffice it to say, they suffered a terrible death at the hands of a man they referred to as The Butcher."

"The Butcher? Then Mary McGinty…"

"Is innocent, and the murderer is still on the loose," I finished with a nod.

"And did any of them identify this butcher?"

"No," I answered. "When I pressed the few that remained

after the gruesome account of their demise, only Mary answered. She said asylum, then disappeared."

"Asylum?" Robert questioned.

"Yes." I raised my eyes to meet his. "It appears we shall have another stop there before returning home."

Robert's brow pinched. "Will she reveal more details there? Or is the killer there?"

"I am not certain. It could be either. In any event, we must return to the asylum as our next step."

"Bloody hell," Robert said as he leapt from his seat and sipped at his brandy. He twisted to gaze at me and Edwin over his shoulder, raising the glass toward his brother. "Thank you for accompanying Lenora. I am most grateful she did not endure this alone."

"I gave her my jacket so that she did not catch a chill," Edwin said, raising his chin.

"Very good," Robert said with a nod before facing me. "Perhaps you should rest, dear. We may delay our departure until you have slept."

"I prefer to go right away. I will rest in the carriage."

"Are you certain? You should not overtax yourself. Undoubtedly, the excursion into the night was quite an ordeal."

"I am all right. Edwin did an admirable job of caring for me," I assured him. "I shall fetch Anne, change, and be ready to proceed."

Robert gave me a tight-lipped nod, still clutching his brandy in his hand. "She is in the bedroom, awaiting you."

He was not pleased, though he realized the course of action was likely the best, lest I be dragged from my bed again, or worse, driven away in a wayward carriage.

I found Anne with her hands clasped in front of her, waiting near the dressing table in the bedroom.

"Good morning, Your Grace."

"Good morning, Anne," I answered as I sat down and she began to brush my hair.

"His Grace was terribly worried about you."

"Yes, I am certain he was. Anne, I have some news." I met her gaze in the mirror for a moment before she broke eye contact and focused on my hair. "Your sister visited me again last night. She is the reason I was missing this morning."

Anne's eyes shot back up to meet mine, an expression of horror on her features.

"She led me back to your former home, where she had gathered several of the victims she had been accused of murdering."

"But she didn't do it!" Anne shouted.

I held up a hand to temper the girl's outburst. "Yes, I know that. It became abundantly clear last night after speaking with the victims."

"Do you mean to say that…" Her voice trailed off, and she clutched a hand to her stomach.

"I spoke with them. A man killed them. Making it impossible for it to have been your sister."

Anne's lower lip trembled as tears filled her eyes. "Are you saying you believe she's innocent?"

"I do," I answered. "And I aim to prove it. It can do little for her now, but perhaps her soul can find some peace if we reveal the true murderer."

Anne nodded her head as she returned her attention to my hair. "Did they tell you who it was?"

"No, unfortunately not. Your sister offered one small clue when I inquired after the killer's identity. She said 'asylum.' We plan to return there today."

"Staghearst, do you mean?"

"Yes," I said with a nod. "It is where I first encountered your sister. Perhaps she will reveal another clue there. Have you any idea why she may lead us there?"

"No, none," Anne answered. "I visited her on two occasions there. She was terribly unhappy."

"I can imagine. Did she say why?"

"At first, she insisted on her innocence. She said the doctor was helping her work through something or another. She would not say what."

"And then?"

"On my second visit, she seemed worse. Agitated, frightened. She grabbed on to me and begged me to help her escape. She kept insisting they would hurt her there."

Anne's features pinched, and her face reddened as tears welled in her eyes. "I feel ever so guilty. I did nothing. And she died."

"It was not your fault," I said, spinning to face her. "You could not have known or done anything to remove her from the institution."

Anne's jaw firmed as she sought to control her emotions. She offered a tentative nod before she retrieved my dress. After changing, I presented myself in the sitting room, and we gathered our things and proceeded to the carriage for another long day of riding.

Robert hired another coachman to take Anne to the castle, along with a note explaining her presence. After settling the matter, he climbed into our conveyance and plopped into the seat next to me.

"Haven't you fallen asleep yet?" he inquired.

"No," I answered.

He snapped his gaze to Edwin. "No doubt you have been babbling at her and keeping her awake."

"I have not!" Edwin insisted, holding his hands in front of him as we lurched forward. "I haven't said two words."

"It is not Edwin," I answered as the buildings rolled past the carriage window. "It is something Anne said this morning."

"Oh? Has she displeased you in some way? You should have said before I sent her on."

"No, no, nothing like that," I assured Robert. "She said she visited Mary twice whilst she stayed at the asylum. Once where she seemed normal and believed the doctor to be helping her. But on the second visit, she seemed agitated and afraid."

"Do you believe her murdered, as was rumored?" Edwin questioned.

"I believe something caused her to change abruptly."

"Perhaps it was not abrupt," Robert conjectured. "How far apart were the visits?"

"I do not know," I said with a sigh, "I suppose I should have asked. Though Anne seemed to find it a marked change with no explanation. Something changed. But what?"

We rode along in silence for a few moments before Edwin spoke up. "When you asked Mary about the identity of the killer, she said asylum."

I bobbed my head up and down.

"Do you believe he visited her? Threatened her?"

"Perhaps. Do you believe we could gain access to the visitor's log?"

Edwin tipped his chin up and grinned at me. "Leave it to me, Lenora, I shall find a way."

Robert shuddered next to me, shaking his head. "That sounds lurid and obscene."

"I shall do what is necessary."

Robert waved a hand in the air. "Please, say no more. There is a lady present."

I smiled at the bickering, realizing it had become less vicious and more playful. Progress, I thought as I let my head rest against the wall and closed my eyes.

* * *

A violent rocking awoke me. I flailed my arms out as the carriage swayed fiercely.

"What's happened?" I questioned, glancing to my side. My jaw fell open as I found the seat empty. "Robert?"

I glanced across from me, finding that seat empty as well. "Edwin?"

My heart raced as quickly as the carriage when I realized I was alone. I glanced out the window, finding the coachman's perch empty also. The horses galloped at full speed, flying uphill through the dense fog at breakneck speeds.

I glanced out the window, attempting to make out my location, when my blood ran cold. High on the hill, Stagheart Asylum loomed. "Again?" I questioned.

My mind wondered how the carriage had managed to get away from Jones, Robert, and Edwin, though I realized Mary had her tricks. She seemed determined to bring me to the asylum.

Before I could reach it, however, the door flung open. Wind blasted into the space, and a ghostly arm reached inside.

"Mary!" I cried as she leaned into the carriage. "Stop this carriage at once! I shall go to the asylum, but you do not need to nearly kill me!"

She clamped her icy fingers around my arm and tugged.

"What are you doing?" I shrieked as she pulled me toward the open door.

"Stop this!" I screamed as wind buffeted my face. Mary's strength overwhelmed me, and I teetered on the edge before she yanked me forward and let go of my arm. I fell head over heels, rolling down the embankment before I came to a stop.

I groaned as I pushed myself off the cold ground and rose to my feet, dusting off my dress. The carriage shot away from me with a sneering Mary still clinging to the outside.

I took a step toward the road, which still swirled with

dust kicked up from the horses' hooves, but lost my footing. I continued to slip backward until I found myself in a familiar area.

I scanned the location, recognizing it as where I had emerged from the underground caves the first time I had traversed them.

With a deep breath, I located the opening I'd exited from previously and stepped inside. Warm light glowed from within the chamber. I spotted the well in the middle. Giving it a wide berth, I scurried across the room and into the passage leading to the water chamber.

Warm light glowed from within it, too. A figure loomed over the water chamber, his head covered with a hood.

My pulse quickened as I spotted them. My foot scraped across the floor as I stumbled forward. The figure twisted to glance over their shoulder before darting away through the other exit. "Wait!" I called.

As I hurried after them, I glanced at the pool of water. Something lay under the surface. I slowed as Mary's voice echoed in the chamber. "Murder."

I fell to my knees and reached inside, my fingers clasping the metal container and hauling it upward. Fabric floated in the water as I tugged.

"My God," I gasped, "someone is inside!"

I rose to my feet, straining to tug the heavy container from the water. As it reached the surface, the identity of the victim became clear. The metal crate slipped from my fingers as I stumbled backward, my eyes wide and a chill running down my spine as I stared at my own face.

CHAPTER 33

I screamed as my eyes snapped open. I stared at two startled faces as the carriage swayed to and fro.

"Lenora! Are you quite all right?" Robert inquired.

I pressed a hand against my chest as I sucked in a deep breath and nodded. "Yes," I gasped out. "Merely a nightmare."

"Another?"

"About Tilly?" Edwin added.

"No," I said with a hard swallow, shoving myself straighter in the seat. "No, not about Tilly."

"What was it, dear?" Robert asked, snaking an arm around me.

"Me," I responded, staring blankly ahead.

"What?"

I recounted the tale of my untimely demise in the underground pool. Robert shook his head, drawing me closer to him. "I certainly hope this is soon resolved. It is becoming too much on you."

"Do you suppose Mary was, indeed, murdered, as was the rumor, and it occurred in the pool below the asylum?" Edwin inquired.

"Must we discuss this when Lenora has endured such a fright?" Robert groused at him.

"Quite all right, dear," I assured him. "And, yes, I am beginning to wonder if this was the case. But how? How did Mary come to be in those chambers?"

"We stumbled upon them once. Perhaps she did, too."

"We had unfettered access to the doctor's chambers to do so. Mary would not have. Nor free access to the music room." My brows knit as I swayed with the moving conveyance.

"Perhaps I am incorrect."

"Wouldn't be the first time," Robert said with a flick of his eyebrows.

"No, I do not believe you are. She has said murder multiple times to me, often whilst in the underground chambers. Twice I have seen a body in the water. And once in the odd metal contraption."

Silence fell between us as we ruminated on the meaning of the clues thus far. Unmasking Mary's murderer would likely reveal the culprit of the other slayings. We needed only reach the asylum and track down the information.

I fidgeted in my seat as the large structure appeared, looming over us on the hill. My nerves refused to allow me to relax as we climbed toward it. Robert would enter first and request a visit with my mother. Edwin and I would then proceed inside and determine the best way to seek out the visitor's log. Edwin remained convinced a wink and smile would do the trick. Given his track record with women, I was inclined to agree.

My mind went over the potential events that might unfold over and over until the carriage slowed to a stop.

"Good luck," Robert said as he stepped to the gravel drive below. He paused for a moment before squeezing my hand

and flicking his gaze to Edwin. "For God's sake, Edwin, take good care of her."

Edwin offered a solemn nod in promise to his brother. My leg bobbed up and down as we waited several minutes before climbing out and crunching our way across the drive and into the large entryway.

A nurse sat behind the large desk. The visitor's guide lay open on the desk in front of her. I licked my lips as we approached the desk and I spotted Robert's signature as the last entry, with my mother's name as the patient to be visited.

"Hello," Edwin said in a husky tone.

"Yes?" the nurse answered.

"We are visitors," Edwin answered, flashing a toothy grin.

"Sign the book. Which patient are you here to see?"

"Uh," Edwin said, waving at me to deal with the book, "do you receive many visitors here? It seems quite lonely." He broadened his smile, leaning onto the desk as I inched the book closer to me. My hands trembled as I flicked a few pages backward, hoping to find Mary's name by luck.

"What are you doing?" the nurse asked, leaping from her seat.

"Oh," I said, feigning confusion, "I seem to have lost the page."

The woman yanked the book back and flipped to the appropriate page before slamming it down on the desk. The inkwell rattled across the marred wood.

"My apologies," I said, "I just feel so…weak." I flung myself toward Edwin as I closed my eyes and faked a fainting spell.

Edwin caught me, breaking my fall. He shouted at the woman, panic lacing his voice. "Oh, my God, Lenora! Do something! Help her! Fetch a toddy or tea or a doctor or something."

Her footsteps scampered across the tile, and a door

slammed. I snapped my head up, grasping the desk to right myself and grabbing the book.

"Let's go!"

"Lenora! What in heaven's name is going on? You nearly fainted!"

"I did not," I said, grasping his arm and hurrying toward the front door. We rushed out into the chilly air, and I climbed into the carriage, with Edwin following me.

"Can you now explain what happened?"

"You were failing miserably," I said as I paged through the book in search of Mary's name. "I improvised."

"Improvised? Lenora, I thought you were ill!"

"I know. It worked wonders to get rid of the nosy nurse. Now, quickly, help me scan these pages for Mary's visitors."

Edwin stared at me for a moment before he nodded and squeezed into the seat next to me. We made quick work of the book, finding Mary's name only twice, with Anne as her visitor in each instance.

"Mary had no other visitors," Edwin said as I flipped the book closed.

"No. So who killed her? How did they gain access?"

"Perhaps..."

I flicked my gaze to Edwin.

"Perhaps Anne," he said with a shrug.

"No," I answered with a shake of my head. "That does not ring true, based on her behavior."

"Perhaps she feels guilty."

I sucked in a breath and shook my head again. "No. The doctor's records indicated her death on the twentieth of October. However, her sister visited her last in August. She could not possibly have killed her.

"Check the twentieth again, perhaps we missed an entry."

I rummaged through the book again, finding the appropriate date, and traced the list of visitors with my finger. "No. No visitors for Mary."

"And only two visitors in total. Could one of them be the murderer?"

I read both names aloud before shaking my head. "No, both women."

"We should not assume Mary's murderer is a man."

"But under our working theory, Mary's murderer is The Butcher. And we know him to be a man. It seems unlikely they are different people."

"Is it, really?" Edwin asked. "Perhaps another patient or one of these visitors had a personal connection to one of the victims and he or she killed Mary."

"Mary did not seem to indicate that. And when asked about where we could find the murderer, she said asylum."

"*Her* murderer, or *the* murderer?" Edwin questioned.

I huffed and hugged the book closer to my chest. "I have no idea. This is becoming more and more difficult to wade through. And I have yet to make sense of whatever may be happening with Sarah or Tilly."

"We need more information. Perhaps we can find more in the patient records."

"How will we get inside? We have likely made an enemy of the nurse charged with keeping the visitor's log."

"You underestimate me, Lenora. Leave it to me."

"We've tried that. It did not work."

"Oh, ye of little faith. I was only half-trying before."

I handed the book back to him. "All right. You gain access to the doctor's office and search through the records for any clues. I shall go to the caves and seek Mary."

"Are you mad? Robert will kill me if I allow you to traipse about on your own."

"You were not given the choice," I said. "Good luck, Edwin."

I departed from the confines of the carriage and hurried down the drive toward where I had emerged when in the underground chambers. I half-walked, half-slid down the hill and searched the fog-laden area for the entrance.

I slipped inside, turning sideways as I navigated the narrow passage and entered the well room. Torches burned brightly inside. My knees wobbled as I recalled my frightening dream. "Only a dream," I told myself before raising my voice and calling out to Mary.

Sobbing reached my ears. I held my breath, scanning the space for any sign of my spirit.

"Mary?" I called again.

The sobbing intensified, seeming to come from the water chamber. I crossed the room, giving the well a wide berth, and squeezed into the passage across the space.

Light shone from the water chamber and movement caught my eye as I entered the space. A woman lay near the pool, soaked through. I raced to her and knelt beside her, patting her cheeks.

"Madam? Madam! Are you all right?"

I stared at her chest, trying to detect if it rose and fell when a shadow loomed over me. I turned too slowly, only catching sight of an object swinging at me. Pain bloomed across my forehead before the world slid from my view and I slumped to the floor.

* * *

My eyelashes fluttered open. My head ached, and my stomach rolled with nausea. Bile crept into my throat, and I swallowed it as I struggled to keep my eyes open. Movement floated around over me.

I realized I lay on my back. I attempted to sit up, but my

head smacked against something cold and hard. I blinked my eyes until the bleariness disappeared. I gasped in a breath as I found myself trapped inside a flat metal cage.

"Hello, my dear Duchess," a voice said. I recognized it but could not place it for a moment. A hooded figure stood across the room. "It seems we have had a bit of a misunderstanding."

"Misunderstanding?" I repeated weakly.

"Yes," the voice answered, throwing back his hood. My heart skipped a beat as I recognized Dr. Merriweather.

"Doctor?" I questioned. My aching head struggled to piece together the facts. Or perhaps it refused to. In either case, comprehension escaped me as he knelt on the ground next to me, attaching a large hook to the metal cage.

"Yes. It seems you felt you had the right to sneak about my asylum. But you do not."

"I–I am searching for someone. A patient was murdered. And the murderer committed several other crimes."

He smiled down at me, but his expression offered me no comfort. Instead, it sent a chill down my spine. "Yes, I know you are. But I cannot let you find him. Or rather…me."

"You?" I squeaked.

The man smiled again before standing and retreating across the chamber. "Yes, my dear duchess. Ironically, I ended up in the care of this asylum after an incident with a fisherman of all things."

He tugged on the opposite end of the chain, and it tugged taut against the hook. I lifted in the air and swung in the air for a moment. The movement turned my stomach, and bile crept up in my throat again.

"Imagine my surprise when I found Mary. She knew me, of course. I had a good run experimenting on all those fellows."

"Experimenting?" I cried. "You killed them!"

"Eventually, yes. But before that, I experimented. It's fascinating how much the human body can sustain before the will to live dies."

I gulped in a sob at his words.

"And I aim to find out just how far. When I realized how easy it would be to kill the real Dr. Merriweather and the few nurses he had in his employ and replace them with my own people, I had to do it. This population gives me an endless supply of people for my experiments."

He secured the chain to a hook on the wall before he wandered over to me. I hung suspended from the ceiling. My eyes slid sideways as a tear rolled toward my hairline.

He raised a finger in the air, his hooked nose giving him an even more sinister look at this angle. "You know, even after having an eye gouged out, the will to live remains strong."

Another sob escaped me, and I flicked my gaze to the ceiling as my fingers searched for a way to open the container and escape.

"Irene, the woman I put into the metal container, which you may have stumbled across on one of your excursions down here, came out fighting even after having an eye poked out. Amazing, really." He grinned, shaking his head as he stared into space as though recalling a special moment.

He paused for a moment before he sucked in a deep breath. "I would love to experiment with your limits, as you are a most interesting woman. But I'm afraid I don't really have the time. So, I will merely need to drown you."

"No," I cried as I pushed against the metal.

"Oh, I completely agree," he said, stalking across the room. "I'm as upset as you are. More's the pity. But I am sorry, my dear duchess. I must be off to convince your husband that you have, once again, wandered off."

"He will not believe you."

"Hmm, I think he will."

I rattled the cage but was not able to shove it open. "He knows about these chambers. He will find the body."

"Hmmm, perhaps. Then I shall have to kill him, too."

A screech escaped me as I kicked my feet. He aimed to leave my children parentless. I could not allow it to happen. I blinked the tears from my eyes as I searched for a way to open the container.

My fingers found a hinge. I grasped hold of it and tried to force the bar from it.

"Goodbye, Duchess!"

The chain rattled as he tugged it from the wall and let it go. I plunged into the icy waters below, smacking against the stone floor. The jolt forced the air from my lungs.

I struggled to pull the hinge apart, but my fingers became numb from the cold. My lungs burned. I tried to push against the metal but could not move it.

Suddenly, the surface came closer. Air smacked me in the face as I emerged from the water. I gasped in a breath, coughing and choking.

"Apologies. I could not resist having just a bit of fun. Down we go."

I gasped in a breath as I fell backward, plunging into the pool again. I continued to struggle to try to release myself while underwater. The surface came closer again, and I rose into the air. Water dripped from my drenched form.

"Again!" The Butcher shouted, his tone bordering on amused.

Water enveloped me, surrounding me before I popped back out. Barely able to get my breath, he let the cage fall back into the water with a slap.

His face loomed over the pool as my lungs began to burn. He waved at me with a smirk before he disappeared from my sight. I struggled to free myself or lift the cage, but I found myself unable to escape.

Water shot up my nose as I fought the urge to inhale and lost. My nostrils burned as my lungs did the same. And my vision began to close to a pinpoint.

CHAPTER 34

My body shook all over. Somewhere in the distance, a voice called to me. "Lenora!"

I tried to answer but found myself unable. What had happened to me? Memories flooded back into my mind. I recalled the burning in my lungs and nose as water surrounded me.

I died. I had drowned, my mind concluded.

"No, Lenora, you do not get to do this to us," a voice wracked with sobs said.

Something smacked into my chest hard. I tried to suck in air but found it difficult. Another blow landed against my bosom. Then another. And another.

A sputtering cough shot from my lips, along with warm water. I rolled, and a hand patted my back.

"That's it, Lenora, that's it."

My eyes fluttered open as I gasped in air and tears flowed freely down my cheeks. "Edwin?" I croaked.

My body rolled backward, and the smiling face of Edwin hovered over me. "Indeed. I have saved you. I am your savior."

Still weak, I tried to reach for him, but my arms felt like lead. He grasped my hand as I tried to lift it and squeezed. "We are even," I breathed.

Edwin smiled at me again as Dr. Applebaum rushed to us and dropped to his knees. "Is she all right?"

"Barely," Edwin told the man. "I found her in the pool of water. She spit out quite a bit of liquid."

Dr. Applebaum grasped my cheeks in his hands and stared into my eyes for a moment before taking my pulse. "Try to sit her up."

Edwin eased me up, keeping a firm hold of me.

"Are you feeling weak? Dizzy? Lightheaded?" Dr. Applebaum inquired.

"No," I answered, clinging to Edwin tightly. "I wish to go."

"Wait, we should not move—"

"Please, Edwin," I said, my eyes pleading with him. Dr. Merriweather had been The Butcher. He had killed the former doctor and his associates. Had Dr. Applebaum been one of his compatriots?

"All right, Lenora. Though you are safe now."

I grasped the side of the water trough that had nearly been my final resting place to steady myself as I prepared to stand when Edwin scooped me into his arms. "I've got you."

He carried me through the small corridor and up the stairs toward the music room. "I thought you hadn't the constitution for this?"

"You have left me with little choice. That stunt was nothing short of unbelievable, Lenora."

"My sincere apologies for nearly drowning."

"And on my watch! Robert would kill me, and then we would have both been dead." He shot me another cheeky grin as he passed through the open panel into the music room.

Given the rather gloomy circumstances and my nerves

remaining on edge about what I would find after my rescue, I appreciated his levity.

Robert rushed forward the moment we entered the room, worry etched into his dark features. "Lenora! My God, what happened?"

"She is all right," Edwin said, passing me off into my husband's arms.

My eyes flitted around the room, finding Dr. Merriweather, or whatever his real name was, sitting in handcuffs, with an officer looming over him.

"You are soaked through! Did you fall into water?"

I shivered as I nodded, unable to articulate the events that had nearly robbed me of my life.

"Quickly, a toddy at once!" Robert shouted at a woman in a dirty peach dress.

"No, wait," I said as he settled me in a chair and continued to shout orders for a fire to be made. He ripped off his overcoat and tossed it over me.

"She nearly drowned, thanks to this character," Edwin said. "Though I got to her in time."

Robert nodded at him as he tucked the jacket around me. "Thank heavens. Good work, Edwin."

I lifted my eyebrows at the sentiment. My almost-death had caused my husband to be civil to his brother for the first time in ages. Edwin brimmed with pride, beaming like a peacock spreading his tail feathers.

"And now, thanks to the Fletcher Agency, this fellow will be going to jail for a very long time," Edwin said, wagging a finger at a grumpy-looking Dr. Merriweather.

"And the asylum patients will receive the proper care they should have received from long ago," Dr. Applebaum chimed in, nudging his glasses up his nose.

"How did you figure it out?" I asked.

"Simple," Edwin answered. "I reviewed the patient notes,

starting with Mary again. The handwriting changed, and the notes became quite odd. We discussed that the first time we read her file."

I nodded at him as I drew Robert's coat closer to me and shivered again. "Yes, I recall."

"I checked the others, and all were the same. All of them changed handwriting and note-taking style at the same time. It indicated to me that a second individual began treating them.

"As I read through the third file, something struck me. The notes mentioned 'water treatment' to 'cleanse the brain.' I recalled you told me about the water pit. And about how you had been presented with bodies inside it."

"He killed more than one person in that water, I am certain," I answered.

Edwin nodded. "Mary among them, I would wager since I found a mention of water treatment in her file, too. Then it struck. Your dream. About finding yourself in the water. It was a warning. The moment I realized, I sought Robert to fetch the police and found Dr. Applebaum to seek you out."

"And not a moment too soon," I said as I eyed Dr. Applebaum warily.

"Don't worry, he is a real doctor," Edwin said. "He came months after all this."

"Indeed," Dr. Applebaum said. "I began to suspect, though I had been told Dr. Merriweather's methods were unique and advanced. I never imagined..."

"But how did you do it?" I asked the man handcuffed in the chair.

"Simple," he answered. "The real Dr. Merriweather was not well-liked. I convinced the others to overthrow him. He and his staff were the first to die. Any other nurses hired on after were none the wiser."

"And a few of the nurses were former patients," Edwin added. "Who would believe a patient here if they suggested this, though? They would merely be thought insane and ignored."

I shook my head at the situation. The man had easily taken advantage of so many helpless people, my mother among them.

"Did you try your experimental treatments on my mother?" I questioned him. "Has she been subjected to your brain cleansing or other foul methods?"

"Oh, no, my dear," The Butcher said. "I dare not. Something is terribly wrong with that woman. Something I cannot fix."

"That will be enough," Robert huffed at him before returning his attention to me. "I think we had better stay at the hotel. The trip home will be far too taxing on you after this."

"No," I pleaded, "please. I want to see the children. I want to be home."

"Lenora, you'll catch a chill in that soaked dress. The carriage is not at all warm."

"I do not care."

"We may give you blankets for Her Grace," Dr. Applebaum suggested.

"Yes, that sounds lovely. Thank you."

After a bit of bickering, Robert relented, but only after insisting I change into a former patient's belongings. I sat in the dress of Mary McGinty with blankets wrapping me like a mummy as we pulled away from the asylum.

I watched the lights blazing from the windows disappear as we journeyed toward our home. Mary McGinty's name had been cleared and the real culprit caught. The Fletcher Agency had solved its first rather odd case.

The fame of it would propel us to be sought after for

many investigations in the future. Though the two I planned to tackle next were Tilly and Sarah.

My mind dwelled on them both as we rumbled along the road. Why could Tilly not visit Blackmoore? Who prevented her? The odd experience I'd had suggested someone stopped her. But why?

And then my dear daughter. Visited by some unknown spirit at her crib. My mother had indicated this had happened to me, too. Visited by a demon, she had told Robert. Was it true, or merely one of her fantastical tales?

Was my little daughter being taunted by a demon at her bedside?

I aimed to find out whilst Edwin enjoyed the fame of being a well-known detective. The thought of Edwin parading about and informing everyone of his conquest, along with the rhythmic wobbling of the carriage, sent me to sleep.

I awoke as Blackmoore Castle appeared on the hill ahead of us, drenched in moonlight. The sight brought a smile to my face as the carriage tilted backward and we began the climb to it.

I happily shed my blankets and hurried into the house to seek out my two children. After the frightening experience, I wanted to hold them both in my arms.

I did not need to search far. As I pushed through the doors into the enormous entryway, I stumbled into a chaotic scene.

Buchanan, our butler, held a crying Sam. The tall man did his best to quiet the child, to no avail. Little Sarah mewled in Nanny West's arms, fussy but not as fretful as poor Sam.

"Your Grace," Nanny West said, her eyes going wide as she spotted me.

Sam swung his head in my direction, spotting me. Fresh

tears streamed from his eyes, and he reached for me, leaning as far as Buchanan would allow him.

I scooped him into my arms and pressed him close to me. "There, there, darling. Whatever is the matter?"

"I am sorry for this scene, Your Grace. I could not do a thing with him. He insists he is too frightened to sleep in his bed. And insisted I bring Sarah along from her crib. Protecting her, he said."

Robert strode in with Edwin. Robert's forehead was crinkling. "What's all this?"

"Something frightened Sam," I said before Nanny could rehash the entire story to him and make another apology. I twisted toward the woman, still holding Sarah. "Give Sarah to His Grace. We shall settle them. I'm certain it is merely our absence that has riled them."

Nanny West offered me a dubious glance but passed the infant off to Robert. We took the children upstairs to my suite, Edwin in tow.

I settled on the chaise with Sam, sitting him on my lap as Edwin squatted in front of him. "What's all this?" he asked.

Sam twisted to face me, and I offered him an encouraging nod. "What has upset you, darling, tell us?"

"I saw Sarah's crib shaking again."

I shot Robert, who had settled into an armchair across the room with a now-sleeping Sarah, a glance.

"How terrible," Edwin said. "It must have been quite frightening."

Sam nodded as I stroked his dark curls.

"Good thing you were there to protect your sister, my boy. You are very, very brave."

"Indeed," I added. "We are all so very proud of you."

"But Mummy, why does it shake?"

"I do not know, darling, but I will find out."

"Please do not make me go back to bed."

"No, of course not, darling. Not tonight. You and Sarah will spend another night with Mummy. But you must promise to sleep."

"I promise," he said with an earnest nod, his gray eyes, so similar to his father's and uncle's, staring up at me.

"And it is well past your bedtime already. Now, let's get you cozy in Mummy's bed for sleep."

"No!" Sam shouted, flinging his arms around my neck.

"Sam, enough nonsense. Do as your mother says," Robert chided gently.

Sam released his grip on me and wiped at his nose. "All right."

I settled him under the covers with a kiss, and within minutes he fell asleep. I returned to the sitting room, pulling the doors slightly closed as I rejoined Robert and Edwin.

"Is this dangerous for them?" Edwin inquired.

I shook my head. "I do not know. But I will find out. I am beginning to wonder if the voice I heard in the well is connected to both this and Tilly. And if the key I found has something to do with that"

"What is the meaning of it in your estimation?" Robert questioned.

I cast my gaze downward for a moment as I weighed my answer. After a breath, I raised my eyes to his. "I wonder if it has to do with the demon that visited my bedside as an infant."

"Lenora," he said with a shake of his head, "your mother may not even have the story correct."

"Correct or not, obviously I have a unique ability. And I very well could have been visited by a nefarious spirit in my youth. Could that nefarious spirit be what is disturbing the children? And what is preventing Tilly from reaching us?"

"How can we find out?"

"Simple," I answered. "We shall investigate."

"Our second case," Edwin said, cocking his head.
I offered him a slight smile and nod. "Our second case."

The details of what would become the Fletcher Agency's second unofficial case, dear reader, are a story for another time. Until then, be well.

Yours, Lenora

THE END

A NOTE FROM THE AUTHOR

Dear Reader,

Thank you for reading this book! *Asylum to a Duchess* is the third in Lenora's series. Lenora is a character I love to write. I enjoy her unique view on life and her forward thinking in an olden time. I especially love the newfound friendship with Edwin.

I hope you enjoyed reading the story as much as I enjoyed writing it! If you did, please consider leaving a review and help get this book and series into the hands of other interested readers!

If you'd like to stay up to date with all my news, be the first to find out about new releases first, sales and get free offers, join the Nellie H. Steele's Mystery Readers' Group! Or sign up for my newsletter now!

All the best, Nellie

OTHER SERIES BY NELLIE H. STEELE

Cozy Mystery Series

Cate Kensie Mysteries
Lily & Cassie by the Sea Mysteries
Pearl Party Mysteries
Middle Age is Murder Cozy Mysteries

Supernatural Suspense/Urban Fantasy

Shadow Slayers Stories
Duchess of Blackmoore Mysteries
Shelving Magic

Adventure

Maggie Edwards Adventures
Clif & Ri on the Sea

Made in the USA
Las Vegas, NV
22 March 2024

87426804R00203